WHAT THE
NIGHT KNOWS

DEAN KOONTZ

RANDOM HOUSE
LARGE PRINT

WHAT THE NIGHT KNOWS

A Novel

Copyright © 2010 by Dean Koontz

All rights reserved.
Published in the United States of America by Random House Large Print in association with Bantam Books, New York.
Distributed by Random House, Inc., New York.

Cover art and design: Scott Biel
Title page art from an original photograph by Joseph Hoban

The Library of Congress has established a cataloging-in-publication record for this title.

ISBN: 978-0-7393-7797-0

www.randomhouse.com/largeprint

FIRST LARGE PRINT EDITION

Printed in the United States of America

10 9 8 7 6 5 4 3 2 1

This Large Print Edition published in accord with the standards of the N.A.V.H.

To Gerda,
who has haunted my heart
since the day we met

Death, the undiscovered country,
From whose bourn no traveler returns . . .

—SHAKESPEARE, **Hamlet**

WHAT THE NIGHT KNOWS

1

WHAT YEAR THESE EVENTS TRANSPIRED IS OF no consequence. Where they occurred is not important. The time is always, and the place is everywhere.

Suddenly at noon, six days after the murders, birds flew to trees and sheltered roosts. As if their wings had lanced the sky, the rain fell close behind their flight. The long afternoon was as dim and drowned as twilight in Atlantis.

The state hospital stood on a hill, silhouetted against a gray and sodden sky. The September light appeared to strop a razor's edge along each skein of rain.

A procession of eighty-foot purple beeches separated the inbound and the outbound lanes of the approach road. Their limbs overhung the car and collected the rain to redistribute it in thick drizzles that rapped against the windshield.

The thump of the wipers matched the slow, heavy rhythm of John Calvino's heart. He did not play the radio. The only sounds were the engine, the wind-shield wipers, the rain, the swish of tires turning on wet pavement, and a memory of the screams of dying women.

Near the main entrance, he parked illegally under the portico. He propped the POLICE placard on the dashboard.

John was a homicide detective, but this car be-longed to him, not to the department. The use of the placard while off duty might be a minor viola-tion of the rules. But his conscience was encrusted with worse transgressions than the abuse of police prerogatives.

At the reception desk in the lobby sat a lean woman with close-cropped black hair. She smelled of the lunchtime cigarettes that had curbed her ap-petite. Her mouth was as severe as that of an iguana.

After glancing at John's police ID and listening to his request, she used the intercom to call an escort for him. Pen pinched in her thin fingers, white knuckles as sharp as chiseled marble, she printed his name and badge number in the visitors' register.

Hoping for gossip, she wanted to talk about Billy Lucas.

Instead, John went to the nearest window. He stared at the rain without seeing it.

A few minutes later, a massive orderly named

Coleman Hanes escorted him to the third—top—floor. Hanes so filled the elevator that he seemed like a bull in a narrow stall, waiting for the door to the rodeo ring to be opened. His mahogany skin had a faint sheen, and by contrast his white uniform was radiant.

They talked about the unseasonable weather: the rain, the almost wintry cold two weeks before summer officially ended. They discussed neither murder nor insanity.

John did most of the talking. The orderly was self-possessed to the point of being phlegmatic.

The elevator opened to a vestibule. A pink-faced guard sat at a desk, reading a magazine.

"Are you armed?" he asked.

"My service pistol."

"You'll have to give it to me."

John removed the weapon from his shoulder rig, surrendered it.

On the desk stood a Crestron touch-screen panel. When the guard pressed an icon, the electronic lock released the door to his left.

Coleman Hanes led the way into what appeared to be an ordinary hospital corridor: gray-vinyl tile underfoot, pale-blue walls, white ceiling with fluorescent panels.

"Will he eventually be moved to an open floor or will he be kept under this security permanently?" John asked.

"I'd keep him here forever. But it's up to the doctors."

Hanes wore a utility belt in the pouches of which were a small can of Mace, a Taser, plastic-strap handcuffs, and a walkie-talkie.

All the doors were closed. Each featured a lock-release keypad and a porthole.

Seeing John's interest, Hanes said, "Double-paned. The inner pane is shatterproof. The outer is a two-way mirror. But you'll be seeing Billy in the consultation room."

This proved to be a twenty-foot-square chamber divided by a two-foot-high partition. From the top of this low wall to the ceiling were panels of thick armored glass in steel frames.

In each panel, near the sill and just above head height, two rectangular steel grilles allowed sound to pass clearly from one side of the glass to the other.

The nearer portion of the room was the smaller: twenty feet long, perhaps eight feet wide. Two armchairs were angled toward the glass, a small table between them.

The farther portion of the room contained one armchair and a long couch, allowing the patient either to sit or to lie down.

On this side of the glass, the chairs had wooden legs. The back and seat cushions were button-tufted.

Beyond the glass, the furniture featured padded, upholstered legs. The cushions were smooth-sewn, without buttons or upholstery tacks.

Ceiling-mounted cameras on the visitor's side covered the entire room. From the guard's station, Coleman Hanes could watch but not listen.

Before leaving, the orderly indicated an intercom panel in the wall beside the door. "Call me when you're finished."

Alone, John stood beside an armchair, waiting.

The glass must have had a nonreflective coating. He could see only the faintest ghost of himself haunting that polished surface.

In the far wall, on the patient's side of the room, two barred windows provided a view of slashing rain and dark clouds curdled like malignant flesh.

On the left, a door opened, and Billy Lucas entered the patient's side of the room. He wore slippers, gray cotton pants with an elastic waistband, and a long-sleeved gray T-shirt.

His face, as smooth as cream in a saucer, seemed to be as open and guileless as it was handsome. With pale skin and thick black hair, dressed all in gray, he resembled an Edward Steichen glamour portrait from the 1920s or '30s.

The only color he offered, the only color on his side of the glass, was the brilliant, limpid, burning blue of his eyes.

Neither agitated nor lethargic from drugs, Billy

crossed the room unhurriedly, with straight-shoul-
dered confidence and an almost eerie grace. He
looked at John, only at John, from the moment he
entered the room until he stood before him, on the
farther side of the glass partition.

"You're not a psychiatrist," Billy said. His voice
was clear, measured, and mellifluous. He had sung
in his church choir. "You're a detective, aren't you?"

"Calvino. Homicide."

"I confessed days ago."

"Yes, I know."

"The evidence proves I did it."

"Yes, it does."

"Then what do you want?"

"To understand."

Less than a full smile, a suggestion of amusement
shaped the boy's expression. He was fourteen, the
unrepentant murderer of his family, capable of unspeakable cruelty, yet the half-smile made him look
neither smug nor evil, but instead wistful and appealing, as though he were recalling a trip to an
amusement park or a fine day at the shore.

"Understand?" Billy said. "You mean—what was
my motive?"

"You haven't said why."

"The why is easy."

"Then why?"

The boy said, "Ruin."

2

THE WINDLESS DAY ABRUPTLY BECAME TURBU-
lent and rattled raindrops like volleys of buckshot
against the armored glass of the barred windows.

That cold sound seemed to warm the boy's blue
gaze, and his eyes shone now as bright as pilot lights.

" 'Ruin,' " John said. "What does that mean?"

For a moment, Billy Lucas seemed to want to explain, but then he merely shrugged.

"Will you talk to me?" John asked.

"Did you bring me something?"

"You mean a gift? No. Nothing."

"Next time, bring me something."

"What would you like?"

"They won't let me have anything sharp or anything hard and heavy. Paperback books would be
okay."

The boy had been an honor student, in his junior
year of high school, having skipped two grades.

"What kind of books?" John asked.

"Whatever. I read everything and rewrite it in my mind to make it what I want. In my version, every book ends with everyone dead."

Previously silent, the storm sky found its voice. Billy looked at the ceiling and smiled, as if the thunder spoke specifically to him. Head tilted back, he closed his eyes and stood that way even after the rumble faded.

"Did you plan the murders or was it on impulse?"

Rolling his head from side to side as though he were a blind musician enraptured by music, the boy said, "Oh, Johnny, I planned to kill them long, long ago."

"How long ago?"

"Longer than you would believe, Johnny. Long, long ago."

"Which of them did you kill first?"

"What does it matter if they're all dead?"

"It matters to me," John Calvino said.

Pulses of lightning brightened the windows, and fat beads of rain quivered down the panes, leaving a tracery of arteries that throbbed on the glass with each bright palpitation.

"I killed my mother first, in her wheelchair in the kitchen. She was getting a carton of milk from the refrigerator. She dropped it when the knife went in."

Billy stopped rolling his head, but he continued

to face the ceiling, eyes still closed. His mouth hung open. He raised his hands to his chest and slid them slowly down his torso.

He appeared to be in the grip of a quiet ecstasy.

When his hands reached his loins, they lingered, and then slid upward, drawing the T-shirt with them.

"Dad was in the study, at his desk. I clubbed him from behind, twice on the head, then used the claw end of the hammer. It went through his skull and hooked so deep I couldn't pull it loose."

Now Billy slipped the T-shirt over his head and down his arms, and he dropped it on the floor.

His eyes remained closed, head tipped back. His hands languidly explored his bare abdomen, chest, shoulders, and arms. He seemed enravished by the texture of his skin, by the contours of his body.

"Grandma was upstairs in her room, watching TV. Her dentures flew out when I punched her in the face. That made me laugh. I waited till she regained consciousness before I strangled her with a scarf."

He lowered his head, opened his eyes, and held his pale hands before his face to study them, as if reading the past, rather than the future, in the lines of his palms.

"I went to the kitchen then. I was thirsty. I drank a beer and took the knife out of my mother."

John Calvino sat on the arm of a chair.

He knew everything the boy told him, except the order of the killings, which Billy had not revealed to the case detectives. The medical examiner had provided a best-guess scenario based on crime-scene evidence, but John needed to know for sure how it had happened.

Still studying his hands, Billy Lucas said, "My sister, Celine, was in her room, listening to bad music. I did her before I killed her. Did you know I did her?"

"Yes."

Crossing his arms, slowly caressing his biceps, the boy met John's eyes again.

"Then I stabbed her precisely nine times, though I think the fourth one killed her. I just didn't want to stop that soon."

Thunder rolled, torrents of rain beat upon the roof, and faint concussion waves seemed to flutter the air. John felt them shiver through the microscopic cochlear hairs deep in his ears, and he wondered if perhaps they had nothing to do with the storm.

He saw challenge and mockery in the boy's intense blue eyes. "Why did you say 'precisely'?"

"Because, Johnny, I didn't stab her eight times, and I didn't stab her ten. Precisely nine."

Billy moved so close to the glass partition that his nose almost touched it. His eyes were pools of threat and hatred, but they seemed at the same time to be desolate wells in the lonely depths of which something had drowned.

The detective and the boy regarded each other for a long time before John said, "Didn't you ever love them?"

"How could I love them when I hardly knew them?"

"But you've known them all your life."

"I know you better than I knew them."

A dull but persistent disquiet had compelled John to come to the state hospital. This encounter had sharpened it.

He rose from the arm of the chair.

"You're not going already?" Billy asked.

"Do you have something more to tell me?"

The boy chewed his lower lip.

John waited until waiting seemed pointless, and then he started toward the door.

"Wait. Please," the boy said, his quivering voice different from what it had been before.

Turning, John saw a face transformed by anguish and eyes bright with desperation.

"Help me," the boy said. "Only you can."

Returning to the glass partition, John said, "Even if I wanted to, I couldn't do anything for you now. No one can."

"But you know. You **know**."

"What do you think I know?"

For a moment more, Billy Lucas appeared to be a frightened child, unsettled and uncertain. But then triumph glittered in his eyes.

His right hand slid down his flat abdomen and under the elastic waist of his gray cotton pants. He jerked down the pants with his left hand, and with his right directed his urine at the lower grille in the glass panel.

As the stinking stream spattered through the steel grid, John danced backward, out of range. Never had urine smelled so rank or looked so dark, as yellow-brown as the juice of spoiled fruit.

Aware that his target had safely retreated, Billy Lucas aimed higher, hosing the glass left to right, right to left. Seen through the foul and rippling flux, the boy's facial features melted, and he seemed about to dematerialize, as if he had been only an apparition.

John Calvino pressed the button on the intercom panel beside the door and said to Coleman Hanes, "I'm finished here."

To escape the sulfurous odor of the urine, he didn't wait for the orderly but instead stepped into the hallway.

Behind John, the boy called out, "You should have brought me something. You should have made an offering."

The detective closed the door and looked down at

his shoes in the fluorescent glare of the corridor. Not one drop of foulness marred their shine.

As the door to the guard's vestibule opened, John walked toward it, toward Coleman Hanes, whose size and presence gave him the almost mythological aura of one who battled giants and dragons.

3

ON THE SECOND FLOOR, ONE DOWN FROM
Billy Lucas, the hospital-staff lounge featured an
array of vending machines, a bulletin board, blue
molded-plastic chairs, and Formica tables the color
of flesh.

John Calvino and Coleman Hanes sat at one of
the tables and drank coffee from paper cups. In the
detective's coffee floated a blind white eye, a reflection of a can light overhead.

"The stench and the darkness of the urine are related to his regimen of medications," Hanes explained. "But he's never done anything like that
before."

"Maybe you better hope it's not his new preferred
form of self-expression."

"We don't take chances with bodily fluids since
HIV. If he does that again, we'll restrain and
catheterize him for a few days and let him decide

whether he'd rather have a little freedom of movement."

"Won't that bring lawyers down on you?"

"Sure. But once he's pissed on **them,** they won't
see it as a civil right anymore."

John glimpsed something on the orderly's right
palm that he had not noticed previously: a red,
blue, and black tattoo, the eagle-globe-and-anchor
emblem of the United States Marine Corps.

"You serve over there?"

"Two tours."

"Hard duty."

Hanes shrugged. "That whole country's a mental
hospital, just a lot bigger than this place."

"In your view, does Billy Lucas belong in a mental hospital?"

The orderly's smile was as thin as a filleting knife.
"You think he should be in an orphanage?"

"I'm just trying to understand him. He's too
young for adult prison, too dangerous for any
youth correctional facility. So maybe he's here because there was nowhere else to put him. Do you
think he's insane . . . ?"

Hanes finished his coffee. He crushed the paper
cup in his fist. "If he's not insane, what is he?"

"That's what I'm asking."

"I thought you had the answer. I thought I heard
an implied **or** at the end of the question."

"Nothing implied," John assured him.

"If he's not insane, his actions are. If he's something other than insane, it's a distinction without a difference." He tossed the crumpled cup at a wastebasket, and scored. "I thought the case was closed. What did they send you here for?"

John didn't intend to reveal that he had never been assigned to the case. "Was the boy given my name before he met me?"

Hanes shook his head slowly, and John thought of a tank turret coming to bear on a target. "No. I told him he had a visitor he was required to see. I once had a sister, John. She was raped, murdered. I don't give Billy's kind any more than I have to."

"Your sister—how long ago?"

"Twenty-two years. But it's like yesterday."

"It always is," John said.

The orderly fished his wallet from a hip pocket and flipped directly to the cellophane sleeve in which he kept a photo of his lost sister. "Angela Denise."

"She was lovely. How old is she there?"

"Seventeen. Same age as when she was killed."

"Did they convict someone?"

"He's in one of the new prisons. Private cell. Has his own TV. They can get their own TV these days. And conjugal visits. Who knows what else they get."

Hanes put away his wallet, but he would never be able to put away the memory of his sister. Now that

John Calvino knew about the sister, he read Hanes's demeanor as less phlegmatic than melancholy.

"I told Billy I was Detective Calvino. I never mentioned my first name. But the kid called me Johnny. Made a point of it."

"Karen Eisler at the reception desk—she saw your ID. But she couldn't have told Lucas. There's no phone in his room."

"Is there any other explanation?"

"Maybe I lied to you."

"That's one possibility I won't waste time considering." John hesitated. Then: "Coleman, I'm not sure how to ask this."

Hanes waited, as still as sculpture. He never fidgeted. He never made a sweeping gesture when a raised eyebrow would do as well.

John said, "I know he was transferred here only four days ago. But is there anything you've noticed he does that's . . . strange?"

"Besides trying to pee on you?"

"Not that it happens to me all the time, but that isn't what I mean by strange. I expect him to be aggressive one way or another. What I'm looking for is . . . anything quirky."

Hanes considered, then said, "Sometimes he talks to himself."

"Most of us do, a little."

"Not in the third person."

John leaned forward in his chair. "Tell me."

"Well, I guess it's usually a question. He'll say, 'Isn't it a nice day, Billy?' Or 'This is so warm and cozy, Billy. Isn't it warm and cozy?' The thing he most often asks is if he's having fun."

"Fun? What does he say, exactly?"

" 'Isn't this fun, Billy? Are you having fun, Billy? Could this be any more fun, Billy?' "

John's coffee had gone cold. He pushed the cup aside. "Does he ever answer his own questions aloud?"

Coleman Hanes thought for a moment. "No, I don't think so."

"He doesn't take two sides of a conversation?"

"No. Mostly just asks himself questions. Rhetorical questions. They don't really need an answer. It doesn't sound all that strange, I guess, until you've heard him do it."

John found himself turning his wedding band around and around on his finger. Finally he said, "He told me that he likes books."

"He's allowed paperbacks. We have a little hospital library."

"What kind of thing does he read?"

"I haven't paid attention."

"True-crime stories? True-murder?"

Hanes shook his head. "We don't have any of those. Not a good idea. Patients like Billy find books like that . . . too exciting."

"Has he asked for true-crime books?"

"He's never asked me. Maybe someone else."

From a compartment in his ID wallet, John extracted a business card and slid it across the table. "Office number's on the front. I wrote my home and cell numbers on the back. Call me if anything happens."

"Like what?"

"Anything unusual. Anything that makes you think of me. Hell, I don't know."

Tucking the card in his shirt pocket, Hanes said, "How long you been married?"

"It'll be fifteen years this December. Why?"

"The whole time we've been sitting here, you've been turning the ring on your finger, like reassuring yourself it's there. Like you wouldn't know what to do without it."

"Not the whole time," John said, because he had only a moment earlier become aware of playing with the wedding band.

"Pretty much the whole time," the orderly insisted.

"Maybe you should be the detective."

As they rose to their feet, John felt as if he wore an iron yoke. Coleman had a burden, too. John flattered himself to think he carried his weight with a grace that matched that of the orderly.

4

THE ENGINE OBEYED THE KEY AND TURNED over smoothly, but then a hard thump shuddered the Ford. Startled, John Calvino glanced at the rearview mirror to see what had collided with the back bumper. No vehicle occupied the driveway behind him.

Still under the hospital portico, leaving the engine idling, he got out and went to the back of the car. In the cold air, clouds of white exhaust plumed from the tailpipe, but he could see clearly that everything was as it should be.

He stepped to the passenger side, which likewise revealed no damage, and got down on one knee to peer beneath the car. Nothing sagged from the undercarriage, nothing leaked.

The knock had been too loud and too forceful to have been of no importance.

He raised the hood, but the engine compartment revealed no obvious problem.

Perhaps his wife, Nicolette, had stowed something in the trunk, and it had fallen over. He leaned in through the open driver's door, switched off the engine, and plucked the keys from the ignition. When he unlocked the trunk, he found it empty.

Behind the wheel, he started the engine again. The thump and shudder were not repeated. All seemed well.

He drove away, under the dripping limbs of the purple beeches, off the grounds of the state hospital, and more than a mile along the county road before he found a section of the shoulder wide enough to allow him to park well clear of the pavement. He left the engine running but switched off the windshield wipers.

The car seat had power controls. He put it back as far as it would go from the steering wheel.

He had stopped in a rural area, flat fields to the left of the highway, a rising meadow to the right. On the slope were a few oak trees, almost black against the tall pale grass. Nearer, between the shoulder of the road and the meadow, stood a ramshackle split-rail fence, waiting for wood rot and weather to bring it down.

A skirling wind shattered rain against the car windows on every side. Beyond the streaming glass, the country scene melted into the amorphous shapes of a dreamscape.

As a detective, John was a cabinetmaker. He started with a theory just as a cabinetmaker started with scale drawings. He built his case with facts as real as wood and nails.

A police investigation, like crafting fine cabinetry, required dimensional imagination and much thought. After interviews, John's habit was to find a quiet place where he could be alone to think about what he'd learned while it remained fresh in his mind, and to determine if any new clues dovetailed with old ones.

His laptop computer rested on the passenger seat. He opened it on the console.

Days ago, he had downloaded and saved the 911 call that Billy had placed on that bloody night. John replayed it now:

"You better come. They're all dead."

"Who is dead, sir?"

"My mother, father, grandmother. My sister."

"Who is this?"

"Billy Lucas. I'm fourteen."

"What's your address there?"

"You know it already. It came up on your screen when I called."

"Have you checked them for signs of life?"

"Yes, I checked them very closely for signs of life."

"Have you had any first-aid training?"

"Trust me, they're dead. I killed them. I killed them hard."

"You killed them? Son, if this is a prank—"

"This isn't a prank. The prank is over. I pranked them all. I pranked them good. Come see how I pranked them. It's a beautiful thing. Good-bye now. I'll be waiting for you on the front porch."

Along the county road came two vehicles behind headlights. Seen through the smeared and misted windows, through the deluge, they had little detail and resembled bathyscaphes motoring through an oceanic trench.

As John watched the traffic pass, the puddled blacktop blazing in their beams, bright reflections coruscating along his streaming windows, the afternoon was further distorted and made strange. He was plagued by confusion, disconcerted to find himself—a man of reason—wandering in a fog of superstition.

He felt adrift in space and time, memory as valid as the moment.

Twenty years earlier and half a continent from here, four people had been murdered in their home. The Valdane family.

They had lived less than a third of a mile from the house in which John Calvino was raised. He knew them all. He went to school with Darcy Valdane and nursed a secret crush on her. He'd been fourteen at the time.

Elizabeth Valdane, the mother, was stabbed with a butcher knife. Like Sandra Lucas, Billy's mother, Elizabeth had been found dead in her kitchen. Both women were wheelchair-bound.

Elizabeth's husband, Anthony Valdane, was brutally bludgeoned with a hammer. The killer left the claw end of the implement embedded in the victim's shattered skull—as Billy, too, had left the hammer in his father's head.

Anthony had been attacked while sitting at the workbench in his garage; Robert Lucas had been clubbed to death in his study. As the hammer arced down, Anthony was building a birdhouse; Robert was writing a check to the electric company. Birds went homeless, bills went unpaid.

Victoria, Elizabeth Valdane's sister, a widow who lived with them, had been punched in the face and strangled with a red silk scarf. Ann Lucas, Billy's grandmother, a recent widow, was punched and subsequently strangled with such ferocity that the scarf—red this time, too—cut deep into her throat.

The women's relationships to their families were not identical, but eerily similar.

Fifteen-year-old Darcy Valdane endured rape before being stabbed to death with the same butcher knife used on her mother. Twenty years later, Celine Lucas, sixteen, was raped—and then butchered with the same blade used on **her** mother.

Darcy had suffered nine knife wounds. Celine, too, was stabbed nine times.

Then I stabbed her precisely nine times. . . .

Why did you say "precisely"?

Because, Johnny, I didn't stab her eight times, and I didn't stab her ten. Precisely nine.

In both cases, the order of the murders was the same: mother, father, widowed aunt/grandmother, and finally the daughter.

John Calvino's laptop directory contained a document titled "Then-Now," which he had composed over the past few days, listing the similarities between the Valdane-family and the Lucas-family murders. He didn't need to bring it to the screen, for he had committed it to memory.

A flatbed truck, transporting a large and arcane piece of farm machinery, roared past, casting up a spray of dirty water. In the murky light, the machine looked insectile and prehistoric, furthering the quality of unreality that characterized this drowned afternoon.

Cocooned in his car, as wind ceaselessly spun filaments of rain around it, John considered the faces of two murderers that phased like moons through his mind's eye.

The Lucas family had been destroyed by one of their own, by handsome blue-eyed Billy, honor student and choirboy, his features smooth and innocent.

The Valdanes, who had no son, were murdered by an intruder whose looks were less appealing than those of Billy Lucas.

That long-ago killer had committed additional atrocities against three other families in the months that followed the Valdane murders. During the last of those crimes, he'd been shot to death.

The journal that he left behind, hundreds of handwritten pages, suggested that he had killed often prior to the Valdanes, generally one victim at a time. He didn't name them or say where those murders were committed. He didn't care to brag— until he started to kill entire families and felt that his work was then worthy of admiration. Aside from the story of his detestable origins, the journal consisted mostly of a demented philosophical ramble about death with a lowercase **d** and about what it was like to be Death with an uppercase **D**. He believed he had become "an immortal aspect" of the grim reaper.

His true name was Alton Turner Blackwood. He had lived under the false name Asmodeus. Itinerant, he had traveled ceaselessly in a series of stolen vehicles or hobo-style in boxcars, or sometimes as a ticketed passenger on buses. A vagrant, he slept in whatever vehicle he currently possessed, in abandoned buildings, in homeless shelters, in culverts and under bridges, in the backseats of twisted wrecks in automobile junkyards, in any shed left unlocked, once in an open grave covered by a canopy raised for a morning burial service, and secretly in church basements.

He stood six feet five, scarecrow-thin but strong. His hands were immense, the spatulate fingers as suctorial as the toe discs of a web-foot toad. Large bony wrists like robot joints, orangutan-long arms. His shoulder blades were thick and malformed, so that bat wings appeared to be furled under his shirt.

After each of the first three families had been savaged, Alton Blackwood had rung 911, not from the site of the murders, but from a public phone. His vanity required that the bodies be found while they were fresh, before the flamboyant process of decomposition upstaged his handiwork.

Blackwood was long dead, the four cases were closed, and the crimes occurred in a small city with inadequate protocols for the archiving of 911 calls. Of the three messages the killer had left, only one remained, regarding the second family, the Sollenburgs.

The previous day, John had solicited a copy of the

recording, ostensibly as part of the Lucas investigation, and had received it by email as an MP3 file. He had loaded it into his laptop. Now he played it again.

When Blackwood spoke in an ordinary volume, his voice was a rat-tail file rasping against a bar of brass, but in the 911 calls, he spoke sotto voce, evidently to foil identification. His whisper sounded like an utterance by the progeny of snake and rat.

"I killed the Sollenburg family. Go to 866 Brandywine Lane."

"Speak up please. Say again."

"I'm the same artist who did the Valdane family."

"I'm sorry. I'm not hearing you clearly."

"You can't keep me on the line long enough to find me."

"Sir, if you could speak up—"

"Go see what I've done. It's a beautiful thing."

In **his** 911 call, Billy Lucas had said, **Come see how I pranked them. It's a beautiful thing.**

To any police detective, the similarities between these two crimes, committed twenty years apart, would suggest that Billy Lucas read about Alton

Turner Blackwood's murder spree and imitated it as an homage to the killer.

But Billy had not mentioned Blackwood. Billy said not one word about his inspiration. Of motive, he said only **Ruin**.

Thunder came and went, thunder with lightning and without. A few cars and trucks seemed to float past as if awash in a flood.

The state hospital was an hour's drive from the city, where John lived and where he had an appointment to keep before he went home. He powered the driver's seat forward, switched on the windshield wipers, released the hand brake, and put the Ford in gear.

He didn't want to think what he was thinking, but the thought was a sentinel voice that would not be silenced. His wife and his children were in grave danger from someone, something.

His family and two others before it were at risk, and he did not know if he could save any of them.

5

USING TWO SPOONS, MARION DUNNAWAY scooped dough from the steel mixing bowl, deftly shaped it into a ball, and deposited it on the baking sheet, where eight others were arranged in rows.

"If I'd ever had children and now had grandchildren, I'd never let them near the Internet unless I was sitting beside them."

She kept a tidy kitchen. Yellow-and-white curtains framed a view of the storm and seemed to bring order even to the chaotic weather.

"There's too much sick stuff too easily accessed. If they see it when they're young, the seed of an obsession might be planted."

She scooped up more dough, spoon clicked against spoon, and a tenth cookie-to-be appeared almost magically on the Teflon sheet.

Marion had retired from the army after serving

thirty-six years as a surgical nurse. Short, compact, sturdy, she radiated competence. Her strong hands attended to every task with brisk efficiency.

"Say a boy is just twelve when he comes across such trash. The mind of a twelve-year-old is highly fertile soil, Detective Calvino."

"Highly," John agreed from his chair at the dinette table.

"Any seed planted in it is likely to thrive, which is why you have to guard against an ill wind that might blow in a weed pip."

Under a helmet of thick white hair, Marion's face was that of a fifty-year-old, though she was sixty-eight. Her smile was sweet, and John suspected her laugh would be hearty, though he doubted that he would ever hear it.

Warming his hands around his coffee mug, he said, "You think that's what happened to Billy— some weed pip from the Internet?"

Having pressed an eleventh ball of dough to the baking sheet, she said nothing as she shaped the final cookie in the batch.

Then she raised her face to the window, staring toward the house next door. John assumed she was seeing beyond that place, imagining the house two doors away—the Lucas residence, the house of death.

"Damned if I know. They were a solid family.

Good people. Billy was always polite. The nicest boy. So very considerate of his mother after the accident that put her in the wheelchair."

She opened the oven. With a quilted mitt, she took out a tray of finished cookies and put it on the sinkside cutting board to cool.

A flood of hot air poured the aromas of chocolate and coconut and pecans through the kitchen. Curiously, instead of making John's mouth water, the smell briefly nauseated him.

Marion said, "I served in field hospitals, battle zones. Front-line emergency surgeries. Saw a lot of violence, too much death."

She slid the tray of neatly arranged dough balls into the oven, closed the door, and took off the quilted mitt.

"I got so I could tell at first sight which ones would survive their wounds, which wouldn't. I could see death in their faces."

From a drawer near the refrigerator, she extracted a key and brought it to the table.

"I never saw death in Billy. Not a glimpse of it. The Internet theory is just twiddle-twaddle, Detective Calvino. Just the jabber of an old woman who's afraid to admit some evil can't be explained."

She gave him the key, which dangled from a beaded chain with a plastic cat charm. The cat was a grinning golden tabby.

Billy's parents loved cats. They'd had two spayed

British spotted shorthairs, green-eyed and frisky, named Posh and Fluff.

When the killing started, Posh and Fluff fled through a cat flap in the kitchen door. A neighbor, at the house across the street from the Lucases, found them shivering and crying under his back porch.

Pocketing the key, John rose. "Thank you for the coffee, ma'am."

"I should have thought to turn the key in the day it happened."

"No harm done," he assured her.

Wondering if the Lucases might have traded house keys with a trusted neighbor, John had that morning made four cold calls before hearing what he hoped to hear from Marion Dunnaway.

"Let me give you some cookies for those kids you mentioned," she said. "The earlier batches are cool."

He sensed that he would disappoint her if he declined.

She put six cookies in a OneZip bag and escorted John to the front door. "I think of going up there to see Billy one day, if he's allowed visitors. But what would I say?"

"Nothing. There's nothing to say. You're better off remembering him as he was. He's very different now. You can do nothing for him."

He had left his raincoat on the front-porch swing.

He shrugged into it, put up the hood, went to his car at the curb, and drove two doors east to the Lucas house, where he parked in the driveway.

Perhaps an hour of daylight remained before the rain washed darkness down the day.

Fat snails, with eye stalks questing, crossed the wet front walkway, venturing from one grassy realm to another. John avoided crushing them underfoot.

To accommodate Sandra Lucas in her wheelchair, the porch offered both steps and a ramp.

He took off his raincoat, shook it, and folded it over his left arm because the only other place to put it was a glider with stained yellow cushions. After Billy finished with his sister and called 911, he had come to the front porch and had sat on the glider, naked and drenched in blood.

In most jurisdictions, after attaining the age of fourteen, children are presumed to have sufficient capacity to form criminal intent. Neither moral nor emotional insanity—as distinguished from men-tal—exempts the perpetrator from responsibility for his crimes.

To the first two police officers on the scene, Billy offered his sister for ten dollars each and told them where she could be found. "Just leave twenty bucks on the nightstand," he said. "And don't have a ciga-rette after. This house is a no-smoking zone."

Now the police-department seal had been peeled

off the front door. Two days previously, long after
the criminalists collected trace evidence and prints,
after a review of that evidence supported Billy's confession in every detail, after the boy was evaluated
by psychiatrists, and after he was remanded to the
state hospital under a preliminary finding of insanity to be reaffirmed or reconsidered in sixty days,
the house ceased to be an active crime scene.

No one from the department would have come
by merely to remove the seals from the exterior
doors. Because the Lucases had no family nearby,
perhaps an attorney, serving as executor, had been
here to review the condition of the house.

John used the key with the dangling cat charm.
He went inside, closed the door, and stood in the
foyer, listening to this home that had become a
slaughterhouse.

He possessed no authority to enter these
premises. Technically, the case file remained open
until Billy could be evaluated in sixty days, but the
investigation was inactive. Anyway, this had never
been John's assignment.

If he'd been unable to discover a neighbor with a
key, his only alternative would have been to force
entry. He would have done it.

With his back against the front door, he sensed
that someone waited for him in one of the surrounding rooms, but this was a false perception. In

other murder houses, after the bodies were removed and the evidence collected, when he returned alone to consider the scene in solitude, he usually experienced this disturbing impression of a presence looming, but it always proved to be unfounded.

6

THUNDER NO LONGER ROARED, AND THE
rain subsided from drumming torrents to a drizzle
too soft to press a whisper through the walls.

According to the real-estate records at the county
assessor's office, the residence had six main rooms
on the ground floor, five on the upper level. As John
stood in the dusky foyer, the house felt larger than
described. The hollow silence had a quality of vast-
ness, as of caverns coiling countless miles through
deep strata of stone.

Eight-pane sidelights flanked the front door, but
the mummified sun, enwrapped by sodden clouds,
would soon be setting.

He waited for his eyes to adjust to the gloom. He
intended to turn on as few lights as possible.

Sometimes the visible aftermath of violence so
disturbed him that he couldn't properly work the
scene. One gang thug capping another in a territo-

rial dispute never fazed him. An investigation in-
volving a murdered family brought him to the
brink.

He wasn't here in an official capacity. This was
personal. Therefore, shadows wouldn't hamper
him. Shadows soothed.

Compassion and pity were desirable in a homicide detective. In some cases, however, a capacity
for intense empathy tended to depress and to dis-
courage rather than to motivate.

In spite of his sometimes anguished identification
with victims, John could have been nothing but
what he was. He became a detective not because he
thought the job glamorous or because the benefits
were generous. He felt **compelled** to follow that
path. His career became a necessity; no alternative
existed either in thought or in fact.

Ahead, on the left, a gray glow might have de-
fined an archway to a living room. Above, a window
on the stairwell landing admitted just enough daylight to suggest a handrail, balusters.

Soon his dark-adapted eyes identified the newel
post at the foot of the stairs. He draped his raincoat
over it.

From an inner sport-coat pocket, he produced a
compact LED flashlight, but he did not at once
switch it on.

He wasn't seeking nuances of crime-scene conditions critical to a prosecution. The premises had been well-tramped; what evidence once existed had been gathered or contaminated, or obliterated.

What he sought was more ephemeral this time, more elusive: a keener intuition than the one on which he currently operated, some insight, some revelation, an enlightenment that would either confirm or put to rest his hunch that the Lucas family would be only the first of four to be massacred.

John followed the dark hall to the kitchen, where the door and casing had been removed to accommodate a wheelchair. The windows were curtained with translucent fabric that filtered the dismal light.

A rancid smell halted him one step past the threshold.

The flashlight fanned a wheelchair near the breakfast bar, the chair in which Billy's mother died when he slammed the knife through her throat.

Now on the floor in front of the fridge, the LED beam revealed the source of the odor. A quart of spilled milk marbled with the mother's blood had congealed into a yellow-and-purple scum peppered with patches of mold. The mess glistened, still not entirely dry.

According to Billy's confession, his mother tried to scream but couldn't raise more than a rasp-and-rattle, a whistling wheeze. She could not summon the help of other family members—or warn them.

As if those sounds had been recorded on the walls, John heard them, imagined in his mind's ear but as real to him as the thunder earlier and as his wife's voice would be when he went home to her.

Sandra Lucas had been disabled in a traffic accident. She coped elegantly with her new circumstances but also volunteered to counsel others in her condition. She gave motivational speeches stressing the importance of family, the strength a spouse could provide, and the reward of being an example of grace and courage for your children.

She bled to death, but drowned, too, from aspirated blood.

The radiant green numerals in the digital clock on the oven had displayed the correct time. Now, inexplicably, the numerals began to flash midnight or noon.

Maybe the electrical service failed for a moment, requiring that the clock be reset. Because he had not switched on any house lights, he wouldn't have been aware of a brief power outage.

He watched the numbers flashing. He watched them and wondered.

The rancid odor seemed to intensify.

After backing away from the odor but not all the way out of the past into the present, John went next to the study. Here, Robert Lucas had been bludgeoned with a hammer while paying bills.

Robert's desk was along the far wall, facing a window, so that he could look up from his work to enjoy a view of the three paper birches in the yard. This put his back to the study door.

Darkness shrank from the flashlight beam, and a collage appeared on top of the desk: an artful scattering of envelopes, invoices, and a sheet of postage stamps against a desk-blotter background, all of it unevenly glazed with a lacquer once bright red, now red-black and rust and purple.

In his audio imaginarium, John Calvino heard nothing of Robert's death cries, perhaps because the first blow had rendered the man unconscious before a sound could escape him.

The flashlight found a spattered pen set on a white marble base, a sprayed windowsill, spotted draperies. The spatter, the spray, and the spotting comprised a kind of scream, a shrill shriek that seemed to arise in John's bones, but this was not a sound that had been made by the victim; this was his own unvoiced cry of moral revulsion.

As he retreated from the study into the hallway, he thought he heard a jingling of tiny bells, a cold silvery sound lasting but an instant. He became as still as any living thing could be still.

The flashlight beam did not quiver on the mahogany floor.

In the sidelights that flanked the front door, the

panes of glass were nearly as dark as the wooden muntins that separated them from one another. The sun had sunk far down the gullet of the storm.

John could not be sure that the sound had been real. He might have summoned it from memory, from twenty years in the past.

He went to the living room, from where the ringing might have come. The double doors—added to the archway after Sandra's accident, to convert this space to a ground-floor bedroom—stood wide open. Bedclothes had been neatly turned down, but Sandra had died before retiring for the night. No one, with or without bells, waited there.

John had no interest in any remaining ground-floor rooms. No one had been murdered in them. The stairs did not creak. At the landing, he paused to gather his resolve.

The worst would be on the second floor. The mother and father had died quickly. But upstairs, the grandmother and the sister had struggled and suffered. Their cries would come to him.

On the landing wall, a print of John Singer Sargent's **Carnation, Lily, Lily, Rose** was spectacular even in the cold LED beam. Two lovely little girls in white dresses were lighting Chinese lanterns under a bower of lilies, in a twilight English garden.

Perhaps the most charming painting of the entire nineteenth century, the scene had often elicited a smile from John when he came upon it in books of art. He didn't smile this time.

As he turned from the picture, he had the impression that one of the girls was sprayed with blood. When he looked again, the blush on her face proved to be light from the Chinese lantern in her hands.

Upstairs, John went to the grandmother's quarters at the front of the house, on the left side of the hall. The door stood open.

No dishwater daylight leaked through the heavy draperies. A combination night-light and air-freshener emitted a peach-colored glow and the fragrance of carnations.

Except for the punch that, to her grandson's amusement, knocked out her false teeth, the assault on Ann Lucas had been bloodless. The aftermath John dreaded waited not here but in the sister's room.

He flicked a switch, lighting a lamp. Half the grandmother's room still lay in shadow. Tangled bedclothes trailed onto the floor.

On the dresser stood a collection of framed photographs. Six featured Billy alone or with others of his family. His open face seemed untouched by deceit. His eyes revealed no hint of dementia.

Celine, the sister, had a face made for mirrors and a smile of such innocence that she looked as if she knew nothing of death and everything of eternity. In a swimsuit at the shore, surf breaking around her ankles, she seemed to be a sprite spun from spray and sunlight. John couldn't bear to look at her.

A taped outline on the carpet marked the position in which the grandmother's body was found. In his confession, Billy had described punching her out as she sat in bed watching TV, dragging her to the floor, and waiting for her to revive before killing her face-to-face.

Staring at the taped outline, John expected to hear desperate sounds of death by strangulation— but he heard instead the silvery tintinnabulation of tiny bells, clear and icy. The tinkling lasted longer than before, perhaps two or even three seconds, and he knew this time the bells were real, not imagined.

In the subsequent brittle silence, he stepped into the hallway and switched on the ceiling fixture. The beveled-glass bowl speared that space with blue-edged blades of light.

Directly across from the grandmother's quarters, the door to the sister's room stood ajar. Darkness beyond.

Again, the bells. Two seconds, three.

He pocketed the extinguished flashlight and drew the pistol from his shoulder rig.

7

CLEARING A DOORWAY UNDER THREAT WAS always the worst. He pushed through fast, found the switch, pistol in one hand but then in both as light bloomed in a pair of bedside lamps. Left to right, head and gun tracking as one, registering few details of the room, focusing instead on target identification and places where someone might be concealed.

A closet offered the only possibility. Two sliding mirrored doors. Approaching himself and the black bore of his weapon, gun in one hand again, reaching toward the door, toward his own reaching reflection, sliding his second self aside. He found only hanging clothes, shoes, boxes on a high shelf.

He still believed the silvery ringing had been real.

He slid the door shut and looked past his reflection at the room behind him, which seemed to be **filled** by the deathbed, by the evil of it, the mattress like the altar of an abattoir religion.

Celine had been sitting on the edge of the bed, one leg bent and her foot on the mattress, painting her toenails. Listening to music through the earphones of her iPod, she could not have heard the struggle in her grandmother's room.

Before throwing open the door and attacking, Billy had stripped out of his clothes and tossed them on the hallway floor. Naked, knife in hand, hot with the thrill of having garroted his grandmother with a tightly twisted red silk scarf, he burst into his sister's room and overwhelmed her. Pain, shock, and terror robbed her of the ability to resist effectively.

The mirror image of the bed filled John Calvino with revulsion, and he heard himself breathing through his open mouth to avoid the coppery smell of the blood-soaked mattress batting that had not yet dried and would not for a long time. But the humid air had a coppery taste—or he imagined it did—that offended worse than the smell, and he clenched his teeth, his nostrils flaring.

Holstering his pistol, he turned to face the abomination, which was immeasurably more terrible than the reflection of it. His disgust was twined now with anger and pity, three threads on a needle sewing this moment into his memory, not only the moment, the scene, but also the raw emotion of it.

Then he could hear Celine, the Celine of his quasi-clairvoyant imagination: crying out in pain and terror, weeping with the shame of violation, pleading for her life, beseeching God to save her, receiving no mercy from the beast who was her brother, receiving no grace until at last, at last, the final thrust of the knife put an end to her misery.

Shaking uncontrollably, hands covering his ears without effect, John turned from the hateful bed, returned to the hallway, leaned his back against the wall, and slid down to sit on the floor. He was in three places simultaneously: this present hallway, this hallway on the murder night, and another house in a distant city twenty years in the past.

Because his father and mother had been artists and art teachers, he had perpetual access to a memory museum of renowned images. Now, before his mind's eye rose a painting by Goya, the chilling and despair-filled **Saturn Devouring His Children**.

John had to sit in silence for a while, letting time past wash out of time present. The horrors of the past and of the present were unredeemable, but he held fast to a hope—wild and unreasoned in its character, but ardent—that the future could be shaped so that it would never **need** redemption.

Although he would have preferred to switch off the lights in Celine's room and retreat from the house, he eventually got to his feet and crossed her threshold once more. He did not, however, look again at the dead girl's bed.

Across her desk spilled glossy magazines published for teenagers and, by way of implausible contrast, a paperback of **The Everlasting Man,** by G. K. Chesterton.

Display shelves held an eclectic collection of things pleasing to Celine. Twenty ceramic mice, the largest no more than two inches tall. Seashells. Glass paperweights. A snow globe containing a quaint cottage.

Bells. Behind the mice, between two plush-toy bunnies in white bonnets and gingham dresses, on a green box in which they evidently had come, lay three miniature silver calla lilies all sprouting from one silver stem. The spathes were exquisitely shaped, but instead of a yellow spike, each enclosed a tiny silver clapper.

The stem, by which the bells could be rung, was dark with dried blood and with tarnish the blood encouraged. If the criminalists had noticed the bells, they would have bagged and taken them.

From a box of Kleenex on the desk, John plucked a tissue. He folded it into a pad and gripped the silver stem, not to preserve evidence—too late for that—but to avoid touching the blood.

On the lid of the green box under the calla lilies, in silver script, were the words **Piper's Gallery.**

Shaken, the bells produced the crisp, cold ringing that he had heard three times since entering the house.

Unable to suppress a tremor in his hands, he placed the bells and the Kleenex in the box, tucked the box in a sport-coat pocket.

Back in the day, Alton Turner Blackwood had carried with him three silver bells, each the size of a thimble, clustered at the end of a handle. They were not shaped like flowers and were not as finely made as those on Celine's shelf of small treasures.

Blackwood had been a psychopathic ritualist with an elaborate post-homicide ceremony that suggested both a strange belief system and obsessive-compulsive tendencies. When everyone in his target family was dead, he returned to the victims in the order the killings occurred and arranged them on their backs. With a drop of epoxy, he glued coins on the cadaver's eyes: quarters that he'd painted black, always with the eagle facing up. In the mouth, on the tongue, he placed a brown disc that the crime lab identified as dried excrement.

Then the killer folded the corpse's hands at the groin, around a chicken egg. To be sure the hands would not release the egg, he tied thumb to thumb and little finger to little finger with string.

Days prior to a slaughter, he prepared the eggs by drilling two tiny holes in each to drain the contents. Then he inserted a tightly rolled slip of paper through a hole into the well-dried, hollow shell. If the body was male, the paper carried the hand-printed word **servus;** if female, **serva**. They were the masculine and feminine forms of the Latin noun that meant "slave."

After the cadavers had been accessorized to suit him, Blackwood had stood over each, ringing his triune bells.

Billy Lucas had not rearranged his four victims but had left them lying as they died. He didn't conduct a ritual using black quarters, dried excrement, or hollow eggs. Evidently, however, he rang the tiny bells.

The delicate silver calla lilies featured no engraving.

On each of Blackwood's bells had been the word RUIN.

John clearly remembered Billy with the almost wistful smile, standing on the farther side of the glass partition.

You mean—what was my motive?

You haven't said why.

The why is easy.

Then why?

Ruin.

John switched off the lights in Celine's room and left the door ajar as he had found it.

In the hallway, he stood listening to the house. No floorboards protested, no hinges creaked. No shadow moved.

He went to Billy's room.

8

THE CASE DETECTIVES—TANNER AND SHARP—
had searched Billy's room, leaving a bit less disorder
than a burglar would have caused.

A few drawers in the highboy were half open.
Tanner or Sharp had rummaged through the
clothes therein, leaving them in disarray.

When they searched between the mattress and the
box springs, they had not entirely disarranged the
chenille spread.

On the nightstand stood a digital alarm clock.
The numbers were not flashing as they had flashed
on the kitchen clock.

John searched the desk, the closet, the nightstand,
with no expectation of finding anything the other
detectives had overlooked.

Previous to his killing spree, Billy Lucas's interests
had been, judging by the evidence, entirely whole-

some. Sports magazines. Video games, but not particularly violent ones.

Bookshelves held a couple hundred paperbacks. John read each spine. Science fiction, fantasy, mainstream fiction: The boy's interests were varied, but he possessed not a single true-crime book.

The computer on the desk was operative. Current department procedure in a case of this kind would have been to make a full backup of every document in the directory and take that, instead of the entire hard drive, for review later. With Billy's confession and his commitment to the state hospital, no detective would have discovered—might ever discover—what the computer contained.

Before reviewing the contents in alphabetical order, John scanned the directory for intriguing key words. In less than half a minute, he found a document titled CALVINO1. Then CALVINO2.

The first contained photos downloaded from an Internet site devoted to serial killers and mass murderers. Here were Tom and Rachel Calvino, John's mother and father. Also Marnie and Giselle, his sisters, at the ages of ten and twelve.

The photos accompanied the account of Alton Turner Blackwood's fourth and final massacre of a family. The document did not contain a picture of the killer; apparently none was ever taken of the drifter during his life, and the postmortem shots in the medical examiner's file were sequestered under a court order that protected young John's privacy and that was never revoked.

For the same reason, John's photo was not included. Besides, the site depicted only victims, and he was the sole survivor.

On the screen, his sisters were so lovely.

Many years had passed since he'd been able to look at photos of them. He had avenged them, for what that was worth. But if he had done something differently on that long-ago night, if he had **not** done a thoughtless thing that he **had** done, one of his sisters or perhaps both of them might still be alive.

Although he loved their faces, he could not bear the sight of them. He exited the document.

The atmosphere in this murder house grew more oppressive by the minute: the rain streaming down the windows, the humid air, a deathly stillness yet a persistent impression that someone listened, waited, and prepared for him in the nearby hallway or in another room.

He closed his eyes and summoned in memory a favorite painting, Pieter Bruegel's **Hunters in the Snow**. This scene of a sixteenth-century Belgian town in a winter twilight, illuminated by a recent snowfall, was full of movement yet serene, somber yet enchanting. Contemplation of it always calmed John—until now.

Johnny.

At the state hospital, the boy had called him Johnny. Having read about Alton Blackwood, the kid knew John had slain the killer.

Here seemed to be proof that Billy patterned his killing spree after Blackwood's murder of the Valdane family twenty years earlier.

When John retrieved the second document, CALVINO2, he discovered five photographs, the first of himself. It was part of a newspaper article about a citation for valor that he and his sometime partner, Lionel Timmins, had received more than two years earlier.

In the picture, he appeared uncomfortable; in fact, he had been embarrassed. Having survived, as a boy, when everyone else in his family had died, he could do nothing as long as he lived that would make him, in the balance, deserving of an award for valor.

He had tried to decline the presentation, but Parker Moss, Area 1 commander—who oversaw Homicide, Missing Persons, and Robbery, in addition to other bureaus, details, and units—insisted he attend and accept. Awards for valor were good PR for the department.

The second photo in CALVINO2 was of Nicolette. Nicky. It was from the website of Lannermil Galleries, a fine-art dealer, the primary representative for her work. She looked radiant.

John's palms were damp. He blotted them on his pants.

The file also contained photos of their son, thirteen-year-old Zachary, and their daughters, eight-year-old Minette—whom they all called Minnie—and Naomi, eleven. These three were snapshots, taken a month earlier, on the evening of Minnie's eighth birthday. The only people present had been him, Nicolette, and the three kids.

John could think of no way that these pictures could have been transferred to Billy Lucas's computer. No way.

Nevertheless, he recognized the document for what it must be: a file of homicidal desire, photographs of targets, the beginning of a murder scrapbook. Evidently Billy had intended at some point to kill them all, just as Alton Blackwood had wasted all but one member of the previous Calvino family.

After exiting the document, John looked at the nearest window down which rain washed in the fading daylight, and he thought of the dark urine flooding across the glass partition between him and Billy.

His disquiet quickened into fear. The house was warm, but he was chilled. He shivered.

He did not feel less of a man or less of a cop for being afraid. Fear was useful if it didn't foster paralytic indecision. Fear could clarify and sharpen his thinking.

Calling up the directory again and scrolling through it, John searched for other document titles that might be surnames. Perhaps Billy had selected and researched other target families.

Whatever the young killer's plans had been, surely they were now of no concern. The security at the state hospital was layered and reliable. He could not escape. The psychiatric board would not deem him cured at least for decades, if ever; they would not turn him loose.

Yet intuition warned John that his family was a target. The taut wire of his survival instinct vibrated, it **hummed**.

When he found no obvious surnames used as document titles, he closed out the program and shut down the computer.

From within the desk came a few bars of a song that John didn't recognize. When he pulled open a drawer, the bars repeated, and he picked up a cell phone that must have belonged to Billy Lucas.

No caller ID appeared on the display.

John waited through fourteen repetitions of the song bite. When the call was not sent to voice mail, the caller's persistence gave him the reason he needed to answer.

"Hello."

He received no reply.

"Who's there?"

Not a dead line. The hollow silence was alive, the caller unresponsive.

The best way to engage in any game of intimidation was to play boldly by the rules of the would-be intimidator. John listened to the listener, giving him no satisfaction.

After half a minute, a single word whispered down the line. He could not be sure, but he thought it sounded like **Servus**.

John waited another half minute before he terminated the call and returned the phone to the drawer.

At the door, when he extinguished the bedside lamps with the wall switch, rhythmic strobes of green light drew his attention to the fact that the clock radio, which had been keeping time when he first entered the room, was now flashing 12:00, 12:00, 12:00. . . .

When he stepped into the upstairs hallway, where he had left the overhead lights on, a more conventional ringing came from a telephone toward the back of the house. After a hesitation, John followed the sound, pushed open a door, clicked on a light, and found the former master bedroom, where much of the living-room furniture was now stored. The phone rang and rang.

He didn't know what might be happening. He

suspected that the worst thing he could do was encourage it, and he switched off the lights, closed the door.

In the hall, at the head of the stairs, he extinguished the ceiling fixtures—and darkness folded around him like great black wings, the landing window offering no relief.

His heart beat faster as he fumbled for the flashlight in one of his sport-coat pockets. The LED beam painted coils of light on the walls, made the pattern in the stair runner seem to wriggle with life, and darkled down the polished-mahogany railing.

Descending past **Carnation, Lily, Lily, Rose,** he was peripherally aware of something new and monstrous about the painting, the Chinese lanterns too bright, their orange color smeared across too much of the canvas, as if one or both of the little girls in white dresses had been set afire, but he refused to look directly.

The telephones shrilled in the living room, study, and kitchen. The pause between each ring seemed to be shorter than usual, the electronic tones harsher and more urgent.

He snared his raincoat from the newel post, didn't pause to put it on. When he threw open the front door, the phones stopped ringing.

Stepping onto the porch, which lay now in the grip of night, he thought he saw a figure on the padded glider to his left, where Billy Lucas had once sat naked and blood-soaked to wait for the police. But when John swept the glider with the flashlight, it proved to be unoccupied.

He locked the house, slipped into his raincoat, found his car keys, and hurried into the rain, forgetting to put up his hood. On his head and hands, the downpour felt as cold as ice water.

In the car, as the engine turned over, he heard himself say, "It's begun," which must have been an expression of a subconscious certainty, for he had not meant to speak.

No. Not certainty. Superstition. Nothing had begun. What he feared would not come to pass. It **could** not. It was impossible.

He reversed out of the Lucas driveway, into the street, fence pickets flaring bright and shadows leaping.

The wipers swept cascades off the windshield, and the rain seemed foul, contaminated.

In the fullness of the night, John Calvino drove home to his family.

From the journal of Alton Turner Blackwood:

I am Alton Turner Blackwood, and I remember. . . .

The south tower was chiseled stairs and stone walls spiraling up four stories to one round room, fourteen feet in diameter. Four pairs of leaded windows, beveled glass, crank handles to open. A truss-and-beam ceiling. From one of the beams, she hanged herself.

The family's fortune started from railroads. Maybe it was honest money then. Terrence James Turner Blackwood—Teejay to his closest associates, who were not the same thing as friends—inherited the whole estate. He was only twenty-one, as ambitious as a dung beetle. He grew it bigger by publishing magazines, producing silent films, developing land, buying politicians.

Teejay worshipped one thing. He didn't worship money, for the same reason a desert dweller doesn't worship sand. He worshipped beauty.

Teejay built the castle in 1924 when he was twenty-four. He called it a castle, but it wasn't one. Just a big house with castle parts plugged on to it. Some public rooms were accidentally lovely. Outside, from every angle, it was an ugly pile.

He worshipped beauty, but he didn't know how to create it.

In one sense, the house was the opposite of Teejay. He was so handsome you could call him pretty. His worship of beauty was in part self-worship. But inside, he was as ugly as the outside of his house. His soul was not bejeweled, but encrusted. Not even Teejay could have named some of the needs that formed that crust.

The immense house was called Crown Hill, after the knoll on which it stood. The 280-acre property lay along the northern coast, which has always been a dangerous length of shore. Every coast is dangerous, of course: Land falls away to the chaos of vast waters.

Jillian Hathaway was the most famous and beloved actress of silent films. She made two talkies, as well. One became a classic: Circle of

Evil. **She supposedly married Terrence Blackwood in Acapulco in 1926. They were never wed. She moved in to the castle that wasn't. In 1929, at the age of twenty-eight, she retired from films.**

Jillian gave birth to Marjorie, her only child, also in 1929. The once-glamorous star hung herself fourteen years thereafter. She was still very beautiful. Even in death, she was very beautiful. Perhaps especially in death.

The Blackwood family continued to produce new generations. Decades later, Anita Blackwood gave birth to Teejay's great-grandson. Terrence, connoisseur of beauty, wanted the deformed infant placed at once in an institution. The father, of course, agreed. But Anita would not allow her son to be discarded like trash.

In time, perhaps she regretted her decision. Over the years, though she taught the boy to read well at a young age, she otherwise distanced herself from him. Eventually she abandoned him at Crown Hill, to the mercy of the merciless old man.

She just went away. No good-bye. They said she had grown scared of the boy, her own boy, repelled by his form and face.

When he was nine years old and abandoned by his mother, the ill-made boy was moved

from the guest house he had shared with her into the round room at the top of the south tower.

The boy wasn't me yet. In time, he would become me.

The boy hated old Teejay. For many reasons. One reason was the beatings.

Another reason was the tower room.

An electric heater made the room warm in winter. Because of the ocean influence, the summer nights were seldom sweltering. A toilet and shower stall were added at some expense. A mattress on the floor made a good bed. There were as many pillows as the boy wanted. A fine armchair and a desk were built right there in the room because they couldn't be hauled up the spiral stairs. Breakfast and lunch were sent up by dumbwaiter. Using an in-house phone, he could request any treat he wished. At night, he could borrow whatever books he wanted from the immense library off the main hall.

The boy was comfortable enough but lonely. The tower room lay high above everything and far from everyone.

In the evening, after others retired, if there were no guests, he was permitted into the house. A late dinner was brought to the boy in the library. He ate off disposable plates with disposable utensils. What might have touched his mouth must never touch another's, although he had no contagious disease.

The staff was forbidden to interact with him or he with them. If a servant violated this rule, he would be fired. The old man paid them exceedingly well not merely to maintain silence toward the boy but also to remain silent about him to the outside world, about him and everything that occurred at Crown Hill. None would risk losing his job.

If the boy initiated conversation, they reported him. Then came the beatings in the privacy of the old man's suite.

He hated Teejay. He hated Regina, too, and Melissa. Regina was Anita's sister, the boy's aunt, the old man's granddaughter. Melissa was Regina's daughter. They were beautiful, as the boy was not, and they could go anywhere they wished, anytime they wanted. Regina and Melissa spoke to the staff and the staff spoke to them. But because Teejay forbid it, neither of them spoke to the boy. Once he overheard Regina and a maid mocking him. How she laughed.

One evening when the boy was twelve, in the library maze, in a far corner, on a high shelf, he found an album of black-and-white photos of Jillian Hathaway. Many were glamour shots of the movie star in elegant gowns and costumes.

The last photo in the album might have been taken by police. The boy suspected old Teejay, then her young husband, took it. In the picture, Jillian hung like a wingless angel from a tower-room beam.

She stripped out of her clothes before climbing on the stepstool and slipping the noose around her neck. The boy had never before seen a naked woman.

The boy wasn't embarrassed to be half bewitched by the nudity of a woman from whom he was directly descended. He lacked the moral training that would allow such embarrassment. He had the capacity to be ashamed of only one thing: his appearance. By cruel experience, he had learned that deformity was the only sin. Therefore his sin was that he existed.

She was some kind of grandmother to him, but nonetheless voluptuous. Her pale breasts. Her full hips. Her slender legs.

He removed the photograph from the album, returned the album to the high shelf, and took the picture to his round room in the tower.

Often the boy dreamed of her. Sometimes she just hung there in the dream, dead but talking to him, though he never remembered what she said after he woke.

In other dreams, Jillian descended from the beam like a spider on a silken thread. She removed the noose from her neck. She held it for a moment above her head, as if it were a halo. Then she tried to slip the loop of rope over the boy's head.

Sometimes it became a nightmare as she struggled to strangle him. On other occasions, he accepted the noose and let her lead him to the stepstool. Although she never hung him, he woke rested from such dreams.

One night the dreams changed forever.

For the first time, he was naked in a dream. Naked, Jillian Hathaway descended but this time didn't stop at his bedside. With the noose around her neck, she slipped beneath the covers, and the rough rope trailed thrillingly across his body. He felt her breasts against him, more real than anything he ever before felt in a dream. The boy woke trembling, wet, and spent.

For a while, he thought it was a thing that could happen only in a dream with a dead woman. Eventually he learned that the photo of a dead woman worked as well as a dream of her.

The boy wasn't me yet. But he was becoming me.

9

THEY LIVED IN A HANDSOME AND SPACIOUS three-story house—four, if you counted the subterranean garage—that no police detective could afford, a consequence of Nicolette's success as a painter, which had been growing for a decade. On a double lot, they had generous grounds for a city house and distance from their neighbors. Made of brick and painted white, with black shutters and a black slate roof, the place appeared Georgian, but it was not a scrupulous example of the style.

John parked in the underground garage, between Nicolette's SUV and the Chevy belonging to Walter and Imogene Nash, the couple who kept the house well ordered and the family well fed. Because mornings were sacrosanct in the Calvino residence, the Nashes came to work at 11:00 A.M. five days a week, and were usually gone by seven.

An elevator served the garage and the three floors

above. But the sound of it would announce his arrival and the kids would come running. He wanted a moment alone with Nicky.

On the drive home, he had called her and discovered she was in her studio, far past her usual quitting time. The master suite and the studio occupied the entire third floor.

In the corner of the garage where a few umbrellas dangled from a wall rack, he hung his raincoat on a hook.

Now that he was home, where life made sense and the madness of the world did not intrude, the events at the Lucas place seemed to have been dreamed more than experienced. He reached into his sport-coat pocket, half expecting the tiny silver bells would not be there.

As his fingers found the small box from Piper's Gallery, three knocks and three more issued from the farther end of the garage, from beyond the parked cars. Sharp, insistent, the rapping knuckles of an impatient visitor at a door.

In spite of fluorescent panels, shadows swagged here and there. None moved or resolved into a figure.

Directly overhead, the rapping came again. John looked at the plastered ceiling, startled—then relieved. Just air bubbles knocking through a copper water line, rattling the pipe against a joist.

From a pocket of the hanging raincoat, he retrieved the six cookies that Marion Dunnaway had presented to him in a OneZip bag.

He unlocked an inside door and stepped onto the landing at the foot of the back stairs. The lock engaged automatically behind him.

The door at the top opened on Nicolette's large studio. Working on a painting, her back toward him, she didn't know he had arrived.

Girlishly slim, brown hair almost black and tied in a ponytail, barefoot, wearing tan jeans and a yellow T-shirt, Nicky worked with the litheness and physical charm of a dancer between dances.

John smelled turpentine and under it the fainter scent of stand oil. On a small table to the right of Nicky, from an insulated mug, the aromas of black tea and currants rose on ribbons of steam.

The same table supported a vase of two dozen so-called black roses that were in fact dark red, darker than a corrupted vermilion pigment in the process of reverting to a black form of mercuric sulfide. The striking flowers had no scent that he could detect.

When painting, Nicky always kept roses nearby, in whatever color her mood required. She called them humility roses, because if she became too impressed with any canvas on her easel—which could lead to a sloppiness born of pride—she needed only to study a rose in full bloom to remind herself that her work was a pale reflection of true creation.

Her current project was a triptych, three large vertical panels, a scene that reminded John of Gustave Caillebotte's **Paris Street: Rainy Weather,** though her painting depicted neither Paris nor rain. Caillebotte's masterly work was an inspiration for her, but she had her own style and subject matter.

John liked to watch his wife at moments she thought herself unobserved. When she lacked all self-awareness, her characteristic ease of action and elegant posture were so pure and unaffected that she became the essence of grace, and so beautiful.

This time, his belief that he had arrived with perfect stealth proved wrong when she said, "What have you been staring at so long—the painting or my ass? Be careful what you answer."

"You look so delectable in those jeans," he said, "it's amazing you've painted something that could be equally mesmerizing."

"Ah! You're as smooth as ever, Detective Calvino."

He went to her and put a hand on her shoulder. She turned her head, leaned back, and he kissed her throat, the delicate line of her jaw, the corner of her mouth.

"You've been eating coconut something," she said.

"Not me." He dangled the bag of cookies in front of her. "You could smell them through an airtight seal?"

"I'm starved. I came up here at eleven, never

stopped for lunch. This bitch"—she indicated the triptych—"wants to break me."

Occasionally, when a picture proved a special challenge to her talent, she referred to it as either a bitch or a bastard. She could not explain why, in her mind, each painting had a specific gender.

"A lovely army nurse baked these for the kids. But I'm sure they'll share."

"I'm not so sure, the little fiends. Why are you hanging out with army nurses?"

"She was older than your mother and just as proper. She's a sort of witness on a case."

John knew many cops who never discussed active investigations with their wives, for fear that evidence would be compromised during beauty-shop gossip or over coffee with the neighbors.

He could tell Nicky anything, with confidence that she would not repeat a word of what he said. She was warm and forthcoming at all times, but regarding his police work, she had the virtue of a stone.

As for his current and unofficial investigation, however, he intended to keep it to himself. At least for the moment.

Nicky said, "Better than a cookie—cabernet."

"I'll open a bottle, then freshen up for dinner."

"I've got maybe a dozen strokes to make and one sable brush to clean, and then I'm done with this bitch for the day."

Another door opened on a large landing at the head of the front stairs. Directly across from the studio stood the door to the master suite: beyond, a bedroom with a white-marble fireplace featuring ebony inlays, a sitting room, two walk-in closets, a spacious bath.

The retreat included a compact bar with an under-the-counter refrigerator and wine cooler. John uncorked a bottle of Cakebread cabernet sauvignon and carried it, with two glasses, into the master bathroom, where he put everything on the black-granite counter between the sinks and poured for both of them.

When he glanced at himself in the mirror, he didn't look the least bit apprehensive.

In his closet, he took the boxed bells from his coat pocket. He put them in the jewelry drawer with his cuff links, tie chains, and spare watch.

He slipped out of his shoulder rig and put it, with the pistol still contained, on a high shelf.

He hung his sport coat on the to-iron rod and tossed his shirt in the laundry basket. He sat on a dressing bench, slipped out of his rain-wet Rockport walking shoes, and set them aside to be shined. His socks were damp. He stripped them off and put on a fresh pair.

These mundane tasks were slowly taking the supernatural shine off the day. He began to think that in time he might find logical explanations for everything that had seemed outré, that what appeared to be malevolent fate in action might look more like mere coincidence in the morning light.

At his bathroom sink, he scrubbed his hands and face. A hot washcloth, like a poultice, drew the ache out of his neck muscles.

As John was toweling dry, Nicky arrived, took her glass of wine, and sat on the wide edge of the marble tub. She wore white sneakers on the toes of which, as a joke during play with Minette a few weeks earlier, she had painted LEFT and RIGHT, each word on the wrong shoe.

Picking up his wine, leaning on the counter with his back to the mirror, John said, "Walter and Imogene are still here?"

"They had a mini-crisis with Preston this morning. He's been hospitalized again. They didn't get here until two o'clock."

Preston, their thirty-six-year-old son, lived with them. He had been through rehab twice, but he still enjoyed washing down illegally obtained prescription medications with tequila.

"I told them to take the day off, no problem," Nicky said, "but you know how they are."

"Responsible as hell."

She smiled. "Not much call for their type in the modern world. I told them you expected to be late, but they insisted on staying to serve dinner and do the initial cleanup."

"Has Minette eaten?"

"Not without Daddy. No way. We're all night owls here, and she might be the most nocturnal of us all."

"The Cakebread's nice."

"Bliss." She sipped her wine.

On her driver's license, her eyes were said to be blue, but they were purple. Sometimes they were as bright and deep as an effulgent twilight sky. At the moment, they were iris petals in soft shadow.

She said, "Preston worries me, you know."

"Doesn't worry me. He's a self-centered creep. He'll overdose or he won't. What worries me is the toll he's taking on his parents."

"No, I mean . . . Walter and Imogene are such nice people. They love him. They raised him well, did all the right things. Yet he became what he is. You never know."

"Zach, Naomi, Minnie—they're going to turn out fine. They're good kids."

"They're good kids," Nicolette agreed. "And Preston was a good kid once. You never know. You can only hope."

John thought of Billy Lucas, the clean-cut honor student and book lover. The rancid puddle of milk and blood. The blood-glazed collage of unpaid bills. The throttled grandmother, the sister's crimson bed.

"They'll be fine. They're great." He changed the

subject. "By the way, something happened today that made me wonder about those snapshots we took at Minnie's birthday party. Did you email them to your folks?"

"Sure. I told you."

"I guess I forgot. To anyone else?"

"Just Stephanie. Sometimes Minnie reminds me of her when she was a little girl."

Stephanie was Nicky's younger sister, now thirty-two and the sous-chef at an acclaimed restaurant in Boston.

"Would Stephanie or your folks have forwarded the pictures to anyone else?"

Nicky shrugged, then looked puzzled. "Why? Suddenly this seems like a gentle grilling."

He didn't want to alarm her. Not yet. Not until and if he could logically explain the reason he was worried.

"At work, I ran into someone who mentioned Minnie in the bunny ears at her birthday party. Someone emailed him the photo. He didn't remember who."

"Well, she's supercute in those ears, and you know how people swap things that tickle them. The photo's probably up on any number of websites. Cute Kids dot com, Bunny Ears dot com—"

"Predatory Pedophiles dot com."

Getting to her feet, she said, "Sometimes you're all cop when half cop would be tough enough."

"You're right. The problem is you never know when it's going to turn out to be a half-cop or an all-cop day."

She rang her glass against his, a single clear note. "You can't go through life always in high gear."

"You know what I'm like. I don't downshift well."

"Let's go have dinner. Later I'll shift your gears **for** you."

She carried her wineglass on high, as if it were a torch with which she revealed the way.

Carrying his glass and the bottle, he followed, inexpressibly grateful for his life with her—and more aware than usual that what is woven will inevitably unweave, the wound will unwind, the raveled will unravel. The thing most worth praying for was that the moment of the **un** would come only when you were old and tired and filled to the brim with this life. Too often, that was not the timetable that Destiny had in mind.

10

BEFORE DINNER, JOHN VISITED WALTER AND Imogene Nash in the kitchen, though not to commiserate with them about Preston's latest fall. They were too self-reliant and possessed too much self-respect to want to be seen as victims, and they were too considerate to want others to shoulder any smallest part of their burden.

Walter toiled as a navy cook for twenty-four years, most of it at a harbor base rather than aboard ship, and Imogene worked as a dental hygienist. When he grew tired of measuring ingredients in hundred-pound and five-gallon increments, when she wearied of staring into gaping mouths, they retired from their professions and, at fifty, went to a school to learn estate management.

In ultrawealthy Montecito, California, they ran a twelve-acre property on which stood a forty-thousand-square-foot main house, a five-thousand-square-foot guest house, horse stables, two swimming pools, and vast rose gardens. Walter and Imogene thrived, managing a staff of twenty, until drunken Preston, then thirty and intending to reunite with his parents for the purpose of negotiating a guilt stipend, had slammed back into their lives by crashing his rental car into the gatehouse, collapsing half the structure, narrowly missing the security guard, and cursing out the owner, who helped extract him from his vehicle before it might burst into flames.

Preston in tow, the Nashes left California and returned to their roots, hoping that by dedicating a year to their son's rehabilitation, they could restore him to a life of sobriety and self-sufficiency. Instead, he became the thing that lived in their basement apartment, sullen and reclusive, occupying himself with video games, smut, and drug-induced stupors. For weeks and even months at a time, Preston remained as elusive as the Phantom of the Opera—until one too many chemical cocktails gave him the screaming whimwhams so bad that he saw evil clowns climbing out of his toilet, or the equivalent.

Even in his silent and reclusive periods, Preston took a toll from his parents. Expectation of his next collapse was almost as emotionally draining as the event itself.

Estate managers usually were required to live on site, but no employer wanted the Nashes to bring along their pale and stubbled basement dweller. Instead of managing a major property and its staff, they were reduced to cleaning house and cooking for the Calvinos, a position they'd held for more than four years. Overqualified, they never acted as though the job might be beneath them; they worked hard and were cheerful, perhaps because work provided escape from worry.

When John entered the kitchen, Walter was plating salads at the center island. Five eight, trim, with steel-rod posture, he might have passed for a jockey if he had been a few inches shorter and ten pounds lighter. His small, strong hands and his economy of movement suggested he would be able to control half a ton of horseflesh with the subtlest pressure of a knee or the slightest tug of the reins.

"There's no need to serve us dinner when we haven't any guests," John said. "You've had a long day."

"You've had a long day, as well, Mr. C," Walter said. "Besides, there's nothing like some extra work to ensure against a sleepless night."

"Well, don't think you're staying all the way through cleanup. The terrible trio can help Nicky and me. We're nearly three-quarters through the year, and they haven't yet broken twenty dishes. We don't want to deny them every chance to exceed their personal best score."

He drew a deep breath, savoring the aromas of

onions, garlic, juniper berries, and well-cooked beef. "Ah, carbonata."

Laying aside her ladle and setting the lid ajar on the stew pot, Imogene said, "You're a regular blood-hound, Mr. C. No wonder you close so many cases."

In youth, Imogene must have been a pocket Venus. Her features were still delicate and her skin as clear as morning light. In spite of her petite stature, she was not now—and likely never had been—fragile either in body or spirit. She had the air of one who could readily assume Atlas's burden if he could not carry it any longer.

"But I don't detect even a hint of polenta," John worried.

"How could you smell polenta through such a cloud of stew? But it's here, of course. We'd never serve carbonata without it."

After another deep breath, he said, **"Piselli alle noci,"** which was an Italian dish of buttered peas and carrots garnished with walnut halves.

To her husband, Imogene said, "He's got a better nose than you do, Wally."

"Of course he does," Walter agreed as he shaved fresh Parmesan on the salads. "After all those years of navy cooking, I've ruined my nose for nuance. Which reminds me, sir, leave the laundry-room door closed, we've got an ugly stink in there. I only discovered it ten minutes ago. I'll deal with it in the morning."

"What's wrong?" John asked.

"I'm not sure. But my best guess is a sick rodent found a way into the dryer exhaust duct and met his fate just on the farther side of the lint trap."

"Wally," Imogene said with some exasperation. "The man's about to sit down to his dinner."

"Sorry, Mr. C."

"No problem. Nothing could turn me off carbonata."

"It's just curious," Walter said, "how the smell came on so suddenly. One minute the laundry room is fine, and a minute later, it reeks."

11

JOHN SAT AT THE HEAD OF THE DINING-ROOM table, Nicolette to his right, Minnie to his left and boosted on a pillow. Naomi sat beside her little sister, Zachary across from Naomi.

For the first time, the sight of his family gathered in one place didn't at once warm John but instead inspired a cold tightness in his chest, a greasy sliding sensation in his stomach. The dining room seemed too bright, although the lighting was the same as ever at dinner, and every window invited hostile observation. The stainless-steel flatware flanking his plate had the sinister gleam of surgical instruments. His wineglass was indeed glass, a potential source of jagged shards.

For a moment, this curious uneasiness threatened to disorient him—until he understood the cause of it. Together, the family was five targets clustered, therefore vulnerable to quick annihilation.

Although he had no incontestable proof that any enemy waged war against him, he was thinking like a man embattled.

His hyperbolic suspicion embarrassed him, and more important, he recognized that if not controlled, it would cloud his judgment. If he permitted his imagination to paint a gloss of evil on all things, he would provide camouflage for true evil. Besides, if you painted the devil on the walls often enough, you got the devil on the stairs, his footsteps approaching.

When John allowed his children to delight him, they soon lifted from him this pall of foreboding.

After grace, during the salad course, the primary subject discussed was the brilliant, the magnificent, the incomparable, the current that's-who-I-want-to-be-when-I-grow-up, Louisa May Alcott, immortal author of **Little Women,** which Naomi had finished reading just that afternoon. She wanted to be Louisa May Alcott, and she wanted also to be Jo, the young writer in the story, but of course she wanted to be herself, embodying all the Alcott-Jo qualities while writing and living in her unique Naomi style.

Naomi seemed destined, as an adult, to appear on Broadway in the title role of a revival of **Peter Pan**. She contained both a tomboy who yearned for swashbuckling adventures and a perpetually breathless girl who saw romance and magic everywhere she looked. She wanted to know how to throw a perfect sinking curveball every bit as much as she wanted to know how to arrange roses to the best effect, and she believed both in Truth and in Tinker Bell. As likely to dance along a hallway as to run it, more likely to sing away a sadness than to sulk, she exhausted the possibilities of each new enthusiasm just as inevitably another one came along to captivate her.

As Walter whisked away the salad plates, Zachary said, "**Little Women** sounds like a giant bore. Why can't you go nuts about vampire novels like every other dorky sixth-grade girl? Then we'd really have something worth talking about at the table."

"I don't find the living dead the least bit attractive," Naomi said. "When I'm old enough to have a boyfriend, I don't want one who drinks my blood. Imagine his bad breath and what a mess his teeth would be. All these girls swooning over hunky vampires, what they really want is to give away their freedom, to be controlled and told what to do and not have to think—and never die, of course. It's sick is what it is. I don't want to be a forever-young living corpse, I want to be Louisa May Alcott."

Minnie said, "It's stupid how she has three names."

"We all have three names," Naomi said. "You're Minette Eugenia Calvino."

"But nobody calls me all three, like you guys said

a thousand times already 'Louisa May Alcott, Louisa May Alcott.' It's stupid."

"Celebrity-shooters always have three names," Zach said. "Like Mark David Chapman and Lee Harvey Oswald. There's a bunch of others, but I can't think of them right now."

"Good," his mother said. "I'd be very disturbed to have a thirteen-year-old son obsessed with three-name celebrity-shooters."

"Zach is totally obsessed with the United States Marines," Naomi said. "He's got like eighty-six books about them."

"I only have thirty-one books about them," Zach protested, "and I'm not obsessed with the marines. I just like military history is all. Lots of people are interested in military history."

"Relax," Naomi said. "I wasn't implying your interest in the marines is a homosexual thing. After all, you're also obsessed with Laura Leigh Highsmith worse than you are the marines."

"Three names," Minnie observed.

John said, "Who's Laura Leigh Highsmith?"

Minnie said, "Is she related to Louisa May Alcott?"

"She's just a girl in my human-head class."

The children were primarily home-schooled. For educational purposes, Naomi went out of the house only to music lessons and to junior-orchestra practices. Zach attended group lessons twice a week as part of an art-institute program for gifted children. Currently he was enrolled in a pencil class to learn the fine points of drawing the human head.

Teasingly, Naomi said, "Hey, does Laura Leigh Highsmith draw portraits of **you**?"

"She's just a challenging subject," Zach said. "Hard to get right. Other than that, she's nobody."

"Are you gonna marry her?" Minnie asked.

"Of course not," Zach said. "Why would I marry a nobody?"

"What's wrong with your face?" Minnie asked.

Naomi said, "It's sure not sunburn. He's blushing."

"I'm not blushing," Zach declared.

"Then it's a bad rash," Minnie said. "Mom, he's got a bad rash."

"Permission to leave the table," Zach said.

John said, "Denied. You've eaten only a salad."

"I've lost my appetite."

"It's the rash," Minnie said. "Maybe it's conflacious."

"Contagious," Naomi corrected.

Minnie said, "Permission to leave the table."

"Why do you want to leave the table?" John asked.

"I don't want no rash."

"He's drawn at least ten thousand portraits of Laura Leigh Highsmith," Naomi revealed.

Zachary had inherited his mother's talent—and

his father's grimace. "What're you doing, snooping in my drawing tablets?"

"It's not like reading a diary, for heaven's sake. I like to look at your drawings, you're so good, and I can't draw for beans. Though if I was a good artist, I'd draw all kinds of things, variety, not a gazillion portraits of Laura Leigh Highsmith."

"You always exaggerate everything," Zach said. "First it's ten thousand, now a gazillion."

"Well," said Naomi, "it's at least a hundred."

"A hundred's a whole lot less than a gazillion."

Nicolette said, "You've drawn a hundred portraits of the same girl, and this is the first I've heard of her?"

"That's a really, really bad rash," Minnie said.

———

For the main course, everyone but Minnie enjoyed the carbonata with polenta and vegetables. Walter served the girl spaghetti and meatballs because she had the culinary stubbornness of the average eight-year-old.

The conversation turned to Italian history, possibly because Naomi noted, rightly or wrongly, that the Chinese invented spaghetti, not the Italians, and Minnie wanted to know who invented meatballs, and to forestall any further diminishment of their Italian heritage, John invented a colorful story that placed the origin of meatballs squarely in

Rome. They talked about Michelangelo lying on his back to paint frescoes on ceilings (according to Minnie, here was another guy with three names—Michael Ann Jello) and about Leonardo da Vinci inventing airships that would have flown if only the technology had existed to build them. Because there was no Italian front for the marines in World War I and because during World War II they served primarily in the Pacific theater, Zachary changed the subject to France in general and specifically to the Battle of Belleau Wood, one of the finest hours in the history of the Corps, while Naomi hummed "The Marine Hymn" and Minnie made surprisingly quiet machine-gun sounds to enhance her brother's anecdotes of war.

For dessert they had lemon cake with layers of ricotta and chocolate. Minnie did not ask for vanilla ice cream instead.

The five of them washed, dried, and put away the dishes without breakage. Unthinkingly, Naomi pirouetted with a stack of clean salad plates, but catastrophe did not ensue.

Had they eaten earlier, there would have been games or contests or a story read aloud. But private time had arrived. Kisses, good-nights, and wishes for sweet dreams were exchanged, and suddenly John found himself alone, walking the ground floor to check that all the exterior doors were locked.

Standing in the dark at a front window, he

watched the lamplit street bubble as if boiling. He had forgotten the rain, but it still fell, without pyrotechnics now, straight down in the windless night. The trees were flourished silhouettes, the yard black. The graceful arc of the porch, styled as an elongated temple portico, was crowded with shadows, but none of them moved or revealed a gleaming eye.

12

ZACH SAT AT HIS DESK WITH HIS ART TABLET, reviewing recent drawings and wondering if he might be turning into a girl. Not the way the usual bonehead in a movie goes walking alone at night in a godforsaken forest where only the terminally stupid would go walking, and he gets bitten by some godawful thing and on the next full moon he morphs into the Wolfman, with no interest anymore in vegetables or cereal grains. If Zach was becoming a girl, it was a less dramatic transformation, slow and quiet, with no thrashing or snarling or howling at the moon.

His room was certainly not a girly room; it was a shrine to the Marine Corps. Crowding the walls were images of a present-day marine in dress blues with white gloves, an F/A-18 Hornet in flight, a supercool V-22 Osprey vertical-lift aircraft, the famous Iwo Jima flag-raising photo. . . . Most striking of all was a print of Tom Lovell's horrifying but thrilling painting of World War I marines attacking German troops in close combat in Belleau Wood: poisonous mist, gas masks, bloody bayonets, facial wounds. . . .

If the marines would have him, Zach intended to be one of them eventually. Even if he was turning into a girl, they accepted girls in the marines now.

His dad's parents had been art teachers, and his mom was a big deal in some quarters of the godawful art world. Zach's talent had two origins, and he knew he ought to use it, but the question was **What should he use it for?** He didn't want to teach art any more than he wanted to cut off his freaking ears and make a sandwich with them. You didn't get to kick much butt teaching art. You didn't get to blow up a lot of things for all the right reasons. And he would never care about what the freaking art-world snobs thought of him. His mom was the only non-idiot among her idiotic art-world friends. He wasn't as nice as his mom, didn't have her tolerance for snotty people, and he couldn't always see the good side of them like she could. If he ever had his own godawful art-world friends, he would end up throwing them out ten-story windows and off overpasses, just to hear them splat.

Being an actual combat marine who, during lulls in the action, found moments to sketch scenes as they had been, as no photographer could ever catch those moments—**that** struck him as important work.

Other kids his age were big on sports stars and pop singers. These days, sports stars and pop singers were as real as steroids and lip-synching. Phonies. Fakes. Something had happened to the world. Everything was plastic. It wasn't always that way.

Zach knew the names of marine combat artists the way other kids knew pop stars. Major Alex Raymond, who had become famous for his **Flash Gordon** comic strip. Pfc. Harry Jackson, who did great work at the Battle of Tarawa. Tom Lovell, John Thomason, Mike Leahy in Vietnam . . .

Zach's determination to make a life in the Corps was almost two years old. For a long time, he didn't give a thought as to why this enthusiasm gripped him, but lately he began to understand.

When he grew up, he didn't want to do boring monkey work just for the bucks. He needed to be part of something where people cared about one another, would die for one another, where they set high standards, where they respected tradition, honor, truth. These were qualities of his family, and the way they lived—to their own rhythm, pursuing their enthusiasms with little interest in the fads of the day, with respect for one another that still left room for poking fun—was something he would need for the rest of his life because he was addicted to it. His family had addicted him to living with purpose and fun. When he became an adult, he wanted his working life to be as much as possible like life in the Calvino family.

And he wanted to be a marine also because of his sisters.

Naomi was hyper but smart, flighty but so talented, frustrating but funny, and sometimes she talked at you until it was like being caught in a flock of fluttering birds, nice bluebirds and canaries, but an infinite number of them, twittering forever. Life with her was often like tumbling through a humongous rotating barrel in an amusement park, **but** when you came out the other end and got your balance, you realized it was better to be in the barrel sometimes than to be stuck forever on some boring dumb-ass merry-go-round moving at like a tenth of a mile an hour with freaking organ music.

And as for Minnie—well, Minnie was Minnie. A couple years back, when Minnie came down with a mysterious illness nobody could diagnose for what seemed like forever but was probably just a week or so, Zach hadn't been able to sleep well or draw well, or think well. Although he wasn't sick like she was, he threw up twice, just because Minnie was sick, like a sympathy puke, though he didn't tell anyone.

Bad things were going to happen to Naomi and Minnie because bad things happened to everyone. Zach wasn't able to protect them from viruses and runaway trucks. But out in the wider world were a lot of evil men and insane dictators, and being a marine was a way to help protect his homeland, his home, his sisters, and their way of life.

Semper Fi.

He hoped he wasn't turning into a girl, because he wanted to be their brother, not their sister. As he paged through recent drawings of Laura Leigh, he wondered about his gender because, although she was seriously pretty and though he had drawn her from observation and from memory more often than Michelangelo had drawn God, Jesus, saints, and angels **combined,** he felt no stirrings of desire for her.

Well, all right, now and then there were stirrings and a couple times the stirrings were so embarrassing that, to distract himself, he chewed on ice cubes until his teeth ached.

But maybe ninety-five percent of his obsession with Laura Leigh had nothing to do with sex. Mostly he felt about her the way he felt about his sisters, but even more so. She seemed so fragile, delicate, slender, so small and vulnerable that Zach worried about her, which struck him as weird because, although petite, she wasn't a **dwarf** with brittle-bone disease, she was a normal size for a thirteen-year-old girl. He wanted to protect her, wanted her always to be happy, wanted everyone to see in her what he saw in her, not just beauty but also merit, virtue, kindness, and a precious something he couldn't even name. His feelings for Laura Leigh were so tender and affectionate that they didn't seem to be the kind of masculine things that a boy should be feeling. Sometimes the sight of her left him breathless, and sometimes when he was drawing her from memory, his throat grew so tight that he couldn't swallow, and when at last he did swallow, though it was just spit, he sounded as if he were a pig taking down an entire apple. Surely only girls—and boys turning into girls—were swept away by their emotions like this.

He turned the tablet to a clean page, propped it on the slanted drawing board atop his desk, and took his pencils from a drawer. He intended to draw only Laura Leigh Highsmith's nose. Her nose was a constant challenge to him because of its perfection.

After Zach sharpened his pencils and arranged them, before he began to commit carbon to paper, from the corner of his eye, he saw something move. He swiveled in his chair and sat watching the door to his closet swing slowly open.

Although the door had never done this before, no expectation of danger passed through Zach's mind. He possessed a good imagination, but it didn't lead him into bogeyman territory, either of the zombie-vampire-werewolf kind or of the guy-in-a-hockey-mask-with-a-chainsaw kind.

In real life, people who wanted to kill you were

one of two varieties, the first being your freaking nutcase true believers who wanted to fly a plane through your window or get their hands on a nuclear weapon to blast you into bone dust. There was nothing you could do about them. They were like earthquakes or tornadoes to an ordinary citizen, so you had to leave them to the marines and not worry about them.

Then you had your everyday criminals who were motivated by envy or greed, or lust, or a desperate need for drugs. They looked so much like law-abiding citizens that more often than not they jammed the muzzle of a gun inside one of your nostrils and demanded your wallet or your booty before you realized they weren't the kind who ever said "Have a nice day."

Neither an al-Qaeda operative nor a convenience-store-robbing junkie could have found his way into Zach's bedroom closet.

When the door drifted to a halt, all the way open, he got up and went to investigate the cause of its movement.

His walk-in closet was deeper than wide, with clothes hanging and shelved along the two longest walls. The overhead light glowed, though he felt certain that he had switched it off earlier.

Toward the back of the closet, a pull-ring on a rope dangled from a trapdoor in the ceiling, access to the crawlspace between the second and third floors. If you pulled the trap open, a wooden ladder unfolded from the back of it.

With the ladder down, a draft sometimes blew out of the space above and into the closet, strong enough to move the door if the latch hadn't been engaged. But now the tightly fitted trap was closed, shutting off the only possible source of a draft.

They didn't live in earthquake country, but like nearly every place on the planet, this city stood above at least one inactive fault. Although a minor temblor might be unlikely, it couldn't be ruled out; however, he hadn't felt the ground move.

Maybe the house had been settling. Houses did that. Maybe it slowly settled in such a way that the closet door no longer hung plumb. Then its own weight might pull it open if it wasn't latched.

No other explanation presented itself. Case closed.

He switched off the light and stepped out of the closet.

Attached to the back of the door was a full-length mirror. Zach solemnly saluted himself, thinking of the day when on very special occasions he would wear dress blues and carry an officer's Mameluke sword in a scabbard at his side.

As he closed the door, leaving the mirror to reflect only the dark closet, he listened to the latch click solidly in place. He was then overcome by a vague sense that something about his reflection, as he saluted, had not been right.

Maybe his salute or his at-attention posture had been sloppy. He had practiced them a lot when he was eleven, less when he was twelve, and lately not at all because when you were still **years** away from being a **real** marine, practicing such things too much seemed childish.

He returned to his chair at the desk, in front of the blank page of art paper, and picked up his pencil. He called forth the memory of Laura Leigh Highsmith's singular and exquisite nose, and contemplated it with the hope of a sudden insight that would precisely define **why** it was so exquisite.

As far as he knew, there were no hairs in her goddess nose. He had never glimpsed any bristling from it, nor had he ever seen a ray of light catch a hair shape in the shadowy ovals encompassed by her porcelain-smooth nares. Of course he never walked right up to her and peered up her nostrils, so he couldn't be sure they were in fact hairless.

"Idiot," he said.

She was human, so of course she had hairs in her nose. She would die or something if she didn't have hairs in her nose. Her nose might be as hairy inside as a freaking gorilla's armpit. Hair or the lack of it had nothing to do with why her nose was a work of art beyond his talent to depict.

Hoping for inspiration, he set to work with his

stupid pencil and the stupid blank sheet of paper. As slowly he drew, he thought of Laura Leigh, of course, but he also thought from time to time of the somehow-wrong reflection, and even though the latch had firmly engaged, he half expected the closet door to swing open again.

13

NAOMI HAD A WALK-IN CLOSET LIKE ZACH'S but somewhat bigger, and on the back of the door hung a full-length mirror, a really splendid beveled-edge **looking glass** of such sparkling clarity that she half believed, when the stars were aligned properly, that the mirror might become a doorway between her world and a magical realm into which she could step and pursue fabulous adventures and her true destiny.

This world where she had lived for eleven years was magical, too, in so many ways, if a person was perspicacious enough to notice the numerous wonders of it. **Perspicacious** was her new favorite word. It meant "having keen insight," an almost uncanny ability to see through—and to comprehend—what is dark and obscure. Unfortunately, there was a terrible shortage of perspicacity these days but veritable oceans of dark and obscure.

Anyway, this world was magical, but just not magical enough for Naomi's taste. She yearned for wizards, flying horses, talking dogs, rainbows at midnight, and for things she could not even imagine, things that would leave her speechless and her heart swollen, not swollen in a bad way, like with disease or something, but swollen with awe and delight. If she ever had a chance to pass through a mirror or through a door that suddenly appeared in the trunk of a great oak tree, she would go—though of course she would have to take Minnie and Zach and her parents with her, and they were not as likely to want to go as she would be, so she might have to Taser them or something. They would be angry, but later they would thank her.

As she thought about perspicacity and magical realms and how a girl her age might obtain a Taser, Naomi tried on hats in front of the mirror, making several facial expressions under each one until she felt that with her face she reflected the character of the hat. This was an acting exercise she read about somewhere, and while she doubted she would ever be an actress, she definitely had not ruled out the possibility if, in the next few years, a magical door didn't appear for her.

While Naomi mugged in front of the mirror, Minnie sat at her play table, building something with LEGO blocks. She was a whiz with LEGOs, she could build just about anything she wanted, but mostly she put together bizarre structures like nothing in the real world, some of them totally weird abstract shapes that ought to have collapsed but did not.

Naomi and Minette shared a room because in a world practically **crawling** with demented, drooling predators, Minette was too young and defenseless to sleep by herself even though Daddy set the perimeter alarm every night before bed. Besides, Minnie got scared sometimes and refused to be alone. Her fears were fraidy-cat stuff, nothing real, but of course she was still a **child**.

A brimless cloche hat with feather trimming on one side inspired Naomi to look mysterious and dangerous, as if she were a woman on a train between Paris and Istanbul, carrying priceless stolen diamonds in the lining of her suitcase. A blue straw hat with an open crown and a spotted veil said, **I am chic, competent, and have no tolerance for nonsense. I will shoot you with the .32 pistol in my purse, step over your corpse, and mix for myself a positively divine martini.**

Naomi had gotten her collection of hats at vintage-clothing stores while with her mother. Mother enjoyed browsing in such shops, though she never bought anything for herself other than an occasional piece of costume jewelry, which she never wore. She said recycled party and formal-occasion dresses were "hopes and dreams on hangers, moments from lives, delightful and intriguing and terribly sad at the same time." Naomi couldn't get her mind around delightful and terribly sad at the same time, but that was okay because gradually she acquired a fabulous collection of vintage hats.

When the strange thing happened, she was wearing a red straw hat with a narrow upturned brim, petersham band, and bow decoration. She thought the correct expression to match the hat ought to be comic or perhaps prim, but she couldn't find it in her face. She was focused so completely on the hat and her face that the person passing behind her registered only as a quick dark shape that darted from right to left.

Minnie sat at her play table, in plain view, and no one in this house ever entered without knocking and announcing themselves, and there had been no knock, yet someone passed behind her, and Naomi spun around to see who it might be, but no one was there.

The open closet. No one in there, either.

Puzzled, she turned to the mirror again, wondering if something was wrong with her eyes, something dreadful and incurable, so that she would be blind by thirteen, a tragic figure, the blind musician, bravely forging on with her lessons until she became magnificently accomplished because of her fierce dedication to her only remaining pleasure, her music. She might become an international sen-

sation, people traveling from all over the world to
see her play, because her music would be so pure,
the music of the virgin blind girl who performed
melancholy passages with such power that even
gangsters wept like babies, and always at her side
would be her pure-white German shepherd Seeing
Eye dog. She played the flute, but she couldn't con-
jure an image of a concert hall full of people who
had come from all around the world to hear a blind
flautist, so perhaps she would need to stop with the
flute and take up the piano. Yes, she could see herself at the piano, tossing her head dramatically as
the music enraptured her, so tragic, so brilliant, the
audience electrified by her playing, the guide dog
gazing up adoringly at his mistress as her hands
danced across the keys—

The mysterious form flashed behind her again,
from left to right this time, a dark blur. Naomi
gasped, turned to the closet, where the intruder
surely must have gone, but again no one was there.

Minnie had gotten up from the play table.
"What's wrong?" she asked as she came to Naomi.

"I saw someone. A reflection. In the mirror."

"It's probably you."

"I mean besides me, of course. Someone passing
behind me."

"Nobody's here."

"Maybe. I guess not. But still . . . something happened. I saw him in the mirror, sure enough. Real quick. He had to be here in the room with us."

"You better tell me true, Naomi. You trying to spook me?"

Minnie had her mother's black hair but her father's green eyes. As was the case with Daddy, too, this emerald gaze could freeze you in place, like an interrogator's spotlight in a screamproof room deep in a dungeon where you understood that you would lose a finger every time you told a lie. Naomi knew that neither Daddy nor Minnie would cut off her fingers, but when either of them focused this narrow-eyed green stare on her, she never fudged the truth even the littlest bit.

"You trying to spook me?" Minnie asked again.

"No, no. It wasn't spooky. Not much. A little spooky. It was mainly just weird. I thought I might have to be a blind pianist."

"**You're** weird," Minnie said.

"I saw some guy reflected in the mirror," Naomi insisted.

"Really? Swear on the grave of Willard."

Willard, their dog, had died two years earlier. Losing him was the hardest ordeal they ever endured. It still hurt to think about him. He was the best, sweetest, noblest dog in the world, and if you swore the truth of something on his grave and you lied, then you were surely going to burn in Hell with nothing to eat for eternity except spiders and maggots and brussels sprouts.

"I swear," Naomi said, "on the grave of Willard."

Impressed, Minnie peered in the mirror, talking to her sister's reflection. "What did he look like?"

"I don't know. I just . . . it was . . . no details . . . just a blur, superquick, way faster than a person should be, as fast as any animal, but it wasn't an animal."

In the mirror, Minnie's eyes moved from her sister's eyes to survey the reflection of the room behind them. Naomi also studied it.

"Maybe it wasn't a guy," Minnie said, "maybe it was a girl."

"What girl?"

Minnie shrugged. "Whoever."

Across the mirror, the thing swooped. Because Naomi was prepared for it this time, she saw it more clearly than before, but there was not anything to see, really, no face, no arms or legs, just a blur and ripple of darkness, here and gone, **zoom**.

Naomi cried, "Chestnuts!" which was something her grandmother said when she was startled or frustrated, and Minnie said, "Whoa!"

Instead of something, this seemed to have been only the shadow of something, and Naomi looked up at the ceiling light, expecting to see a moth darting about that cut-glass globe, but there was no moth.

When she returned her attention to the mirror, the phantom swooped across the glass again, and she said, "There must be a moth in the room, it keeps flying past the lamp. Help me find it."

Solemnly, Minnie said, "It's not a moth. Not in the room. **It's in the mirror.**"

Minnie was just eight years old, and all eight-year-olds were kind of screwy because their young brains had not yet grown to fill out their skulls or something like that, which was a known scientific fact, so they were likely to say or do anything, sometimes mortifying you, though this was absurd rather than embarrassing.

"You took one too many silly pills this morning, Mouse. How could a moth be **in** the mirror?"

"It's not a moth," Minnie said. "Don't look at it anymore."

"What do you mean it's not a moth? It was like a wing shadow—**swoosh!**—I saw it clearly this time, it must be a moth."

"Don't look at it anymore," Minnie insisted. She went into the closet and began selecting a change of clothes for herself. "Get what you'll wear tomorrow, put everything on your desk."

"Why? What're you doing?"

"Hurry!"

Although Minnie was a fraidy-cat with some empty space waiting to be filled in her eight-year-old skull, Naomi suddenly had the creepy feeling that her sister's advice might be worth heeding. She stepped into the closet and quickly put together an outfit for the next day.

"Don't look at the mirror," Minnie reminded her.

"I will if I want," Naomi said, because she was the older of the two and would not allow herself to be bossed around by a sister so young that she could twist spaghetti onto a fork only if she guided it with her fingers. But Naomi did not even glance at the mirror.

After they put the next day's clothes on their desks, Minnie carried the chair from the play table to the closet. She closed the closet door and braced it shut by tipping the chair backward and wedging its headrail under the doorknob.

"I have to put all these hats away," Naomi said.

"Not tonight."

"But we have to go in the closet **sometime**."

"After we figure what to do with the mirror," Minnie said.

"What do you want to do with the mirror?"

"I'm thinking about it."

"We need to have a mirror."

"We don't need **that** one," Minnie declared.

14

IN THEIR THIRD-FLOOR SUITE, SHE SHIFTED his gears as she had promised, but he shifted hers as well. Their lovemaking didn't have the character of a race toward pleasure but was instead an easy and familiar journey, full of affection and tenderness, fueled less by need than by devotion, and the final stretch a long sweet coast to the finish and the flag thrown down, and joy.

Until he met Nicolette, John had been incapable of a sexual relationship or at least incapable of pursuing one. The killing of everyone in his family by Alton Blackwood, rapist and murderer, had knotted sex and violence in young John's mind, so that it seemed to him that all desire was savage lust, that the gentlest longing for connection and release was in fact a sublimation of the urge to destroy. Blackwood's sexual satisfaction had been a prelude to murder; and for years John felt that his own ecstasy would be an affront to the memory of his mother and his sisters, that a climax reduced him to brotherhood with their killer. His ecstasy would inevitably remind him of their humiliation and agony, and he could no more find pleasure in climax than in stabbing or shooting himself as they had been stabbed or shot.

If Nicolette had not come along, John might have traded his police uniform for a monk's habit long before he achieved the rank of detective. She restored to him the understanding that desire is corrupt only if the soul is corrupt, that the body and the soul can both be elevated by giving pleasure in a spirit of love, and that an act of procreation is in its essence always a grace.

After the events of the afternoon, he expected to pass the night awake and restless, but in the shared warmth of the sheets, lying on his back, her hand still in his, he listened to her breathing change as she found sleep, and soon he, too, slept.

In the dream, he visited the city morgue as he had visited it many times in real life, though now the corridors and rooms lay in an eerie blue half-light, and he was—or so it appeared—the only living person in this ceramic-tiled, air-conditioned catacomb. The offices and file rooms and hallways were hushed, his footsteps as soundless as they would have been in a vacuum. He entered a chamber where the walls were lined with the gleaming faces of steel drawers, refrigerated body drawers in which the recently deceased awaited identification and autopsy. He thought that he belonged here, that he had come home, that one of the drawers would roll open, chilled and empty, and that he would feel compelled to climb into it and let Death kiss away the last breath in his lungs. Now the stillness relented to a single sound: the solid hammer strike of his heartbeat.

Retreating to the door by which he'd entered, he discovered that it no longer existed. Turning in a circle, he saw no other exit, but in the center of the room stood something that had not been there before: a slanted autopsy table with blood gutters and reservoirs. On the table lay a corpse under a sheet, a corpse with motivation and intention. A hand appeared from out of the white shroud, and by its great size, by its long spatulate fingers, by its knobby wrist as graceless as the gears of a nineteenth-century machine, the identity of the cadaver was revealed. Alton Turner Blackwood pulled the sheet off himself and cast it to the floor. He sat up and then descended from the table, standing fully six feet five, lean and bony yet powerful, his malformed bat-wing shoulder blades straining at the yoke of his shirt, subtly insectile, as if they were features of a bug's exoskeleton. John's heart beat harder than before, harder than fast, a stone pestle pounding a stone mortar, steadily hammering his courage into dust.

Blackwood wore what he had worn on the night he invaded the Calvino house: black steel-toed boots similar to ice-climbing boots with the sole crampons removed, khaki pants with four front pockets, and a khaki shirt. He lacked the wounds that had killed him, and appeared in the condition that John had first encountered him on that night.

His face was not so deformed as to be freakish, but he suffered from the degree of ugliness that, in most people, evoked pity but without tenderness. On the heels of pity, discomfort arose at the thought of inadvertently offending by staring or by an ill-considered word, followed by a distaste that compelled people to turn guiltily away, an antipathy that was intuitive rather than considered.

Snarls of greasy dark hair lay close to his scalp, his eyebrows bristled, but his face appeared beardless. His skin was pale where it wasn't pink, as smooth as the flesh of a baby doll yet unhealthy and not at all an asset, seemingly without pores and therefore unnatural. The proportions of Blackwood's long face were wrong in ways John could not fully define, beginning with a slab of brow that beetled over deep-set eyes. His hatchet nose, elongated ears reminiscent of the goatish ears of a satyr, jawbones as flat and hard as chisel blades, too-thin upper lip and too-thick lower one, sharpened his countenance to a spade of a chin that he raised in the haughty manner of Mussolini, as if at any moment he might chop at you with his face.

His eyes were so black that no differentiation existed between pupils and irises. Sometimes it seemed that only the whites of his eyes glistened and had substance, that the black must not be color but instead absence, holes in the eyes that led back into the cold and lightless hell of his mind.

Blackwood took three steps away from the autopsy table, and John retreated three steps, until he backed into a wall of body drawers. The killer's yellow-toothed grin, a wolfish sneer, seemed to be the prelude to a bite.

He spoke, his deep raspy voice transforming ordinary words into obscenities: "Your wife is sweet, your children sweeter. I want my candy."

Around the room, the big drawers flew open, and the dead came forth, legions in the service of Alton Blackwood, who reached for John's face as if to tear it off—

He woke, sat up, stood up, damp with sweat, his heart knocking hard enough to shake him. He felt certain that the house had been violated.

Two indicator lights shone on the security keypad—one yellow, one red. The first meant that the system was functioning, the second that the perimeter alarm—but not the interior motion detectors—

was engaged. No one could have entered without triggering the alarm.

His sense of imminent danger was nothing more than a remnant of his nightmare.

In the glow of Nicky's clock radio, John could just make out her shape beneath the sheets. She did not stir. He had not awakened her.

Near the door to the adjoining bathroom, a night-light fanned the floor, and tiny variations in the wool yarn of the tufted pile stippled the illuminated carpet with nubby shadows.

He had fallen asleep naked. He found his pajama bottoms on the floor beside the bed, and pulled them on.

The door to the master bathroom opened onto a short hallway flanked by their walk-in closets. Quietly, he closed the door behind him before clicking the wall switch.

He needed light. He sat on Nicky's vanity bench and let the fluorescents fade his memory of Alton Turner Blackwood's double-barrel stare.

When he glanced at the mirror, he saw not only a worried man but also the boy who he had been twenty years earlier, the boy whose world imploded under him and who might never have found the fortitude and resolution to make a new world for himself if he had not met Nicky when he was eighteen.

That boy had never grown up. During a few minutes of horror, an adult John Calvino had been formed, and the boy had been left behind, his emotional maturation arrested forever at fourteen. He had not evolved gradually from boy into man, the way other men experienced their passage out of adolescence; instead, in crisis, the man had **leaped** from the boy. In a sense, the boy, so abruptly left behind, remained in the man almost as a separate entity. It seemed to him now that this part of himself, this unevolved boy, must be the source of his adolescent fear. Fear that the similarities between the Valdane and the Lucas murders, twenty years apart, could not be explained by police work and cool reason. The inner boy, as imaginative and as thrilled by the supernatural as were all fourteen-year-olds, insisted that the explanation must lie beyond the power of reason and must be otherworldly.

A homicide detective could not entertain such ideas and still do his work. Logic, deductive reasoning, and an understanding of the human capacity for evil were his tools, the only ones he needed.

The nightmare from which he had awakened was not that of a grown man. Boys dreamed such comic-book scenarios, boys with their newfound fear of death that came with hormonal changes as surely as did an interest in girls.

John's and Nicky's cell phones lay on the granite

top of the vanity, recharging in a duplex plug. His cell rang.

Infrequently, he was called out at night on a murder. But the summons usually came on the third line of the four-line house phone, which was his private number. Charging, the cell phone should have been switched off. No caller ID appeared on the screen.

"Hello?"

His mellifluous church-choir voice at once recognizable, Billy Lucas said, "Did you have to throw away your shoes?"

John's first thought was that the boy must have escaped from the state hospital.

He put his second thought into words: "Where did you get this number?"

"Next time we meet, there won't be armored glass between us. While you're dying, I'll piss in your face."

Conversation would serve only Billy; he was not likely to answer what he was asked. John did not respond.

"I remember them soft against my tongue. I liked the taste," Billy said. "After so long, I still remember the sweet and slightly salty taste of them."

John stared at the cream-colored marble floor with its diamond inlays of black granite.

"Your lovely sister, your Giselle. She had such pretty little training-bra breasts."

John closed his eyes, clenched his teeth, and swallowed hard to quell his rising gorge.

He listened to the killer waiting, to a gloating silence, and after a while he seemed to be listening to a dead line.

When he attempted to ring back his caller with *69, he had no success.

15

THE WIDE NIGHTSTAND BETWEEN THEIR BEDS accommodated two reading lamps. Minnie left hers on the lower of two settings, the goose neck straight, so that the cone shade directed soft light at the ceiling. One of the little fraidy-cat's dreads that sometimes tested Naomi's saintlike patience was bats, specifically the possibility that a bat might get tangled in her hair, not only clawing and chewing open her scalp but also driving her insane so that she would have to pass the rest of her life in an asylum where they never served dessert. In this case, Minnie probably wasn't worrying about bats, even though she had adjusted the lamp to the bat-banishing angle.

They were both reclining against piles of pillows, a position from which they could see the closet door and the barricading chair.

Although their parents expected a great many things of the Calvino brood, going to bed at an established hour was not one of them. They were permitted to stay up as late as they wished, for any purpose except to watch TV or play video games; however, they must be showered, dressed, and ready for breakfast with their mother and father promptly at 7:00 A.M. and alert during their home-schooling, which began at seven forty-five.

This coming Saturday, like every glorious Saturday, they would be allowed to sleep in as late as they wished, and breakfast would be an individual responsibility. Of course, if the shadowy thing swooping through the mirror was as hostile as Minnie seemed to think it must be, they might not survive until Saturday, in which case Saturday breakfast would be moot.

"Maybe we should tell Mom and Daddy," Naomi said.

"Tell them what?"

"Something's living in our mirror."

"**You** tell them. Hope you like the nuthouse."

"They'll believe us when they see it."

"They won't see it," Minnie predicted.

"Why won't they see it?"

"Because it won't want them to see it."

"That's the way it would be in a story, not in real life."

"Real life's a story, too," Minnie said.

"What does that mean?"

"It doesn't mean nothing. It just is."

"But what are we going to do?"

"I'm thinking," Minnie said.

"You've **been** thinking."

"I'm still thinking."

"Chestnuts! Why am I waiting for a pathetic eight-year-old to figure out what we should do?"

"We both know why," Minnie said.

The chair under the knob of the closet door looked less sturdy than Naomi would have liked. "Did you hear something?"

"No."

"You didn't hear the doorknob turning?"

"Neither did you," Minnie said. "Not this time, not the nine times you thought you heard it before."

"**I'm** not the one who thinks a flock of bats will carry me off to Transylvania."

"I never said flock or carry off, or Transylvania."

A disturbing idea rattled Naomi. She eased up from her pillows and whispered, "There's a gap under the door."

Minnie whispered, "What door?"

Whisper discarded, Naomi said, "**What** door? The closet door, of course. What if it comes out of the mirror and slips under the door?"

"It can't come out of the mirror unless you ask it."

"How do **you** know? You're in third grade. I've been through third grade—the spectacular tedium of it—I finished it in three months, and there was no lesson about shadowy things in mirrors."

Minnie was silent. Then: "I don't know how, but I know. One of us needs to invite it."

Sinking back against her pillows, Naomi said, "Well, that's never going to happen."

"You can invite it all kinds of ways."

"What ways?"

"For one thing, by staring at it too much."

"Mouse, you're just making this up."

"Don't call me Mouse."

"Well, you are making it up. You don't know."

"Or if you talk to it, ask it a question, that's another way."

"I'm not going to ask it beans."

"You better not."

The room seemed colder than usual. Naomi pulled the blanket under her chin. "What kind of thing lives in a mirror?"

"It's a people, not a thing."

"How do you know?"

"I know in my heart," Minnie said so solemnly that Naomi shivered. "He's people."

"He? How do you know it's not a she?"

"Do you think it's a she?"

Naomi resisted the urge to pull the covers over her head. "No. It feels like a he."

"It's definitely a he," Minnie declared.

"But he who?"

"I don't know he who. And don't you ask him who, Naomi. That's an invitation."

They were silent for a while.

Naomi dared to look away from the closet door. Backlit by a streetlamp, silvery worms of rain squiggled down the windowpanes. The scarlet oak on the south lawn loomed huge, its glossy green leaves here and there reflecting the lamplight as if crusted in ice.

Eventually, Naomi said, "You know what I've been wondering?"

"Something weird, I bet."

"Could he be a prince?"

"You mean Mr. Mirror?"

"Yeah. If he's a prince, the mirror might be a door to a magical realm, a land of tremendous adventures."

"No," Minnie said.

"That's it? **No.** Just like that?"

"No."

"But if he lives beyond the mirror, then there's got to be another world on that side. The fabulous world beyond the mirror. That sounds like a magical but true thing, doesn't it? It could be like in all those stories—an heroic quest, high adventure, romance. My destiny might be to live over there."

"Shut up when you say that," Minnie said.

"Shut up when you say shut up," Naomi bristled. "You can't know my destiny. I might live over there and be queen one day."

"No one lives over there," Minnie said solemnly. "Everyone over there is dead."

16

WEARING A DARK-BLUE ROBE OVER HIS PAJAMA bottoms, John stood before the gallery in his ground-floor study. There were photos of the kids when, as infants, each had come home from the hospital, and others taken on every birthday thereafter, a total of thirty-five pictures. Soon the gallery would be continued on the next wall.

The girls liked to come in now and then to recall favorite birthdays and to make fun of the way each other had looked when younger. Zach was less inclined to enjoy photographs taken when he was a toddler and a grade-schooler because they didn't comport with his image of himself as a young man in preparation to be a tough marine.

More than he could have expressed even to Nicky, John looked forward to seeing his daughters become women, because he believed that each had a great good heart and would change her small corner of the world for the better. He knew they might surprise him but would always delight him by the way they lived their lives. He knew, as well, that Zach would become anything he wanted to be—and in the end would be a better man than his father.

One of two windows in the study provided a view of the flagstone terrace and the deep backyard, which now lay in absolute darkness. Their house stood on a cul-de-sac, on a street that was a peninsula between two converging ravines, quiet and sequestered for an urban home. Beyond their back fence, the land dropped off steeply, into brush-choked woods. On the farther side of the ravine, the lights of other neighborhoods were smeared and faded by the rain. Between the study window and that distant glow, nothing could be seen: not the terrace or the lawn; not the arbor twined with climbing roses; not the great deodar cedar, its boughs drooping gracefully.

Although not remote, the house was sufficiently secluded to allow a rapist-murderer, hot with need and icy with determination, to come and play and go with little risk of being seen by neighbors.

Also out there in the dark lay Willard's grave. City ordinances forbade the interment of animals on a residential lot unless they were cremated. An urn containing their beloved golden retriever's ashes was buried under a black-granite plaque beyond the rose arbor.

The girls had suffered such grief at the loss that they remained reluctant to risk losing another. But perhaps the time had come to bring a new dog into their lives. Not a golden retriever who counted everyone his friend, but instead a breed with a greater reputation for aggressively protecting its family. Maybe a German shepherd.

At his desk, John switched on his computer and sat in thought for a minute before keying in the number for the state hospital. The voice-mail system offered options, although the reception desk and various offices were closed until eight in the morning. He pressed the number for psychiatric-ward security.

A man answered on the second ring.

John pictured the stark security vestibule on the third floor, where Coleman Hanes had taken him just the previous afternoon. He identified himself, learned that he was speaking with Dennis Mummers, and inquired if Billy Lucas had escaped.

"Where did you get that idea?" Mummers asked. "Nobody's ever walked away from here, and I'd bet a year's wages nobody ever will."

"I assumed he didn't have a phone. But I got a call from him."

"Phone in his room? Of course he doesn't."

"If legal counsel wants to talk to him without coming out there, how is it done?"

"He's fitted with restraints and taken to an obcon room that has a no-hands phone."

"What's obcon?"

"Observed-conference room. We watch him through a window, but it's a privileged conversation, so we can't hear what he's saying. He's in restraints and he's watched to be sure he doesn't pry anything out of the phone, anything sharp that might be a weapon."

"He called me a little more than ten minutes ago," John said. "On my home-office line. He must have gotten possession of a phone."

Mummers was silent for a moment. Then: "What's your number?"

John gave it to him.

"We'll have to toss his room," Mummers said. "Can I get back to you in half an hour?"

"I'll be here."

While he waited to hear from Dennis Mummers, John went online to a series of dot-gov sites, accessing information available to the public, but also restricted information that he could view only with his police pass code.

The need had arisen to confirm that Coleman Hanes was the man he appeared to be. John had given the state-hospital orderly the unlisted number that Billy Lucas had called, and he could think of no other way that the killer could have obtained it.

In minutes, he ascertained that the Marine Corps emblem tattooed on the palm of Hanes's right hand was not in support of a fraudulent persona. The orderly served admirably in the Marine Corps, was decorated and honorably discharged.

Hanes had no criminal history in this state or in any state with which it shared information. Even his driving record was without a blemish.

The truth of military service and the lack of a police record did not clear him of having colluded with Billy Lucas, but it made the possibility less likely than it otherwise might have been.

When Dennis Mummers called back, he said, "Billy doesn't have a phone. Are you certain it was him?"

"His voice was unmistakable."

"It is distinct," Mummers acknowledged. "But how often have you spoken with him before your visit here?"

Deflecting the question, John said, "He mentioned something to me that only he could know, related to my interview with him."

"Did he threaten you?"

If John confirmed the threat, they would expect him to file a report, and if he did so, they would learn that he had no authority to involve himself in the Lucas case.

"No," he lied. "No threat. What did Billy say when you searched his room for a phone?"

"He didn't say anything. Something's happened to him. He kind of cratered. He's funked out, withdrawn, not talking at all to anyone."

"Is there a chance maybe someone on the staff might have allowed him to use their cell phone?"

"Depending on the circumstances," Dennis Mummers said, "that could be a reason for dismissal. No one would risk it."

"In this work, Officer Mummers, I've learned some people will risk everything, **everything,** for the most trivial of reasons. But thank you for your assistance."

After he hung up, John went to the kitchen, where he turned on just the light in the exhaust hood over the cooktop.

Most of their friends drank wine, but for the few with a taste for something stronger, they kept a small bar in a kitchen cabinet. Certain that he could get back to sleep only with assistance, he poured a double Scotch over ice.

He was disturbed less by the threat Billy Lucas had made than by the last words the murderous boy had spoken on the phone.

To the best of his recollection, John had never shared with the police any of what the murderer of his parents and sisters, Alton Turner Blackwood, had said before he died. John had been mute with grief and terror, but Blackwood had tried to distract him with talk.

The next-to-last thing Blackwood said on that long-ago night was word for word the last thing Billy said on the phone less than an hour earlier: **Your lovely sister, your Giselle. She had such pretty little training-bra breasts.**

17

ZACH DREAMED THAT HE WOKE IN HIS DARK bedroom and saw a blade of amber radiance slicing out of the closet, under the door. In the dream, he lay staring at this narrow brightness, trying to remember if he had extinguished the closet light before going to bed, and he decided that, yes, he had turned it off.

He switched on his nightstand lamp, which left most of the room still in shadows, and he got up from the bed and slowly approached the closet, behaving exactly like your typical bonehead in a brain-dead horror movie where everyone dies because everyone is terminally stupid. When he put his hand on the doorknob, the light in the closet went out.

Someone or some godawful **thing** had to be in there to operate the switch, so the worst of all dumb-ass moves would be to open the closet without having a weapon. Nevertheless, Zach watched his hand rotate the knob, as though he had no control over it, as though this also must be one of those movies in which a clueless dork undergoes a hand transplant and the hand has a mind of its own.

This was when he began to realize he was dreaming—because his hands were the same pair with which he'd been born, and they always did only what he intended them to do. With that fluid transitional dissolve common to dreams, he never opened the door, yet abruptly it stood wide, and he was poised on the threshold of the pitch-black closet.

Out of that lightless hole, enormous hands seized him, one by the throat, the other gripping his face, meaty palm crushing his nose, stoppering his mouth, his scream, his breath.

He seized the hand that cupped his face, frantic to break free, the wrist as massive as a horse's hock, hard gnarl of bones, thick tendons. Cold, greasy fingertips bigger than soup spoons digging at his eyes, and no breath, no breath—

Sucking breath at last, Zach startled up in bed, the nightmare bursting away like a shattering shell.

The thunder of his heart pealed through him, but even as his dream fear quickly subsided from its peak, he saw that the fright-flick scenario of his sleep played out also in the waking world. In the true darkness of the real room, the blade of amber light knifed through the crack between the bottom of the door and the floor.

Earlier, when the door swung open on its own, he dismissed it as the house settling, the door out of plumb and moved by gravity. When it seemed, as an afterthought, that something had been wrong with his reflection when he saluted himself in the mirror, he didn't dwell on it, didn't hurry back to take a second look, because he recognized who were the actual-factual, sure-enough villains in the world and didn't need bogeymen to distract him from worrying about **real** evil.

Some quality of the just-ended dream changed him. Suddenly he knew a kind of fear he hadn't felt before, or maybe it was a kind that hadn't rocked him in so long that his memory of it faded the same way that his memory of infancy had receded beyond recall.

Most nightmares were less ordeals than they were entertainments, infrequent rides through a funhouse of the mind. You drifted in your stupid gondola past one weird tableau after another until one of the horrors turned out to be real and the totally improbable chase was on. After a brief terror, you woke, and if you were able to remember the details, they were usually ridiculous and they made you laugh, just a brainless spookshow no scarier than the kind of half-assed monsters you'd find in a TV cartoon for little kids.

This freaking dream had felt as fully real as the room into which he awakened: the cold, greasy hardness of the assaulting hands; the pain of his nose pressed flat, nostrils pinched; the sense of suffocation. Even now, a lingering ache in his eyes suggested that the soup-spoon fingers had been real and would have gouged him blind if he hadn't thrashed up from sleep.

He switched on the nightstand lamp and sprang out of bed, though not to rush the closet as the idiot Zach had done in the dream. In the corner near his desk stood a replica of a Mameluke sword, which he drew from a highly polished nickel-plated scabbard.

Modern-day Mamelukes were strictly for show, cool badges of rank carried by officers during ceremonies of various kinds. This one was stainless steel, the ricasso engraved, the quillon and the pommel handsomely gilded. And like any ceremonial sword, the edge was dull and useless as a weapon. The point wasn't battle-sharp, either, but it could still do damage that the edge of the blade couldn't.

Standing to the side of the closet, Zach threw open the door with his left hand, the Mameluke ready in his right. No assailant flew into the room to test the point of the sword.

The walk-in closet harbored no one, but it did hold a surprise. The ceiling trapdoor had been dropped, the folding ladder unfolded. Between the second and third floors, the dark crawlspace waited for him.

Zach hesitated at the base of the ladder, peering up, listening. He detected only the susurration of the ring burners in the two gas furnaces that heated the second and third floors, a hollow whispery sound like the roar of a waterfall heard from a great distance.

The crawlspace was actually a half floor, a five-foot-high service mezzanine, so you could almost stand erect. It housed the two furnaces, humidifiers, a few hundred feet of flexible ductwork running every which way, copper water lines, both iron and PVC drain pipes, and who the hell knew what. Just the farther side of the trap, you could switch on garlands of work lights, which were used whenever plumbers or electricians needed to go up there to perform periodic maintenance or to make repairs.

Little more than a month before, a geeky exterminator with bug eyes and a long mustache like insect antennae had climbed into the service mezzanine to search for signs of vermin. Instead of rats, he found a nest of squirrels that entered through a torn vent screen.

Nothing as innocent as a pack of squirrels had opened the trap and put down the ladder while Zach slept.

He didn't lack the courage to search the space

above; however, he would have to be the bonehead
of all boneheads if he went up there at night with
no weapon other than a cool but cumbersome dull-
edged sword. He needed a good flashlight, too, because the strings of bare bulbs by which repairmen
worked didn't chase the shadows out of every corner. The following afternoon, after lessons and
lunch, he might climb into the service space, have a
look, poke around, see what he could see.

Maybe he would tell his father. They could search
the mezzanine together.

With his left hand, Zach lifted the bottom of the
ladder and folded back the lowest of four hinged
sections, whereupon a clever automatic mechanism
took over and accordioned the whole thing onto
the back of the trapdoor, which swung up into
place with a thump.

He stood in the closet for a while, until the pull-
ring on the trapdoor rope stopped swinging like a
pendulum, and then another minute or two. No
one tried to put the ladder down again.

Exterior doors were kept locked even during the
day. Dad said bad guys weren't like vampires, they
didn't hide from the sun, they were up to no good
24/7, so you never did anything to make their work
easier. No one could have sneaked inside and ascended to the mezzanine to hide.

More likely, the settling of the house that brought
the closet door out of plumb was also to blame for

this. Because of a slight shift in the structure, the weight of the ladder and gravity could have overpowered the spring-loaded closure, causing the trapdoor to drop open and the ladder to unfold on its own.

In fact, that must be exactly what had happened. Any other explanation was stupid kid stuff for gutless bed-wetters.

Before killing the closet light, he studied himself in the full-length mirror. He slept in briefs and a T-shirt. Although not superbuff, he wasn't by any definition scrawny. Yet he appeared smaller than his image of himself. His legs seemed thin. Pink knees, pale feet. The sword was too big for him, perhaps for any thirteen-year-old. He didn't look laugh-out-loud, bust-a-gut stupid, but he for sure didn't look anything like a guy on a recruiting poster, either.

After turning off the closet light, he braced the door shut with his desk chair, although doing so embarrassed him a little.

He placed the sword on his bed and slipped beneath the covers, only his head and right arm exposed. His hand lay lightly on the hilt of the Mameluke.

For a few minutes, he considered the nightstand lamp, but at last he decided that leaving it aglow was what a spineless jellyfish would do, a fully wilted wimp. He had no fear of the dark. Zip, zero, nada. No fear of darkness itself, anyway.

With the lamp out and the gloom relieved only by the pale-gray rectangles of curtained windows and the clock-radio light, Zach became convinced that, as earlier in the night, something had not been right about his reflection. He assumed that he'd lie awake until morning and that before dawn he would figure out what troubled him, but after a while an avalanche of weariness overcame him. As he was carried down into sleep, he saw himself in the mirror, pale feet and pink knees and too-thin legs, all of that quite true and right even if dismaying. Then he realized that the eyes in his reflection were not gray-blue like his eyes really were, but black instead, as black as soot, as black as sleep.

18

BAREFOOT AND IN A BLUE ROBE, SIPPING Scotch to foil insomnia, John paced the kitchen by the light of the stove hood, brooding about the events of the day. Sooner or later, he would have to share his suspicions with Nicky. But considering the bizarre and fantastic nature of what he would be asking her to believe, he wanted to lay out his case only when it seemed ironclad. They were as close as a husband and wife could be, committed to each other, with full trust in each other, but of course he could not tell her that invisible little creatures from Mars were living in the attic and expect her immediate belief even though she couldn't see them.

So much of what happened during this past day could be dismissed as psychological phenomena arising from the profound emotional trauma of the murders that occurred twenty years before. In any homicide investigation or in a court of law, such evidence would be considered hearsay at best, delusional at worst.

The tiny ringing bells that he heard in the Lucas house could have been an auditory hallucination. Yes, he had found the calla-lily bells in Celine's room, but no one had been there to ring them. He believed that, sitting at the desk in Billy's room, he had heard the murderous boy's cell tone, and he thought he had heard a faint voice say **Servus,** but without a witness to corroborate these experiences, they could have been auditory hallucinations, as well.

John knew that he had not imagined the recent call from Billy, and he assumed an investigation of telephone-company records would confirm an incoming call at the time he had received it. But nothing about Billy Lucas was apparently supernatural, nothing that supported the idea tormenting John: the possibility that Alton Turner Blackwood—his spirit or anima, or ghost, or whatever you wanted to call it—must be in the world once more, and must be somehow in the process of restaging the brutal murders he committed twenty years earlier, with the Calvino family as his fourth and final target.

The peculiar things he had seen were either in his peripheral vision or were arguably insignificant. While passing the print of John Singer Sargent's **Carnation, Lily, Lily, Rose** on the staircase landing in the Lucas residence, he glimpsed—or thought he did—one of the little girls in the painting sprayed with blood, the next time set afire. He had to acknowledge that in his agitated state of mind, he could have imagined those manifestations in the image. And the digital clocks in the Lucas kitchen and in Billy's room, suddenly flashing high noon or high midnight, were not irrefutable evidence that an entity from outside of time had been present; they were not evidence of **anything**.

Nicolette knew what had happened to John's family and that he killed their murderer on that same night of monstrous evil. He had told her every detail of the event in order that she might understand the psychology—the anguish, the guilt, the quiet paranoia, the dread that lingered—of the man she intended to marry. He withheld from her only one thing, which he would have to reveal when and if he told her why he now feared for their lives.

The kids knew John was an orphan. When asked how he had come to be alone in the world, he didn't quite lie to them, but implied that he was abandoned in infancy, knew nothing of his folks, and grew up in a church home for boys. He suspected that all three sensed some tragedy untold, but only Naomi now and then raised the subject, for she assumed, as was her nature, that orphanage life must have been marked by sweet melancholy yet also by grand adventure; if her father's past might be filled with romance in the classic meaning of the word, she yearned to be told about every thrilling episode.

When Minette turned eighteen, John intended to tell all three kids the truth, but he saw no reason to burden children with such a fearsome and disquieting tale. He knew too well what it was like to make one's way through adolescence in the shadow of primal horror. He intended—and now hoped—that they would grow up without that abomination seeded in their minds.

When he finished the Scotch, he rinsed the glass, left it in the sink, and went to the adjoining dayroom. Here Walter and Imogene Nash took their lunch, made out their shopping lists, and did their planning related to the maintenance of the house.

He sat at the walnut secretary, on which lay their spiral-bound month-by-month planner. He opened the book where it was paperclipped, to a two-page spread for the month of September.

Serial killers, especially obsessive ritualists who selected their targets with some care, like Blackwood, might kill at any time if the opportunity arose, but their major crimes usually occurred at regular intervals. The periodicity was often related to phases of the moon, though no one knew why, not even the sociopaths themselves.

Alton Turner Blackwood had not been strictly guided by the lunar calendar, but he had not been far off that schedule. The number thirty-three had meant something to him: He had murdered each of the families thirty-three days after murdering the previous one.

Billy Lucas massacred his family on the second of September. Counting from there in the day planner, John determined that the next slaughter, if it transpired, would be on the night of October fifth, only hours less than twenty-seven days from now. The third family would die on the seventh of November.

And if his superstitious expectation was fulfilled, the fourth family—he, Nicky, the children—would be scheduled for extermination on the tenth of December.

He was only mildly surprised when he discovered that the last of the four events fell on the night of Zach's fourteenth birthday. John had been fourteen when his family had been murdered by Blackwood. The synchronicity confirmed the validity of his dread.

After closing the day planner, he phoned the homicide-division personnel office to leave a message, taking a second sick day. He also called Lionel Timmins, his sometime partner, and left a similar voice mail on his cell phone.

The laundry lay at the farther end of the dayroom from the secretary. John found his attention drawn to that closed door.

He remembered Walter Nash warning him about an "ugly stink" in the laundry room. Perhaps a rat crawled in through the dryer exhaust duct and died in the machine.

Or perhaps not.

It's just curious how the smell came on so suddenly. One minute the laundry room is fine, and a minute later, it reeks.

In his current state of mind, John Calvino sensed a deadly spider spinning somewhere nearby but out of sight. Every detail of his day seemed to be a silken fiber in an elaborate surrounding web. Nothing could be dismissed as insignificant. Each occurrence related to all others in ways visible and invisible, and soon the spiral and the radial filaments would begin to vibrate as the architect of this ominous filigree circled toward the hub, toward the prey it hoped to trap there.

The longer he stared at the laundry-room door, the more gravity it exerted on him. He felt pulled toward it.

Another development or two, which need not have an obvious supernatural quality, which need only be strange and inexplicable, might snap the remaining threads that tethered him to the mooring mast of logic that was essential to any police investigation, and superstition would cast him adrift as surely as a dirigible was pulled aloft by its swollen helium ballonets. He had chosen a law-enforcement career and then the homicide division as a lifework of atonement for being the sole survivor in his family. He had proved to be a formidable detective in part because he possessed a talent for taking a few threads of evidence and from them reasoning his way to a correct picture of the entire tapestry of a crime. He did not know how he could proceed with confidence if ever reason failed him.

Reluctantly, as if the floor beneath him were a high wire and he an inexperienced aerialist certain of a fall, John rose from the walnut secretary and went to the laundry room. He opened the door and crossed the threshold.

The foul, strong, pervasive stench was that of Billy Lucas's uniquely repulsive urine, unmistakable in its singularity, which Coleman Hanes, the orderly, had attributed to the boy's regimen of medications. In his mind's eye, John saw the dark disgusting yellow-brown stream sheeting down the armored glass.

The ceramic-tile floor appeared spotless. No puddle of urine, not even one drop of filth.

Holding his breath, he looked in the washer and dryer. They had not been fouled.

He opened the cabinet doors on either side of the machines. The shelves were dry.

He looked at the surface-mounted, four-faceted ceiling vent from which warm air flowed. No dark fluid dripped from those angled vanes. Anyway, urine could not be in the heating system, for if it were, the stench would not be confined to this one room.

No urine was present, only the sulfurous stink of it.

Backing out of the laundry room, John closed the door. He switched off the dayroom lights and returned to the kitchen, where he drew deep breaths of clean air.

At the sink, he pumped soap from the dispenser and lathered his hands. Although he had touched nothing that required this sanitizing, he rinsed his hands in the hottest water he could tolerate, for as long as he could endure the sting.

The stench in the laundry room undid the effect of the Scotch. His nerves were tightly wound again. In the deep lake of his mind, schools of dark expectations darted in a frenzy that he must quell not merely to sleep but also to be able to keep his family safe.

He clicked off the stove-hood light and in full darkness went to the French door that offered access to the flagstone terrace and the backyard. He raised the pleated shade that provided privacy and stared out at the rain-smeared lights of distant neighborhoods beyond the wooded ravine.

The threat did not wait in the ravine. Although blinded by the night, John knew that nothing lurked anywhere across the unseen lawn, neither under the deodar cedar nor among its needled branches, nor in the playhouse that its limbs embraced. No enemy watched this house either from Willard's grave or from within the rose arbor.

He recalled the hard and inexplicable thump that had shuddered through his Ford when he had been parked under the main-entrance portico at the state hospital, when he had started the engine to leave.

Hours later, in the garage under this house, after he hung up his raincoat, three knocks and then three more had issued from the shadows and then from within the plastered ceiling. At the time, he attributed the noises to pockets of air vibrating through a copper water line.

Now intuition, as real as the marrow in his bones, told John Calvino that the knocking was instead an unseen visitor finding its way into a house that was strange to it, much as a blind man might be heard exploring new territory with his white cane.

The enemy did not lurk in the night. The enemy was already in the house.

Although he might be deemed a mental case if he made the claim out loud, John knew that when he came home, he had brought something with him.

From the journal of Alton Turner Blackwood:

The boy in the round room, high in the stone tower, hid his photograph of the beautiful dead movie star in all her naked glory, and always handled it with care. His one treasure.

He simmered with resentment of the old man, Teejay Blackwood. Of Anita, his mother, who abandoned him to his constrained life at Crown Hill. Of Regina, his mother's sister, and of young Melissa, Regina's daughter, who could go where they wished on the estate at any time of day or night, who never spoke to him, who mocked him to servants and laughed at him behind his back.

For the longest time, his resentment didn't grow into full-blown anger. It remained only a bitter brooding over insults and injuries.

Fear of being beaten restrained his anger.

And he dreaded having his few freedoms taken away. There was a subcellar with which he had been threatened more than once, a kingdom of silverfish and spiders.

He also feared what might lie beyond the 280 acres of Crown Hill. The old man often told him that in the world beyond, he would be called a monster, hunted down, and killed. In the early years, when his mother seemed to care about him, she also warned him against yearning for a life outside the estate. "If you leave here, you'll destroy not only your life but also mine."

The raven taught him freedom.

One hot June twilight, the boy cranked open all four windows in the tower room to encourage a cross-breeze.

With a flutter, the raven landed in the orange light that bathed the sill of the west window. With one sharp obsidian eye, the bird studied the hard-faced, graceless boy in his armchair with a book.

The bird cocked its head this way, that, the other. It assessed everything. Then it flew across the round room, out the east window, into the purple sky.

The boy believed his winged visitor wasn't merely a bird. Raven first, but spirit also, an omen, a harbinger.

From a bowl of fruit, he selected three grapes. With a knife he cut each grape in half to free its scent. He put the pieces side by side on the western windowsill.

He suspected that if the bird was more than a bird, it would return for this fleshy offering. As the orange light thickened to red, the raven alighted on the sill.

The boy watched it eat the grapes, and it watched him watching it. When the bird flew across the room once more and out the eastern window, the boy felt they had conducted a wordless conversation. A profound communion had occurred. But what it meant, he didn't know.

The next day at twilight, the raven appeared again, accepting more grapes. On the following dusk, quartered strawberries.

That third evening, two hours after the berries, the bird returned, the first time it visited after dark.

Sitting in lamplight, the boy stared at the bold raven on the shadowed sill, and the raven stared at the boy, and after a while the boy perceived that the creature had come to offer him something. But what? For half an hour, he waited, wondering, and then he knew. The bird had come to offer him the night.

Before the raven flew across the room, the

boy was on his feet, striding toward the east window. An instant after the bird sailed through the open casement, the boy clutched the center post with one hand and leaned out so far that he risked a fall.

As the raven glided down from the tower and away, moonlight glimmered wetly on the glossy black wings, scapulars, and tail feathers, as if the bird were a spill of ink that wrote the boy's future on the wind.

He hurried to the oak door, threw it open, and raced down the winding stairs. His footfalls were the drumming of a dragon heart, his urgent breathing echoing gustily off coiled-stone walls, like exhalations of fire.

Although he had long slept by day and lived in the late night, the easier to avoid the others whose company he was denied, he had never ventured from the house and the most immediate of the grounds. The time had come, the raven with its offer, the night and all its possibilities.

On these 280 acres were meadows and deep woods. Vales and hills. Rock formations and caves. Two streams and a pond. Although he could not set foot off the estate, before him waited a fenced world ripe for exploration.

And because the family and the servants slept, they would dream on unaware of how far he roamed and of what he did. He might do anything, anything, and they would think he walked the public rooms of the house or huddled in his tower, if they thought of him at all.

Always, he had been a shambler or a tottler, a clumsy construct of knobby joints and crude bones, stilting along in a praying-mantis gait. But suddenly in this night, racing across the east lawn in the wake of the liberating raven, the boy discovered a strange grace in his ungainly body.

Although, in the movies, the grim reaper was nothing but bones within his robe and cowl— as in Jillian Hathaway's famous Circle of Evil— the harvesting spirit was shown to move effortlessly, to flow, to glide as if skating on a slick of blood. Now, as the raven circled over the boy, carving the fat moon with its pinions, he too flowed, glided, skated across the lawn, into a meadow, toward the woods.

The boy was not yet me. He had one thing to learn and one thing to do. Then he would become the man that I am now.

19

THE RAIN DIMINISHED DURING THE NIGHT and ended as dawn broke. By the time John turned off the county highway onto the beech-lined approach road that served the state hospital, the cloud cover was worn thin, but it was nowhere threadbare enough to reveal blue sky.

On the hilltop, the institution huddled fortress-like, its parapeted roof resembling battlements, its windows wider than arrow loops in a castle wall but not by much, as though the place had been designed to defend against the sanity of the outside world rather than to keep its disturbed or even insane patients from wreaking havoc beyond its walls.

He parked under the portico again and displayed his POLICE placard on the dashboard.

On the telephone hours earlier, Dennis Mummers, who manned the third-floor security desk during the graveyard shift, said something about

Billy Lucas that required this second visit. When John asked about the boy's reaction to the search of his room, the guard's response did not at first seem significant. Later, it did.

He didn't say anything. Something's happened to him. He kind of cratered. He's funked out, withdrawn, not talking at all to anyone.

Karen Eisler, smelling of break-time cigarettes and wintermint breath freshener, entered John in the log at the reception desk.

Because he had spoken to Coleman Hanes en route, not more than twenty minutes earlier, the orderly did not have to be paged. He was waiting when John arrived.

In the elevator, Hanes said, "I'd still prefer you saw him in the conference room, like yesterday."

"If he's in total withdrawal, a wall of armored glass between us only makes my job harder."

"I can't leave anyone alone with him in his room, as much for his protection as for the visitor's."

"No problem. Stay with us."

"We've put him in restraints for your visit. I don't think it's necessary, the way he is now, but it's the rule."

In the security vestibule, John surrendered his service pistol.

Walking the third-floor hall, Hanes said, "He stopped eating last evening. This morning, he's refused liquids. If this keeps up, we'll have to force-feed him. That's an ugly thing."

"You don't have a choice."

"It's still damn ugly."

Billy's room—pale-blue walls, white ceiling, white tile floor—contained a safely upholstered chair without tufting or welting and a yard-square molded-plastic table tall enough for dining. A four-foot-wide concrete shelf protruding from a wall served as a bed, made comfortable with a thick foam mattress.

Lying on his back, head propped on two pillows, Billy did not react when they entered.

The restraints consisted of nylon-mesh netting that wrapped his torso, keeping his arms crossed on his chest, and between his ankles a trammeling strap to which the upper-body netting was secured.

John stood over Billy for a moment, hoping not to see what he expected to see, but he saw it at once, and the sight so affected him that his legs grew weak and he sat on the edge of the bed.

Coleman Hanes closed the door and stood with his back to it.

The boy's once fiery eyes were burnt out, still blue but as without depth as the glass orbs of a cheap doll, lacking their former intensity of feeling, their challenge and arrogance. Billy stared at the ceiling, but perhaps he did not see it. Although he blinked from time to time, he never changed focus, his steady stare like that of a blind man lost in thought.

His face remained as smooth as before. But his fresh-cream complexion had in less than a day curdled into a pallor. A gray tint shadowed the skin in the hollows of his eyes, as if those two fierce flames, now extinguished, had produced a residue of ashes.

His hair looked vaguely damp, perhaps with sweat, and his pale forehead appeared greasy.

"Billy?" John said. "Billy, do you remember me?"

The gaze remained fixed, not on the ceiling but on something in another place, another time.

"Yesterday, the voice was yours, Billy, the voice but not the words."

The boy's mouth hung open slightly, as though he had exhaled his final breath and waited with the patience of the dead for a mortician to sew his parted lips together.

"Not the words and not the hatred."

Body as limp as a cadaver prior to rigor mortis, Billy did not strain whatsoever against the restrictive netting.

"You were just a boy when he . . . walked in. Now you're just a boy again. You see? I understand. I know."

Billy's silence and stillness signified not mere indifference, but instead a mortal apathy born of despair, a retreat from all feeling and all hope.

"You were the glove. He was the hand. He has no further use for you. He never will."

How strange it felt to say these things, almost stranger than believing them.

"I wish I knew why you instead of someone else. What made you vulnerable?"

Even if one shiny fragment of the boy remained among the crazed ruins on the dark floor of his mind, even if one day he cared to live and if he spoke again coherently, he might not know why or how he had become an instrument of destruction in the service of the thing—all right, say it, **the corrupted spirit**—that had once been Alton Turner Blackwood.

"If you, why not anyone?" John wondered, thinking forward to the tenth of December, three months hence, when he might need to defend his family against the entire world. **Anyone** he encountered might be the glove in which the monstrous hand was next concealed. "If you . . . why not me?"

His biggest fear was not that something otherworldly had come home with him the previous day.

His biggest fear was that some flaw or weakness in himself would prove to be a door through which he might be entered as easily as a murderer, with a glass cutter, could enter a locked house.

To Billy he said, "You must be very broken now. He wouldn't leave you whole. One good boy in a million pieces."

John put one hand on Billy's forehead, expecting

to find him feverish. But though greasy with a scrim of sweat, the pale skin felt cold.

"If you find a way to talk and if you want to talk, tell them to call me," John said, without much hope that it would happen. "I'll come back. I'll come back right away."

He could see himself reflected in the boy's flat blue eyes, seeming to be transparent as he floated upon those irises, as if he were a man who had two spirits and was engaged in a double haunting.

Smoothing the lank hair away from Billy's brow, he whispered, "God help you. God help me."

In the third-floor corridor, after Coleman Hanes closed the door to the room, he said, "What the **hell** was that about?"

Heading toward the security vestibule, John said, "How long has he been like that?"

"Since late yesterday afternoon. What's this glove and hand business?"

"He became like that immediately after I left? An hour after, two hours?" John pressed.

"Soon after. What is this, what did you want in there?"

"Like twenty minutes after, ten after, five?" John rapped on the window in the security-vestibule door.

Hanes said, "Right after, I guess. I don't know to the minute. Are you going to tell me what you were doing in there?"

As the guard buzzed them into the vestibule, John said, "I don't talk about evidence in an open case."

"This is an open-and-**shut** case."

"It's technically open."

Hanes's usually pleasant face became a storm warning. He kept the pending thunder out of his voice, making a conscious effort to speak more softly. "Nine times he stabbed his sister."

John retrieved his pistol from the guard and holstered it. "If he comes out of the trance or whatever it is, if he wants to talk to me, I'll come back."

Hanes loomed, intimidating. "He doesn't belong out there. Not ever."

"That's not what this is about," John said as he pushed the elevator-call button.

"It sure sounded like that's what it's about."

"Well, it's not. Call me if he comes around. Call me whether he asks for me or not." The elevator door slid open, and John stepped into the cab. "I can find my way out."

"That's not the rules," the big man said, staying close behind him, crowding him. "I have to escort you."

After a silence, between the second and the ground floors, John said, "My son wants to be a marine. Any advice for him?"

"You remember her picture?" Hanes asked.

"Your sister? I do. I remember."

"I don't guess you'd remember her name?"

"I remember all their names. She was Angela, Angela Denise."

John's memory and his words clearly did not allay the orderly's suspicion.

In the lobby, as they walked past the reception desk toward the main entrance, Hanes said, "Twenty-two years, she's still dead—and the guy who did her, he's got this woman admirer, she writes a blog about him. He's got followers."

"Billy Lucas is never going to have followers."

"Oh, yes, he will. They all do. Every last sick damn one of them."

Hanes spoke the truth.

John said, "I can only tell you that isn't what this is about. I'm not his champion. He'll never be freed either from these walls or from what he saw himself do."

Still unappeased, Hanes followed John through the front doors, jostling him—perhaps unintentionally—when he fished his car keys from a sport-coat pocket.

The dropped keys rang off the pavement, and Hanes snatched them up. He held them in a clenched fist.

The orderly's eyes narrowed in his bleak brown face. " 'What he saw himself do'? That's a strange choice of words."

John met the other man's stare but only shrugged.

"The way you were with him in there," Hanes said.

"What way was that?"

"Sad. No. Not sad. Almost . . . tender."

John stared at the fist that held the keys, the fist of a man who had been to war and no doubt killed in self-defense.

Then he looked at his own hands, with which he had killed Alton Turner Blackwood twenty years earlier, with which he had wounded two men and killed another during his years of police work.

He said, "There was a brilliant artist, Caravaggio, he died back in 1610, when he was only thirty-nine years old. In his time, he was arguably the greatest painter in the world."

"What's he to me?"

"What are you to me or me to you? Caravaggio led a troubled life, brought to trial eleven times. He murdered a man, had to go on the run. Yet he was profoundly religious. He painted masterpiece after masterpiece on Christian themes, among other things."

"A hypocrite," the orderly said.

"No. He knew his faults, despised them. He was a tormented man. Maybe **because** he was tormented, he rejected the classical idealism of Michelangelo that other painters still embraced. He portrayed the human body and the human condition with a realism no one before him ever dared. The figures in his religious paintings aren't ethereal and idealized. They're deeply human, their suffering explicit."

"What's the point of this?" Hanes asked impatiently.

"I need my car keys. I'm explaining why you should give them back to me. One of Caravaggio's paintings is called **The Crucifixion of Saint Peter**. Peter is shown as a post-middle-aged man with a thick body and a worn face. There's Peter nailed to a cross, three men lifting it, hauling it erect. There's darkness and menace in the picture, such violence. The expression on Peter's face is complex, compelling, you can't stop staring at it. A man like you or me . . . we should see that painting for the first time alone, no one watching. Study it, give it an hour, and Caravaggio will show you the horror of what we are but the glory of what we could be, he'll take you from despair to hope and back again. If you let him . . . he'll reduce you to tears."

"Maybe not," Hanes said.

"Maybe not. But maybe so. Here's the thing. I admire Caravaggio's talent, the genius and hard work he brought to it. I admire the faith he tried—and often failed—to live by. But if I'd been a cop in his time, I would've chased him from one end of Europe to the other till I caught him, and I'd have seen him hanged. A hundred works of genius aren't compensation for the murder of a single innocent."

Hanes had a searchlight stare, and after a silent assessment, he relinquished the keys.

John rounded the car to the driver's door.

The orderly said, "Your son, he wants to be a marine—what's his name?"

"Zachary. Zach."

"Tell him, it'll be the best thing he'll ever do."

"I will."

"Tell him, he'll never regret one moment of it, except maybe the moment he retires from it. And one more thing."

John waited at the open car door.

"Someday I'd like to know what that was about in there."

"If I'm around at Christmas, come have dinner with us."

"Deal. How do you spell 'Caravaggio'?"

After spelling it, John got in the car and drove away.

In a few weeks, the purple beeches in the median strip between the two lanes would change to a rich shade of copper.

By Christmas, these trees would be bare.

He remembered other purple beeches in a park, their copper-leafed limbs draped with an early snow, a dazzling display.

Willard had been alive then, romping in a foot of white powder with the kids. The retriever and the trees had been the same shade of copper.

Again, he brooded about getting a German shepherd or another protective breed. But then he realized that perhaps an animal, as easily as a human being, could be the glove in which the hand of Alton Turner Blackwood might be hidden.

Weary from too little sleep, John wondered what condition he would be in by the tenth of December, Zach's birthday, when and if a dead man came to visit.

20

FOR NICOLETTE, THE MORNING WAS FINE, full of family, but the waking nightmare came at half past noon.

Mornings in this house were sacrosanct, beginning with breakfast prepared by Nicky and attended by all five Calvinos before John went off to work. During these early hours, no phone calls were made or accepted. Interruptions of routine were seldom sanctioned.

At seven forty-five, Nicky took the kids to the second-floor library, where she oversaw their lessons until lunch. They were a lively bunch, as eager to learn as to joke and tease and sass. Usually they engaged in too much of the latter three activities, yet always—frequently to Nicky's surprise—a satisfying amount of learning occurred.

This morning, the conversation around the breakfast table was different from the usual chinfest, more subdued, and the children were less lively during lessons, as well. Nicky attributed their uncharacteristic reticence to their late dinner the previous night and to the fact that they must have subsequently settled down to sleep hours later than usual.

At noon, Walter and Imogene offered options for lunch, and as this was the one meal of the day that **wasn't** a family event, Nicky took her Caesar salad with sliced chicken breast and a cold bottle of tea to her studio on the third floor. She didn't want to suffocate her ducklings. They needed time with one another, no adults around. They certainly needed time alone, too, if only to discover if they were going to be healthy saplings who found solitude nutritious or bratlings who, when left alone, blew things up for sport. She didn't mind if they suffocated **her**. They could hang out in her studio while she painted and they could quack at her nonstop, and she would relish every minute of it, though this proved to be a day when Zach took his lunch to his room and the girls retreated to theirs.

No out-of-house music or art lessons were scheduled for the afternoon, but Leonid Sinyavski, their math tutor, would be in-house from two o'clock until four. With his wild head of Einsteinian hair, bushy eyebrows, bulbous nose, and expansive belly, dressed always in a black suit and white shirt and black tie, he looked like a former circus clown who had decided to get serious. He was a dear man who seasoned his mathematics with magic tricks, and the urchins adored him, which was a good thing, because although Nicolette had a solid background in history and literature and art, she was no less undone by math than Samson by a barber.

In her studio, Nicky put the bottle of tea on the table that held her humility roses and sat on a stool to eat her salad while she studied the triptych that she suspected-hoped-believed was more than half finished. It looked like crap, which was okay because every painting in process seemed like crap when she returned to it on a new day. The longer she assessed a seemingly crappy canvas, the better it appeared, until sooner or later it didn't seem to be crappy anymore. Or if it continued to seem crappy, often it was the kind of crappy that had the potential to be transformed into something quite wonderful if only she could shift her sluggish talent into a higher gear, find that sweet spot between bitter self-doubt and dangerous overconfidence, and **get it done**.

John was one of the figures in the painting. He often appeared in her work. He wouldn't recognize himself at first—if at all—because the face on the figure differed from his. This face was one that Nicolette imagined he might have had if his adolescence hadn't been shattered by horror and violence, if his family had lived. She had painted him with many faces over the years because she had never known a man who held within him so many potentialities for goodness, even greatness.

At breakfast, before John left for the day, he had been a bit reticent, too, like the kids. Sometimes an investigation challenged him or emotionally involved him to such an extent that he lived half a step apart from everyone else, sometimes even from her, distracted by the scattered pieces of the puzzle that the murderer left behind.

Currently his primary case concerned a high-school teacher, Edward Hartman, who had been beaten to death in his cottage by the lake. Clues pointed toward the instructor's students, though not to one in particular. John's parents had been teachers—and murdered—so Nicky supposed he might be less himself for a while, until reason and intuition led him to a suspect and to case-clinching evidence.

Curiously, however, he had not mentioned the murdered teacher to her in perhaps a week, though he usually bounced ideas off her throughout the course of an investigation. If she didn't know how committed he was to his work, she might have thought he had reached a dead end in the Hartman case.

After she finished the salad, Nicky stepped out of her studio, crossed the third-floor landing at the head of the stairs, and went into the master suite, to the bathroom.

A month earlier, she'd undergone surgery to remove an abscessed tooth with roots fused to the jawbone. Although she had always been a twice-a-day flosser, the oral-surgery experience encouraged her to be obsessive about dental hygiene, and now she flossed after every meal.

With her tongue, Nicky could feel the gap where the tooth had been extracted. Eventually, when the bone repaired itself, she would receive an implant to fill the hole.

Because the storm clouds had begun to tatter, the clerestory windows high in the walls admitted enough sunshine that she didn't switch on the bathroom lights.

She drew a glass of cold water and put it aside.

Flossing, she bent over the sink, closed her eyes. Two minutes later, finished, she opened her eyes, saw scraps of lettuce and tiny shreds of chicken in the porcelain basin, and felt virtuous. She took a mouthful of water from the glass, rinsed, and spat.

When she put down the glass, raised her head, and grinned at the mirror to look for any obvious remaining bits of lettuce, she saw a man standing close behind her in the bathroom.

Crying out, Nicky swiveled to confront him. No one was there.

Shadowy and half-glimpsed in the clerestory light, he had seemed real nonetheless, tall and stoop-shouldered and scarecrow-strange. He could not have fled the bathroom, however, in the split second during which she turned toward him.

She took a deep breath, blew it out, and with it a small nervous laugh, amused that she had spooked herself.

When she turned once more to the mirror, the man was not behind her, as before, but now appeared—a dark shape, a shadowed face—in the looking glass where Nicky's reflection should have been.

A rough voice said something that sounded like **Kiss me,** a blast of arctic air slammed into Nicky, the mirror exploded in a thousand shards, and darkness took her.

21

SIX SCREWS IN THE FRAME OF THE FULL-
length mirror held it to the back of the door in the
girls' closet. On her knees, using a screwdriver,
Minette extracted them, starting with the two in
the bottom corners.

Naomi had gotten over the scare of the night before. Sister Half-Pint had infected Naomi with
spookitis, which was one of the dangers of sharing a
room with a sibling who both was colossally imma-
ture and yet had Daddy-green eyes that looked
right into you and sometimes made you think she
was the only third-grader in the world who knew
everything. Of course Mouse knew only about
enough to fill a teaspoon, she was your typical
eight-year-old ignoramus, as sweet as a sister could
be but tragically naive and dismally unsophisti-
cated. In the clear light of day, Naomi knew, as she
had **always** known, even in the grip of the mass

panic Minnie had fomented, that no sinister creature had been moving through the mirror, that she
had been right to say it was a moth shadow in the
room behind her, a moth currently tucked into a
corner somewhere and sleeping.

Naomi stared into the mirror now, as her sister
worked on the screws, and she saw nothing scary or
even unusual. In fact she was pleased to see that she
looked rather pretty, maybe even more than merely
"rather," though she would have to do something
enormously more stylish with her hair if she hoped
ever to enchant a prince, because a prince would
have a highly refined taste in all things and would
be very discriminating when it came to such matters as his lady's hairstyle.

"If we have to do anything at all, which I don't
think we do, why don't we just cover the mirror?"
Naomi asked. "This is a lot of work. Just covering it
so we can't see the mirror man and so he can't see
us—the mirror man who probably doesn't even
exist—won't that be good enough?"

"No," Minnie said.

"What do you know about it?" Naomi said. "You
don't know beans about it. I'm the one who knows
about magic mirrors. I've read like sixteen thousand
stories about magic mirrors. You've never read one."

"You read one to me that time," Minnie reminded her. "It was as dumb as scum."

"It wasn't as dumb as scum," Naomi said. "It was

literature. You were a second-grader then, you didn't understand. It was too sophisticated for a second-grader."

"It was pages and pages and pages of barf," Minnie insisted, putting aside the first screw. "I thought I'd never want to hear a story again."

"We could just hang a blanket over this thing."

"And you'd all the time be lifting it to peek at the mirror."

"I would not," Naomi said. "I have plenty of self-control. I am **disciplined**."

"You'll all the time be lifting it to peek, and sooner or later the mirror man will be there, and you'll start yammering at him about whether he's a prince, and he'll suck you into the mirror, and you'll be over there with the dead people forever."

Naomi let out a long-suffering sigh. "Honestly, dear Mouse, you are going to have to go into fraidy-cat rehab."

"Don't call me Mouse," Minette said, putting aside the second screw. She got to her feet and went to work on the next pair.

Naomi said, "What are Mom and Daddy going to say when they find out the mirror's missing?"

"They're going to say, 'Where's the mirror?' "

"And what are we going to say?"

"I'm thinking about that," Minnie said.

"You **better** be thinking about that."

Extracting the third screw, Minnie said, "Why

don't you put your gigantic eleven-year-old brain to work on it?"

"Don't be sarcastic. Sarcasm doesn't become you."

"Anyway, maybe they'll never know we took the mirror down."

"How could they not know? They have **eyes**."

"Who cleans our room?" Minnie asked.

"What do you mean who cleans our room? **We** clean our room. We're supposed to learn personal responsibility. Personally, I've learned enough personal responsibility to last a lifetime, so someone else could clean my room for a while, but **that's** never going to happen."

Putting the fourth screw with the first three, Minnie said, "After Mrs. Nash washes and irons our clothes, who brings them up here and puts them away? Who makes our beds every day?"

"We do. What's your point? Oh. You mean, if we keep the closet door shut, then it'll be a century before they realize the mirror's gone."

"Or at least a couple months," Minnie said as she placed the stepstool in front of the mirror. "When I take out the next screw, the mirror's gonna slip. Hold it tight for me." She climbed onto the stool. "Hold it tight."

Holding the mirror, staring into it, Naomi said, "What are we going to do with it when we take it down?"

"We're gonna carry it along the hall to the storage

room where Mom and Daddy keep all that junk, and we'll put it behind some of the junk so nobody won't even see it."

"Or we could save a lot of work and instead put it mirror-side down under your bed."

"I don't want the mirror man under my bed," Minnie said. "And I don't want him under your bed, 'cause you'll crawl under there to talk to him, and he'll come out of the mirror into our room. We'll be toast. One screw left. You holding it with both hands?"

"Yes, yes. Hurry up."

"Be careful it doesn't fall and break. If it breaks, maybe that lets him out of the mirror."

The sixth screw came loose, Naomi didn't let the mirror fall, Minnie put the stepstool away, and together they lowered the long pane of glass onto the bedroom carpet.

As Minnie closed the closet door, Naomi stood over the face-up looking glass, peering down into the reflected ceiling, intrigued by her face seen from this unusual angle.

The mirror dimpled like water dimpled when you dropped a pebble into it. Concentric circles spread outward across the silver surface.

"Bullcrap!" Naomi exclaimed, which was something her grandmother rarely said when the word **chestnuts** wasn't emphatic enough. "Minnie, look at this!"

Gazing down at the mirror, Minnie watched two, three, five new dimples and sets of concentric rings form, as if the glass were a pool and rain were falling into it.

"Not good," Minnie said, and went to the play table where her lunch sandwich waited on a plate with a sprig of sweet green grapes.

"You can't just go away and **eat,**" Naomi protested. "Big weird stuff is happening here."

Minnie returned with the sprig. She plucked one of the grapes, held it over the mirror, hesitated, and dropped it.

The plump green fruit plopped through the mirror as it would have sunk through the surface of a pond, and disappeared.

22

IN HIS BEDROOM CLOSET, ZACH PULLED ON the rope that opened the overhead trapdoor, and the ladder unfolded to his feet.

Since finding the ladder in this position the previous night, he'd thought through the possibilities, and he'd decided that the answer to the mystery was entirely mechanical, as he first suspected. A settling house shifted the trap mechanism slightly, and now from time to time it might drop open and the ladder unfold because its own weight could cause it to release spontaneously.

He didn't need to ask his dad to help him search the service mezzanine between the second and third floors because there wasn't anyone in the stupid mezzanine to find. The previous night, his nerves had been fried because of the freaking dream in which the big hands had tried to tear off his face and gouge out his eyes, those fingertips as big as soup spoons. He was a little disappointed in himself that he'd been rattled by a moronic dream. A few times over the years, he'd dreamed of being able to fly like a bird, soaring above everyone, above the city, but he'd never taken a dumb-ass leap off a roof to see if he could actually go lighter-than-air, and he never would, because dreams were just dreams.

Now he was going to search the service mezzanine not because a bad guy was lurking around up there, scheming and cackling like some Phantom of the Opera wannabe, but just for the principle of it, to prove to himself that he wasn't a chickenhearted, gritless jellyfish. He had a flashlight and a whacking big meat fork with a bone handle, and he was ready to explore.

After he'd gotten a sandwich and some fruit from Mrs. Nash and had brought his lunch to his room, he'd waited until he knew that she and Mr. Nash would be in the dayroom, having **their** lunch, before he returned to the kitchen to sneak a knife. He opened the wrong drawer, one containing meat forks and skewers and serving utensils, and just then he heard Mrs. Nash coming—saying, "It's no trouble at all, I'll get it, dear"—so Zach grabbed a killer fork and closed the drawer and split before she saw him. The stupid thing wasn't a knife, but it had four- or five-inch tines with wickedly sharp points, so even if it wasn't anything a marine would be issued in combat, it wasn't a total weenie weapon, either.

Holding the handle of the fork in his teeth with the tines to one side, as if he were an idiot pirate looking for a turkey dinner to carve up, the flashlight in his left hand, he climbed the ladder. At the top, he sat on the frame of the trap opening and switched on the strings of work lights that looped throughout the mezzanine.

This space had a finished floor, particleboard with a laminated Formica surface, so you could either scoot around easy on your butt or knees, or you could shuffle around in a crouch. The ceiling height was five feet, and Zach stood five feet six, probably going to be six feet like his dad, so he had to prowl the place in a stoop.

In addition to the garlands of work lamps and his flashlight, there were screened ventilation cutouts in the walls, to prevent dangerous mold from growing in here—and to allow squirrels to chew their way in now and then if they felt like it. The daylight didn't exactly pour in through the screens, just more or less dribbled. The flashlight peeled open the darkness wherever the other lamps didn't reach, but the movement of it also caused shadows to slide and twist and flutter at the periphery of your vision so you felt something was stalking you out there at the edge of things.

The mezzanine contained more machinery and ducting and pipes and valves and conduits than the engine room of a freaking spaceship. A maze, that's what it was, full of softly humming systems and clicking relays and the rushing-air sound of pressurized natural gas burning in the furnaces. The air smelled of dust, hot-iron gas rings, and aging preventative insecticide sprayed in the corners by the pest-control guy with the cockroach-feeler mustache.

Holding the flashlight in one hand and the fork in the other, Zach was maybe in the middle of the maze when the work lamps blinked off and when he heard the distinctive sound of the trapdoor thumping shut between the mezzanine and his closet. The night before, when his nerves were fried and when he imagined all kinds of things that might happen if he climbed up here to conduct a search, this was not one of the scenarios that occurred to him.

His flashlight died. The beam faded, faded, faded, and then went out altogether.

Zach wasn't such a complete bonehead that he believed the loss of both sources of light at the same time must be a coincidence. This was mortal trouble, sure enough, and in mortal trouble you needed to stay calm and **think**. You didn't survive freaking Guadalcanal or Iwo Jima, or the horrors of old Belleau Wood, by screaming for help and running blindly this way and that.

The service mezzanine might be a maze, okay, but every maze had an exit, and he remained pretty sure of his position relative to the trapdoor. The ventilation cutouts didn't reveal anything, but the faint glow of them at points around the perimeter served as markers to further guide him. Tiny red, green, yellow, and blue indicator LEDs on the furnaces and the humidifiers would also help him find his way back to the trapdoor.

His biggest concern, bigger than the darkness and bigger than the twisty nature of the return route to safety, was that someone must be in the mezzanine with him. Simple gravity might drop open an out-of-plumb, out-of-balance trapdoor, but gravity couldn't in a million years pull it up and close it again. And gravity didn't have fingers to switch off the work lamps.

If some foaming-at-the-mouth maniac had decided to live secretly in the mezzanine, quieter and nuttier than squirrels, he couldn't be a **benign** maniac.

Zach continued to grip the dead flashlight tightly in his left hand because it might serve as a secondary weapon, a club with which he might be able to bash an adversary even as he forked him. In the heat of battle, you sometimes ran out of ammunition and your bayonet snapped, and then you had to fight with makeshift weapons. Of course, he'd never possessed a gun with ammunition or a bayonet; he **started** with makeshift weapons, but the principle still applied.

For a while, Zach stood motionless, waiting for the enemy to reveal his position. The only sounds were the low background noises of the furnaces and the other equipment. The longer he listened, the more those ticks, clicks, and hisses sounded like insects conspiring with one another, as if he were in some kind of godawful hive.

He told himself that the assumption of mortal danger might not be correct, that some joker might be playing games with him. Naomi was capable of trying to frighten him. She might have climbed into the mezzanine to switch off the lights, descended, and put up the ladder. The brother-sister competition to make each other appear to be a geek or an idiot tended to wax and wane, and it had waxed lately, but their pranks were mostly good-humored. This didn't feel the least bit good-humored. This felt threatening. Besides, if the culprit was Naomi, she would not have been able to contain herself more than ten seconds after closing the trapdoor, she would be down there in his closet, laughing her stupid head off right now, in full loon mode, and he would hear her.

Inaction began to seem like a loser's strategy.

Maybe this crawlspace guy was a supertuned stealth machine, highly trained in the ancient Asian secrets of silent motion, like a ninja assassin or something. The light-footed bastard might be on the move, closing on his clueless target, yet as hushed as a dandelion puffball drifting on a breeze.

Zach knew a lot about the military strategy that had won many famous battles in numerous wars, but applying military strategy to a one-on-one creep-and-kill in a dark crawlspace quickly turned out to be difficult, maybe even impossible.

To his chagrin, Zach felt his heart beating harder, faster. By the second it became increasingly difficult to maintain the stillness necessary to listen for his adversary. He grew convinced that someone approached him from behind, now from ahead, now from the left, the right. If he remained where he stood, he was essentially dead on his feet, a corpse waiting to happen.

Lightless flashlight and two-pronged fork held in front of him, crouching lower to avoid ceiling-suspended ducts and pipes, he turned and began to inch back the way he'd come. Something brushed the top of his head, but he knew it wasn't anything alive, and he bumped into a sheet-metal panel on a furnace, which pealed hollowly like the fake thunder of stage-show sound effects. The flashlight knocked against a wood post. The floor creaked underfoot. The steel tines of the fork stuttered against another metal surface. The harder he tried to be quiet, the noisier he became.

Zach's heart **boomed,** the loudest noise he made, at least to his own ears, although his breathing wasn't exactly hushed. He was virtually **snorting**. At the same time that he grew ever more frantic to escape the darkness, he became increasingly mortified by his poor self-control, and he fought against descent into flat-out panic.

Blindly, he felt his way between something and something else, intuitively turned right, into a pitch-black pocket of the maze where not even an LED indicator light relieved the gloom, and the cool air abruptly plunged twenty degrees, maybe thirty, pricking shivers from him. He froze, not as a consequence of the cold air but because he sensed that someone crouched immediately in front of him, that he'd come face-to-face with his unknown adversary. Although he couldn't see anyone in this blackout, he **knew** a man loomed, a man big and strong and not in the least afraid of him.

No. Get real. Stay cool. Just his imagination running wild. There was nothing in front of him but more darkness, which he could prove easy enough by thrusting fiercely at the void with the fork. The two long tines sank into someone, into a freaking **wall** of meat. No one cried out, no one grunted in pain, and Zach wanted to believe he'd stabbed something inanimate.

That hope was instantly dispelled when a hand, as slick and cold as a dead fish, closed around his wrist, **engulfed** his wrist, as big as the hand that tried to tear his face off in the dream. He couldn't pull free. He sensed the man seizing the shank of the fork, wrenching the tines out of himself. Zach held desperately to the handle. If he lost control of the weapon, he'd be stabbed with it—relentlessly stabbed, gouged, torn.

Inches from Zach's face came a cruel voice speaking in a low hoarse whisper: **"I know you, boy, I know you now."**

Zach's cry for help couldn't press past his lips, but instead fell like a stone into the well of his throat, seeming to block his airway, so he could neither exhale nor inhale.

To Zach's surprise, the brute knocked him backward, the fork still in his fist, and he fell on his back as the iciness instantly melted from the air. The work lamps brightened, as did the beam from the flashlight still clutched in his left hand, and shadows flew away to farther corners.

Gasping, he sat up, alone in the light, alive and alone, the fork thrust forward defensively in his right hand. The shank of the weapon was bent at a severe angle from the handle, and the two long steel prongs were twined together as if they were ribbons.

23

THE SECOND GREEN GRAPE DROPPED FROM Minnie's fingers and passed without a sound through the surface of the mirror. Concentric waves lapped outward from the point of impact, but the grape did not bobble to the surface as it would have done in water.

Spooked but also exhilarated, Naomi said, "**Pig fat!** Minnie, we have to show Mom and Daddy, they've gotta see this, there's somewhere else inside the mirror, this is like the biggest big news ever, this is so **huge**." **Pig fat** was an expression of her own invention, so she wouldn't always have to rely on her grandmother's **chestnuts** and **bullcrap**. "It's not such dumb scum now, is it, huh, is it, when it's real in front of your face?"

As Naomi started toward the door, Minnie said, "Wait," in that way she sometimes had that was older than eight.

Returning to the mirror, standing over it, Naomi said, "What?"

"We'll see."

In addition to the wavelets made by the grapes, rings of ripples appeared continuously from end to end of the mirror, like raindrops briefly and gently cratering the surface of a pond. Now that phantom-rain activity declined . . . ceased. The silver surface became calm.

Minnie plucked a third grape from the sprig, held it between thumb and forefinger, hesitated until Naomi began to fidget with impatience, and at last dropped it. The plump fruit hit the mirror, bounced, raised no ripples, rolled across the hard surface, and came to a stop against the frame.

"What happened?" Naomi demanded.

"Nothing happened."

"Wow, brilliant, I **see** nothing happened, I've got two eyes. Why **didn't** something happen, where did the magic go?"

"You said show Mom and Daddy, and it doesn't want them to see."

"What doesn't want them to see?"

"It."

"It what?"

"The it-what in the mirror, which could be just about anything, except I don't think it's your lah-dee-dah fairy-tale prince."

Deciding to let the **lah-dee-dah** pass without a

withering retort, Naomi said, "Why doesn't it want them to see the magic?"

Minnie took a slow step back from the mirror and shook her head. "Because the magic isn't magic, it's something else, and it's really, really bad. If Mom and Daddy see, they'll take the mirror away from us, and the mirror doesn't want to be taken away from us."

"The mirror wants to stay with us? Why?"

"Maybe it wants to eat us," Minnie said.

"That's **so** big-baby silly. Mirrors don't eat people."

"This one ate grapes."

"It didn't eat them. They passed **through** it."

"They passed through it to where it ate them," Minnie insisted.

"Not all magic is black magic, Miss Gloomy Bloomers. **Most** magic is about wonder and adventure, new horizons and learning how to fly."

"This isn't magic," Minnie insisted. "This is the kind of weird stuff that's **real**."

Stooping, Naomi reached for the grape that had failed to penetrate the glass.

"Don't touch the mirror," Minnie warned. "Only the grape. You better listen to me, Naomi."

Naomi snatched up the grape, popped it into her mouth, then gave the mirror a quick pat.

"Don't be dumb," Minnie said.

Chewing the grape, swallowing, Naomi again patted the mirror with her fingertips to prove that she did not possess the fraidy-cat gene that made her sister a superstitious basket case, that she was capable of exploring a scientific phenomenon like this with a clear mind and healthy curiosity.

"You make me crazy," Minnie said.

Grinning, Naomi patted the mirror a third time, longer than before: **pat-pat-pat-pat-pat-pat-pat**. "Maybe there's a shark swimming in there, looking for more grapes to eat, and it'll come up and bite off my fingers."

"Something a whole lot worse than any shark," Minnie declared. "It'll bite off your head, and **then** what am I gonna tell Mommy and Daddy?"

Instead of patting the mirror again, Naomi pressed her right hand flat against the shiny surface and held it there.

Suddenly her hand went cold, and the mirror spoke or something within the mirror spoke, its voice ragged, wet, ferocious, sharp with hatred: **"I know you now, my ignorant little bitch."**

The words literally stung Naomi, a volley of hot needles lancing out of the mirror, swiftly sewing through her arm, into her shoulder, up her neck, stitching across her scalp. She cried out, snatched her hand away, and fell backward on the floor.

Minnie scrambled to her—"Your hand, your

hand!"—certain there must be fingers missing, torn flesh and bristling bones, but Naomi remained whole: no blood, no burn, not even so much as needle pricks stippling the palm of her hand.

The sting was emotional as well as physical, because Naomi had never before been the recipient or the dispenser of such rage and hatred. She loved the world and the world loved her, and all anger was but a momentary irritation, a fleeting exasperation, one petty vexation or another that evaporated soon after being expressed. Until the voice spoke of her with such fury and contempt, she had not fully comprehended that someone might exist who ardently desired that she should suffer humiliation, great pain, and even death. She didn't need to infer those ill wishes in the voice of the unknown speaker, for they were implicit in the viciousness with which he had spoken.

She and Minnie sat on the floor, hugging each other, reassuring each other that they were all right, untouched and undaunted, and only gradually did Naomi come to realize that her sister hadn't heard the voice. The man spoke only to her, through her contact with the mirror, and somehow the **intimacy** of this communication made it worse, creepier, more threatening.

Minnie expressed no doubt that the voice had been real or that it had said to Naomi exactly what she reported that it said. For her part, Naomi no longer questioned that the mirror must be a portal to some kind of hell rather than a door to Narnia, and she was as eager as Minnie to get it out of their room. In the rush of daily life, they were eight and eleven years old, they were as different from each other as salt from pepper, but in either a pinch or a serious crisis, they were sisters first and last.

Again Naomi wanted to tell their folks, but Minnie said, "It'll sound like a big steaming bowl of the usual Naomi. Besides, I've got my own reason for not running around yelling about ghosts and stuff."

Naomi was about to take offense, but the second thing Minnie said was more interesting. "What reason?"

"You can't waterboard it out of me. And you **know** that's true."

The mirror had a smooth wooden back, and the girls agreed to lay it flat and slide it along the carpet rather than carry it, in part because it was heavy but also because they could push it with the toes of their shoes, with less need to touch it.

When they got to the storage room, however, they would have to lift it in order to tuck it away behind a bunch of other junk, where no one would notice it. They had no work gloves, but they did have white gloves for special occasions, like church at Easter, and they put those on before proceeding with the task, to avoid accidentally touching bare fingers to the mirror.

Daddy was at work. Mom was in her studio. Mr. and Mrs. Nash were finishing their lunch or cleaning up the kitchen.

Only Zach might step out of his room and see them toeing the mirror along the hallway, but Naomi was confident they could handle Zach with one fib or another. Fibbing wasn't like telling whoppers that could land you in Hell. Fibbing was lying lite, sort of like the caffeine-free diet cola of lying, so your soul didn't gain any serious weight of sin from it. They would have to fib, because Zach would never believe that grapes had fallen through a mirror or that something in the mirror had threatened Naomi. Zach liked to keep things real; now and then, when Naomi was particularly enthralled with some fabulous new idea or possibility, when she was compelled to share every detail of it with everyone, Zach sometimes said, "Let's keep it real, Naomi, let's get it earthbound."

After Minnie opened the door, scoped the hallway, and found it deserted, they slid the mirror out of their room. Using only their feet, they worked it quickly to the east end—the back—of the house. The reflection of the ceiling sliding ahead of them made Naomi a bit dizzy. Minnie said, "Don't look at it." But Naomi continued to look, because the more she thought about the voice from the mirror—**I know you now, my ignorant little bitch**—the more she worried that by pressing her hand to the looking glass and defying Minnie's plea to be cautious, she had **invited** the mirror man to cross over from his side to theirs, that now he might rise out of the silvery glass.

She had thought of herself as a girl absolutely **loaded** with perspicacity; but now it didn't seem very perspicacious of her to have done what she had done.

The storage room was the smaller of two guest bedrooms. It was three-quarters full of boxes and small items of furniture in rows with passage-ways between them. The end tables and chairs and chests and lamps, used in a previous house, were out of style in this one, but Mother was reluctant to dispose of them because they were still things that she liked and about which she was nostalgic.

They stood the long mirror on its side. Naomi pulling, Minnie pushing, hands protected by Easter Sunday church gloves, they slid this door-to-a-not-so-magical-kingdom past all the other junk and hid it behind the final row of boxes.

Mission accomplished, they returned to their room, examined their gloves to be sure they weren't soiled, and put them away.

Professor Sinyavski would arrive in little more than an hour to torture them with math.

"I'm too emotionally wrung out for math," Naomi declared. "I'm **exhausted,** the strain has just been too severe, my strength has been utterly consumed. I'm **fatigued,** there's nothing left in me for math."

"Eat your sandwich," Minnie said, pointing to the lunch plate on Naomi's desk. "You'll feel better."

They had left the closet door open. The absence of the mirror now posed a problem for Naomi.

"I won't know how I look. I won't know if my clothes match, if my hair's properly combed, if some outfit makes me look fat. I could have a smudge of something on my face and not know and make a fool of myself in public."

"But without a mirror," Minnie said, "you gain like three hours a day to do something else."

"Very funny. Hilarious. Yes, giggle yourself sick, go on, give yourself a massive hernia. But a mirror is absolutely essential to a civilized life."

Giggles spent, Minnie said, "There's mirrors in the bathrooms, and there's one in the hall, and there's a big one down in the living room. There's lots of mirrors."

Naomi was about to explain that the other mirrors were much less convenient, but another and troubling thought struck her. "How do we know the mirror man isn't in those other mirrors?"

"We don't know," Minnie said, and this was clearly not a new idea to her.

"He couldn't be."

"Maybe he could. Maybe he couldn't."

Naomi shook her head emphatically. "No. Not **every** mirror can be an enchanted doorway to wherever. Magical things are magical because they're rare. If everything was magical, magic would be ordinary."

"You're right," Minnie said.

"If **every** mirror was a doorway to someplace fantastic . . . well, then there'd be confusion, chaos, pandemonium! The sky would be full of flying horses, and trolls would be running wild in the streets."

"You're right," Minnie said. "It's only that one mirror."

"You really think so?"

"Yeah. And it's gone, so now it's safe to sleep at night."

"I hope so. But what if I'm wrong?"

"Eat your sandwich," Minnie said.

"Can I have your pickle?"

"No. You have a pickle already."

"I wish I would've asked for two."

"You already ate one of my grapes, and the mirror ate two," Minnie said. "Nobody gets my pickle."

"So keep it. I don't want your crummy pickle anyway."

"Yes, you do," Minnie said, and ate her gherkin with much crunching and lip smacking.

24

HAVING RETURNED TO THE CITY FROM THE
state hospital, John parked in front of a store on
Fourth Avenue. Above the entrance, silver script on
the sign matched the script on the green box that
contained the calla-lily bells: **Piper's Gallery**.

These two blocks of quaint brick buildings offered specialty shops of many kinds. The caliber of
the vehicles snugged against the curbs suggested an
upscale clientele.

Shagbark hickories lined the street, trunks gray
and flaking. Their dark-green leaves would be deep
yellow in a few weeks, and when they shed, the
pavement would appear to be paved with gold.

Three customers were browsing in the store, two
forty-something women in stylish pantsuits and a
young man whose face seemed to be set in a perpetual dreamy smile.

John expected a gift shop, and it was that, but it

was something else as well—though he could not quite define its retail niche. The merchandise seemed to be an incoherent mix, yet he suspected that a theme must connect each line of goods to the others. Although the regular customers appeared to understand that leitmotif, to John it became increasingly elusive the more he browsed through the store.

The items on the display tables were of high quality. Exquisite crystal animals: bears, elephants, horses. Coiled crystal snakes, lizards, tortoises. Cats outnumbered other mammals. There were many owls, as well. Goats, foxes, wolves. Another table presented clear and colored crystal forms: obelisks, pyramids, spheres, octagons. . . .

Past a table of magnificent geodes stood a collection of gold-plated and silver bells, small and superbly detailed. All were shaped as flowers, not just calla lilies but also tulips, foxgloves, fuchsias, daffodils. . . . Some were single bells, others triune, and the foxglove was a seven-bloom spill along a gracefully curved stem.

There were soaps, candles, oils of numerous scents, and the walls were lined with shelves holding thousands of small green jars of dried herbs. Angelica, arrowroot, caraway, basil, borage. Figwort and fever root. Marjoram and mayapple. Rosemary, sage, sweet cicely. Some jars contained powdered weeds: burdock, creeping buttercup, fireweed, nettle, shepherd's purse, and thistle. Others had stranger names: wonder of the world, High John the Conqueror, **mombin franc**.

As he familiarized himself with the store, he became aware that the two women in pantsuits were intrigued by him and curious about what items attracted him. They watched surreptitiously, conversing in murmurs and whispers, not realizing he was alert to their interest.

He was not a man whose looks turned women's heads. Furthermore, he lacked the aura of authority and the air of perpetual suspicion that made so many cops recognizable to one another and that common citizens often perceived at least unconsciously. His ordinariness in fact gave him an advantage as a detective, especially if he needed to conduct surveillance.

When John looked up from a display of silver jewelry featuring animals, he saw the young man watching him from another aisle, that abiding half-smile reminiscent of a porpoise.

He supposed Piper's Gallery might be one of those stores that fostered a sense of community among its regular customers. Certain specialty merchants had a knack for making their patrons feel like members of an extended family. In which case, these three sensed that he was unfamiliar with the store, and like any group of insiders in a world of outsiders, they were entertained by his reactions.

After circling the premises, he came to a cashier's station at the back, opposite the front door, where a clerk sat on a stool. She was reading a slim volume of poetry, and she finished a quatrain before closing the book and smiling at him. "May I help you?"

An attractive, freckle-faced brunette of about fifty, she wore no makeup. Her lustrous hair was drawn into a ponytail that looked as if it might reach to her waist. Hanging on a short chain, a silver ring encircling a silver sphere nestled in the hollow of her throat.

Police ID usually elicited a subtle reaction that John could read as easily as a newspaper headline. In this case, he could tell nothing from the woman's response; she seemed as indifferent to the sight of a badge as she might have been to a library card.

"Is Mr. or Mrs. Piper available? Or is Piper a first name?"

Her smile was as fresh and wholesome as her appearance. But John thought he detected smugness in it, a faint trace of haughtiness, a discreet disdain closer to pity than to dislike.

Or perhaps his paranoid mood shaded her smile with a quality it did not contain. To have any success as a detective, he must remember that what was perceived was not always what had been seen, that an observer was part of the scene he observed. Only a perfect lens did not distort, and no human being could achieve perfection.

"Piper," said the clerk, "isn't anyone's name in this case. It's a title. I'm Annalena Waters. I own the place."

From a coat pocket, John produced the box containing the calla-lily bells. He had cleaned the blood from the silver stem, though the tarnish remained.

"I see by the display, it's a regular item in your inventory. Do you sell many of it?"

"Quite a few of the entire line, but not that many of any one flower. There are seventeen different kinds. And the calla lily is the most expensive."

"If you sold a set of bells like these to someone recently, might you be able to describe him?"

"This is about the Lucases, isn't it?" asked Annalena Waters.

"Then you recognize this particular set? The bells were found in the girl's room. I believe the boy carried them with him from murder to murder."

Her face seemed unaccustomed to a frown and aged with the strain of it. "How strange. Why do you believe he did such a thing?"

"I'm not free to discuss evidence in the case. But you do recall selling these bells to him?"

"Not to him. To Sandy. His mother."

John had assumed the boy bought the bells under the influence of Blackwood's invading spirit. They had been circumstantial evidence of a supernatural aspect to the case. Now they were just bells.

Annalena said, "Sandy was my customer ever

since the accident that put her in the wheelchair. She was such a lovely person. What happened to the family—it's too awful to think about."

"Were you surprised that Billy could do such a thing?"

"I'm still not sure he did."

"He confessed."

"But he was such a kind and thoughtful boy. There wasn't any violence in him, not any anger. He usually came with his mother. He was so attentive to her, so caring. He adored her."

"When did she buy the bells? Recently?"

"Oh, no. Maybe two, three months ago."

Returning the bells to the box, John said, "Why would Sandra Lucas buy a set of bells?"

"For one thing, they're beautiful. The artist does fine work. And they produce such a sweet sound. Some people call them fairy bells. We call them reminder bells. They remind us that Nature is beautiful and sweet, that life will be more beautiful and that we will be healthier when we live in harmony with her."

"The dried herbs, weeds," John said, "are they for homeopathic remedies?"

"Not primarily homeopathic," Annalena said. "They're useful in all forms of alternative medicine."

"That's what the store is about, huh? Alternative medicine."

"Natural therapies," she explained. "Fill your home—your life—with the beauty, the aromas, the sights and sounds of nature, and you will prosper in all ways. Or is that too New Age for you, Detective?"

"I keep an open mind, Ms. Waters. I keep a wide-open mind."

In spite of the sincerity of his answer, he thought he saw again that most gentle arrogance in her smile, that disdain akin to pity.

Outside, as John opened the driver's door of his car, he looked at the shop and, through the large windows, saw the women customers and the young man with the dreamy smile gathered at the cashier's station, not as if lined up to make purchases, but as if consulting with Annalena Waters.

The rain clouds had mostly unraveled. The sun ruled the sky, but shadows gathered under the shagbark hickories, and the afternoon seemed darker than it was.

25

NICOLETTE WOKE FROM A DEEP DARKNESS IN which lesser darknesses moved, and she found herself alone at the bottom of a well, light high overhead but shadows here, and cold stone for a bed.

As her disorientation passed, she realized the light came from the clerestory windows that faced away from the westering sun of the afternoon. She remembered the exploding bathroom mirror.

Wary of the danger of shattered glass, she moved circumspectly, anticipating the brittle notes of shards falling from her onto the limestone floor. There was no such glassy music, and when she touched her face, she found no embedded splinters, no wounds, no blood.

No debris crackled underfoot as Nicky rose. She discovered the mirror intact.

The undiminished memory of the looming figure, the strange and shadowed face where her reflection should have been, chilled her now just as the blast of arctic air, out of the disintegrating mirror, chilled her then.

On the black-granite counter lay the loop of waxed floss with which she had cleaned her teeth, and beside it stood the tumbler of water with which she had rinsed her mouth. The scarecrow figure had seemed as real as these everyday objects.

She switched on the lights. In the clear depths of the mirror, she was the sole presence.

When she consulted her wristwatch, she realized that she had been lying on the floor for longer than an hour.

Such a period of unconsciousness suggested a serious knock on the head, the danger of concussion. She did not feel concussed—no dizziness, no blurred vision, no nausea—and when she explored her skull with her fingertips, she found no tender spot.

Brooding about what had happened, she rinsed the drinking glass and dried it with paper towels. She returned it to the drawer from which she had gotten it earlier.

As she threw the paper towels and the length of floss in the small trash can, her tongue found the hole from which the first molar on the lower left side had been extracted a month earlier. She knew at once a possible explanation for the man in the mirror and the exploding glass.

The oral surgery had taken a few hours because

every speck of the fused roots of the broken-off tooth had to be drilled out of the jawbone. Her periodontist, Dr. Westlake, prescribed Vicodin for the post-operative pain, which was sharp and persistent. Nicky took the drug only twice before experiencing a serious adverse effect, a rare idiosyncratic reaction: frightening hallucinations.

Those visions were different in substance but akin in feeling to the apparition in the mirror. She had not taken Vicodin in twenty-six days, but it must somehow be the culprit in this case.

She would have to call Dr. Westlake to inquire if a flashback hallucination was possible after so much time. She knew that some drugs remained in the body, at least in trace amounts, weeks after being taken. Such a possibility disquieted her.

In the library, Zach and Naomi and Minnie sat at different tables, and Leonid Sinyavski cycled from one to the other, providing different levels of instruction, yet making them feel as though they were a class of equals.

Math was a sport to Zachary. The problems were games to be won. And good math skills would be crucial if he became a marine sniper targeting bad guys at two thousand yards. Even if he didn't qualify for sniper training or if he decided against it, military strategy was intellectually demanding, and knowledge of higher mathematics would always be super-useful no matter what his specialty.

He liked Professor Sinyavski: the cartoony white hair bristling every which way, those bizarro eyebrows like huge furry caterpillars predicting a hard winter, the rubbery face and the exaggerated expressions meant to drive a point home, the way he made you feel smart even when you were stuck in stupid. But this time Zach couldn't concentrate on geometry. He wished away the two-hour session with such intensity that of course it crawled past like twenty hours.

All that he could think about was the encounter in the service mezzanine. The bent shank of the fork. The braided tines. The low, hoarse whisper: **I know you, boy, I know you now.**

The incident either happened or it didn't.

If it happened, some godawful supernatural presence lurked in the mezzanine. No real person could be stabbed and not bleed. No real person could twist the stainless-steel prongs of a big old meat fork as if they were blades of grass.

If it **didn't** happen, then Zach must be mentally ill.

He didn't believe he could be flat-out insane. He didn't wear an aluminum-foil hat to prevent telepathic aliens from reading his thoughts, he didn't eat live bugs—or dead ones, either—and he didn't think God was talking to him and telling him to kill everyone he saw who wore blue socks or something. At worst, he might be having delusions, moments of delirium, like because of some stupid blood-chemistry imbalance. If that was true, he wasn't really even halfway nuts, he was just the screwed-up victim of a medical condition, and no danger to anyone except maybe to himself.

The damaged meat fork seemed to disprove the delusion theory. Unless he imagined the fork along with everything else.

To accept the supernatural explanation would be to acknowledge that there were things you couldn't deal with no matter how strong and smart and brave and well-trained in the art of self-defense you might become. Zach loathed admitting such a thing.

But to accept the mental-illness explanation, he would have to admit a similar and even more dis-tressing fact: that no matter how smart and coura-geous and well-intentioned you were, there was always a chance that you would not become the person you envisioned yourself being, because your own mind or body could fail you.

In either case, a supernatural invasion of the ser-vice mezzanine or some half-assed madness, sooner or later he would need to have a conversation with his parents about the situation, which was dead sure to be almost as just-kill-me-now mortifying as the conversation he had with his dad about sex a year or so previously.

Before he sat down with his folks to reveal that he was either a superstitious idiot or a foaming-at-the-mouth lunatic in the making, Zach wanted to think further about what had happened. Maybe he would arrive at a **third** explanation that would obviously be the correct one and that would spare him embarrassment.

To make a point, Professor Sinyavski pulled a small red ball from Minnie's left ear, turned it into a trio of green balls in front of their eyes, and juggled the three until somehow they all became yellow without anyone noticing when it happened.

To Zachary, this kind of prestidigitation no longer qualified as magic. His world had changed a little while earlier; and now reality encompassed things that once seemed impossible.

⁂

Naomi doubted that any human being really understood math, they simply all pretended to have it down pat, when in truth they were every bit as confused by it as she was. Math was nothing but a giant hoax, and everyone participated in it, everyone **faked** a belief in math so they could be done with the hideous classes and the drudgery of the hateful homework and get on with life. The sun came up

every morning, so the sun was real, and every time
you inhaled you got the air you needed, so the atmosphere was obviously real, but half the time
when you tried to use math to solve the simplest
problem, the math absolutely **would not work,**
which meant that it couldn't be real like the sun and
the atmosphere. Math was a waste of time.

Not only was math a waste of time, it was also im-
mensely boring, so she pretended to understand
what dear Professor Sinyavski prattled on about,
and she pretended actually to listen to the sweet
man. Mostly she had him bamboozled, which suggested a future as an actress might indeed be in her
cards. While she handily deceived the genius Russian into believing he had her attention, Naomi actually thought about the enchanted mirror they had
secreted in the storage room, and she wondered if
they had been too hasty about removing it from
their bedroom.

I know you now, my ignorant little bitch.

In memory, as clear as anything on a CD, she
could hear the creepy voice that had spoken to her
and to her alone, and it still scared her. But she realized now that she should not have judged the nature of the entire vast and fabulous land beyond the
mirror from evidence consisting of merely eight
words spoken by a perhaps evil but certainly rude
individual. There were many rude people on this
side of the looking glass, too, and evil ones, but this

entire world wasn't rude and evil. If a magic kingdom truly waited beyond the mirror—a real magic kingdom, not just another Disney World—it would be populated by all kinds of people, good and bad. She had probably heard the voice of a wicked wizard, perhaps the sworn archenemy of the kingdom's good and noble prince, in which case he had probably spoken to her with the sole intention of scaring her off, chasing her away from the prince, who needed her at his side, and from her glorious destiny.

For more years than she could remember, for **eons,** Naomi dreamed of finding a doorway to a more magical world than this one, and now that she finally discovered precisely such a portal, she allowed a typical eight-year-old booby with a still-developing brain to spook her from pursuing the adventure for which she'd been born. You had to be so careful with peewee siblings. In spite of their laughable big-baby ways, they could be so convincing that they infected you with fraidy-cat flu before you realized it was contagious.

Later, this evening, after Minnie went to sleep and could no longer spread her plague of panic, Naomi would return to the storage room to investigate the mirror further. She wouldn't try to step into it or reach through it. She wouldn't even touch it. But she owed it to herself, to her future, to see if she could contact the prince who might wait for her in the world beyond. The wizard—or whatever he might be—had essentially phoned her through the mirror, and she had received his call. Maybe if she placed the call, if she faced the mirror and asked for the prince, for the rightful ruler of that land, he would speak to her, and her life of great magic would begin.

⸺⸙⸻

Minnie could see that Naomi schemed at something. She could tell that Zach worried about something.

Some kind of big trouble was coming. Minnie wished that good old Willard, the best dog ever, were still alive.

26

THE INTERIOR OF THE LUCAS RESIDENCE seemed less bright than it should have been, as though the sin of murder so thickened the air that sunshine could pierce only inches past the window-panes.

Room by room, John turned on every light for which he could find a wall switch. He could not bear to tour the house in shadows again.

The living room, converted to a bedroom for wheelchair-bound Sandra, had not interested him before because no one had been killed there. Now he circled through it in search of items that might have been purchased at Piper's Gallery, and he found them everywhere.

On her nightstand stood a crystal cat. In a semi-circle around the animal were three green candles of a kind sold by Annalena.

The nightstand drawer contained a dozen bottles

of various herbs in capsule form. There were sticks of incense, a porcelain holder in which to fix them, and a box of wooden matches.

John saw the corner of something dark protruding from between Sandra's two bed pillows. A red sachet plump with a perfumed cloth.

He assumed the sachet would smell sweet, but the scent proved to be faint and vaguely unpleasant. He could not identify the fragrance, and the more often that he held it to his nose to inhale, the more his stomach turned with incipient nausea.

Bookshelves surrounded a fireplace above which a flat-screen TV was mounted. Instead of books, the shelves held crystal cats of different kinds, crystal spheres and obelisks.

The Lucases owned two real cats that had fled the murder house on the night: British spotted short-hairs named Posh and Fluff.

On an end table stood a geode, its hard black crust filled with red crystal spears. In the shop, it would have dazzled, but here it looked like a snarling maw bristling with hundreds of bloody teeth.

What had sparkled in the Fourth Avenue store instead darkled in this house. What had been cheerful there had here become cheerless.

Across the width of the mantel were clear-glass cups holding fat candles, most of them green, a few blue, and one black.

Elsewhere on the ground floor, he found Piper's Gallery items in the kitchen. A pantry shelf crammed full of double-stacked jars of exotic dried herbs. A crystal sphere on a redwood stand at the center of the dinette table, three half-melted candles encircling it.

In the study, where Robert Lucas was murdered with a hammer, there were no candles or crystal pieces, nothing from the gallery.

Upstairs, the grandmother's room was also free of Annalena's merchandise.

John dreaded returning to Celine's room, where to his mind's ear the bed was as saturated with screams as with blood. But he needed to know if she possessed items from Piper's Gallery. He would have overlooked them on his previous visit, unaware that they might be significant.

He found nothing, and he was further convinced that the calla lilies had been left there by Billy after he rang them over his sister's corpse. Celine was his fourth and final victim.

In Billy's room, among the shelves of paperbacks nestled a pair of crystal lizards—one green, one clear—and a blue obelisk. On his nightstand a volcanic-rock geode featured deposited purple crystals of amethyst. A pair of three-inch-diameter scented blue candles in glass holders stood on his desk.

None of those things had seemed significant before. Now they intrigued John.

Apparently only the disabled mother, Sandra, and her son—who supposedly adored her—had bought in to Annalena's theory of natural therapies that would help them to "prosper in all ways."

This mattered, but John could see no reason that it should. He sensed that these objects had not brought the Lucases into greater harmony with nature but, to the contrary, had in some mysterious way endangered them. If he could discover **why** that was true, he would better understand the threat to Nicky and the kids, and he would have more hope of protecting them. His intuition told him as much, and intuition never failed him.

Throughout this second search of the house, he half expected to hear the silvery ringing of the calla-lily bells. The sound did not arise, perhaps because the entity that came with him from the state hospital the previous day was no longer his fellow traveler, but waited for him at home.

As John pored through the boy's desk drawers again, a voice that was not otherworldly said, "Breaking and entering, Calvino?"

27

KEN SHARP WAS ONE OF THE DETECTIVES who had caught the Lucas call. The case belonged to him and his partner, Sam Tanner, and of everyone in Robbery-Homicide, they were the most jealous of their turf.

When Sharp entered Billy's room, he seemed less puzzled than offended. Head shaved to hide creeping baldness, eyes set deep, nose hawkish, having a tendency to flush with impatience as readily as with rage, he possessed a face better suited to intimidating scowls than to smiles of friendship.

"What the hell are you doing here?" he asked.

"A neighbor had a key."

"That's **how** you got in. I'm wondering why?"

Twenty years earlier, the police and the courts protected John from reporters who were in those days marginally more responsible and less invasive than the aggressively sensational crew currently running the media circus. His role in Blackwood's death was more suggested than described, and his status as a juvenile ensured his privacy. In the wake of his loss, he was allowed to fade into his grief and guilt, and the orphanage became a wall between his future and that night of horror. Even when he went to the police academy, the background report on him reached no further into the past than to his departure from St. Christopher's Home and School at the age of seventeen years six months, where his record had been exemplary both in terms of academic achievement and discipline.

If they knew his full story, some would suggest that his ordeal might make him psychologically unfit to be a homicide detective. Was not his choice of this career an indication of an obsessive focus on his loss? Did it not suggest in his pursuit of every murderer that he might be seeking symbolic revenge for the slaughter of his family? And in that case, could he be trusted to treat every suspect with a presumption of innocence, or was he likely to abuse his power as an officer of the law?

The moment he revealed the events of that long-ago night, his life and the lives of his wife and children would change. His ability to function as a detective would be diminished, might even be more profoundly affected than he believed, in ways he could not predict. And of all the people in

Robbery-Homicide, Ken Sharp was the least likely to treat John's revelations with discretion.

Sitting on the edge of the desk, his mood far less casual than his posture suggested, Sharp said, "And just minutes ago I heard you've been up to the state hospital twice to see the butcher boy. You told them you were assigned to the case."

That was a harder blow to John's credibility than being caught searching Billy's desk.

"No. I didn't tell them I was the go-to guy. I will admit . . . I let them make that assumption."

"You did, huh? Why the hell did you, John?"

Sooner rather than later, he would have to tell someone about the eerie similarities between the murders of the Valdane family two decades earlier and the recent massacre of the Lucases. He was morally bound to warn that the crimes of Alton Turner Blackwood were perhaps being imitated half a continent away from the place where they were once committed. He didn't know how he could deliver that warning without mentioning his suspicion that this case had a supernatural dimension, an assertion that might require him to be suspended and to undergo a psychiatric evaluation.

Sharp's face looked boiled. "An orderly up there says maybe you think Billy's innocent, you think he's some kind of victim himself."

"No. That's wrong. I know he did it. But it's not that simple."

"Hey, pal, it's as goddamn simple as anything gets. He's naked on the front porch, drenched in blood. He says he did them all. His prints are on every weapon. The lab says his semen was in the sister. What you've got here is you've got the **definition** of an open-and-shut case."

This was neither the time at which nor the audience to which John would have chosen to make his revelations, but he could not avoid telling at least some of his story to Sharp.

Rolling shut the desk drawer he had been searching, switching on Billy's computer, he said, "I have reason to believe the killer—the boy—intended to murder more families than his own."

"That would be a noisemaker if it's true. What reason?"

"First, I want you to understand why I poached your case. My own family is one of the others he intended to kill."

John did not look up from the computer to see Sharp's reaction, but he heard both surprise and skepticism in the man's voice.

"Your family? How's he know your family? He never said anything about whacking a cop's family."

"There's a document on this computer," John said, "photos of my wife and kids. It's the start of a murder scrapbook."

On the computer were **two** documents of interest—CALVINO1 and CALVINO2—the first of which would crack the lock on John's past whether he wanted that door flung open or not. He could see no way to show Ken Sharp the second document but not the first.

"Why'd you come here in the first place?" Sharp asked. "How'd you know this thing was on his computer, you should look for it?"

John scrolled down the alphabetized directory—and found no documents with his name as their titles. He scrolled to the top and down again: **A, B, C,** into the **D**s.

"It's not here. It was right here last night, my name in the title, and now it's not."

"A murder scrapbook of your family, and now it's gone? Where's it gone?"

In his own voice, John heard how sincerity could sound like slippery evasion. "It's been deleted. Someone must've scrubbed the directory."

"Who? I mean, Billy sure as hell didn't come back and scrub it."

"I don't know who." John couldn't say there had been a ghost in the machine, literally a ghost. "But someone did it."

Sharp got up from the edge of the desk. His expression was dark, but his face brightened to the high pink of fresh-cut ham.

"Give me the keys you got from the neighbor."

Instead of fulfilling that request, John exited the directory, switched off the computer, and said,

"You've got a full backup of the hard drive in the evidence locker. Load it up, look for two documents—Calvino 1 and Calvino 2."

"John, for God's sake, what you've done is possible criminal trespass, I shouldn't even be here myself with the investigation closed now. Seems like you've got a screw loose about this case, I don't know why, but it's my case, mine and Sam's, and I want those keys."

As he produced the key ring with the dangling-cat charm and surrendered it to Sharp, John said, "Load the backup. Look for those documents. Do it, all right? Other families are in jeopardy, Ken. Not only mine."

"For one thing," Sharp said, pocketing the key, "no one's ever escaped from the high-security floor of the state hospital."

"There's always a first time."

"For another thing, Billy Lucas is dead."

The news struck John harder than he might have expected. He recalled the broken boy as he had been only that morning: arms restrained by netting, in a trancelike thrall of grief and despair.

"Dead—when?" he asked.

"Less than an hour ago. I got a call from Coleman Hanes. That's when I learned about—you."

"How did he manage to do it?"

"He didn't. Not suicide. There'll be an autopsy.

Right now it looks like maybe it was a cerebral hemorrhage."

The past was a weight John Calvino had always carried. Now it was worse than a weight, it was a noose, and he felt the roughness of it around his neck.

"What's going on with you, John? We don't run the ball the same way, but we're on the same team, and you've always seemed like you have enough of the right stuff."

"I'm sorry, Ken. I shouldn't have tramped your heels like this. I'm in a strange place. Maybe I'll tell you later. Right now I've got some thinking to do."

He went down through the murder house, and Sharp followed.

On the staircase landing, John paused only briefly to look at **Carnation, Lily, Lily, Rose.** The two little girls in white dresses looked happy in the garden with the Chinese lanterns, happy and safe and unaware that Evil walked the world.

From the journal of Alton Turner Blackwood:

The boy and the world would never be in harmony, but the boy and the night became as one. The boy flowed through the woods and meadows of the night, and the night flowed through the boy.

After that first exhilarating excursion, which ended minutes before dawn, he carried a small flashlight with him for those places where moonlight couldn't reach and for those nights when the sky was moonless or brightened by only the thinnest crescent. He never used the flashlight within sight of the house.

Over the next few years, the boy's night vision improved to an uncanny degree. The more time he spent out in the world between dusk and dawn, the better he could see even when the sky was overcast and the stars were only legend. He used the flashlight less and less, and his trust of the night was rewarded when the night increasingly, generously opened itself to him.

Once, kneeling at the edge of the deep pond, listening to fish take insects off the surface and wondering whether he might be quick enough with his hand to snatch one of those closest to the bank, he glimpsed his vague reflection in the inky water. But his eyes were not dark as human eyes should have been in such conditions. In them shimmered the faintest gold of animal eye-shine; his eyes drank in the weak glow from a quarter moon and the far twinkle of stars, and magnified them to assist his vision.

However far the boy went or how late he roamed, the raven stayed with him. He was sure it did. Sometimes he saw it backlit by the moon or detected its silhouette gliding across a star-speckled vault. From time to time, he glimpsed its moonshadow undulating across the land.

And if for periods of time he didn't see the bird, he always heard it. The flap of pinions. The whoosh of rigid wings in a gliding dive. The disturbance of leaves as it preceded him tree limb to tree limb through the dismal forest. Its low resonant prruck, its baritone brronk, its occasional bell-clear cry.

The raven was his companion, his tutelary, his familiar. The raven taught him about the night, and the boy began to learn what the night knows.

The land welcomed the boy as entirely as the darkness did. The fields, the woods, the stream, the pond, every vale and every hill and every thrusting mass of rock. He could walk any deer trail, make a new trail of his own, thrash through a thicket of any composition, and come to dawn without a burr or thistle in his clothes, without nettle rash or poison ivy. No insect ever bit or stung him, nor any snake. He could ascend steep inclines of loose shale as quietly as he could make his way up slopes of grass. No vine tripped, no bramble snared. He was never lost. He roamed the night land as though he might be some goat-legged, goat-eared, horned god who ruled all wild things.

In time, he began to kill two or three nights a month. Mostly rabbits. They appeared before dusk, coming out of their burrows, into meadows, to nibble on tender grass and flavorful weeds. The boy sat in the meadow to wait for them, sometimes catching the musky smell of them before they arrived. His own scent was by this time familiar to everything that ran or hopped, or crawled, or slithered. He could sit on a rock or log with such perfect stillness and for so long that they feared him no more than they feared the thing on which he sat. When they wandered close, he seized them, either to strangle them or snap their necks, or stab them with his knife.

He dispatched them neither to feed upon them nor to take their pelts for trophies. At first he killed to assert his authority over the land and every living thing that it produced. Later, he killed the animals from time to time because he didn't yet dare kill people, though he knew the day would come when all warm-blooded creatures would be game to him.

Larger and stronger and quicker than he had once been, the boy also had the power to lure and mesmerize. Deer came to him on narrow trails, at pinch points between steep rocks and phalanxes of trees, their eyes shining brighter than his own—and succumbed to his well-sharpened, furiously swung, and relentless hatchet.

On mornings that followed a lethal spree, as dawn neared, he stripped to wash himself and his killing clothes in the pond. He laid the garments to dry on a shelf of rock above the water, and dressed again in the unstained clothes that he had worn into the woods the previous twilight.

One moon-drenched night in his fourth year

under the sign of the raven, when the boy was sixteen, as he sat on a throne of weathered rock in a meadow, resting from violent labor, savoring the rich odor of fresh blood, a mountain lion eased out of the brush into shorter grass, and stared hungrily at him. Of all predators in North America, short of the polar bear that was a ruthless killing machine in its arctic realm, the most deadly were the grizzly bear and the mountain lion.

The confident boy met the big cat's gaze without fear and with no intention of fleeing from it. He could feel the raven circling in the night overhead. After a lingering assessment, the mountain lion chose to retreat, vanishing into the tall brush from which it had appeared.

He knew then that whether or not he might be the goat-legged god of this land, he was for certain Death with an uppercase D. The cat recognized him as such even though the boy wore no cowled robe and carried no scythe.

One thing he had learned earlier in this fourth year under the sign of the raven was that if you surrendered yourself entirely to the wilderness and to the night, you became aware of things unseen, ancient and immeasurably powerful presences with savage hungers and dark intentions, that roamed ceaselessly, almost dreaming, that were immortal and therefore never impatient, that were content to wait for the unwary to cross their path. He suspected they existed in cities, too, everywhere that humanity had been or was or would be, but were more evident here in the quiet of the wild, to one who had the heart to acknowledge them.

He was as unafraid of these unseen but immense presences as he had been of the mountain lion. In fact, they were as he wished one day to be: the true royalty of this world, users and corrupters, the hidden rulers of this troubled Earth, princes of a secret order. They were to all other predators what the mountain lion was to a mere house cat. If the boy could not one day become one of them, he would settle for being used by one of them to wreak the violence and chaos that they cherished.

For a few weeks following the encounter with the lion, the boy didn't kill anything. As the desire began to build again, he found the graveyard.

He was about to learn the one more thing he needed to know—and do the one more thing that must be done—to throw off the mantle of boyhood and become me.

28

LATER THAT DAY, LONG AFTER DARKFALL AND dinner but well before midnight, Naomi squirmed so impatiently under the covers that she feared she would wake her sister in the other bed. She wanted to be sure Minnie was sleeping soundly before she risked sneaking out to visit the mirror—and the prince!—in the storage room, but if she delayed another minute, she would positively burst. Most of the time, she was a paragon of patience, which she **had** to be with a shrimp sister hanging on her skirts all day, but even saints had their limits, and Naomi didn't claim to be a saint. She wasn't a monster, either. She was good enough by most standards, and she didn't expect to spend centuries upon centuries in Purgatory—or even a month—assuming that she ever died.

Since the afternoon math lesson with the nice but interminable Professor Sinyavski, Naomi had been thinking about how to take the initiative with the mirror. Instead of waiting for something in the looking glass to appear or to speak to her, which is what she had done thus far, she should speak to the prince, reach out to him and express her desire to help him save his kingdom from the dark powers by which such kingdoms always seemed to be plagued. Otherwise, she was allowing the dark powers to use the mirror exclusively, like a supernatural Black-Berry or something. She felt that it was extremely perspicacious of her to recognize that she should stop being passive with the mirror and become aggressive.

Finally she turned back the covers, got out of bed, and quietly extracted the flashlight from under her pile of pillows, where she had hidden it earlier and where it had been making her uncomfortable for the past hour. She didn't switch on the flash nor did she don a robe over her pajamas, for fear that Sister Half-Pint—who sometimes seemed to have the sharp senses of a hyperalert dog—would be torn from sleep by the slightest rustle and come panting after her to spoil everything.

With admirable stealth, Naomi navigated the nearly lightless room without a blunder, eased open the door, stepped barefoot into the hall, and closed the door behind her with only the softest click of the latch. Resorting to the flashlight now, she hurried to the east end of the hallway, regretting that she wasn't wearing a cape, like those that heroines often wore in Victorian fantasies, because nothing looked more splendidly romantic than a cape billowing out behind a girl racing into the night on a clandestine mission.

In the storage room, she switched on the overhead light, wishing that she had instead a candelabra with a dozen tapers that made light and shadows leap mysteriously across the walls. Three steps from the threshold, she realized that the mirror no longer lay hidden but had been dragged into the open and propped upright against a stack of boxes. Two steps farther, she saw that the looking glass didn't reflect anything, that it was black—**black!**—as if it were an open doorway beyond which lay the moonless and starless night of a land oppressed by something . . . by something . . . by something too terrible to name.

Naomi marveled at the absolute blackness for a longish moment before she noticed the sheet of stationery on the floor in front of the mirror, a page so creamy and thick that it might have been vellum. On sight, she knew that it must have come from out of the mirror, from the once-happy kingdom that now suffered under the brutal yoke of something . . . of something unspeakable. No doubt the message would be of earth-shattering importance— or so she assumed until, stooping to pick it up, she recognized Minnie's neat printing, which ought to have been the childish scrawl of an average eight-year-old but was not. The note said: DEAREST NAOMI, I PAINTED THE MIRROR BLACK. GO BACK TO BED. IT'S OVER NOW. YOUR DEVOTED SISTER, MINETTE.

The first thing Naomi wanted to do, of course, was prepare a bucket of ice water with which to wake the devoted titmouse, but she restrained herself. Because she was on a fast track to adulthood, becoming remarkably more self-possessed and wonderfully mature every day, Naomi realized that by admitting she had found the fingerling's smarty-pants note, she would be acknowledging the sorry lack of self-control that sent her racing to the mirror in the middle of the night. She could too easily imagine Minnie's deadpan expression of smug satisfaction—**pig fat!**—so she vowed right then and there, on her honor and her life, not to give Miss Peewee the pleasure of knowing that the note had been found.

She placed the sheet of creamy paper on the floor precisely as she remembered that it had been, and she silently retreated from the storage room and along the hallway, pleased by her superior cunning. Without benefit of the flashlight, she entered her room, returned to her bed, and lay smiling in the dark. Until she wondered if—and then became convinced that—the occupant of the second bed was no longer Minnie.

In Naomi's absence, something could have happened to poor little Minnie, and now the thing that had happened to Minnie could be lying in the sweet child's bed, in her place, patiently waiting for the surviving sister to go to sleep before rising to devour her, as well. Naomi dared not lie lamblike in the blackness, meekly waiting to be eaten alive, yet she dared not switch on her bedside lamp, because the instant she confirmed the presence of the beast, it would even sooner gobble up every last morsel of her. The only thing to do was stay awake until dawn and hope that sunshine would send this creature of the night fleeing to some deep lair.

Half an hour later, Naomi fell asleep, then woke uneaten in morning light. The new day proved less eventful than the previous day, which set a pattern for the following month. The raw-voiced presence—**I know you now, my ignorant little bitch**—did not appear in the bathroom mirror or the hallway mirror, or anywhere else. No more grapes disappeared through seemingly solid objects.

As day after uneventful day passed, Naomi wondered if her only chance for grand exploits in a fantastic alternate universe had come and gone without her having been able to seize the opportunity.

For compensation, she still had magical stories to read, her flute, the junior orchestra, her unique family, the dazzling autumn leaves in this gorgeous semi-magical world, and her imagination. As the days flew by, the scarier aspects of the recent events seemed less scary in retrospect, and Naomi gradually became aware that she had conducted herself with more valor and intrepidity and dashing style than she had recognized at the time. She stopped worrying that she had botched her one chance for glory, and she knew an occasion would eventually arise in which she could—and would—fulfill her singular potential as an adventurer.

Minnie knew that Naomi found the note. One corner of it was bent. And Naomi had held the thick writing paper so tightly that her fingers dimpled it in a few places.

By herself, Minnie dragged the painted mirror behind the boxes once more. Good riddance.

She folded the note and kept it as a souvenir.

Days passed, and nothing weird happened. Still more days, and still nothing.

The spooky stuff hadn't come to an end forever. They were in the eye of a hurricane. This calm was misleading; the storm remained all around them.

Minnie possessed some natural knowledge of

such things. She seemed to have been born with a sixth sense; and it had always been her little secret.

Since the incident with the mirror, she now and then sensed that she was being watched by something that didn't have a body, therefore didn't have eyes, yet could see.

She thought it must be a ghost, but she sensed that it was not an ordinary ghost or maybe not **only** a ghost. So at first she thought of it as the watcher.

Sometimes the watcher's stare was almost like a touch, a sliding hand along her neck, along her arm, along her cheek and chin.

Usually but not always, this feeling came over her when she was alone. She tried not to be alone except when she went to the bathroom or took a shower.

The eyeless watcher didn't prowl just the house. It was outside, too, in certain secluded places.

One day in the backyard, she started to climb the ladder to the playhouse in the branches of the enormous old cedar. Suddenly she knew the watcher waited up there.

She refused to believe that a thing without a body could hurt her. But she didn't want to be alone with it in that high place, to feel its stare, and to have no way out except the ladder. She might fall and break her neck. And that might be exactly what it wanted.

The arbor was draped with climbing vines, and pooled within it were shadows and the fragrance of roses, the last blooms of the year. Lingering there one afternoon, she felt the watcher enter the tunnel.

Although the day was windless, the roses shuddered, as if the thorny vines winding through the crisscrossed lattice were trying to pull loose and reach for her.

Inside the arbor, with the roses trembling and petals falling, Minnie felt the watcher brush past her, and by that contact she knew that it called itself Ruin. This seemed to be a peculiar name, yet she was certain that it was the right one. Ruin.

For as long as Minette could remember, she had from time to time felt unseen presences that other people didn't feel. Occasionally she got a glimpse of them. Presences. Spirits. People who weren't alive anymore.

They weren't always where you expected them to be. They didn't hang around graveyards.

Two of them were in a convenience store where Mom stopped now and then. Minnie could feel both of them. She had seen one, a man with part of his face shot off. Something bad happened in the store a long time ago.

Minnie usually stayed in the car.

When she was little, the presences sometimes scared her. But she learned that they were all right if you just ignored them.

If you stared at them too long or if you spoke to them, that was an invitation. If you didn't invite them, you could go months and months without seeing one.

Ruin was the first in years that kind of scared her. Ruin was different somehow.

She was usually alone when she became aware of Ruin watching, but sometimes it watched all of them when they were having dinner or playing games. That was the worst.

Although aware of the presences when they were near, Minnie never knew what they wanted, what they might be thinking or feeling, if they thought or felt anything at all.

In the case of Ruin, however, especially when it watched all of them, she knew exactly what it was feeling. Hatred. Hatred and rage.

Anyway, Ruin was a ghost or some kind of spirit new to her, new but nonetheless a spirit, and spirits could not harm her or anyone else. If she ignored it, if she did nothing to invite it, then it would have to go away.

⸻

After math with old Professor Sinyavski, in the late afternoon of the day Zach had encountered something in the service mezzanine that tested his sphincter control—**I know you, boy, I know you now**—he returned to his room and discovered that the stupid meat fork, which he had hidden under some stuff in a bottom desk drawer, had been restored. **Presto!** The previously wrecked shank was no longer bent. The tines were straight, not twined together. The polished steel bore no indications of ever having been stressed.

This suggested that of the two explanations for the incident—either supernatural or delusional—the latter was more likely. Nuts. He was nuts. Loony, loco, crackers, screwy, one shoe short of a pair.

Maybe for his own good, he should sign himself into a monkey house, wear one of those monkey jackets with the long sleeves that tied behind your back, and be entertained by stupid freaking monkey thoughts swinging through his empty skull.

Or not.

Being able to consider the idea that he might be insane pretty much ruled out madness. Raving lunatics never wondered if they were lunatics; they believed the other six billion people in the world were lunatics and that they themselves were pillars of reason.

Instead of convincing Zach that what happened in the service mezzanine must have been a delusion, the restored fork ticked him off and made him more determined than ever to learn the truth about what was happening in this house. He knew when he was being jacked around. He wasn't a dog so dumb that he didn't see the leash. He wasn't a naive idiot who would happily chow down on cow pies because someone told him they were chocolate cake.

With insanity off the table, one explanation remained: something supernatural. If a supernatural force could screw up the meat fork, then it was a no-brainer that the same supernatural force could make it right again.

Any alternate theory would now have to identify a human villain, some clown with a self-serving reason for replacing the twisted fork with an identical but undamaged utensil.

Zach gave himself a week to think and to see what might happen next. He thought, all right, but nothing happened. The trapdoor didn't fall open by itself, and the ladder didn't self-deploy. Every night, feeling like a wuss, he braced his closet door with a chair, but the knob never rattled and nothing in there turned on the light.

His parents were the high command, and he was a grunt. A grunt didn't go to the high command with a wild story about a ghost in the service mezzanine unless he had the ghost in chains.

Zach gave himself another week. And then another.

He began to wonder if that one episode was going to be the whole of it. Some half-assed ghost rides in from the hereafter, plays with a stupid light switch and a trapdoor ladder, screws up a meat fork, fixes the fork, gets bored, and splits for some other ghost gig. That scenario seemed even more lame than the usual brain-dead horror movie full of boneheads doing every wrong thing to get themselves killed.

But if it was finished, that would be okay with Zach. He wanted to be a marine, not a ghostbuster.

⚬⚬⚬

Dr. Westlake doubted very much that Nicolette's idiosyncratic adverse reaction to Vicodin could continue to manifest three and a half weeks after she took her last dose. But he wanted to research the issue and get back to her the next day.

She said nothing about the hallucination to John. She hoped to avoid worrying him.

The following day, when Dr. Westlake called, he all but ruled out the possibility that her latest experience could be related to Vicodin; however, he wanted her to have a complete blood workup, just as a precaution.

Nicky never fretted about anything. Brooding about possible calamities seemed to be ingratitude. Her life was bright with family and love, her paintings were acclaimed and sold for excellent prices, and in return her minimum obligation included being happy and giving thanks for her good fortune.

Always, even during darker times, she'd been cheerful, hopeful. Surely life was too short to waste any of it in the expectation of disaster. Even when Minnie had been ill and the malady difficult to diagnose, Nicolette prayed but didn't dwell for a moment on darker possibilities, on **any** possibility except Minnie's complete recovery.

She wasn't a Pollyanna. She knew terrible things happened to the best of people, to people far better than she would ever be, even to people as good and as innocent as Minette. But she also **knew** that the power of the imagination could shape reality. Every day she made real on canvas the scenes that would be otherwise confined forever to her mind; therefore, it seemed a half step in logic to believe that the imagination might **directly** influence reality, without the physical intervention of the artist, that what was feared obsessively might manifest in the real world. Worry wasn't worth the risk of worry's possible consequences.

Returning to her painting with enthusiasm, she finished the triptych during the week she waited to learn the results of the blood workup. The painting turned out well, perhaps as good as anything she'd done to date, and the laboratory tests confirmed that she was in good health.

She started another picture. A second week passed, a third, and she experienced no more hallucinations. Happy with her work, Nicky became convinced that regardless of what Dr. Westlake said, the weird episode in the bathroom indeed had been related to Vicodin, one last spasm of its influence in her system, and that she would be troubled no further.

Although aware of a persistent tension in John, she had seen its like before. She assumed that when at last he nailed the killer of the schoolteacher and closed his current case, his stress would be relieved.

As September waned and then October dawned, the beautiful autumn revealed no blemish except for Nicky's dream. She woke from it nearly every night, with no memory of its characters or story, yet certain that it was always the same dream. Because she never woke in fear and routinely returned to sleep without difficulty, she didn't believe this dream qualified as a nightmare, but sometimes it left her with an unclean feeling so that she rose to wash her face and hands.

She had a vague recollection of being the object of desire in the dream, of being wanted desperately by someone whom she did not want in return. The intensity and persistence of whoever wanted her and her unrelenting resistance left Nicky exhausted when she woke, which is perhaps why she never had trouble falling asleep again.

When he arrived home after relinquishing the key to the Lucas house, John learned from Walter Nash that the stench in the laundry room had relented as abruptly as it had arisen. "Doesn't seem to be any reason to dismantle the dryer," Walter said. "Whatever the stink was, it must not have been a decomposing rat. It's a mystery for the moment, but I'll keep thinking on it."

Over dinner, Nicky and the kids seemed subdued, but John thought his own mental state must be the damper on the evening. Billy Lucas was gone and with him any hope that he might one day answer further questions. Worse, John was found in the Lucas house without a valid reason, and he revealed his concern that his family might be targeted for murder, a fear that must have appeared irrational to Ken Sharp. He could not predict how the day's events would affect his ability to protect Nicky and the kids, but he knew his options would be fewer.

The following morning, he returned to work and to the case of Edward Hartman, the high-school teacher who had been beaten to death in his lakeside home. Lionel Timmins, the partner with whom he shared responsibility for the investigation, had been chasing leads during John's two sick days; over coffee in an unused interrogation room, Lionel brought him up to date.

Timmins was black, fourteen years older than John, three inches shorter, forty pounds heavier, and so broad in the upper torso that some other cops called him the Walking Chest. He had been married, but his obsessive commitment to his job led to a divorce before any kids came along. His elderly mother and her two spinster sisters lived with him; and although he was devoted to those ladies, no one with a healthy survival instinct would ever call Lionel a mama's boy.

In countless ways, John and Lionel were different from each other, but in one way they were more alike than any other two detectives in the division: Homicide investigation was less a job to them than it was a sacred calling. As a sixteen-year-old, Lionel had been charged with the brutal murder of a woman named Andrea Solano, during the course of a burglary. The state tried him as an adult, the jury convicted him, and the judge sentenced him to life imprisonment. While he was in prison, his beloved father died. After Lionel spent six years in a high-security cell, the real burglar-murderer was arrested in another case and tied to the Solano killing by evidence in his possession; eventually, he confessed. Without that lucky break, Lionel would have rotted in prison. Released, the crime expunged from his record, he became a cop and eventually a detective with two compelling goals: first, to put murderers behind bars, on death row if they deserved it; second, to be sure that, at least on his watch, no one hung a murder conviction around the neck of an innocent man.

As partners, they were friends but not best buddies, largely because they spent less time together than other paired detectives. They worked as a team, but they did not ride in tandem. Both were devoted family men when at home, which they preferred to the world beyond those walls, but at work they were loners, each with his unique style of investigation, each impatient with the accommodations that same-car partners inevitably had to make for each other. They divvied up leads, accomplished twice as much as they would if yoked together, backed up each other when the task required that, compared notes at the end of every day, and had the highest case-closed record in Robbery-Homicide.

The Hartman assignment should have been engaging; the victim was a teacher, as John's murdered parents had been. But he was not able to focus as sharply as necessary. He was distracted by thoughts of the Lucas murders and by fear of October fifth, which would be the date of the next killings if the crimes of Alton Turner Blackwood were indeed being replayed. The Hartman investigation swiftly became the poorest effort of his career.

Six days after returning to work, he received a summons to the office of Nelson Burchard, chief of detectives. Ken Sharp had filed a report about John's visits to Billy at the hospital, the illegal entries at the Lucas house, and their conversation in Billy's room.

Burchard employed a wise-old-uncle managerial style and rarely raised his voice. As a disciplinarian, he preferred to approach the situation as alternately a caring surrogate father, an understanding colleague, and a therapist. He was stout within the physical limits of the department, white-haired, with a face made for dinner-theater comedies about twinkly-eyed older men who were assumed to be a bit daft because they claimed to be Santa Claus or angels who needed to earn their wings.

In order to explain his actions, John had to reveal what had happened to his family when he was fourteen. The story earned him Nelson Burchard's pity, which he didn't want and which seemed both genuine yet unctuous. The man's cloying earnestness made John's revelations even harder to disclose than he expected.

As caring as he might have been, Burchard also saw at once that an experience of such horror at a young age might seed psychological problems that could make a career in Robbery-Homicide particularly taxing, problems that might not sprout and ripen until they were, so to speak, fertilized by a case disturbingly reminiscent of the long-ago trauma.

"I understand your concern that Billy was imitating Blackwood. But he **did** turn himself in. If he intended to kill again, he wouldn't have done that." Burchard leaned forward in one of the armchairs in the counseling corner of his office. "Did you really worry that he might escape the state hospital?"

"No. I don't know. Maybe." Although John could not have avoided telling Burchard about what happened twenty years earlier, he found it impossible to raise the theory that a murderous spirit might have operated through Billy Lucas. **Possession** was not a word any defense lawyer would ever use or any judge ever countenance. "The striking similarities between the Valdane and Lucas massacres wasn't something I could ignore. I just . . . I had to know. . . . I'm not entirely sure why, but I had to know if Blackwood inspired Billy."

"You told Ken Sharp there were documents on the boy's computer—they indicated your family was one of his targets."

"There were. I saw them the first time I was in the house. But someone deleted them."

Burchard's jolly face remained in a Christmas Eve expression, though his eyes now twinkled less with goodwill than with the glint of a forensic surgeon's scalpel. "Ken reviewed the backup CDs made of the computer's hard drive. There aren't any documents about your family on those, either."

The armchair seemed like an execution-chamber chair. John wanted to get up and move around. He remained seated and said nothing.

"The backup CDs were secure in the evidence locker," Burchard said. "You don't think someone could have gotten to them?"

"No. I don't. Not in the locker. I can't explain it, sir. But I stand by what I said that I saw."

As if it pained him to look at John just then, Burchard turned his attention to a window and the steel-gray sky. "Whatever the boy's intentions might have been, he's dead. There'll be no more killing of families now."

"October fifth," John said. "That's the day. Or would have been if his murders were an homage. Blackwood's homicidal periodicity was precise. Thirty-three days."

When he looked at John again, Burchard said, "But he's dead."

"What if he didn't do it alone?"

"But he did. There's no evidence anyone else was in that house when it all went down."

"I'm just wondering if—"

"It's not your case," Burchard interrupted. "How's the Hartman job coming along?"

After a hesitation, John said, "I'm sure Lionel's making progress."

"But you?"

John shrugged.

"You're my Thoroughbreds, you and Lionel. But . . . presenting yourself at the state hospital as the case detective. Trespassing twice in the Lucas house. Maybe all this has knocked you off your stride. Would you say it has?"

"Not so that I can't regain my footing."

"You drive every case hard, John. Maybe you need time to rest and think. Time to put this behind you." As John began to protest, Burchard raised a hand to halt him. "I'm not talking about a formal suspension. Nothing that'll wind up on your ten card. You just ask for a thirty-day leave without pay, I'll authorize it right now."

"If I don't want a thirty-day leave?"

"I'd have to pass Sharp's report upstairs to Parker Moss."

Moss was the Area 1 commander, a good enough cop but at times a by-the-book sonofabitch.

"And then what?" John asked.

"Maybe a review-board hearing, but probably not. For sure, he'll want mandatory psychological counseling and an evaluation. Because of the undisclosed childhood trauma."

"I'm not coming unwrapped."

"I don't believe you are. Which is why I'd prefer dealing with it this way. But if it gets to Moss, he'll follow protocols."

"You want my tin and my piece?"

"No. On unpaid leave you still follow off-duty rules. You carry at all times, you're plainclothes auxiliary."

Under the circumstances, it was important to John to be able legally to continue carrying a concealed weapon.

"All right," he conceded. "But what'll you tell Lionel?"

"That's up to you."

"Family matters," John decided.

"He'll want to know more than that."

"Yeah. But we never pry at each other."

"Then it's family matters," Burchard said.

"It has the virtue of being true."

"You'd be uncomfortable lying to him?"

"Couldn't do it," John said.

On unpaid leave, he had little more to do than to anticipate October fifth. That he became increasingly restless and apprehensive day by day was no surprise.

Determined to spare Nicolette and the kids needless anxiety, he avoided telling them about his thirty-day leave. He left in the morning as if for work, killed time at movies that didn't entertain him, at libraries where he learned nothing he needed to know, on ten-mile walks that failed to tire him.

He no longer entertained any doubts about the supernatural nature of the threat if only because nothing else could explain how Billy had known the next-to-last thing that Alton Turner Blackwood said before John killed him: **Your lovely sister, your Giselle. She had such pretty little training-bra breasts.**

Nevertheless, he harbored a small hope that he kept afloat with prayer and with his long-embraced belief that the concept of fate had no validity. With the proper exercise of free will, he could see his wife and children safely through this troubled time. Such conviction, even if tenuous, was essential to hold fast to sanity.

If October fifth passed without murders to match Blackwood's second slaughter, if the pattern of the past changed, John would never need to tell the kids—though perhaps one day he would tell Nicky—that he had endured thirty-three days of gut-twisting dread.

If instead the murders occurred, he would share everything with Nicky and together they would decide what to do. But if the ghost of a homicidal psychopath really could return from the grave and use a human being as a puppet, there seemed to be no weapon that any man or woman could employ against it.

Walking the grid blocks of the city, rambling the lakeside park, and during movies that he only half saw, John was gnawed by a sense of helplessness not only in regard to the defense of his loved ones but also because he could do nothing to warn whatever family might be the second in this current killing spree.

Twenty years earlier, after the Valdanes, the Sollenburgs had been Blackwood's next target.

Their master suite lay at the farther end of the house from other bedrooms, the main living spaces intervening: convenient for a murderer who planned to kill his targets in a certain order and who hoped not to alert the fourth and final victim when executing the first three.

The parents, Louis and Rhoda, had been murdered in their bed, beginning with the husband. Louis was shot once in the head while sleeping. The presence of steel-wool fibers in the wound indicated that the killer had fashioned a homemade silencer for his 9-mm pistol.

Perhaps the muffled gunfire woke Rhoda or perhaps she woke when Blackwood switched on the light. He shot her twice as she sprang off the bed, and she died on the floor.

With no scream from either victim and the gunfire adequately muffled, Blackwood was able to make his way across the house at his leisure, taking the time to savor the murders he had just committed and to anticipate with dark delight the brutalities soon to come.

The homemade silencer deteriorated quickly. He carried a pillow from the parents' bedroom to further suppress the sound of the shot with which he killed Eric, the fifteen-year-old son, in his bed.

With three dead, Blackwood was alone with seventeen-year-old Sharon Sollenburg. Subsequently, the medical examiner estimated that she had been shot more than four hours after her brother was killed.

The humiliations and cruelties that the girl suffered during those four hours, as reported in the autopsy, sickened even homicide detectives who thought they had seen everything but discovered now a more savage and inventive monster than they had known before.

Her suffering did not end when Blackwood shot her. The ratio of high serotonin to lower free histamine levels in the wound indicated that she had taken at least half an hour to die.

Torn candy wrappers and smears of chocolate on the upholstery suggested that her murderer sat in an armchair and ate three Almond Joy bars while he watched life fade from her. Blood on the wrappers indicated that he had not washed his hands between his games with the girl and his snack.

Like the victims at the Valdane house, all four Sollenburgs were left with black quarters epoxied to their eyelids, carefully shaped coins of dried feces on their tongues, and specially prepared hollow eggs in their bound hands.

Twenty years later, in this great city, there must be thousands of families consisting of father, mother, son, and daughter. There was no way to know who might be marked for death.

Furthermore, it could be wrong to assume the killer would not seek a family of five instead of four, one with two or three girls instead of a single daughter. After all, the widowed aunt who was part of the Valdane family, two decades ago, was a grandmother at the Lucas house in the here and now, and the ages of one set of victims were not identical to the ages of the other. The methods of murder and certain other details were the same, but the scenarios were not in every aspect identical.

This entire state did not have half enough police to mount protective surveillance of every family in the city that might be targeted.

As September became October, the green trees of summer dressed themselves in the spectacle of autumn. Purple beeches became bright copper, and frisia turned even more orange than the yellow buckeye. Silver-leafed poplars paid out a dividend of gold, and the enormous scarlet oak on the south yard of the Calvino property lived up to its name for the first time all year.

Late on the afternoon of October fourth, on the eve of the dreaded date, when John came home early from pretending to work, the house was transformed. He felt the difference the moment that he got out of the car in the basement garage, a freshness to the air, a curious perception that everything was cleaner than it had been, a sense that a pall had been lifted from the place. This feeling only increased as he ascended through the residence.

He had been weighed down by worry and had not realized that an oppressive aura had settled on the house itself. For weeks, the rooms had felt less harmonious in their proportions than before; the lamps and ceiling fixtures had appeared to be dialed down even when all the dimmer switches were at their highest settings; the artworks and the furnishings had seemed tired and in conflict with one another; and although the air had not reeked of Billy Lucas's urine, it had been stale, like the air in a moldering old museum, thick with dust and history. He realized all of that only in retrospect, now that the house was bright and welcoming once more.

Perhaps no one else felt the change as profoundly as did John, for only he suspected—all right, **knew**—that something had come home with him from the state hospital twenty-six days earlier. If Nicky and the kids weren't consciously aware that the house had been under a kind of cloud that had now dissipated, they must have felt the difference because they were all livelier and merrier at dinner than they had been for days. The rapid conversation

had its old bounce—from wit to badinage, to persi-
flage, and back again.

The food tasted better, too, and the wine, not because Walter and Imogene had outdone themselves,
for their standards were always high, but because
the familiar cheerful atmosphere of the house had
been restored, which was an essential spice that, like
salt, enhanced the flavor of all things. If something
otherworldly had been here the past three and a half
weeks, that presence was now inarguably gone.

Once he had convinced himself to embrace the
unknown, to accept that a malevolent spirit might
find its way back into the world and into his life,
John had imagined that the haunting would
progress as it did in books and movies. First came
subtle moments of strangeness for which reasoned
explanations might be fashioned, and then ever
more bizarre and fearsome manifestations escalated
to the third act, when the terror would reveal its
true ferocity and the invaded house would become
a hell on Earth. Until now he had not considered
that a haunting might peter out between the first
and the second acts, that the ties binding the
haunter and the haunted might be as vulnerable to
weariness and indifference as were so many relationships in which both parties were living.

John entertained this hopeful thought only
through the soup and partway through the entrée.
Long before dessert, he realized the invading spirit

had not dissipated or departed forever. By whatever means such entities traveled, whether by magic or by moonlight, or on wheels of sheer malevolence, this one had gone in search of its next Billy Lucas, for the glove in which it would conceal itself to murder another family. With that blood ceremony completed, it would return.

29

MACE VOLKER IS A DELIVERYMAN AND A THIEF. Now thirty, he has delivered flowers for a florist since he was nineteen, and he has been stealing since he was eleven. He has never been caught nor has he even once come under suspicion, for he is blessed with a gentle and open face, a most appealing voice, and a fearless nature, all of which he uses as instruments of deception no less artfully than a concert pianist uses his supple, nimble hands.

Mace shoplifts, picks pockets, burglarizes homes. He doesn't steal solely or even primarily for financial reasons but mainly for the thrill. Stolen cash and goods have a powerful sensual appeal and feel better to him than the silky skin of a beautiful woman. He can't achieve climax merely by caressing stolen money, but he can become fiercely aroused by the texture of it, sometimes teasing himself for an hour or more, into a sweat of desire, merely by handling purloined twenties and hundreds. A psychiatrist might say Mace is a fetishist. He has had a few girlfriends, but only to see how much he can steal from them: money and possessions, honor and hope and self-respect. Generally he turns to prostitutes for satisfaction, and the best sex is always when he steals from them the money with which he paid for their services.

There are ten doors into Mace Volker: his sensitive and thieving fingertips.

Twice a week, he delivers flowers to the Calvino house, roses for Nicolette's studio, and occasionally a dining-table arrangement. This fourth of October, shortly before five o'clock, he has three dozen long-stemmed yellow roses for the artist, each dozen in its own plastic sleeve. He is not taken when he rings the doorbell, but by his index finger on the button, he is known and wanted.

Walter Nash signs for the flowers. Because Walter's arms are filled with the bundled roses and the greens that come with them, Mace assists him, upon leaving, by pulling the front door shut from outside. **Taken.** Mace isn't aware that he is no longer alone, that he is now a horse with a rider that might in time dismount without ever making itself known to him—or that might choose instead to ride him to death.

Deliveries concluded, Mace returns the van to the florist's shop where he works. Ellie Shaw, the owner, is behind the cashier's counter, totaling out the register, and Mace hands in his clipboard manifest, with the signatures of those customers who received the flowers. Ellie is in her late thirties and quite pretty, but Mace has never really seen her as a woman because she is his boss and, therefore, he can't use her and steal from her without serious consequences. As they talk briefly about the day, Mace imagines her naked, which he has never done before—other women, never Ellie—but to his surprise and alarm he also vividly envisions her strangled with a striped necktie, her swollen grayish tongue protruding from her mouth and her dead eyes wide in the final look of terror with which she rewarded her enthusiastic murderer. This fantasy pumps him rigid with desire.

Rattled by this vision and afraid that Ellie will notice his condition, he mentions a nonexistent engagement with a young lady and flees to his car in the employee parking lot. Behind the wheel and on the move, wondering at his savage flight of imagination, Mace stops at a traffic light where a young woman and a girl of about ten stand hand in hand, waiting to cross the intersection. With graphic detail and an intensity that rocks Mace, he suddenly sees them both naked, stepping into the street—but then bound to chairs in a rough room, raw and red and carved like scrimshaw.

So as not to alarm the horse unnecessarily, the

rider reins in its tendency to envision objects of its desire in conditions of total subjugation and physical ruin. In truth, Mace Volker is shocked by his hallucinatory episodes but not entirely repelled. He is, after all, a thief who is thrilled by the act of stealing rather than by the gain received from what is stolen; and he will realize now that the ultimate act of theft is the taking of a life. This realization may have an interesting effect upon the deliveryman's future criminal career.

Having burglarized a house during his lunch hour and having taken some good diamond jewelry that he hopes will bring him as much as twelve to fifteen thousand dollars, Mace drives now to a tavern he knows in a part of the city that was once on the skids but is being gentrified. This is the kind of neighborhood in which a white-collar bar isn't a dive and serves as a respectable front for a fence who, paying hard cash for stolen merchandise, also finds the streets safe enough that he doesn't need to worry about being hijacked when coming or going. The tavern has a black-granite and mahogany facade. Inside, the booths and bar stools are occupied by more upwardly mobile young couples than young loners.

Mace gets a bottle of Heineken, no glass, from the bartender, who knows him and who uses the house phone to seek permission for him to go to the back office. After receiving the bartender's thumbs-up, Mace pushes through the swinging door into the small kitchen, which produces only sandwiches, French fries, and onion rings. A door at the farther end of the fragrant room leads to a narrow staircase with a ceiling-mounted camera at the top that covers his ascent. On the upper landing, he waits for a moment at a steel door before it opens and he is ushered inside.

This is the reception room. The office of Barry Quist, tavern owner and fence (among other things), is through an inner door. Here in the first room is a table on one edge of which sits a beefy man in shirtsleeves, his shoulder rig and pistol in plain sight. Another guy in shirtsleeves, equally solid and well-armed, has opened the door for Mace. He closes it and, though he knows Mace doesn't carry, he pats him down for a weapon before he returns to a chair on which lies an open issue of **Sports Illustrated**. These two men are always with Barry Quist, but Mace has never heard their names. He thinks of them as One and Two, One being the behemoth who opened the door. They look like men who, in a fight, will not shirk from committing any cruelty and will be stopped by nothing short of a bullet in the brain. With six straight-backed chairs in two groups separated by a tall magazine rack holding a collection of glossy publications, the place resembles a dentist's waiting lounge—if you wanted a dentist who would knock your teeth out with a hammer.

On the table lies a pistol with an extended magazine, which evidently belongs to the man currently doing business with Barry in the fence's office. Beside the pistol lies a sound suppressor, which can be screwed onto the barrel.

In one of the straight-backed chairs sits a stunning blonde who also belongs to the man now with Barry. Two has come out from behind the table and is sitting on it so that he can chat her up. Evidently they know each other, and the guy she has come with is named Reese. Two speaks to her as if he is a concerned friend: "All I'm sayin' is get from Reese as much as you can, as fast as you can. He wants everything he sees, and he's always movin' on." The blonde says she knows her guy, she's got him by the pecker and she knows how to make him heel like a well-trained poodle. Two shakes his head and says, "If he got all the money in the world and he laid every woman worth the time, then suddenly he'd start wantin' little boys. He's never gonna stop wantin' what he doesn't have or can't have."

The inner door features an electronic lock, and it buzzes a moment before Reese comes into the reception room. He is a crocodile in a five-thousand-dollar suit, his claws given a civilized shape and a coat of clear polish by a manicurist, his wide mouth designed for efficient consumption, his eyes restless with hunger. He consults his twenty-thousand-dollar wristwatch in such a way that he displays it for others to admire. But his expression sours at the sight of it, as if recently he has seen a more expensive watch and is dissatisfied with this instrument that has previously so pleased him.

Reese has many doors by which he can be entered, but the eyes are the easiest. **Taken.**

As flower deliveryman Mace Volker, now only himself, proceeds into Barry Quist's sanctum sanctorum to negotiate a price for the stolen jewelry, Reese Salsetto recovers his pistol as well as the precision-machined sound suppressor, which fits in a separate sleeve of his custom shoulder holster. His rider is content for the moment to use neither spurs nor reins, and Reese is unaware that he is no longer the master of himself. To Brittany Zeller, the blonde, he says, "Let's go, Puss."

Crossing the kitchen and then the busy tavern, Reese is aware that every man's attention is drawn irresistibly to Brittany. Every man covets her and envies him.

They have a seven-thirty dinner reservation at one of the city's finest restaurants, where he is a valued customer. In the street, at his Mercedes S600, Reese tells Brittany that he wants to move the reservation to eight o'clock, so they will have time to go back to his place first. He explains that he has

bought something wonderful for her birthday—
three days hence—and he's so eager to see how she
likes it that he can't wait until then to give her the
gift. They'll have a martini together at home and go
from there to the restaurant.

This change of plans is the desire of Reese's rider,
but it is so subtly encouraged that Reese doesn't detect the pressure of the bridle or feel the bit between
his teeth. Already, the rider knows everything about
its horse: Reese's history, hopes, needs, desires, every
secret in the nautilus turns of the popinjay thug's
twisted and corrupted heart. In all those inter-
wound darknesses, the rider has discovered a family
that will be a pleasure to reduce to bloody ruin. Its
expectation had been that four or five changes of
horses would be necessary before a target family
would be found. But Mace Volker to Reese Salsetto
is all that's needed.

Home, to Reese, is a flashy penthouse apartment
neither as large as he feels that he deserves nor on
quite as high a floor as he desires. But this building
is one of the finest, and in another year, he will ascend to higher and much larger quarters. The style
is plush Art Deco, the furnishings of the best quality. The decor was provided by a woman whom
Reese believes to be the classiest and most talented
interior designer in the city largely on the basis of
her British accent.

While Brittany goes directly to the corner bar in the living room to mix a pair of Grey Goose martinis, Reese proceeds to the bedroom to retrieve the diamond-and-emerald necklace that is her birthday present. He can't resist stepping into the master bathroom for a quick look in the mirror, to assure himself that his pocket handkerchief is properly presented, his necktie precisely knotted, and his hair in place.

Because the time has come to take absolute control of the horse and to smother every expression of its will, the rider allows itself some fun. After the fop assesses his appearance with satisfaction, his reflection changes in a blink, and instead of himself, he sees Alton Turner Blackwood, whose spirit feet are in Reese Salsetto's stirrups. Hunched back, sharp chin, brutish jawbones, half-ripe and entirely cruel mouth, black-hole eyes with enough gravity to pull whole worlds to destruction. Even Reese, a fearless sociopath, cries out in fear, but his cry is soundless, for he no longer has control of his body. He is a prisoner in his own skin, shackled by bones he once controlled, a powerless observer behind the windows of his covetous eyes.

Reese joins fetching Brittany in the living room, not with her gift in hand but with the sound suppressor fitted to the barrel of his pistol. When she turns toward him, offering a martini, he shoots her twice in the abdomen and once in the chest. The shots make a shushing sound, as if admonishing Brittany to die quietly.

Although the rider is a connoisseur of torture and relishes the humiliation and the pain of others, it wastes no time with Brittany Zeller because she is too hard for its taste, too knowing, long in the process of extinguishing her own light. Instead, the rider yearns to rend what is tender, to corrupt what is innocent, and to destroy what shines.

Leaving the dead blonde in the living room, Reese Salsetto—under the firm control of his rider—returns to the master bedroom, takes a box of ammunition from a nightstand drawer, and replenishes the extended magazine of the pistol, which when fully loaded holds sixteen rounds.

A family is living its last hours. Father, mother, son, and daughter. The mother, seen in Reese's memory, is succulent and sure to be exciting, but the eighteen-year-old daughter is luminous and untouched, a rare flower the despoiling of which will be a fine achievement. He will kill the father, then disable the son and force him to watch the use, abuse, and ruination of the mother and the girl.

Reese says aloud, "You've been wanting the girl yourself, Reese, and now you'll have her."

He turns out the living-room lights.

The re-enactment continues, and this time everything will be done right, as it had almost been done back in the day. The promise to John Calvino will be kept. The Promise.

Reese says, "It's warm and cozy in the skin again. Don't you think so, Reese? Aren't you warm and cozy, Reese?"

In the kitchen, he stands staring at a rack of knives. They will have knives at their house. He can carve the girl with their cutlery.

As he turns out the kitchen lights and retreats along the entry hall to the foyer, Reese says, "This will be such fun, Reese. Don't you think it'll be fun?"

30

ON THE EVENING OF OCTOBER FOURTH, Zach sat in his room, drawing a nightmare when what he really wanted to be drawing was Laura Leigh Highsmith, especially her lips.

Following the recent weirdness, life had defaulted to normal so completely that Zach had returned the restored meat fork to the kitchen drawer from which he had secretly taken it. Already the edges were worn off the memory of the encounter in the service mezzanine. He abandoned both of his original explanations—supernatural or insanity—and convinced himself that a logical answer would present itself if he just stopped being a bonehead and focused on **real** things like math, cool military history, and Laura Leigh Highsmith, goddess, and let his subconscious eventually puzzle out the truth of what had happened.

His half-assed expedition into the stupid mezzanine embarrassed him because now he seemed to have been like some little kid playing slay-the-dragon with a trash-can lid for a shield and a fence picket for a sword. That was a game of his when he was an idiot five-year-old. His dad, in a rare but spectacular failure of parenting wisdom, captured slay-the-dragon on stinking video and from time to time, much to Zach's mortification, reran the whole sordid featurette to the delight of old Naomi and Minnie who, of course, called him Saint George for days afterward. Sometimes Zach wondered just how much humiliation a person could take before he finally stopped thinking that he could **ever** be a marine.

Anyway, life returned to almost mind-numbing normality until the nights of October second and third, when he dreamed twice about the freaking freak with the ginormous hands. This time the dream didn't take place in pitch-blackness but at night in a carnival with all the amusement rides ablaze with neon and blinkers, spotlighted show tents, and strings of colored lights festooning the concourse from one end of the midway to the other. Zach saw the shambling monstrosity with the humongous hands this time, and the guy was the kind of ugly that makes ordinary ugly people feel like prom kings and queens.

In the first dream, all the amusement rides were turning and whipping and undulating, but no one was aboard any of them, and the dumb-ass cliché of a nightmare carnival was dead silent, as if it were in a vacuum. The only people anywhere on the grounds were Zach and Ugly Al. He didn't know how he knew the guy's name was Al, but that's what he kept thinking in the dream, and of course Ugly Al chased him all through the stupid carnival, almost nailing him again and again. This dream should have been as basically boring as yogurt, because over the years Zach had been chased in other nightmares by way uglier idiot bogeymen than Ugly Al, but it kept getting scarier until Zach burst into a show tent, hoping to hide, and suddenly there was **music**.

He was in a sleazy striptease show, and women in G-strings and pasties were on the stage. It was the first time he ever remembered being embarrassed in a nightmare. The strippers weren't moving in a sexy way, but jerkily, clumsily, and then Zach realized they were dead women, zombie strippers, all women Ugly Al had killed. They had stab wounds and gunshot wounds and worse, and when Zach turned to run from the tent, Ugly Al was **right there,** maybe three feet away.

The freak was dressed in a khaki shirt and khaki pants with lots of pockets, and he wore black Nazi boots with shiny steel toes, and from one of his pockets he withdrew this knife that was so sharp it could cut you if you just looked at it. The godawful bump-and-grind music was still playing, and Ugly Al spoke in a low voice that made you wish you had quills and could curl up in a ball like a porcupine. He said, **"Come here, pretty boy. I'm gonna cut off your peepee and shove it down your throat."** Then Zach woke in a sweat, with a superbad need to go to the bathroom.

The next night, the carnival was the same and silent except for one desperate voice. Ugly Al didn't chase Zach this time. Naomi was somewhere on the midway, crying out to Zach for help, voice far-away and frightened. Ugly Al hunted Naomi, and Zach wanted to warn her, for God's sake, to be quiet, but he had no voice of his own. He searched frantically for Naomi around the Tilt-a-Whirl, behind the Whip, around the Tip Top and the Caterpillar, under the silently turning Ferris wheel, past the snow-cone and the cotton-candy stands, in sideshow tents and game arcades, her voice always somewhere that he wasn't—and then she screamed.

Zach saw Ugly Al dragging Naomi by her hair, dragging her along the sawdust-carpeted concourse, Naomi silent now, doing nothing to resist. Zach almost caught up with them, got close, close enough to see that where Naomi's eyes should have been there were these coins, quarters, **black** quarters, and something dark in her mouth, her hands tied together, thumb to thumb, little finger to little finger, with a chicken egg cupped in them. Worst of all—he should have seen it first, but he saw it last—worst of all was the knife, the cut-you-if-you-looked-at-it knife, shoved to the hilt in her throat. Zach tried to scream, couldn't, and Ugly Al raced away at high speed, dragging dead Naomi. The carnival concourse telescoped out, suddenly going on to infinity, and Ugly Al dragged Naomi away into forever while Zach fell farther and farther behind, screaming soundlessly until he woke up screaming into a pillow.

He hoped he wouldn't dream of the freak three nights in a row.

The mood in the house had changed this afternoon. Dinner was the best time they had in a while, everyone with something interesting to say, quick and funny. Zach knew the rest of them felt it too, as if for weeks the air was thick with a pending thunderstorm and everyone waiting for lightning, and this afternoon the weather changed.

Now, alone in his room, he finished his fourth half-assed pencil portrait of old Ugly Al. Each of the four looked somewhat different from the others, and none caught the full-on weirdness of the guy. When you were drawing from a dream, you were working with less even than a memory, so Zachary couldn't beat himself up too much for getting it only three-quarters right.

He sprayed the portrait with fixative, tore it out of the tablet, and started to draw Laura Leigh Highsmith's lips, the full purse of the mouth from the philtrum to the suggestion of the chin muscles. He worked from memory now, not just from a dream, and in this case his memory was as sharp as if he had been drawing from real life.

Reading a book in bed, Naomi sat propped against a sumptuous pile of pillows so feathery they seemed capable of levitating like great slow birds and carrying her aloft with them. Until recently, when she read in bed, she wore mere pajamas, pathetic childwear, but not anymore. Now she sat attired in a Vietnamese **ao dai,** a flowing tunic-and-pants ensemble made of colorful silk, which she discovered during an all-girls shopping afternoon with her mother and Minette. This exotic garment— deliriously glamorous and drop-dead chic—was infinitely more appropriate for her than were kiddie pajamas, now that she was closer to twelve than to eleven. The **ao dai** served as day and evening wear, it was not for sleeping, but she intended to sleep in it anyway, and in the two others now in her wardrobe. A mere child sleeps in a wrinkled mess of cotton, drooling, hair disarrayed, but a young lady strives to look her best even when unconscious.

Minnie, who would be an exasperating child for **years** yet, sat at her play table, bagged in a typically dumpy pair of jammies with, of all things, a precious teddy-bear pattern. She worked intently on one of her bizarre LEGO-block structures, all strange angles and cantilevered sections that should have collapsed but didn't.

"What is that funky thing?" Naomi asked.

"I don't know. I saw it in a dream."

"**That's** where they come from? Buildings you see in dreams?"

"Not the other ones. Just this. But it's not a building. It's something. I don't know what. And I don't have it right, either."

"Don't you ever dream about unicorns and flying carpets and wishing lamps?"

"No."

Naomi sighed. "Sometimes I worry myself sick about you, Mouse."

"I'm good. I'm fine. Don't call me Mouse."

"You know what? I could be your dream coach! I could teach you how to dream right, with golden palaces and crystal castles and a fabulously colorful tent city around a desert oasis, wise old talking turtles, geese that fly underwater but swim through the

air, and ice skating in the moonlight with the hand-
somest boy ever but he turns out to be a kind of
griffin except all lion and just the wings of an eagle,
and he flies over a shining city with you riding on
his back."

"No," Minnie said, concentrating on the LEGO
thing.

"I'd be a **great** dream coach!"

"Aren't you reading a book?"

"It's a great book. It's about this very cultivated
dragon who teaches this savage girl how to be civilized because she's got to become a Joan of Arc to
her people. Should I read it out loud?"

"No."

"Then what **do** you want? Sometimes, dear child,
you are quite inscrutable."

"I want some silence so I can think about this
thing."

"Yes, of course, being a whiz at LEGOs is just like
being a chess master, such profound strategy re-
quires absolute silence."

"Absolute," Minnie agreed.

Ensconced in her lavish mound of pillows,
Naomi returned her attention to the book, wondering why on earth she even tried to be a responsible
older sister, why she struggled to lift this benighted
little squirt out of the sandbox when, clearly, not
even a cultivated dragon could have done the job.

———— ⁂ ————

The new mood in the house encouraged Nicolette, but around a tiny grain of frustration, her mind began to secrete a black pearl of worry. Intuition, intense but unspecific, warned her that the children were in some way at risk. Curiously, this concern began with a difficulty she was having with her current painting.

She seldom returned to work in her studio following the post-dinner family time, but this evening she wanted to study the canvas that was in progress, perhaps for a couple of hours.

John was understanding, as always. He said that he would read in the library and that she shouldn't be concerned if he came to bed late, as he felt so wide-awake he might be in the grip of insomnia.

She took a snifter of brandy to her studio, though she rarely had anything to drink except wine at dinner, and though she had never previously wanted— or needed—brandy to assist her in the evaluation of a problem painting. She put the snifter on the tall table with the yellow roses that had been arranged by Imogene a few hours earlier.

Taped to the upright of the easel, above the current canvas, was a photograph of Zach, Naomi, and Minnie, taken two weeks earlier. For the photo, Nicky had carefully posed them framed by the living-room archway, and this group portrait was the subject of her latest work.

She had planned a painting informed by John Singer Sargent's **The Daughters of Edward Darley Boit:** light in the foreground fading to deep shadow, depth of field, and spatial mystery against which the clarity of the children's character would be explicit.

In the painting as in the photo, the kids stood in an unexpected order, not in ascending age and not girls together. Naomi was in the hall, in the foreground, arms crossed and feet planted apart, a power stance, challenging the artist, the world. Behind and to the right of Naomi, Zach posed casually in the archway, hands in his pockets, self-possessed. Farthest from the artist, within the living room, stood Minette in a white dress, luminous in shadow, entirely clear.

The spaces and the details of the clothing were nearly complete, and the quality of light was almost as Nicky wanted it, though she had not yet done the fine work on the faces, which were currently just cranial structures and muscle masses, otherwise eerily blank. She had come to a halt because the painting wasn't saying what she intended that it should say.

Among other things, she meant to show personality expressing itself powerfully regardless of distance from the viewer or the nature of the lighting. Each child should be known equally well for the person—for the grace—that she or he was. Nicky intended the painting to be a quiet but moving celebration of individuality.

Instead, it felt like a painting about **loss**. As if she were re-creating her children not from a photograph but from her memory of them after they were dead.

This perception at first annoyed her, then disturbed her, and finally filled her with an abiding disquiet. She told herself that the unfinished faces were the cause of her uneasiness, those blank bone and muscle masses, but she knew better. She had worked in this manner before, toward a culmination in faces, without any problem.

For the past three days, the painting increasingly projected the theme of loss until she could not study it long before disquiet escalated into a gnawing anxiety. In the brushstrokes she had laid down, she could see—could **feel**—the less acute but more enduring grief that is called sorrow, as if she had done this work years after some unthinkable tragedy.

She had never labored on the canvas while in a somber mood. She approached the picture with enthusiasm, affection, and love. At all times, she worked with pleasure, which often rose to a condition of delight. Yet the piece appeared despairing, as though an artist with a darker set of mind had come in every night to rework the portrait.

The photograph, a computer printout on a full sheet of paper, was different in many ways from the canvas because she never had any intention of merely reproducing it in paint. Now she peeled it off the upright of the easel to inspect it closely.

She had instructed the kids to remain deadpan, because she did not want to paint from a shot in which they were mugging for the camera; she intended to supply each with his or her most signature expression. Maybe they subtly defied her instructions, assuming just enough expression to influence her subconsciously. But, no, each was as deadpan as could be.

Then she noticed the shadowy figure.

The photo had been taken in the evening, with overhead light in the hallway but only one table lamp aglow in a corner of the living room beyond the archway. Behind Minnie, everything faded to darkness, and the only thing to be seen in that gloom was a tall mirror on the farther wall, which was expressed only as a pale shimmer of reflected light, its baroque frame invisible. In that dim rectangle loomed a dark figure that could not be any of the kids or Nicky because none of them was positioned to reflect in the mirror.

She carried the printout of the photo to the slanted draftsman's table in one corner of the studio. A large lighted magnifying lens, fixed to the table on a swing arm, brought the mysterious figure into fuller view. The silhouette lacked features, but it appeared to be a tall, stoop-shouldered man.

No one but she and the kids had been present. No one had watched from the hallway, and no one other than Minette had actually been in the living room. Zach, the nearest to Minnie, stood in the archway, on the threshold of the chamber.

Nicky's uneasiness grew the longer she studied the silhouette. She cautioned herself that what she saw might not be a person but a trick of lighting or a reflection of some item of furniture in the living room.

At the time, she had taken five other shots that she deemed less desirable than the one she used at the easel. She retrieved printouts of them from her desk and brought them to the draftsman's table to study each under the big magnifying lens.

In four of the five photos, the figure appeared as a shadow in the mirror. It could not be a reflection of an inanimate object that happened to resemble the silhouette of a tall man, because from shot to shot it subtly changed position.

Nicky thought back to the imagined murky presence in the master bathroom and the shattering mirror that hadn't really shattered, the hallucination that she persisted in attributing to an adverse reaction to Vicodin. She sensed that the first figure and this one in the living-room mirror must be related, but she could not see how. The first had been a moment of delirium, but this one could be seen in five of six photographs, as real in its way as any of the three children, **yet no one had been there**.

After reviewing the photos again under the magnifier, Nicolette remained baffled, but her intuition bored with a sharper bit, drilled deep, and worry welled up.

31

BRENDA SALSETTO WOBURN SAT WITH HER twelve-year-old son, Lenny, on the living-room sofa, watching TV. Lenny liked being with his mom more than he liked being anywhere else, and with Brenda the feeling was mutual. He was her Down syndrome boy, as sweet and true as anyone she had ever known, wise in his way, always surprising her with his observations, which were as clear and thought-provoking as they were uncomplicated.

Davinia, seventeen, was studying in her room, and Jack, Brenda's husband, worked in the kitchen, testing a recipe for veggie lasagne that, if it turned out well, would be the next night's dinner. Jack was a parks-department supervisor, a good man who had become a fan of the Food Network. He discovered that he possessed a previously unrecognized culinary talent.

The family movie on TV featured talking dogs,

and Lenny giggled frequently. Brenda should have been relaxed; but she was not. For the past five days, she had been preoccupied with how to respond to something her brother had done and something unspeakable that he might have intended to do.

Brenda feared her younger brother, Reese. She knew that after she left home when she was eighteen, Reese molested their sister, Jean, from the time the timid girl was seven years old until she committed suicide at eleven. Brenda had no proof, only something Jean said to her on the phone a few hours before she hung herself, so long ago. She had more reasons to despise her brother than to fear him, but her fear of him was great.

She tried with some success to minimize their contact over the years. But she knew that if she rejected him outright for any reason or without expressing a reason, her repudiation would be a boil in his mind, festering over weeks or months until bitter resentment darkened into anger, anger into rage, rage into fury, and he would be swept to a violent reaction. He wanted everything that he didn't have and wanted it with a frightening vehemence, not just material possessions but also admiration and respect, which he believed could be gotten with intimidation and brute force as surely as could money.

A few days earlier, Reese came to visit in the early afternoon of a school holiday, when Jack and

Brenda were at work. Only Davinia and Lenny were home. He came with comic books and candy for Lenny, a wristwatch set with diamonds for Davinia. Never before had he been alone with the kids and never had he brought them anything. Davinia knew the wristwatch was an inappropriate gift, too expensive, its very value an improper insinuation. Reese played at being a loving uncle, which he had never been before, and found every excuse to press close to Davinia. He held her hand, his touch lingered over her bare arms, admiringly he smoothed her hair away from her face. Instead of kissing her chastely on the cheek, he kissed the corner of her mouth, and his lips would have brushed across hers if she had not pulled away.

Davinia was a bright but inexperienced girl who dated little and then only boys as innocent as she. Her beauty was enchanting, especially because it was a beauty equally of body, mind, and soul—and because in her humility she didn't understand the power of her appearance. She was capable of finding joy in small things, in the flight of a bird or a cup of tea, and she had told her parents that she might choose a religious life in one sisterhood or another.

Brenda wondered what horror might have occurred during Reese's unannounced visit if, shortly after his arrival, Jack's sister Lois had not stopped by unexpectedly. Davinia was his niece, but that relationship meant nothing to a man who considered his little sister to be fair game and drove her to self-destruction. Brenda had seen him watch Davinia with lascivious interest, but she had been in denial of the possibility that he might act on his desire. Davinia was not as delicate as she looked, not emotionally fragile; but rape might do more than devastate her, might destroy her. Brenda was at times physically ill with the thought of it.

She and Jack were currently deciding whether she should give up her job to be sure the kids were never alone in the house. They had taken other steps to prevent the unthinkable. But Reese was clever, cunning, bold, without moral constraints, and unpredictable.

A slight draft motivated Brenda to get another afghan from a chair across the room. As she passed a window, Reese's Mercedes pulled in to their driveway. He drove too fast, stopping with a bark of brakes.

At once, Brenda suspected her brother intended to cause some kind of trouble. If he didn't intend it, he would foment it anyway. She shouted toward the kitchen, **"Jack, Reese is here!"**

She hurried Lenny to his sister's room and told them to lock the door. Maybe she was overreacting. Maybe Reese had come back only to get the diamond wristwatch that he refused to take when Davinia tried to return it to him.

Reese Salsetto—more accurately, the rider that owns him now—raps lightly on one of the four windowpanes in the back door, and waves at Jack, who is doing women's work in the kitchen, preparing something for the oven. Wiping his hands on his apron, Jack frowns as he approaches the door, but Reese gives him a sheepish grin and tries to look as if he has come to apologize for something, because Jack and Brenda are the kind of self-righteous prigs who at any one time have a thousand reasons why they should receive apologies.

Jack opens the door and says, "Reese, we've got to talk about some things," and Reese says, "No, we don't," and shoots him twice with the silencer-equipped pistol. As if the muffled shots require an equally discreet response, Jack drops as quietly as a sack of laundry, and Reese steps over the body, closing the door behind him. This is the Sollenburgs redux, husband and wife and son shot dead, and then the daughter used in ways that she has never comprehended that she might be used. Although the assault begins on the evening of the thirty-second day after the Lucas murders, Reese and his rider will not be done with Davinia Woburn until well into the morning of October fifth, six or eight hours from now.

Brenda, succulent mother of the much-desired

piglet, hurries into the kitchen, and Reese, speaking for himself **and** for his ventriloquist, says, "When I'm done with her, she'll hang herself like Jean." But his taunt comes at an unexpected cost when Brenda raises a .38 revolver in a two-hand grip and pops him three times, the third time in the throat. The mount dies under the rider.

Brenda is a good woman who would have rescued her sister, Jean, if she had known what Reese intended, but her failure to save her sister has left her with a settled anger that has simmered in her for all these years. The bitter anger is the stirrup that might allow her to be mounted, and because she curses Reese as she kills him, the way into her is through the mouth.

She feels the rider enter and struggles fiercely to resist, reeling backward against a bank of cabinets, door pulls gouging at her back and buttocks. The rider encourages her anger, for if anger can be raised to fury, and if fury and terror crowd out all other feelings, she can be taken. Unlike many others who do not fully understand the nature of their rider, this woman knows it, not by name but for what it is. She sees at once the consequences of being taken, that it will ride her to her children and force her to abuse, torture, and murder them, and last of all to degrade herself in as many ways as its rich imagination can invent.

Just as her spine begins to feel like an accommodating saddle, she finds another emotion besides rage and terror, and she recalls the prayer of Saint Michael, which she hasn't said since adolescence.

This sudden vomitous spew of pious words will not repel her new master, because it now rules her spine and will soon have control of her bones down to the marrow. The rider is moments away from using her voice for a cry of triumph when she turns the revolver on herself and squeezes off a round that punches through her chest, past her heart, ricochets off her sternum, off a clavicle, and lodges under her left scapular. White-hot pain magnifies her terror but entirely evaporates her rage. And as she falls to the floor, in the humble recognition of her mortality, she casts off her rider.

Recklessly, the son and the exquisitely ripe daughter respond to the shots, as though even weaponless they can halt the violence, perhaps with—what?— his guileless tears and with her pure heart. They are naive, helpless, the colt and filly, thinking meat machines that think too little. The rider wants the boy, for with the boy, the juicy piglet can still be reduced to a ferociously used, broken, despairing **thing**. But the boy is only twelve and, more to the point, he has a condition that renders him the next thing to a perpetual innocent, with no corruptions adequate to serve as grips for a mounting. The weeping girl cannot be saddled, either. The rider can only watch with escalating fury as Davinia directs the boy to call 911 and as she kneels beside the fallen mother, competent in spite of her tears, gently elevating the mother's head to improve her breathing.

No ride exists here, nothing to be taken but the house itself, its fleshless bones a poor substitute for a living host. A haunt is never a fraction as sweet as a possession, but soon other possible hosts will arrive, and there is no danger that this house will become a prison. Furious, the spirit takes the house with such force that a loud **boom** passes through the walls, windowpanes rattle, draperies flap on rods, glasses and dishes clink and clatter on the kitchen shelves, and two oven doors fall open like gaping mouths.

32

DETECTIVE LIONEL TIMMINS KNEW THAT
some in the department, among themselves, called
him the Walking Chest, and still others called him
the Dog, because he had a bulldog face and he was
difficult to shake loose when he got his teeth in a
case. He had his teeth in this one, and he didn't like
the taste of it.

Because this was Homicide South, within the
Lake District and only two blocks from his home,
he caught the call and arrived behind the ambu-
lance as its siren wound down to silence and the
paramedics threw open their doors, the earliest he
had ever arrived at a crime scene.

The medics stabilized the wounded—the husband critical, the wife less serious but not good—
and took them away as four uniforms arrived to
secure the scene. Lionel managed to ask a few ques-

tions and get answers from the woman before they carried her out.

The girl, Davinia, had called an aunt to take her and Lenny to the hospital. Lionel waited with them in the living room.

Wrenched with grief but determined to be brave, the boy held fast to his sister's hand, so innocent of evil until now that his sudden education was a painful thing to see.

The girl was remarkable, a delicate rock. Although slender and only about five feet four, she seemed tall, strong, sure. Although her eyes, like her brother's, glistened with tears, hers didn't spill as his did. Lionel well knew that beauty was power, but her power had a deeper source.

Davinia provided the identity of the dead man in the kitchen and spoke frankly but not angrily about his visit five days earlier. She produced the unwanted diamond wristwatch, which looked like a year's wages.

"I want to be rid of it," she said. "It's a terrible thing."

"This isn't evidence, I can't take it," Lionel said. "Your mother shot him in self-defense. There won't be any trial of anyone."

"Can't you put it with his body?"

"No. Some charity might be the place for it."

Neither Davinia nor Lenny had seen events unfold in the kitchen, but from the time line they could provide, Lionel deduced the order in which the shootings occurred.

The aunt appeared, the children went with her to the hospital, and the criminalists arrived to sift the scene.

A flash report on Reese Salsetto revealed one conviction and much suspicion. He had served a year in prison when, if all were known, he might have deserved a century.

The criminalists came quickly to the determination that Reese shot Jack Woburn with the 9-mm pistol fitted with a sound suppressor and that Brenda Woburn killed Reese with her .38 revolver.

According to Brenda, she stumbled, fell against some cabinets, and shot herself after killing her brother. Lionel and the lab boys found it difficult to believe that a woman proficient enough with a handgun to put three centralized rounds in a man at a distance of even just fifteen feet would accidentally shoot herself in the chest.

Furthermore, though Reese might be a hothead, he had managed to conduct more than a decade of criminal enterprise with only one arrest and one conviction. Even if, as Brenda had said, he molested their younger sister, Jean, when he was a teenager, reason argued that he would have tried to get to his niece in a way that was as circumspect as his behavior with Jean—and more in accord with the weasely business with the wristwatch. Reese cared too much about Reese to try to kidnap the niece by launching a reckless assault on the entire Woburn family.

Leaving the kitchen to the techs, the uniforms outside chasing away curious neighbors and swapping bullshit stories, Lionel walked the rest of the downstairs, touching nothing, studying everything. He was troubled that the facts of the shooting scenario were beads on a string of irrationality and therefore, though facts, were worth no more than the weak filament on which they were strung.

Something else bothered him, too, but he couldn't identify the source of his uneasiness until, standing in the dining room, he saw movement from the corner of his eye. He turned to watch the pendant crystals swaying on the simple chandelier above the table. In the absence of a draft, with no vibration to be felt or heard, the easy pendulum motion of the crystals seemed inexplicable. Perhaps more curious was the lack of uniformity in their arcs: some swung north-south, some east-west, others to different points of the compass. The crystals slowed and stopped as he watched—and then he turned toward a noise behind him. It was a mere rustle, it could have been anything or nothing, but some quality of it caused his neck hairs to prickle. He realized that in addition to the weaknesses in the crime scenario, the other thing that bothered him was the house.

He did not know what he meant by that.

Some houses had a history that colored your feeling about them: murder houses, for instance, in which innocents had been tortured and slaughtered. The shootings in the kitchen didn't qualify because they were too clean, insufficiently perverse. Lionel knew nothing about the history of this house, and based on the impression that Lenny and Davinia made on him, he doubted this was a family with dark secrets.

A house could subtly abrade your nerves if the proportions of its rooms were wrong, if the colors were harsh, if items of furniture clashed with one another. But this architecture was harmonious, the colors pleasant, the furniture homey and of a kind.

Waiting for the rustle to repeat, Lionel knew what bothered him about the house: a feeling of being watched. In spite of having been railroaded for murder and having spent six years in prison, he wasn't prone to paranoia. In his work, he relied on a sober instinct for danger, and the only thing that plucked his fear wire was the thought of losing his mom or one of the aunts who lived with him.

Overhead, floorboards creaked as someone crossed an upstairs room. The family was at the hospital. The criminalists were in the kitchen and had no reason to venture to the second floor.

He returned to the hallway and stood at the foot of the stairs, looking up, listening. A soft thump might have been a door closing above or only a settling noise. Another thump.

Lionel ascended to the second floor and conducted a casual but thorough search. The room doors were all open or ajar, and he toed or elbowed them wider, to pass through. Light switches chased darkness but nothing else, no intruder.

The final room at the end of the hall seemed to be Davinia's. The decor was feminine but not frilly, almost austere. Her books proved to be of a more serious nature than he might have expected.

She had been doing homework at a table that served as her desk. Her computer remained on.

The screen saver consisted of ceaselessly shifting shapes in gold, red, and a variety of blues. He had never seen anything quite like it, and in fact it was beautiful, worth watching for a minute, almost mesmerizing.

Although he expected the shapes to remain mysterious, fluid and continuously changing, the blues and golds suddenly coalesced into a handprint on a purling red background, as though someone flattened a palm against the inner face of the screen.

Lionel found himself in the desk chair without realizing that he had sat down. He watched, almost as an observer of someone else's action, as his right hand moved forward to match itself to the handprint on the screen.

On contact, Lionel felt a cold quivering against his palm and spread fingers, merely an odd vibration at first, but quickly growing into a vigorous squirming sensation, as if his hand were pressed against a mass of newborn snakes. Just as his curiosity gave way to alarm, something nipped lightly at the pad of his thumb, a fang prick but not a full bite, as if one of the imagined serpents were testing his susceptibility to their venom. He snatched his hand away from the screen and shot up from the chair.

No puncture marked his thumb.

He was as disturbed by his expectation of a wound as by the phantom nip. His revulsion at the cold squirming sensation lingered although he had touched nothing worse than a smooth glass surface. Intellectually, he understood that the foul sensation of squirming serpents must have been the consequence of some rare kind of static charge, but he still felt as though he had touched something alien and vile.

The shapes on the computer were amorphous once more. Lionel watched for five minutes, waiting for the handprint to appear again, assuming that it must be a programmed feature of the screen saver, but his vigil went unrewarded. Finally, he switched off the system in case there might be an electrical problem with it.

In the upstairs hall, he stood listening.

He still felt watched.

Lionel Timmins wondered if he had been working too hard lately.

33

ALTHOUGH HE COULD DO NOTHING TO IDEN-
tify and protect the family at risk, indeed **because**
of his helplessness, John Calvino knew sleep would
elude him. He sat in a library armchair, trying to
lose himself in the latest book by one of his favorite
authors, but his mind would not relent from its obsession. He read page after page, turned from chapter to chapter, but the story failed to become as
vivid to him as the memory of what Alton Blackwood had done to the Sollenburgs, the homicides
that might this night be repeated.

At eleven-thirty, he put the book aside and
phoned the Robbery-Homicide watch commander
to learn if anyone had been called out on an unusual 187—murder—during the evening. He seldom checked in like this, but his call was not
entirely out of character, either. Only anxiety, not
intuition, compelled him to pick up the phone.

The thirty-third day did not begin for another half an hour, but Blackwood's crimes two decades earlier twice bridged the midnight hour. For whatever reason he kept to a thirty-three-day schedule, the killer sometimes failed to wait for that magic day to arrive. His desire, his need, his **hunger** for violence could drive him to an early start, though he always finished his work according to his sacred calendar.

When John learned from the watch commander about the shootings at the Woburn house hours earlier, he knew this could be the one, **must** be the one, even if it seemed to have gone wrong for Blackwood. The Sollenburgs and the Woburns were both families of four; in each instance, the parents were shot; and the Woburns had one son and one daughter, just like the Sollenburgs.

He turned off the lights in the library and hurried upstairs to tell Nicky that he was going out on a case, which was not a lie even if it might not be strictly the truth. This case was not his, but it **was** Lionel's case, according to the watch commander. And John had a legitimate—if personal—interest in it even if he had completed little more than half of his thirty-day leave, about which he had **also** managed to tell Nicky neither the truth nor a lie.

Her studio was dark, and in the master bedroom, John found her sound asleep in the soft light of her bedside lamp. On her nightstand stood an empty brandy snifter beside a copy of the complete poems of T. S. Eliot, which she had read often.

She failed to stir when he whispered her name. He wrote a note and placed it in the empty brandy glass.

Sleeping, Nicolette looked as innocent as a child, and if the only transgressions that counted were those done with the **intent** to transgress, then she was perhaps as blameless as the children she had brought into the world.

At half past midnight, when John arrived in the ICU visitors' lounge at St. Joseph's Hospital, Jack Woburn's sister Lois was text-messaging a status report to relatives. The exhausted boy slept on a thinly padded three-seat couch.

The daughter stood at a window, gazing out at the night and the city. She turned to John, and he knew beyond doubt that the Woburns were meant to be the family with which the Sollenburg murders would be restaged. Blackwood was consecrated to the ritualistic destruction of what was both beautiful and innocent, two qualities of this girl, as they had been qualities also of John's lost sisters, Marnie and Giselle.

As he introduced himself to Davinia, his voice trembled and broke, so that she must have wondered why the suffering of her family—strangers to him—should evoke such emotion. He could not tell her that he was thankful for her survival not only as anyone should be thankful that the life of another was spared, but also because her escape from their otherworldly enemy gave him hope that his family might likewise be saved.

When Lois completed her BlackBerry message, she shared with John the news she texted to relatives. Brenda Woburn had undergone a forty-five-minute surgery for her gunshot wound, had come through brilliantly, and had recovered from anesthesia. She was lying now in an ICU bed. They expected soon to be allowed to see her for a few minutes. Jack Woburn remained in surgery, his prognosis grave.

John sat with them, hopeful that after the children had been allowed to see their mother, he would be permitted a couple of minutes with her, as well.

<hr />

The four uniformed officers, who are dealing with onlookers, return to the house one at a time to check on the progress of the techs or to use the half bath off the ground-floor hall. Patrolmen, technicians, crime-lab photographer, morgue-wagon jockeys all touch doorknobs, doors, and door casings not directly related to the crime scene. They touch the flush on the half-bath toilet, faucet handles, light switches. By these contacts, they are known and assessed.

All are more accessible than Lionel Timmins, two offer easy mounts, and the easier of these is Andy Tane, a uniformed patrolman. Andy sometimes uses the threat of arrest to receive free services from prostitutes, scouts teenage runaways for pimps, and takes a finder's fee for each girl he conveys to them. When he was little, his mother called him Andy Candy. He likes the hookers to call him that, as well, when he uses them. He also accepts bribes from other criminal entrepreneurs either for pretending to be unaware of their activities or for actively assisting them.

Andy Candy Tane is known in full when he enters the house by the front door to use the half bath. When he flushes the toilet, he is **taken,** which in his case is by far the most appropriate moment. Andy is tall and strong, thirty-six, a worthy horse for the ride ahead.

After the morgue wagon departs with the body of Reese Salsetto, only one pair of uniforms is needed until the criminalists leave and Lionel Timmins locks the house. Andy Tane and his partner, Mickey Scriver, are the first unit released from the scene.

Andy and Mickey are on a four-day-a-week, forty-hour schedule—cruising the streets, on the lookout for bad guys, catching calls as they come—from 6:00 P.M. until 4:00 A.M. They usually take a dinner break at eight if they're not in the middle of a collar or responding to a priority code.

They have been together only two weeks; and though Mickey is still trying to figure out if the partnership will work, Andy already prefers a change, a partner more flexible, more **nuanced**. Mickey is ex-army, his head full of self-limiting words like **honor** and **duty**. He's ambitious, intending to make a rep in this rolling-blue work and then move up to plainclothes, possibly the narcotics bureau, not because the big bribes are there, which is why Andy might consider it if he were ambitious, but because that is where the action is. Mickey Scriver likes action. He wants to do work that "makes a difference in the community." Andy loathes action as much as he loathes the community; and he would by now loathe Mickey if not for his sense of humor.

Andy's previous partner, Vin Wasco, had been on the take, too, which made it a lot easier for Andy to conduct his own business. But Vin has gone under the knife for a benign brain tumor. Although doctors say he will make a complete recovery, Andy will be amazed and disappointed if Vin doesn't fake himself into a full, lifetime disability pension.

At half past midnight, there are fewer places to catch dinner than at eight o'clock. Mickey suggests takeout from an Italian place that does good sandwiches, because if they eat in the car, they're ready to take a priority-code call if they get one. Mickey of course is always happier swinging the hammer than polishing it. Mickey goes into the joint alone to place their orders because Andy doesn't want any restaurant owner in his precinct to see him paying for a meal. He and Vin never paid. But Mickey acts like there's no alternative to paying, as if the tight-assed sonofabitch not only has his lily-white heart set on promotion to plainclothes in Narcotics but also on sainthood.

When Mickey returns with two bags of takeout—a meatball-and-cheese sub with Sicilian slaw, a steak-and-cheese sub with regular slaw, two bags of potato chips, two large Cokes—Andy doesn't want to be seen eating in the damn parking lot. Carpenters, plumbers, gardeners, and the like eat in their vehicles, and Andy strongly believes that it brings disrespect to the uniform when people see their law-enforcement officers chowing down in cars like common laborers.

Three blocks from the restaurant, at Lake Park, Andy pulls around the chain and stanchions that close the entry road until morning, drives on the grass far enough to reconnect with the pavement, parks on the sward near the shore, and leaves the engine running but kills the headlights. The lake isn't so big that it's a great blackness. Shore lights shimmer on dark water, and there's a view if you're into that kind of thing.

Andy claims he needs to take a leak, says he'll be right back, and walks to the edge of the embankment. Dark grass slopes ten feet to a pale beach at which black water gently laps. The moon rocks in the cradle of the lake. At this hour and in this chill, the park is deserted. Andy pretends to start to piss, does a double take that maybe he oversells, takes two steps down the slope, and then hurries back to the patrol car, zipping up his fly as he goes, to Mickey's window, which the saint is already cranking down.

"I think there's a deader on the beach," Andy says.

"Maybe it's a drunk," Mickey says around a mouthful of steak and cheese.

"You don't see too many naked blondes sleeping off a bender on the beach. Gimme a flashlight."

Mickey gets out of the car with two flashlights. Because he's Mickey and hot to trade his shirt badge for a walleted one, he takes the lead, hurrying toward the spot where Andy had pretended to kill the grass with his bull stream.

Ridden as authoritatively as any horse in all of history before him, Andy Tane draws his pistol and squeezes off two rounds. Shot in the back, the dutiful and honorable Officer Scriver collapses facedown, his flashlight rolling on the close-cropped grass. Andy comes in fast behind him, the swivel holster on his utility belt slapping against his thigh, to pump a third round in the back of good Saint Mickey's head, point-blank.

This will most likely be the last night of Andy Candy's life; therefore, there's no reason for him to dispose of the body or work out an alibi. He returns to the cruiser, throws the bags of takeout from the car, and drives out of the park.

Some horses require more effort to be ridden than do others. In horror, some buck and kick, metaphorically speaking, when they see themselves committing atrocities. Others, like Reese Salsetto, actually feel liberated by their new master, and respond less like ridden beasts than like conspirators. They are thrilled that they have been freed from the last constraints that hobbled them, from the fear of death, and may now be the fully revealed and ruthless apostles of chaos that they have longed to be.

Andy Tane is neither horrified nor exhilarated. His thousands of corrupt acts—bribe-taking, facilitating white slavery, rape by intimidation, running a protection racket with his badge—have been committed without the ardor and the glee that would have fermented his soul into a thick, dark, intoxicating devil's brew. Instead he has done his evil in the unimaginative and plodding manner of a dull-minded bureaucrat, in the process poaching the leaves of his soul until they are nothing but a cup of weak tea. Incapable of either outrage or delight at the acts his rider forces him to commit, Andy Tane can react only as the coward he has for so long been, retreating into a kind of automatismic trance, allowing himself to be used while retreating from all awareness of what he has been forced to do.

He knows to which hospital the Woburns were taken, and there as well he will find the boy and girl, the unfinished business that his rider is determined to address.

After Brenda Woburn's children and sister had been allowed, as a group, to spend ten minutes with her, the head nurse in the ICU was hesitant to admit John. His badge didn't impress her. But his powers of gentle persuasion, long practiced with witnesses, and his earnest assurances convinced her to give him three minutes.

"But I'll be timing you, and I mean just three," she warned.

When John slid the curtain aside from Brenda Woburn's bed bay and then pulled it closed behind him, she did not open her eyes. She seemed to be fast asleep.

Her heart, respiration, and blood pressure were being monitored, but she was not on a ventilator. An intravenous drip maintained her body fluids and sugar level. She received oxygen through nasal cannulas.

Tendrils of her short dark hair, damp and pasted

flat, looked like the checks and X's of some game played on her pallid brow with felt-tip markers. The deep hollows of her eyes seemed exaggerated, resembling those of luckless travelers in movies about survival on a desert trek along a route where every oasis was a mirage. Her lips were bloodless.

John spoke her name three times before she opened her eyes. Her gaze resolved on him as he identified himself. She was on painkillers, but the effect was more apparent in the slackness of her face and in her lethargy than in her eyes, which were clear, focused, and suggestive of alertness.

"You must've had handgun training," he said. "Three mortal hits. Not a round wasted. That's more than luck. Even if they never make an issue of it, they won't believe you accidentally shot yourself."

She stared at him. Her voice was parched: "What do you want?"

Mindful of his three-minute limit, he went to the heart of it: "Twenty years ago, four families were murdered in my hometown. The fourth was my family—both my parents, two younger sisters."

Unblinking, she stared at him.

"I killed the killer. Now I have a family of my own. . . ."

The light from overhead did not paint a flat sheen on her eyes but fell away into them.

"A family of my own now, and I'm afraid it's happening again. You must've seen the news . . . the Lucases."

Brenda Woburn blinked, blinked.

"They were killed exactly the way that first family was killed twenty years ago. The second family back then, the Sollenburgs—the father, mother, and son were shot to death. In that order. Daughter was raped. Tortured. For hours."

The soft beep and the spiking light pulse of the ECG monitor tracked an increase in her heartbeat.

"I don't want to distress you," John said. "But I need to know something. I'm not here as a cop. I'm here as a husband and father."

The automatic sphygmomanometer showed a rise in Brenda's blood pressure.

"Why did you shoot yourself?"

She licked her lips. Her gaze slid to her left, to the hanging IV bags, past them to the heart monitor.

"Billy Lucas didn't kill his family," John said. "Your brother, Reese, didn't kill your husband."

Her stare returned to him.

"You can tell me. Please. Tell me. Why did you shoot yourself?"

"Suicide."

"You meant to kill yourself? Why?"

"To stop it."

"Stop what?"

She hesitated. Then: "Stop whatever it was. Stop it from taking me. Control of me."

And here was the revelation. Mere truth and yet extraordinary. Confirmation.

"Cold and crawling, slithering. Not just in my head. Everywhere in my body. Skin to bones."

"You reacted so fast."

"No time. It knew me, **all** of me. In an instant. But I knew some of it, too, how it wanted Lenny dead, Davinia not dead . . . not right away."

John thought of his sisters, stripped and brutalized, and his legs felt weak. He leaned with both hands on the bed railing.

Brenda shuddered as though recalling the cold slithery invader fingering the marrow in her bones. "What was it?"

"The killer I killed twenty years ago."

They stared at each other. He suspected that she might wish, as he almost did, that they were insane, delusional, rather than to know that such a thing as this could be true.

"Is it over?" she asked.

"For you. Maybe not for me. Unless by casting him out, you broke the spell, stopped the cycle, something. Then maybe it could be over for me, too."

She reached out to him with her left hand. He took it, held it.

34

RIDDEN LESS LIKE A HORSE THAN LIKE A MA-chine, withdrawn to a coward's perch in a back room of his brain, Andy Tane parks the patrol car near the entrance of St. Joseph's Hospital. In the main lobby, half the fluorescent lights are doused. The information desk is not staffed at this hour. The gift shop is closed. No one is in sight.

Maybe he should have parked at the ER entrance. But he knows how to find his way to the emergency room by an interior route.

At this late hour, even the ER is deserted, except for three patients. A heavyset woman sits at the only open registration window. A middle-aged couple, she in a blue-and-white exercise suit, he in tan jeans and a white T-shirt, sit watching the blood-soaked towel wrapped around his left hand, waiting to be taken seriously by someone.

Politely because politeness will more quickly get

him what he wants, but with official solemnity, Andy apologizes to the heavyset woman and interrupts the registration clerk—ELAINE DIGGS, according to her breast-pocket badge—to inquire as to the whereabouts of two gunshot victims, Brenda and Jack Woburn. Elaine Diggs consults her computer, makes a quick phone call, and reports, "Ms. Woburn is in the ICU. Mr. Woburn recently came out of surgery and is in post-op recovery."

As an officer of the law, Andy Tane is familiar with the layout of the hospital. The ICU is on the tenth floor. The operating rooms are all on the second floor, as is the recovery room, where patients are taken after surgery until the anesthesia has worn off and their vital signs are stable.

Jack Woburn's vital signs will not be stable much longer.

———∞∞∞———

After visiting Brenda Woburn in the ICU, John Calvino stopped in the adjacent visitors' lounge to leave his card—his home and cell numbers written on the back—with Davinia Woburn and her aunt Lois. Lenny remained asleep on the austere couch.

"Your mother's a brave woman," John told the girl.

Davinia nodded. "She's my hero. She always has been."

"She may want to call me. I'm always available, day or night."

"We just heard Daddy's out of surgery," Davinia said. She was radiant. "He's going to be all right."

She seemed to John like a cross between Minette and Naomi, though he could not say why. He wanted to hug her, but he hardly knew her.

"It's looking better, anyway," said Lois. "They'll probably be bringing Jack up here in another hour, maybe sooner."

"That's great," John said. "That's wonderful. Remember—day or night, if your mother has anything more to tell me."

He followed the corridor to the elevator alcove. Six stainless-steel doors, three on each side. According to the indicator boards, two cars were downbound, one was ascending, one was in the basement, and two were at the ground floor. He pushed the call button, and a car on the ground floor headed up.

Officer Andy Tane pushes through the swinging door to the post-op recovery room. The place is quiet and softly lighted. The air smells of an antibacterial cleaning solution.

The only patient present is Jack Woburn. He's lying on a gurney, a sheet drawn up to his shoulders. He's sleeping, hooked to a heart monitor and a ventilator.

Jack doesn't look good. He could look worse.

In an alcove off the recovery room, a nurse sits at a computer, typing. She doesn't see Andy enter.

After killing Mickey Scriver, Andy reloaded his service pistol. You always want a full magazine when you're after a bad guy, and you especially want a full magazine when you **are** the bad guy. He puts the muzzle under Jack Woburn's chin and fires one round.

The hard crack of the shot spins the nurse in her chair, and she springs to her feet just as the airborne blood and tissue soil the white-tile floor. She sees Andy, his gun drawn, and she's too stunned to scream. She dives out of sight, scrambling for whatever pathetic cover the alcove offers, **then** she lets out a scream, and she's got a good one.

Because Andy's rider has no interest in the nurse, Andy turns away from her and leaves the recovery room. The elevator car in which he ascended from the ground floor is still on 2. The doors slide open the moment he pushes the call button. Inside, he presses DOOR CLOSE on the control panel to hurry the process, then presses 10, and the car rises toward satisfaction.

⁘

According to the indicator boards, two cars were on the way up, the first a floor behind the other. When one of them arrived, John boarded it and pressed the button marked LOBBY.

Just as the doors began to close, a nurse hurried into the alcove, hoping to catch the car. John jammed his thumb on the DOOR OPEN button to accommodate her.

"Thanks a bunch," she said.

"No problem."

As the doors sighed shut a second time, he heard the **ding** of another car arriving on the tenth floor.

Passing the open doors to the ICU visitors' lounge, Andy's rider sees Jack Woburn's nagging bitch of a sister—as Reese Salsetto had thought of her—and the exquisite girl whom it's still got a chance to ruin, such a deliciously creamy little twist, and the moon-faced boy sleeping on a couch.

The girl and the woman see Andy, but they have no reason to wonder about him. He will deal with both sluts when the oh-so-heroic, self-sacrificing mother is forced to finish what she started by her own hand: dying.

He proceeds twenty feet to the end of the corridor, where the door to the intensive-care unit is locked. He presses the intercom button to call a nurse. When one of them replies, asking if she can help him, he glances back to be certain that the hallway is deserted and that no one can overhear him, and then he says, "It's a police emergency."

A nurse arrives to look at him through the window in the door. Andy taps his badge impatiently. Opening the door but blocking his entrance, she says, "What emergency?"

Andy puts a hand on her shoulder, and even though she tries to shrug his hand off, the rider knows her entirely in the instant. It could take her if necessary. Her name is Kaylin Amhurst, and she is an extremely cautious angel of death who over the years has decided that certain patients have been too much of a drain on the medical system and has euthanized eleven of them, the most recent being a woman named Charlain Oates.

Andy says, "Charlain Oates was only fifty-six and had a damn good chance of recovering."

Stunned, eyes protuberant, mouth sucking for breath that she can't draw in, like a fish drowning in air, Kaylin Amhurst backs away from him.

Sixteen beds occupy the perimeter of the room. A monitoring station stands in the center, where two other nurses are at work.

"Go to your station, Nurse Amhurst, and wait for me," Andy says, in the cold tone of voice that he uses with any perpetrator.

Of the sixteen beds, seven are unoccupied, and curtains are drawn around the other nine. But Andy's rider knows in which bay Brenda Woburn waits, because that, too, was learned from Kaylin Amhurst when the whole of her was read at a touch.

It doesn't want to use his gun a lot, preferably not

at all, because gunfire will alert those in the visitors' lounge, with whom it will deal next. It must not scare off the delectable girl and then have to smell her down like a hound snuffling after a bitch in heat.

As Amhurst retreats to the monitoring station, the other two nurses look up, perplexed. One of them frowns, wondering what Andy's doing in here, but no doubt she assumes that he wouldn't have gotten past the angel of death unless his mission was legitimate.

At Brenda Woburn's bay, he pulls back the curtain, then closes it after himself. Awake, alert, she turns her head toward him, but she isn't alarmed because he is a policeman, after all, sworn to defend and protect.

He leans over the low bed railing and says, "I have wonderful news for you, Brenda. I'm going to suck Davinia's sweet tongue right out of her mouth."

Andy is a large man, solidly muscled, with big fists. As the woman tries to rise from her pillows, he hammers her throat with everything he's got— once, twice, three times, four—crushing her larynx, her airway, rupturing arteries.

⁕

The nurse from the tenth floor got off at the eighth, and an orderly boarded, pushing a wheeled cart holding several white boxes. He was Hispanic, thirty-something, with an overbite, teeth as square and white as Chiclets, and he looked familiar.

He pushed the button for the sixth floor and said, "Remember me, Detective Calvino?"

"I do, but I don't know from where."

"My brother's Ernesto Juarez. You cleared him of killing his girlfriend, Serita."

"Yeah, sure, you're Enrique, Ricky." The orderly grinned and nodded, and John said, "How's Ernesto doing these days?"

"He's okay, he's good. It's four years, but he's still grieving, you know, it was hard for him. Half the family thought he did it, you know, and he's never quite got over they didn't have faith in him."

At the sixth floor, Enrique kept a thumb on the button that held the door open, while John got caught up on where Ernesto was employed these days and what his hopes were.

Working homicides, you usually recognized your guy the first time he walked on the scene, and it was only a matter of discovering what mistakes he made, so you could hang him. You did not often get a chance to clear someone who was innocent but who looked guilty from sixteen different angles, and it was satisfying when it happened.

With her throat crushed, she can't breathe, so her heart races and her blood pressure spikes. Monitors sound soft alarms.

Andy turns away from the bed, and as he reaches for the curtain, a nurse—not the angel of death—whisks it open, steel-bead glides clicking softly in the track. She says, "What're you doing?"

He punches her in the face, and she goes down, and he steps over her. His rider is exhilarated, striding toward the door to the corridor, the ultimate prize within reach.

Kaylin Amhurst cowers against the central monitoring station, as pale as any of her patients after she euthanized them. The third nurse is on the phone, and Andy hears her say "security," but he's rolling now. The outcome is inevitable.

When he steps into the corridor, drawing his pistol, no one in the visitors' lounge has heard anything from the ICU. No one has come out here to investigate.

They're still in the positions where he last saw them. Entering the room, he shoots the dozing boy twice, point-blank, and the kid is dead in his sleep. Aunt Lois starts up from her chair as if she can somehow stop him. He pistol-whips her to her knees and then kicks her flat.

He is between the girl and the door. She can't get past him, but she stands defiant, scared and at a dramatic physical disadvantage, yet ready to defend herself. If she has some fight in her, she will claw and bite. Although the rider doesn't care what happens to its horse, there isn't time for a prolonged struggle. It doesn't want to shoot her because it still has a good chance to use her, which is an important part of doing this **right**.

So Andy Tane snatches the four-inch can of capsaicin spray out of its pouch on his utility belt and, from a distance of eight feet, he squirts her twice. The first stream catches the outer corner of her right eye and sweeps across her left. The second stream spatters her nose and—as she cries out in surprise—splashes into her mouth.

The girl is instantly disoriented, virtually blind, everything a bright blur, and she's desperately wheezing, overwhelmed by a sense of suffocation, though she is not suffocating. Andy has been sprayed with an aerosol projector as part of his police training. He knows how it feels. He knows how helpless she is now.

Holstering his pistol and the aerosol can, he moves around Davinia. He seizes her from behind, pulls her against him, and encircles her neck with his left arm. It's not a full choke hold because he doesn't complete it by gripping his left wrist with his right hand. But he's got her tight. She's not going anywhere he doesn't want her to go.

The fumes from the capsaicin spray burn in his nose, but direct contact is necessary for a serious effect. He has no difficulty breathing or seeing.

At the small of the girl's back, he grabs the belt of her jeans. Using that handle, pushing up on her chin with the arm that's around her neck, he lifts her off her feet. She kicks backward feebly and claws at his forearm, but he tightens the choke hold for a moment, which panics her because already she has trouble getting her breath, and she relents.

Pulling her tight against him, holding her off the floor, he carries her out of the visitors' lounge. Although seventeen, she's petite and weighs no more than a hundred pounds. He could carry her a couple of city blocks if he needed to do so.

In the corridor, the door to the ICU is closed. But to the right, maybe fifty feet away, a group of people in white uniforms—three nurses, two orderlies—are hesitantly venturing this way, in response to the shots and the girl's cries. They halt when they see him.

To further confuse them, he shouts, "Police! **Stay back!**"

Given a closer look at the girl, they won't be able to believe she is a threat to anyone, so Andy Tane isn't going to carry her through them to the elevator alcove. Anyway, there's a more direct route to where his rider wants him to go. Across the hall from the ICU lounge is a fire exit. The door features a push-bar handle. He slams through with the girl, onto the tenth-floor landing.

If he goes down, he won't get to his car and away before he's stopped. His best chance to do what he wants with her is to go up.

———— ∞ ————

Enrique Juarez said good-bye to John, took his thumb off the DOOR OPEN button, and pushed the stainless-steel cart into the sixth-floor elevator alcove.

The doors closed, and the car descended once more. Between the fourth and third floors, a voice arose in the elevator shaft, evidently from another car that shared it. Someone talking loudly. Agitatedly. As if on a phone. The car passed. John thought it had been ascending, the voice fading on the rise.

35

OFFICER TANE, WHIPPED AND SPURRED BY HIS secret rider, half carries and half drags the pepper-sprayed and gasping girl up two flights of concrete stairs toward the last floor in the building. Up there are not merely the administrative offices but also the corporate offices of the parent company and two conference rooms. The rider has learned this not from Andy Candy but from Kaylin Amhurst, the one-nurse death panel and Jack Kevorkian acolyte.

The upper door opens into a windowless, wood-paneled receiving vestibule containing no furniture. Only three elevators come to this final floor. Opposite the fire exit are double doors to a reception lounge. It's locked at this hour. Corporate officers don't work the graveyard shift. Andy draws his pistol. Fires two rounds not into the door that features the lock assembly, but into the one that receives the deadbolt. Chunks, chips, splinters of wood explode. The mahogany disintegrates around the bolt. He kicks the door open.

Startled by the shots and backspray of debris, the girl screams. She has no volume, but the effort exacerbates her breathing. She's wheezing, choking, gagging at the same time—and still struggling, but weakly.

An alarm sounds, not a siren—this is a hospital, after all—but a soft **beep-beep-beep** followed by a recorded voice: **"You have violated a restricted area. Leave at once. The police have been called."**

With his left arm still around the girl's neck, Andy forces her through the doorway, into the reception lounge. Big desk with a granite top. Chairs. Coffee table with magazines. Large posters of impressionist paintings.

Two closed doors lead out of the room. The one to the left will open on a hallway that serves the rest of the eleventh floor. The one straight ahead is to a conference room. He manhandles Davinia through the second door.

The recorded voice continues to warn him of the seriousness of his trespass.

Andy Tane is figuratively and literally a horse, as strong as one, but his rider brings to him the additional supernatural strength of a furious and obsessed spirit. Once in the conference room, Andy throws the girl aside, out of his way. She hits the floor, tumbles, knocks her head against the wall.

Andy switches on the lights, slams the door, twists the thumb-turn that drives home the deadbolt. He says, "Now she's ours, Andy Candy. Now she's all ours."

John stepped out of the elevator and crossed the deserted lobby, which was hushed in the fluorescent half-light. The faint squeak of his shoes on the polished travertine sounded like the plaintive whimpers of a wounded animal.

He glanced at a few high-placed cameras, certain that primary public spaces of the hospital were monitored around the clock by guards at a central station. He understood the need for security in a world gone as wrong as this one, but the prospect of an oncoming universal surveillance dismayed him. He suspected that, ironically, society would be less safe under such a regime.

The automatic doors slid open. He stepped out, into the portico, and stood for a moment, breathing deeply of the cool night air, which seemed country-fresh to him in his current mood.

The restaging of the Sollenburg killings with the Woburn family had been thwarted by a quick-thinking woman skilled with a handgun. This bane, this ordained threat, this curse, whatever it should be called, was not a fate set in stone. If the Woburn family could be saved, so could the Calvinos. In fact, the disruption of the new cycle of crimes might have already broken the spell. The best-laid plans of men most often failed or withered short of fulfillment, and a curse was indeed a kind of plan.

A police car was parked in the outer of the two lanes, between the portico columns. John's Ford stood in front of the cruiser, which had not been there when he arrived.

The hospital driveway continued straight along the front of the building, beyond the portico. At both ends, it curved out toward the street.

The building faced east. The ER entrance lay on the west side. Maybe that farther entrance bustled with activity, but here in the east, long after visiting hours, the night was uncannily quiet, not just the hospital but also the light-stippled buildings of the city beyond, rising toward a moon-ruled sky.

He stood there, enjoying the coolness and the quiet city.

<hr />

Blinking to clear her stinging eyes, weeping copiously, breathing slightly better but not easily, spitting out the bitter hotness of the capsaicinoids administered by the aerosol projector, Davinia crawls past the long conference table. She frantically paws at the chairs, trying to find the end of them and something else, maybe something she can use as a weapon.

Andy Tane doesn't need to find a weapon. He's a walking weapon: his fists, his teeth, the singular viciousness of his rider. Besides, he possesses two deadly weapons. One is the pistol. On his braided utility belt are the swivel holster with the gun, two leather pouches each holding a spare magazine, a Mace holder, a handcuff case, a key strap from which also dangles a gleaming nickel-plated whistle, and a flap-covered holder with two sleeves for pens. He carries one pen and, in the second sleeve, a slim switchblade knife. The blade isn't issued by the department. It's not even legal. It's a drop knife that he can plant on a suspect to explain an otherwise unjustifiable shooting.

By the lightest touch of the inset button on the mother-of-pearl handle, the blade springs out. Five razor-edged inches. A point keen enough to pierce animal hide.

The question is time. There's not enough precious time both to deflower her and to cut her up alive. One or the other. Debauchment or disembowelment. Ravish or butcher. Either will be a pleasure for the rider. The recorded voice of the alarm is still hectoring. The police are coming. The hospital security guards will be here even sooner, in minutes, and they also will be armed. Rape or cut. The object is to terrorize. Break her spirit. Reduce her to a god-less despair.

Cut is the answer. Of all the many things you are, the face—unconcealed, unconcealable—is the fore-most. Your face is what other people first think of when they think of you, whether your face is fit for a freak show or you possess angelic beauty. Cut apart her face to cut away her sense of self, to cut away her hope. Cut away this exquisite face that by its very existence mocks all faces less beautiful, and by the cutting make a mockery of all beauty, of all that is fair or fine or full of grace, of all creation.

Having reached the last chair, the end of the long table, the crawling girl finds empty floor and then a console, where she pulls herself to her feet. As Davinia rises, Andy Candy Tane and his rider ap-proach her with the knife and with an order of dis-figurement in mind: first the ears, then the nose, the lips and then the eyes.

The pounding at the locked door comes sooner than he expects, and the pounding at once escalates to kicking. The rider has assumed a few minutes will be devoted to one-sided hostage negotiation. But perhaps the three murdered Woburns and the gun-battered aunt on lower floors have disabused these authorities of their modern preference for dis-cussion, concession, and business as usual. Andy can't win a shootout with them, so his options no longer include either rape or cut. There is now nothing but to kill, and by killing fulfill this phase of the Promise.

Only a step from the girl, he throws away the knife, draws his pistol, and turns toward the floor-to-ceiling-view windows that offer a panoramic city scene. One, two, three shots. A giant pane dissolves outward, and a night breeze shivers in through the exploding glass.

He turns toward lovely Davinia as she swings toward him. In her game of blind-girl's bluff, on the console she has found a slender two-foot-high bronze sculpture of a caduceus, which has long been an emblem of the medical profession: the staff of Mercury, who was the messenger of the gods. Unable to see Andy but sensing him near, she swings the caduceus, surely hoping for his head, but bludgeoning his right arm instead. His hand spasms and the gun flies from it.

His fractured arm would fail him now if he were just Andy Tane. But he is also something else, and his rider overrides his pain. The girl swings again, the caduceus cuts the air, but Andy ducks. He goes in low, jams her against the console, seizes her wrist, the slender wonder of her supple wrist, and forces her to drop the bronze.

The sound of wood splintering. The **boom** of impact and the wood splintering. They are breaking down the door. The thirty-third day is barely an hour old, the work is nearly finished, and they are breaking down the door.

Andy takes the girl in his arms, the sobbing girl, all the sweetness of her in his arms. Pulls her close. Lifts her a few inches off the floor. With both hands, she pummels his face, her fists as light as feathers. He says, "My bride in Hell," and rushes with her toward the shattered window, staggers toward the window and the city and the night, toward a darkness beyond the night where no stars shine and where no moon has ever risen.

—⁂—

As John unlocked his car, he heard a muffled report simultaneous with the brittle crack-and-jingle of a bursting window, followed by two louder sounds that were definitely gunshots. He looked toward the south end of the hospital, perhaps two hundred feet away, as a rain of glass glimmered down the lighted facade of the building from the highest floor. Instinct and training prompted him to run toward the trouble even as the glass fell, and he kept moving when the debris shattered further on impact, becoming icy puddles on the driveway.

Almost halfway to the scene, shock halted him when two people leaped from the opening where the enormous window had been, as if confident of their ability to fly. In the first instant of the fall, however, John realized the girl was the captive of the man, fighting to escape him even as ruthless gravity ensured that her struggle to survive would be futile. Upon his first glimpse of her high in the night, he knew her by her long blond hair, by her yellow blouse and blue jeans. He had seen many terrible things in his life, but this plunge was as much an abomination as any. For a fraction of their plummet, the flywheel of time seemed to cycle more slowly than usual, and they appeared to come down with an eerie grace. It was possible to think, to pray, that because of some fluke in the laws of physics, they would sink like a stone through water, not like a stone through air, and touch down in the manner of circus aerialists, **en pointe** and with flourishes. This brief illusion was dispelled by an acceleration that John could clearly see. When they met the pavement, the sound resembled a distant detonation, the **whump** of a mortar round shaking the earth just beyond a hill.

Over the years, John had investigated several suicides that might have been murders, and two were jumpers. They had dispatched themselves from heights less than this, ninety feet in one case, a hundred in the other, but this must be 130 feet or more. In each case, the cadaver was recognizably human but not recognizable as the person whom it had once been. Depending on angle of impact, the skeleton snapped and folded—or bloomed—in unpredictable ways. The cracked pelvis could be compressed into the rib cage. The spinal column might become a pike, piercing the head instead of supporting it. For an instant, breaking bones became clashing swords. Even if the jumper did not land on his head, the stress of impact translated upward through the compacting body, reconfiguring the facial bones until the structural incongruity could be greater than that in a portrait by Picasso.

Had the pair fallen eleven stories into sandy earth or into dense feathery shrubs, they might have had one chance in a thousand of surviving. But at such velocity, stopping abruptly on concrete, they were as doomed as bugs encountering the windshield of a speeding car. The presence of skilled medical personnel mere steps from the point of impact mattered no more than the sea of air that torn lungs could not process.

Although no aid could resuscitate the dead, John's reaction to the **whump** at the end of the fall surprised him. Over a hundred feet from the impact site, less than a hundred from his Ford, he turned and sprinted toward the car. He wasn't fleeing from the intolerable fact of Davinia's death or from the horror of looking upon her and her equally pulverized assassin. Neither was he concerned about the ramifications of his presence here when he was supposedly on unpaid leave and removed from all police work. He had never before in his life run from anything.

He didn't fully comprehend the reason for his flight until he was behind the wheel, turning the key in the ignition. The kamikaze who killed himself in order to murder Davinia, the jumper, must have been in the condition of Billy Lucas when the boy wasted his family. A puppet. A glove in which the hand of Alton Blackwood was concealed. In the fall or at the moment of death, the controlling spirit might become disembodied once more. John did not know how it traveled, what rules limited its journeying in this world, if any. He had brought it home from the state hospital without, as far as he knew, hosting it in his body. It seemed to be able to attach itself to a place—a hospital, a car, a house— as readily as it could enter and conquer a person. Or **some** people. The previous afternoon, he felt its absence in his home, an elevation of mood, the return of the former sense of harmony. If he could escape the hospital grounds without bringing the spirit, it might find its way to his home without hitching itself to him, but at least he wouldn't be responsible for its return.

Madness. Running from a ghost though he would never run from a man with a gun.

He popped the hand brake. Shifted gears. Tramped the accelerator hard. The car shot north along St. Joseph's driveway. Bounced through a drainage swale. The street. No traffic. He hung a hard left, tires squealing.

Terror and pity speared his heart. All reason abandoned, he was in the fevered grip of savage superstition.

Or maybe modern society was a cave of noise and frantic motion, in which primitives congratulated themselves on their knowledge and reason, when in fact they had forgotten more truth than they learned, had abandoned true sophistication for the lighter burden of studied ignorance, trading reason for the cold comfort of ideology, for the promise that the sound and fury of life signified nothing.

Even for this late hour, the avenues seemed strangely still, as if the entire populace had perished. No moving vehicles in sight. No pedestrians. Not a single homeless insomniac pushing a shopping cart full of junk possessions toward some hallucinated shelter. Nothing moved except steam rising from the slots in a manhole cover, numbers changing on a digital clock above the entrance to a bank, a flying saucer spinning on a giant automated billboard, a cat slinking along the sidewalk and vanishing into an alleyway, and the Ford racing away from what could not be escaped. . . .

They must all be dead, not just Davinia. Jack, Brenda, Lenny, perhaps even the aunt. In retrospect, John realized that the jumper, who carried the girl to her death, had been wearing a uniform. The patrol car parked in the portico. Perhaps one of the responders to the original call from the Woburn house had become a vehicle for Blackwood after Reese Salsetto failed him.

Two families slaughtered. Two more marked for destruction. Sixty-six days to prepare to defend his wife and his children against an irresistible force.

Easing up on the accelerator, he pulled to a stop at the curb and parked on a street of pricey shops and posh restaurants.

Suddenly the sedan seemed confining. He threw open the driver's door, got out. He walked a few steps forward from the car and leaned against a parking meter.

In memory, Davinia Woburn stood before him in the ICU visitors' lounge, and he tried to hold fast to that radiant image of the girl. Inevitably, the lounge dissolved into a memory of the rain of glass and the plummeting pair, Davinia's hair unfurling like a pale flag, the brutal impact and the bodies seeming to spill like a viscous oil across the pavement.

Holding the parking meter with one hand, he leaned forward and vomited into the gutter. He could purge his stomach, but he could not expel from memory the image of the girl plunging to her death.

36

THE RIDER INTENTLY WATCHES DAVINIA'S terror-stricken face on the way down from the eleventh floor and dismounts Officer Andy Tane a fraction of a second before impact. It reels back along the line of their fall like a yo-yo coming home on its string, returning through the missing window. Three hospital security guards, having broken down the conference-room door, stand paralyzed by shock, astonished that the patrolman has leaped to his death with the girl in his arms.

No human structure in this world provides a solid barrier to the rider. All made by man is porous and accommodating. The rider enters the conference-room floor and travels swiftly through the walls and ceilings, through pipes and cables and conduits, wherever it wishes. Anything ever built by human hands is sufficiently infused with human spirit to sustain a haunting presence, to anchor the spirit to this world. This rider in particular feeds on the human spirit. Now the hospital is its surrogate body until it selects another man or woman, every steel beam a bone, Sheetrock its flesh. Without a horse, it has no eyes but still sees, has no ears but nevertheless hears. It watches, listens, learns, and prowls, an immaterial ghoul in a material world, with the numerous hungers of corrupted human nature but with other and more ferocious hungers of its own.

A patient pushes a call button for the nurse—and is known. A nurse closes the door to a pharmacy closet—and is known. An orderly opens the door to a supply room, a maintenance man wipes a bathroom mirror, a weary resident internist in the ER sits in a chair and leans his head back against the wall, a night-shift systems engineer taps a gauge on a basement boiler—and they are known better than anyone else in this world knows them, more completely than they will ever know themselves.

Some of these people are not vulnerable, cannot be taken and ridden. Others have enough weaknesses—or one weakness so profound—that they can be mounted. None of them appeals to the rider. The police swarm the building, and some are interesting. TV, radio, and newspaper reporters gather in the portico, a potential pool of fine horses.

The hospital administrator, Dr. Harvey Leopold, arrives with one objective, to ensure the reputation of St. Joseph's isn't damaged by the murders. A public-relations whiz, Leopold doesn't keep the press waiting in the cold night, but instructs hospital security to welcome them into the lobby for a press conference. Nelson Burchard, chief of detectives, participates in this event only because he can't persuade Dr. Leopold to delay it an hour in order that the facts of the case can be more fully ascertained and marshaled.

During the remarks by the two men and during the question-and-answer session that follows, the rider cruises the city press corps, seeking opportunities to know them. It samples quite a few before settling on Roger Hodd of the **Daily Post**.

Hodd is an alcoholic with a mean streak, a narcissist, and a woman-hater. He has alienated his adult children. His first two wives despise and revile him, and the feeling is mutual. He expects his current wife to file for divorce soon. He is most easily entered by the mouth. **Taken.**

The rider has a use for Hodd, but at this time it is not a cruel use. It rides him lightly. The reporter does not even realize that he is no longer alone in his skin.

37

AFTER SECURING THE WOBURN HOUSE, LIONEL Timmins went to Reese Salsetto's apartment building with keys he had taken off the dead man's body. He hoped to find photos or other evidence to confirm that Salsetto had been erotically obsessed with his niece. The man was dead. Brenda Woburn would not be charged in such an obviously justified act of self-defense. But Lionel abhorred loose ends even in open-and-shut cases certain never to be brought before a judge.

The limestone-clad exterior of the building featured carved window surrounds, and the interior of the lobby offered marble on every surface except the faux-silver-leafed ceiling. This was not a residence for old money, catering instead to the look-at-me rich.

Ronald Phipps, the night doorman—sixtyish, white-haired with a neat white mustache—was so distinguished in appearance and manner that Lionel was saddened to see him in a tacky uniform better suited to the foppish colonel of a banana republic in a comic operetta. He looked like a once-wealthy banker supplementing his Social Security income after losing his fortune.

Phipps appeared not the least surprised to hear that Reese Salsetto had shot someone and, in return, had been shot dead. Nor did he seem worried about the reputation of the building, perhaps because Salsetto wasn't the only or even the most colorful resident at this address. His concern was that proper procedures be followed. He called the non-emergency number for the police to confirm that the ID Lionel presented was legitimate. In spite of the hour, he phoned the general manager of the building to get permission to allow the detective to enter the Salsetto apartment.

Lionel could have asserted his authority and gone at once to the twelfth floor, leaving the doorman to follow procedures in his wake. Six years in prison taught him patience, however, and he was loath to demean the old man.

These days, human dignity was everywhere under assault. Lionel chose not to contribute to that war effort.

When he received permission and went up to Salsetto's apartment, he found the door unlocked and ajar, as if Reese had left in a hurry.

According to Phipps, Salsetto lived with his "fi-ancée," Ms. Brittany Zeller. Although **fiancée** had not been given the slightest ironic inflection, Lionel suspected, because of a quickening of the doorman's blinking, that the title had just then been conferred on her for propriety's sake.

Standing on the threshold, he called out to her twice. No one answered.

He entered the apartment, switching on lights as he went. In the living room, a well-dressed blonde sprawled on the floor, on her back, the carpet under her dark with blood.

Cautious about contaminating evidence, Lionel stepped just close enough to the woman to be sure that she was dead. Her wide-open right eye stared fixedly and her left was more than half closed, as if she had winked seductively at Death when sud-denly he loomed.

Retreating to the hallway, Lionel phoned head-quarters, reported the crime, and triggered the dis-patch of the medical examiner's and the crime lab's crews. This was going to be a long night.

While waiting for the criminalists, Lionel went to the master bedroom. This seemed the most logical place to begin searching for photos of Davinia Woburn or other evidence that Reese Salsetto had been erotically obsessed with her. Within two min-utes, he came across extensive evidence of **other** crimes.

Immersed in what he found, Lionel didn't hear the techs arrive until one of them hailed him from the bedroom doorway. None of them had been at the Woburn house earlier, so he brought them up to date, explaining how the two crimes were connected.

As the M.E.'s team and the lab crew set to work, Lionel returned to the bedroom. Before he could continue to examine the evidence he had uncovered, his cell phone rang.

The caller was Nelson Burchard, chief of detectives. "I'm at St. Joseph's Hospital. I need you here quicker than a goose can crap. One of our jakes, Andy Tane, he was at the Woburn house, he followed the family to the hospital and murdered them all."

Lionel thought of the sweet boy with Down syndrome and the angelic girl, and he felt as if he had taken a punch in the stomach.

"I need someone here to cover my position," he told Burchard, and explained that he had found a dead woman in Salsetto's apartment.

"What the hell's happening?" Burchard wondered. "Are we becoming the murder capital of the country in one night?"

From the journal of Alton Turner
Blackwood:

Three weeks after the mountain lion
acknowledged his status, the boy found the
graveyard in a clearing surrounded by a wall of
pines.

He had crossed this ground often during the
years that he was apprenticed to the night.
Nothing about it previously intrigued him.

The oval clearing measured about sixty feet
end to end, forty at its widest point. Wild grass
tended to be long and silky. Here it was
scrubby, bristling, growing every which way
instead of in the uniform fashion ordained by
rain, by prevailing winds, and by the
predominant angle of sunlight. The grass
wasn't aggressive enough to choke off invading
weeds, and the earth was soft underfoot.

He entered the clearing in a peach-and-

scarlet twilight and therefore couldn't overlook
the digging that had been done recently by an
industrious animal, perhaps a wolf or a
bobcat, or possibly a pack of raccoons. Strewn
in a patch of torn raw earth were human
bones. A complete skeletal hand missing only
the end phalange of the thumb. The radius and
ulna of a forearm.

As the twilight bled away, the boy stood
beside the excavation, staring at those bones,
which in the purple shadows seemed to glow as
if irradiated. The stars came out before he
turned away from the evidence—this must be
more than mere remains—and made his way
back to the house.

A secluded building with stone walls and
embrasured windows, well removed from the
main house, served as the estate workshop,
containing woodworking machines, numerous
tools, and the landscaper's equipment. Teejay,
patriarch and sportsman, also kept his hunting
and fishing gear in this structure.

The boy found a Coleman lantern in a
carrier with a can of fuel, a packet of spare
cloth mantles, and a box of wooden matches.
He took this carrier, a spade, a pick, and,
under a rising moon, returned with them to
the distant clearing in the woods.

He sensed the raven high in flight, but he

heard only a conclave of owls hooting to one another from their different podiums in the surrounding forest.

By the ghostly light of the hissing gas lantern, the boy mined the shallow grave with care. He proceeded cautiously not out of any respect for the deceased but because of concern that he might miss or destroy something that identified the remains. He had no intention of bringing in the police. He hoped to ID the dead only to satisfy his curiosity. The body appeared to have been interred in a pit no deeper than three to four feet.

To hasten decomposition and to counteract any malodor that would attract animals, the corpse had been laid in a thick bed of powdered lime and covered with a lush blanket of the stuff. The white lime had caked, hardened, combined with other minerals to form crystals, and become veined with yellow and gray. But it did the job. The bones were clean and bleached.

On close inspection, some bones were pitted, as well—pitted, pocked, etched with peculiar whorls. This suggested the murderer's recipe called for acid of some kind to be added to tenderize, to hasten decomposition.

The skull revealed death by bludgeoning, both parietal bones having been staved in. The brain that had been pierced by shards of the skull was long gone to poisoned soil. Only a few scraps of rotted clothing remained. But perhaps the body had been interred many years earlier.

For whatever reason the raccoons or other animals had burrowed into the grave, they had not been drawn by the scent of carrion. As he dug, the boy could detect nothing other than a faint persistent odor of lime, a separate and fainter astringent scent that might have arisen from the breakdown of the acid, and underneath all, the smell of damp earth.

Carrying the lantern, he searched the clearing and gradually came to see the subtle waffle pattern of regular depressions that time, weather, and snarls of scraggly grass couldn't entirely disguise. He had found not one grave, not evidence of just a single crime, but an entire graveyard without headstones, with no memorial flowers except for the stunted blossoms on the stems of withered weeds.

He was much stronger now than when, years earlier, the raven had selected him, and the earth was soft. He dug faster, with less care than before.

The well-limed earth disgorged the remnants of those on whom it previously had gorged. In every case, there were no fragments of a casket, only bones, scraps of fabric, the rubber soles of dissolved shoes.

The boy found three deteriorated skulls of babies killed so soon after birth that the fontanel of each, the soft spot at the top of a newborn's head, had not yet closed and hardened. Infant bones were too soft to survive long in a grave. There were only a few smooth white discs and lozenges, like water-worn stones, that might have been fragments of hip bones and scapulars.

The third adult skeleton was not the last waiting to be found, but the boy didn't disinter a fourth. No flesh remained on these bones, either, but he knew how long the deceased had been resting in this hole. Seven years, two months, and a few days.

As this was the most recently interred of his discoveries, the scraps of clothing not yet dissolved were larger and retained more color than those in other graves. He recognized the dress that his mother had been wearing the last day he had seen her.

The boy stood over this discovery for a while, considering his life in the guest house with his mother, comparing it to his life in the tower after she apparently abandoned him.

Long ago the owls had moved on to feed in

moonlit fields, and the surrounding forest seemed to be asleep and dreaming.

The lantern hissed as if calling serpents to it, and the mantles—incombustible little bags filled with gaslight—pulsed softly.

The boy did not tremble, although he watched his shadow shiver slightly across the stunted grass and the excavated earth of the secret graveyard.

The light played masquerade with his deformed shoulders and with his misshapen head, costuming his shadow in a robe and cowl. When he lifted the pick, the shadow appeared to lift a scythe.

The boy wasn't the goat-legged, horned god of anything, as once he wished to be. He was Death, and just being Death might be a most satisfying life.

38

RETURNING HOME AT 2:46 A.M., JOHN USED his cell phone to call the home-security computer and switch off the alarm as he arrived at his garage door.

When he got out of the car in that subterranean space, the house still felt free of the oppressive presence that for weeks had been in residence. But with the Woburn family dead, the hateful spirit would soon find its way back here.

Spirit. He arrived at his conclusion logically, and the evidence of its accuracy appeared irrefutable now. Yet sometimes he rebelled against it. **Spirit. Ghost.** He wanted to think of it in other terms. **Corruption. Infection. Disease.** Or turn to psychologists for answers that would persuade him to deny what he knew to be true.

And **that** was the most remarkable thing about

this rebellion: A part of him would have preferred the comfort of psychiatric theory and jargon to the truth, not only because the truth put before him an enemy who might be impossible to defeat, but also because truth in this instance was an embarrassment to the modern mind. In this age, faith remained acceptable, but recognizing a **dark** supernatural aspect to life could make a rational man feel foolish and gullible. The Evil of all evils thrived on the denial of its existence.

The last time he tried Scotch to settle his nerves, the night of the first day that he had gone to the state hospital to see Billy Lucas, the whiskey had not helped him. Nevertheless, he went up to the kitchen and poured a double shot over ice. His hand shook, and the neck of the Chivas bottle rattled against the rim of the glass.

In thirty-three days, another family would be destroyed. There was no way to determine the target or in what person the spirit would be concealed when it attacked.

Brenda Woburn felt it trying to take possession of her. **Cold and crawling, slithering . . . Everywhere in my body . . . Skin to bones.** She had been able to resist it—but only by extreme measures.

Evidently, the spirit had been unable to invade either Lenny or Davinia. Otherwise, it would have used one of the kids against the other, probably Lenny against his sister.

The factor that inoculated for possession was not youth. Billy Lucas had been only fourteen but vulnerable.

John doubted that Lenny's limited mental capacity vaccinated him against possession. Davinia was highly intelligent—yet inaccessible.

Not having met the boy, having spoken with the girl too briefly, John did not know what qualities brother and sister had in common. He suspected innocence must be one. The girl seemed exceptional, gentle, kind. Perhaps the boy had been equally so.

With his Scotch, John walked the perimeter of the ground floor. He stood at windows in dark or dimly lighted rooms, searching the night, though he knew that he would find nothing suspicious. No more killing for a while. No killing here for the next sixty-five days.

Yet the compulsion to patrol was irresistible. He would be a watchdog for the rest of his life, as he had been since the night that, because of his foolishness, he facilitated the massacre of his family. His penance was eternal vigilance; never again would he know the peace of the blameless.

Minette, Naomi, and Zach seemed innocent to John, basically good kids, not morally immaculate but free from serious weaknesses. He not only loved his children, he was also proud of them. He could never credit the possibility that any of them might be a glove to hide the hand of Alton Turner Blackwood.

Perhaps no adult was innocent. But Nicolette was as virtuous as anyone he knew, charitable and kind. She was strong enough and tough-minded enough to be as resistant to possession as Brenda Woburn.

The weakest link in the Calvino chain was John himself. That assessment seemed to him as true as it was terrifying.

In the kitchen again, he poured two more ounces of Scotch.

Between leaving St. Christopher's Home and School when he was seventeen and meeting Nicky a year later, he had spent a few months drinking most lunches and dinners: Seagram's shooters chased with beer, an efficient route to oblivion. Without the emotional support of the staff at the school, without family or friends, he turned to the kind of spiritualism in which the spirits came in bottles sealed with tax stamps. He had an inheritance—his parents' life-insurance, equity from the house—but it seemed like blood money. He saw an ironic kind of justice in spending it on his self-destruction, glass by glass. He wasn't old enough to buy his own poison, but there were hobos to buy it as his agents, for a generous commission. He called them his kindly executioners, and if they had been able to purchase cyanide, he might have added it to the shopping list he gave them.

Fortunately, he made a lousy drunk because he had no practice at it and no heart for it. Oblivion was not as easy to attain as he expected. Drunk, he became grotesquely melancholy, more focused on his loss than when sober. Shooters and beer proved to be not a fast track away from memory but instead a direct route to the obsessive and vivid recollection of every wrenching experience he wanted to erase from his mind.

Alone in his apartment, in the depths of intoxication, whether sitting at the kitchen table or collapsed in a living-room recliner, he became garrulous, talking to beloved ghosts and to himself. At a certain point, when the floor ceased to be safely horizontal, when it canted like the deck of a ship, when the shapes of things no longer appeared to be right—walls curving inward toward the top, ceiling swelling down like a distended belly—and when the tall curved spout at the kitchen sink seemed as sinister as a cobra poised to strike, young John talked to God.

He perceived these monologues as rants of theological genius, as challenges to the wisdom of the Maker of the universe, as brilliant prosecutorials that demolished the very concept of a benign Creator, as jeremiads so logically argued that God could make no satisfactory response.

One night, although he was no less drunk than usual, he suddenly heard himself as an impartial witness might have heard him, and he was humiliated not only by the mush-mouthed and rambling nature of his screed but also by the sophomoric character of his arguments and accusations. He put a hand to his mouth to silence himself, but the hand fell away from his lips in an angry gesture. He kept talking, now with even less intelligence and coherence. His rant became so tedious, repetitious, and petty that his humiliation thickened into mortification. Yet still he chattered on, as though his tongue owed no obedience to him; he could not halt the insane gush of words. In every expression of grief, he heard a total self-absorption that made him cringe. In every whiny lament, he recognized the voice of a self-pitying wretch. Every tiresome accusation revealed the immaturity of a useless boy who lacked the courage to accept the blame for his own actions, who did not possess the fortitude to carry his guilt like a man.

When mortification deepened into shame, he finally found the will to shut off the torrent of words. He lurched to his feet and staggered to the bathroom, where he knelt at the toilet. Instead of words, vomit gushed forth, such a hideous stream that the next day he remembered it had been

black, although surely it could not have been that dark.

He had not been drunk since that night. Wine with dinner never brought him close to inebriation. Seventeen years of sobriety. Now he stared at the second serving of Chivas Regal—and he emptied the glass into the sink.

With or without Scotch, he would not be able to sleep. He feared that he would dream of the plummeting girl.

He had no idea what he should do next. He felt adrift, unable to imagine how he might make his family safe.

Asking for guidance, he went to the kitchen door and stepped out onto the flagstone terrace at the back of the house. The night chill might clear his head and help him think.

The air was crisp, cold, but not so frigid that it made him uncomfortable. He breathed deeply and exhaled a pale plume.

A few sinuous threads of cloud slowly slithered out of the north. The moon rode deep in the west, sailing toward a far shore, but still softly illuminating the yard.

John wished his family might be saved by the simple expediency of boarding a ship or a plane with them and traveling to some distant port. But a creature who had taken the long journey back from death would not be daunted by mere mountain ranges or seas, or national borders.

He stepped off the terrace and followed a flagstone path to the rose arbor. The last flowers of the season had wilted, withered, and turned brown. The leaves were dead. The thorny trailers needed to be cut back to encourage a crop of lush blooms the following year. In moonlight, the looping brambles were a black-and-silver tangle of barbed tentacles.

Three steps from the threshold of the arch, John was halted by the sudden perception that the arbor might be dangerous. Unaffected by the night chill, now the hairs on the nape of his neck stirred as he drew near the lattice tunnel. A cold foreboding skittered down his spine, vertebra to vertebra, with quivering centipedal haste.

The interior of the twelve-foot-long arbor was darker than the surrounding night. But John could clearly see the moon-washed lawn at the farther end. No one waited in the tunnel.

After the events at the hospital, John's nerves were raw, and he felt perpetually under an imminent threat, although Zach's fourteenth birthday was sixty-six days away. If he allowed himself to be spooked by every dark place, to be suspicious of every closed door and blind corner, he would be worn out and useless when trouble finally came. He

must resist the tendency to see Alton Turner Blackwood in every shadow.

He took another step toward the arbor but again
halted, alarmed, when something brushed against
his legs, not lightly but with force. Low, from right
to left. Some animal. He turned, seeking it in the
gloom.

Again, it brushed against him, and even as it
passed, he looked down and saw nothing. He felt it
against his knees, his shins, yet it remained invisible.

As John backed away from the arbor, fallen leaves
rustled and flew up from the grass to his left. They
had blown here earlier from the scarlet oak on the
south yard. But at the moment, the still air lacked
the breath to make leaves tremble, let alone to tumble them and toss them up from the lawn.

The disturbance continued across the deep yard,
circled back toward John, looped around him,
raced off again, as if a little wind devil were funnel-
ing this way and that, except the leaves were not
spun up in a vortex but were scattered at random.
As he watched, he began to feel that the phenomenon had a frolicsome quality; it wasn't related to his
fear of the arbor, and in fact it seemed to him that
this thing that was **not** a wind devil had warned
him away from that latticework tunnel.

While he watched, the phenomenon diminished.
The whirl of leaves settled, and the night grew still
once more.

As the last leaves floated to rest on the grass, John thought he heard a familiar sigh of pleasure, one he hadn't heard for a long time. If **this** had been a ghost, it had been a blithe spirit. Filled with sudden wonder, remembering their golden retriever that had died two years earlier, John whispered, "Willard?"

39

WHILE SITTING IN HIS CUBICLE AT THE **DAILY Post,** writing an account of events at the Woburn house and at St. Joseph's Hospital, Roger Hodd takes hits from a flask of tequila and lime juice. Long ago, he lost interest in journalism, but the weirdness of this story keeps him more engaged in the writing than usual.

His rider, of which Hodd remains unaware, inspires certain turns of phrase and clever edits that lift the piece above the reporter's usual fare. The rider wants its work to be well described, although this isn't the reason it took possession of Hodd.

Shortly after dawn, when the copy has been filed, Hodd goes home to his third wife, Georgia. She is an odd combination: an incurable romantic and a rehabilitation therapist specializing in recovery from addiction. Having all her life idealized and romanticized newspaper reporters, Georgia married

Roger Hodd knowing he was a heavy drinker, because she believed that she—and she alone—could cure him of his addiction and inspire him to write stories that would bring him a Pulitzer.

Hodd has always known that she would fail in this quest, and now she knows it, as well. Only after the wedding did she discover that Hodd would win a gold medal in narcissism if it were an Olympic sport and that he is not just a drunk but also a mean one. The violence that he perpetrates is psychological and verbal rather than physical. Georgia is particularly galled that she, with all her education and background in psychology, is so vulnerable to his torment. She has cried herself to sleep many nights and has lost eleven pounds since they were married ten months previously.

Sometimes she fears that she might be addicted to this abuse if not to Hodd himself, a fact the rider learns as Hodd wakes Georgia with a sour-tequila kiss. The reporter paws clumsily at his wife in a pretense of lust when in truth he is too intoxicated to perform. She is repulsed by his condition, as he knows full well, which is why he continues to fumble at her pajama tops, trying to bare her breasts.

Hodd thinks Georgia will soon seek a divorce, but the rider knows everything about her from the kiss, including that she has spent less time thinking about a divorce than about ways of killing her husband that will not bring suspicion upon her. Georgia is an easy mount, and the rider changes horses during a sloppy kiss. It encourages Hodd to pass out as it leaves him, and it also implants in his mind a come-to-me curse.

Georgia is as incognizant of her rider as was her husband. She showers, dresses, eats breakfast, and sets out for her office at New Hope Rehabilitation Hospital. She has a series of scheduled sessions with patients, but because she is more than an hour early, she has time to write a discharge letter for one of them, releasing him three days before he concludes the thirty-day course of treatment to which he committed himself. The decision to release this patient is her rider's idea. Georgia is easily manipulated into believing that the decision originates with her and that it is the correct thing to do.

When she proceeds to the patient's room to present him with his discharge, Preston Nash is surprised to hear that his addiction to prescription medications is entirely psychological and that he is cured of it. When, in gratitude, he clasps both of Georgia's hands in his, the rider **knows** him. Preston is eager to return to the basement apartment in his parents' home, call his dealer, and once more climb aboard the pill train. Preston listens attentively, however, as Georgia gives him post-discharge instructions, her twenty-four-hour contact number, and her best wishes for a clean-and-sober life.

The rider encourages Georgia to offer her hand to

Preston, and on this second shake, it transfers from the mare to its new mount, leaving her with a come-to-me curse. Preston packs and calls a taxi. Unaware that he now shares his body with another, he smiles all the way home.

By the time he arrives, his parents—Walter and Imogene—have left for work at the Calvino residence. Preston is annoyed to find that they have aggressively cleaned his two rooms and bath in the basement. He is capable of cleaning his own quarters. The fact that he has never done so only means that he doesn't share their neurotic obsession with maintaining an antiseptic living space. Antibacterial cleaning solutions, which eventually wind up in sewers and dumps and storm drains—and ultimately in the water table—are polluting the earth. Besides, if you are constantly cleaning and using Purell and avoiding contact with microbes, you aren't building immunity to them, and you are certain to be in the first wave of mass deaths when the inevitable plague strikes.

Preston expects the plague will be first, followed by the death of the oceans. Then the nuclear war arising from a vicious conflict over the shrinking food supply, and finally the asteroid impact. His hope is to survive as many catastrophes as possible, assuming that prescription medications and electricity remain available.

He is eager to return to his video games, pornography, and drug cocktails. But his rider has a task for him first.

Suddenly Preston is inspired to prepare for the day when his parents might attempt to control him financially by scheming to have his SSI disability checks taken away from him. Someone out there is probably foolish enough to employ a thirty-six-year-old man with no skills, but Preston isn't so foolish as to accept a job. Life is too short for work. Especially with the planet-wide plague coming. One way to replace that lost SSI income would be to steal it. Indeed, theft is the only course of action that makes sense to him.

The homes of prosperous people contain a variety of valuables. Preston's father and mother manage the household—whatever the hell that means—for a prosperous artist and her husband. They carry keys to their employers' home.

To this point, even though he has been without drugs and booze for twenty-seven days, Preston is sufficiently clear-minded to follow the sequence of thoughts through which his secret rider guides him. But he arrives at an insoluble dilemma and is so deeply disappointed that he wants only to get wasted and play video games until his eyes bleed. The hitch: There is no way to get at his parents' keys to the artist's house. They guard the Calvino keys more closely than they guard those to their own home, and carry them at all times. Walter and Imogene are as obsessive about responsibility and duty as they are about cleanliness. They are so neurotic that an entire thousand-page psychology textbook could be devoted to them. They're sick, they really are, they make Preston nuts.

This is the problem with life. Nothing is easy. It's just one damn thing after another. The line between where you are and where you want to be is never straight and simple to follow. There are always walls you have to get around, fences you have to climb over, and when you go around and over all of them, then there's suddenly a damn ravine in front of you, a canyon, an **abyss**.

Because Walter and Imogene touched many surfaces in the Calvino house while the rider inhabited the place, it knows them to their core. It knows they keep a spare Calvino key taped to the underside of a dresser drawer in the master bedroom of this house. Although Preston doesn't have any knowledge of this key, his rider induces in him a dim memory of it, and with renewed excitement, Preston ventures upstairs to find this treasure.

With key in hand, Preston sets out for the nearest locksmith to have it copied. He's not permitted to drive his parents' second car, but neither he nor his rider hesitates to do so. Because Mrs. Nash's boy is sober at the moment and because his rider gently represses Preston's impulse to speed, to run stop-lights, and to gesture rudely at other drivers, no cars are struck and no pedestrians are run down.

Although his parents would not be easy mounts, their son is no harder to control than a child's rocking horse.

After Preston returns to the house, replaces the key that he stole, and hides his three copies in his apartment, he telephones his pill guy, Dr. Charles Burton Glock, who has several medical degrees under different names from a variety of third-world countries. He orders prescriptions for his three favorite mood elevators. Dr. Glock is delighted to hear Preston is safely home from rehab. He generously offers free delivery on this initial order.

Preston's relationship with Dr. Glock is the most meaningful of his life. His disability caseworker gave him the doctor's name and number, the doctor certified his disability; and now the doctor assures his freedom from phantom pain and all worry.

Dr. Glock has interests in a few pharmacies around the city, and delivery is faster than you can get a pizza, though of course, the pharmacist doesn't have to bake anything.

The primly dressed young woman who brings the order looks like a door-to-door witness for an outreach religion, but when the rider conspires to have Preston touch her hand when paying for his order, it finds she will be easy to occupy. Her name is

Melody Lane, but there is no melody in her heart, only a thrilling dissonance, and the rider realizes that she will be more than just a means of transport.

At the rider's direction, Preston asks Melody to wait a moment. He returns to his apartment and retrieves one of the three keys to the Calvino house. Upon returning to the woman, he holds out the key to her.

As it departs one horse to mount the next, the rider leaves a come-to-me curse, but Preston is aware neither of the curse nor of having been ridden.

With genuine bewilderment, as the woman takes the key from him, Preston says, "I don't know why I'm doing this."

"I do," Melody says as she pockets the key. "Surely it's not the first thing you've ever done that seems to make no sense."

"You're right about that."

"I'll be seeing you," she says, and leaves the house, closing the door after herself.

Before knowing Melody for what she is, the rider initially intended to use her only to get back to the Calvino house. But she is so interesting that it decides to stay with her a few hours and also to incorporate her into its mission.

Melody is pretty but not strikingly beautiful, fresh-faced, with direct brown eyes, an appealing smile. She is demure, almost shy. She seems modest and gentle. Her quiet voice falls pleasantly on the ear, and altogether her manner charms and inspires trust. Such a disguise serves any monster well, but it is especially helpful in avoiding suspicion if you are, like Melody, a murderer of children.

She may very well be essential to the certain destruction of the Calvino family.

40

HAVING GOTTEN NOT ONE MINUTE OF SLEEP during the night, John claimed at breakfast that he felt weary, out of sorts, as if the flu might be coming on, which was true as far as it went. He allowed Nicky to think he had called in sick, but of course he was already on an unpaid leave.

He retreated to his study on the first floor with an insulated pot of caffeine-free coffee. For a while he stood at a window, gazing at the backyard.

On the grass blazed the leaves of the scarlet oak, like scales shed by a dragon. **Dragon scales** sounded totally Naomi, and when John thought of her, he smiled. Maybe she hadn't inherited **all** of her fanciful imagination from her mother.

The scattering of fallen leaves lay undisturbed. In daylight, no spirit, blithe or otherwise, capered through them.

He didn't know what to think of the incident

with the leaves. In the dark, after a generous serving of Chivas Regal, the presence—first warning, then playful—had seemed as real as the plume of his crystalized breath in that cold air. But now . . .

He wondered why it was easier to believe in a malevolent spirit than in a benign one. Sometimes it seemed that the human heart, this side of Eden, feared eternal life more than death, light more than darkness, freedom more than surrender.

With a mug of coffee, he sat in his armchair, put his feet on the footstool, and pretended for a while that he would methodically think through the ticking threat of Alton Turner Blackwood until he understood how to disarm it. But weariness was a sea in which he sank, and thinking became as arduous as walking on the ocean floor with a world of water pressing down relentlessly.

He dreamed of a surreal journey in a world of falling scarlet leaves, falling girls, falling blades of guillotines, the leaves no longer leaves at all but laminas of blood cast into the air from the severed neck stumps, and then not either laminas of blood or leaves but sheets of paper, pages from a book, and something important on them that he must read, **must** read, except that they floated away as he tried to pluck them from the air, slipped through his fingers as if they were smoke, just as the girls slipped through his hands as he stood at a cliff's edge and tried to save them, Davinia and Marnie and Giselle, girls at the brink, turning to smoke in his hands but then suddenly flesh-and-blood girls again as they plunged, plunged, Minette and Naomi, all the girls plunging away from him, down and down through a rain of scarlet leaves and book pages and glittering blades of merciless intent, then no leaves or pages or blades but only snow, girls falling through night snow and slamming into a snow-mantled street—**Whump!**—with lethal force, girl after girl—**Whump! Whump! Whump!**—and already on the street, on his back in the snow, staring with the steady eyes of a dead man, staring up at the falling girls, lay Lionel Timmins, the girls plunging to their deaths around him—**Whump! Whump!**—and heavy snow falling into Lionel's unblinking, sightless, frozen eyes.

"John?"

Someone shook him by the shoulder, and when he opened his eyes, he thought he must still be dreaming, because Lionel Timmins leaned over him.

"John, we have to talk."

The dusting of snow on Lionel's face was, on second look, white beard stubble. He hadn't shaved recently.

Sitting up straighter in his chair, swinging his legs off the footstool, John said, "What're you doing here? What's going on, what's happening?"

Perching on the stool, Lionel said, "That's what I need to know, partner. What the hell is going on?"

John wiped his face with both hands, as if sleep were a cocoon from which he emerged and he were pulling off the gossamer remnants that still clung to him. "When did your beard go white?"

"Years ago. That's why I try to shave twice a day. Makes me look like Uncle damn Remus or something. Listen, what is this—you gave Mrs. Fontere your card with all your phone numbers?"

"Mrs. who?"

"Fontere. Lois Fontere. Jack Woburn's sister."

"Oh, yeah, all right. Aunt Lois."

Filaments of sleep, like threads with a static charge, clung to John, tangling his thoughts. He needed to be wide awake with Lionel.

"I'm on this all night," Lionel said, "now I just find out from her you were at the hospital."

"How's she doing?"

"She's a mess, but she's alive. John, you were at the hospital just **minutes** before Andy Tane blew all his fuses."

"Was he the one? Tane? The one who jumped with the girl?"

"He did all of them. Including Mickey Scriver, his partner."

"I saw them fall. Walking to my car in the portico, heard the shots, the glass breaking."

Lionel's flat expressionless stare was one that he sometimes used with witnesses and often with suspects, to make them wonder how much he knew. "You saw them fall."

"She was a fine girl. A good girl."

"You saw them fall and you—what?—just drove away?"

As John rose from the chair, Lionel got up from the footstool.

"You want some coffee?" John asked.

"No."

"Something else?"

"No."

John went to the gallery wall on which were hung the birthday photos of the kids. Lionel followed him, but John focused on the photographs.

"You're on leave, John. Are you still on leave?"

"Yes."

"Then why are you dogging this case? Why did you want to talk to Brenda Woburn?"

"I wasn't there as a cop. It was a personal matter."

"After midnight. In the ICU. The woman's recovering from a gunshot, surgery—and you stop by for a chat? A woman I don't think you met before that moment?"

John didn't reply. He studied a picture of Naomi on her seventh birthday. She wore a tam-o'-shanter. One of her enduring enthusiasms was hats. He cherished Naomi for many reasons, but certainly on his top ten list was the intensity of her love for the world and the passionate delight that she could take in the most mundane things, almost a **rejoicing**.

"John, there's major heat on this. One of our own kills his partner, four other people, then himself. The press is foaming at the mouth. This isn't my case alone. There's a little task force. Sharp and Tanner—they're part of it."

John turned from the photographs. "Do they know I was at the hospital?"

"Not yet. But I might have to tell them. John, why are you on a thirty-day leave?"

"A family thing. Like I told you."

"I wouldn't think you'd lie to me."

John met his stare. "It's not a lie. It's just incomplete."

"Ken Sharp implied you tried to horn in on the Lucas case."

"What exactly did he say?"

"Just that if you come back from leave, he won't work with you on the Tane investigation. He wanted me clear on that."

"It's not a problem."

"All he said was he doesn't want a repeat of the Lucas house, doesn't want to go into Tane's place and find you cooking dinner."

The "cooking dinner" reference was a euphemism, a suggestion that John had been cooking the crime scene, planting evidence. Ken might have reached that conclusion after talking to the orderly,

Coleman Hanes, at the state hospital, who suspected that, in spite of the boy's confession, John believed Billy Lucas must be innocent.

Lionel said, "Were you really in the Lucas house unofficially?"

"Yes."

"What the hell? Why?"

John glanced at the hall beyond the open study door. He didn't want to be overheard. "Let's go outside."

The air was cool, but the day chilled only in the shadows. They sat in the sun, on wrought-iron chairs, at a table on the terrace.

As succinctly as he had laid out his case for Nelson Burchard, John told Lionel about the Blackwood murders twenty years earlier, about the loss of his family.

Lionel did not respond with the cloying earnestness of Burchard. He knew that pity could be an insult. He said only "Shit," and in that one vulgarity, he expressed genuine sympathy and a touching depth of friendship.

As John listed the uncanny similarities between the recent Lucas murders and the Valdane-family massacre two decades earlier, Lionel listened with interest. But when the discussion turned to the fact that three of the Sollenburgs had been shot, that twenty years later three of the Woburns were shot as well, and when John noted that in each instance the

daughter was murdered last, Lionel blinked in confusion until he blinked himself into a frown.

"You think there's some link between these cases?"

"They were thirty-three days apart, like back
then. I warned Burchard—thirty-three days."

"Thirty-three days could be coincidence."

"It isn't."

The sky was pale, the sun a white instead of a
yolk, as if a high, finely diffused pollution muted
the natural colors.

Leaning forward, arms on the table, Lionel said,
"What're you trying to tell me? I don't get it. Help
me make the leap."

Although he risked sounding like a man seeking a
psychiatric-disability pension, John was desperate
for an ally. "Thirty-three more days will put us at
November seventh. Blackwood's third family was
the Paxtons. Mother, father, two sons, two daughters."

"You mean this is somehow copycat stuff? Alton
Blackwood's crimes redone?"

A faint breeze quivered the scarlet leaves on the
half-sered autumn grass, but neither the cascading
boughs of the deodar cedar nor the rose brambles
on the arbor stirred whatsoever.

"If a third family is murdered on November seventh, then the fourth will be on December tenth."

Lionel shook his head. "There were two different
killers. Billy Lucas, Andy Tane. They're both dead."

The glass top on the wrought-iron table reflected the faded sky, a hawk gliding in a narrowing gyre.

"And in the Sollenburg case," Lionel continued, "in all those cases back then, a girl was raped and tortured."

"Billy Lucas raped and tortured his sister, Celine."

"But Davinia Woburn wasn't."

"Reese Salsetto was going to do the Woburn family. If Brenda hadn't shot him, he would have shot her and the son. Then he would have done to the girl precisely what Alton Blackwood did to Sharon Sollenburg."

"I'm still lost. You can't seriously be saying Billy, Reese, and Andy conspired to re-create the Blackwood crimes?"

"No. They didn't have to know one another if each of them had a secret partner and if that partner was the same in each instance."

"But there's no evidence of any perp but Billy in the Lucas house. And for sure, nobody but Andy Tane went out the window with that poor girl."

"Nobody we could see," John said.

Exasperated, Lionel leaned back in his chair. "Who are you, man, and what've you done with my plain-talking partner?"

Watching the circling hawk reflected in the table, John said, "I went up to the state hospital twice to see Billy Lucas."

"Well, that'll put a bee up Ken Sharp's ass."

"He knows. The first visit, Billy called me Johnny, though he'd been told only my last name."

"We don't need Sherlock to figure out that one."

"That night he called me on an unlisted number he hadn't been given. Using a phone they say he didn't possess. He said something to me that was word for word something Blackwood said right before I killed him. Something I've never told anyone. Something only Alton Blackwood could know."

For a long moment, Lionel was as silent as the pale sky and the white sun and the gliding hawk in the glass.

At last he said, "I don't do **X-Files** cases, and neither do you. Come in from the Twilight Zone—okay?"

John looked up, met his eyes. "How do **you** explain something as weird as what Andy Tane did?"

"I don't know yet, but I will eventually. I found a connection between Reese Salsetto and Andy. The answer is there. I just have to work it out."

Surprised, John said, "What connection?"

"Salsetto was a comer, a pusher and booster and grifter and paperhanger. You name a scam, he was working it. And he had a fixer list as long as King Kong's dick—cops, all kinds of city officials. I found a ledger under the false bottom in his nightstand drawer. He recorded every bribe he paid—amount, date, time, place, to whom. In half the cases, when the payoff was made in a parking lot or a park or anywhere outside, Salsetto had someone on his team get a photo of the envelope being passed. If he ever needed to turn state's evidence to save himself, he figured to have so much crap on so many people that a prosecutor wouldn't just cut him a deal for no prison time, he'd adopt him and call him son. Andy Tane is on that list a lot, and so is his former partner, Vin Wasco. I think maybe somehow Salsetto's sister Brenda and her husband were involved in something with Reese, and with Tane."

"They weren't like that."

"Maybe they were. Maybe they were in something with Reese and Andy, and it went wrong in a big way. Reese lost his cool, which he had a habit of. Reese dead, Andy Tane sees his world falling apart, too, and he goes for revenge and a quick exit, something like that."

John looked at the sky, and the hawk was gone. He had only seen it reflected in the table. He wondered if there had been a real hawk or only the reflection of one.

"I know it sounds good to you now," John said, "but it won't come together that way. The hinges aren't where you think they are."

"I'd rather spend my time looking for hinges than for a ghost or whatever it is you're talking about."

"If another family's murdered on November seventh, what'll we do then?"

"Keep looking for hinges. If your explanation is right, what could we do anyway?"

"Maybe nothing," John acknowledged.

Lionel surveyed the big yard, lingered on the deodar cedar. He looked tired, not merely weary but worn down and prematurely aged by a life in Homicide.

When he looked at John again, he said, "Listen, man, that's a hell of a thing you've been carrying with you all these years, your whole family killed. You shared it with anybody till now?"

"Nicky knows. She always has. Not the kids. Only Nicky until Burchard and you. But I didn't go as far with Burchard as suggesting . . . that it's Blackwood himself again. Do you have to tell him?"

Lionel shook his head. "No. But how much longer are you on leave?"

"About ten days."

"Maybe you should extend it till you work this out for yourself. Till you get your head straight about it. You know what I'm saying?"

"Yeah. Maybe I'll ask for another thirty days."

Lionel started to slide his chair back from the table, but then he pulled it in again and leaned once more with his arms on the thick glass top. "I feel like I let you down."

"You never have. You didn't now."

"Couldn't be easy for you to say what you're really

thinking when you're thinking something as far out as this."

"I had to take a deep breath and swallow hard," John admitted.

"See, the problem is, I remember all those old movies, they were old even when I was a kid, where something goes bump in the night, and it's not even something supernatural, but the black guy always says 'Feets don't fail me now,' and does a fast shuffle for someplace safe. Used to embarrass the hell out of me when I saw that."

"Me too."

"So I won't be what I can't be."

"Tell your mom I think she did an amazing job."

"You mean, considering what she had to work with."

John smiled. "It's a flat-out miracle."

As they rose from their chairs, a breeze sprang up. All across the yard, fallen leaves slid and tumbled over one another, adding to drifts of leaves against the rose arbor and against the fence between the yard and the wooded ravine. It was just a breeze.

41

AFTER THE MORNING LESSONS WITH THE kids, Nicolette retreated to her third-floor studio, intending to make significant progress on the painting in which Zach, Naomi, and Minette were prominently featured. She'd had an excellent night of dreamless sleep. She felt rested and buoyant. Yet when she returned to the unfinished canvas, she was as disturbed by it as she had been the previous evening. It still struck her as being about loss, despair, which was far from her intention.

She decided not to address the troubling canvas for a few days and instead to do some preliminary composition sketches for another picture. She moved the vase of yellow humility roses and the thermos of fortifying tea from the tall table by her easel to another tall table by the draftsman's board.

More often than not, she worked in a silent studio. Art was not just images but also a kind of music in her mind, and sometimes real music could be a distraction from the inner melody.

That morning, however, she had watched the news while dressing for the day, had seen the terrible story about the rampaging cop and the murdered family, and had been unable to stop thinking about it. In the silent studio, the photo of Davinia Woburn, shown on TV, kept coalescing in Nicky's mind like the visage of a ghost materializing from a cloud of ectoplasm. She programmed a few hours of Connie Dover CDs, haunting Celtic music to distract her mind from the haunting face of that tragic child.

In spite of the news and the disturbing painting of the kids, the mood of the house remained felicitous. As inexplicable as it had been persistent, the oppressive pall of recent days, which lifted the previous afternoon, was gone—until ten minutes past two o'clock.

As Nicky refined a third iteration of the preliminary sketch, the atmosphere in the house changed so distinctly and suddenly that she glanced at her watch as she might have done to mark the exact moment of a car crash in the street or the first note of a doomed airliner's shrieking descent.

She started to get up from the draftsman's table, as though some urgent situation demanded her attention, but then she hesitated and sat down again. She'd heard no alarming noise. No screams. No anxious shouts. The house sailed on as calmly now as it had at 2:09.

On reconsideration, she acknowledged that the mood shift surely must be hers, internal. A house couldn't change moods any more than it could change its mind.

Nevertheless, the suddenness of the transformation seemed strange. Nicky wasn't a manic-depressive. She didn't abruptly drop off cliffs of emotion or feel her heart soar like a helium balloon.

Instead of picking up her pencil, she sat listening to Connie Dover sing "The Holly and the Ivy," which charmed her bar by bar. When she began to draw again, however, she couldn't entirely shake the feeling that somewhere in the house, something wasn't right.

***

After Lionel Timmins left, John thought he wouldn't be able to nap anymore. When he sat with the **Daily Post** in the armchair in his study, however, he soon put the paper aside.

In sleep, he walked vast subterranean chambers and endless corridors of cold stone, climbed and descended chiseled staircases that curved like Mobius strips: an exitless architecture that said, **Your quest is hopeless, your strength inadequate, your escape plan useless.** He trudged alone except for one moment when a cruel voice spoke to him out of the labyrinth: "Ruin." It was as intimate as Lionel's voice when he had leaned over the armchair to shake John's shoulder, and it woke him, but only briefly, long enough to blink at the clock on the desk. He had been asleep less than an hour. It was 2:10 in the afternoon. He dropped once more into the maze that was carved from a mountain of tombstone granite.

———

Because that afternoon there would be neither a math session with old Sinyavski nor an out-of-house art class with Laura Leigh Highsmith and her radically perfect mouth, Zach went down to the small gym on the garage level to work out with free weights. Although more buff than most thirteen-year-olds, he would be fourteen in two months, signing up for the marines in maybe three and a half years, so he couldn't slack off. He needed to jam the freaking weights like a starving monkey in an experiment pumping a handle for treats.

Weights were stupid, but lots of things were stupid that you had to do to get where you wanted. He shifted his brain to Neanderthal, where he could concentrate narrowly on dumbbells, on barbells, and on trying to avoid torsion of the testicles during certain exercises. He recently read about torsion of the testicles, and it sounded like about as much fun as being circumcised with hedge clippers.

For about forty minutes, he rocked great, pumped like a starving but careful monkey, until he was soaked with a godawful lather of reeking sweat, his motion smooth and rhythmic, his form correct. The humiliating and fully weird Rubber Boy moment came when he was lying on the bench, pressing the weights high, arms extended straight up and locked in the eighth repetition in a set of ten. He began to bring the bar down toward his chest, and suddenly it seemed to weigh three times what it should. His arms quivered, he couldn't control the barbell, he strained harder, his arms seemed to turn to rubber, and the bar came down on his freaking throat instead of on his chest, right on his Adam's apple. Wimp.

Zach had for totally damn sure not put too much weight on the stupid bar. He didn't do bonehead things like that. He increased the weight only when his dad was there to spot him, to help if the new poundage overwhelmed. He felt as if some superfreak was pushing **down** on the bar, like a **reverse** spotter who wanted to crush his windpipe. He could half hear this crazy wicked laughter inside his head, not his laughter, a mean ugly laugh. The thing in the service mezzanine—**I know you, boy, I know you now**—would have a laugh like this.

Zach strained so hard he could feel his pulse hammering in his temples, eyes bugging out, throat swollen with his effort, so like in maybe two minutes he would die from a crushed airway or from a stupid artery popping in his idiot brain. Couldn't take the stress longer than that. He checked the wall clock for his time of death—2:10 now. If he held out two minutes, he'd die at 2:12, because this wasn't San Quentin, the freaking governor wouldn't call the warden at the last minute like in those dumb-ass prison movies. Zach was crying, damn-damn-damn, not with fear or self-pity, really, but because he was straining so freaking hard that tears popped from his eyes like sweat popped from his pores.

When the clock of doom ticked from 2:10 to 2:11, the weight of the barbell abruptly returned to normal. Zach thrust it off his throat, racked it with a **clang,** and sat up on the edge of the bench, gasping, shaking. When he wiped his surprisingly cold hands across his face to slough off the sweat, he discovered he had strained so hard that his nose was bleeding.

⎯⎯∽∝∽⎯⎯

Sometimes Naomi enjoyed reading in the queen's eyrie. That was what she called the second-floor window seat in the guest bedroom. The space was about eight feet long and almost three feet deep, with plush cushions and piles of comfy decorative pillows, which allowed her to recline elegantly, regally, as if she were the queen of France in a chaise longue, taking a much-deserved respite from the rigors of being a benevolent ruler to adoring subjects. Three French windows looked into the massive oak and down on the south lawn, which the tree had recently begun to carpet with scarlet leaves. **Très belle.**

Only eighty pages remained in the novel about the cultivated dragon who was tasked with civilizing a savage young girl and turning her into a Joan of Arc who would save an imperiled kingdom. Naomi was eager to finish the tale and begin the sequel. The story was kind of like **My Fair Lady** but with sword fights and derring-do and wizards, and instead of Professor Higgins, you had a dragon named Drumblezorn, which made the whole thing just fabulously more interesting without sacrificing literary quality.

Immersed in the story, Naomi was rudely yanked back to reality by a sudden burst of wind that thrashed the oak and rattled a storm of leaves, like scarlet bats, against the windows. Startled, she peered out into the red chaos, half expecting to see a funnel cloud. The whirling leaves clicked and hissed and tap-tap-tapped across the glass for at least a minute, such a beautiful spectacle but also a bit disquieting. This was one of those moments that wise Drumblezorn called is-but-is-nots, when ordinary objects and forces—leaves and wind—created an effect that appeared to be entirely ordinary but was not, when the hidden reality beneath the apparent reality of our world rose almost into sight.

In front of the window seat stood a tea table and two chairs, creating a charming conversation area where Minnie Half-Pint always steadfastly refused to play ladies-at-tea and improvise worldly dialogues. The whirling wind died as suddenly as it arose, and when the leaves fell away from the windows, Naomi turned her attention once more to her book—and from the corner of her eye saw a woman sitting in one of the nearby chairs. Startled but not alarmed, Naomi gasped and leaned forward from the bank of decorative pillows.

The stranger wore what might have been antique clothing: a simple ankle-length tunic dress with bishop sleeves, a high round neckline, gray with blue piping. She was pretty, but she did nothing to accentuate her attributes. She wore no makeup, no lipstick, no nail polish, and her unstyled brown hair hung straight and drab, as though she might be some kind of Shaker or Amish person.

In a soft, gentle, and magically musical voice that mesmerized Naomi, the woman said, "I am embarrassed and greatly sorry if I startled you, m'lady."

M'lady. Whoa! Naomi knew instantly, even more instanter than instantly, that this was beyond a mere is-but-is-not moment, that here was Something Big unfolding just when she thought she might never experience any adventure outside of what she found in books.

"I would have preferred not to come to you by way of the wind and the tree, with so much drama. But the mirror was painted over, m'lady, leaving me with no other door."

"My sister," Naomi said, "she's only eight, you know how it is, her skull's not totally full of brains yet, she's a fraidy-cat. But—what am I going to do?—I love her anyway."

She realized she was babbling. There were a gazillion questions she should ask, but she couldn't think of any; they blew around in her mind like a tumult of leaves and wouldn't remain still so that she could grab one.

"My name is Melody," the woman said, "and when the day comes, it will be my great honor to serve as your guardian and your escort home."

Honor? Guardian? Escort? **Home?**

Putting aside her book, swinging her legs off the window seat to sit on the edge of it, Naomi said, "But this is my home. Isn't it my home? Well, of course it is. I've lived here since . . . since I've lived here."

Leaning forward conspiratorially, Melody said, "M'lady, for your own protection, the memory of your true home has been repressed by a spell, as have those same memories in your brother and sister. The agents of the Imperium would long ago have found you if you knew from where you came, and the assassins of the Apocalypse would by now have run you down."

All that sounded thrilling and romantic and precisely the most desirable degree of scary, and Melody almost **glowed** with sincerity, and her stare was direct and unwavering and piercingly honest, and her plain-Jane manner wasn't what could be expected of some faker. But although Naomi couldn't put her finger on the problem, she felt that something wasn't quite right with this scenario.

As if sensing her lady's doubt, Melody said, "Your true home is a kingdom bright with magic, which you have long suspected."

With that declaration, the woman raised one arm and pointed to the ceiling with her index finger, as if calling down some power from on high.

Every drawer in the dresser, the highboy, and the nightstands flew open as far as they might without crashing onto the floor, and the book about Drumblezorn levitated off the window seat three feet, four, five. When the woman closed her raised hand into a fist, every drawer slid shut—**thump, thump, thump, thump, thump!**—and the book flew across the room, slammed into a wall, and fell to the floor.

Electrified, Naomi shot to her feet.

Rising also, Melody said, "In a month or slightly

more, m'lady, the circumstances in the kingdom will be ripe for your return, all your enemies destroyed, the way made safe. I've come today only so that you will be prepared when I appear again on the night that we must travel. At that time, your memory will be restored, and it will be most essential then that you do as I, your servant, request."

In all the years that she fantasized about a moment of revealed destiny like this, Naomi had imagined a thousand times a thousand clever responses to such a messenger, but she had never expected to be speechless. She heard herself speaking disconnected syllables that might have been the start of words, and then she managed to stammer full words but couldn't put them in coherent sentences. Feeling not at all like a m'lady but very much like a pathetic eight-year-old half-pint booby, she finally said, "Does do Zach Minnie know, like you told me, does you did you tell them, and my parents?"

Melody dropped her voice to a whisper. "No, m'lady. You are the supreme heir to the kingdom, and only you need to be prepared ahead. It would be too dangerous for all of you to know until the very last assassins of the Apocalypse are rendered powerless. This must be your secret, and you must guard it well until the night I return, or else you and everyone you love might die."

"Chestnuts!" Naomi declared.

Pointing to the windows, Melody said, "Regard the tree, m'lady. Regard the tree."

As Naomi turned toward the windows, the wind from nowhere burst into the calm day again and shook the great oak as if to shatter it and cast its broken limbs against the house. Stripped from branches, flocks of scarlet leaves flew against the windows, with a sound like wings beating frantically against the panes. The exhibition was scary but, oh, so beautiful as well: sunlight and shadow playing on the glass, trembling multitudes like crimson butterflies.

As the wind abruptly died, Naomi remembered Melody and turned to her, but the woman was gone. Evidently she had departed by way of the wind and the tree, whatever that meant.

The door to the second-floor hallway stood slightly ajar. Naomi couldn't recall if she had left it that way, but she didn't think so.

She ran out of the guest bedroom, glanced left, right, and found the hallway deserted. She listened for rapid footsteps on the front or back stairs, but she heard none.

In the guest room once more, she hurried to the book that had levitated and flown. She snatched it off the carpet. She dashed to the window seat and knelt on the cushions to watch the last leaf in the glorious multitude settle toward the lawn. Pressing her forehead to a cold pane of glass, straining for a glimpse of Melody dwindling through the branches toward some magical realm or an impossible door closing in the trunk of the oak, she saw nothing more than a big beautiful old tree readying itself for winter.

Her heart raced and she thought it might never stop racing. She was exhilarated although confused, delighted but frightened, totally convinced yet riddled with disbelief, amazed, astonished, eager but wary, impetuous, cautious, buoyant but sad as well, as close to crazy as she had ever been.

Naomi couldn't imagine how she could keep such a secret for one week, let alone for more than a month, for one **day,** let alone one whole week. On the other hand, she knew in her heart she was a protagonist, not an antagonist, not the secondary female lead who might or might not go over to the dark side, who might lack the perspicacity to do the right thing. She was the true lead, the right stuff, a veritable Joan of Arc who could be mentored by dragons but never-ever defeated by them. Perhaps she should have her hair cut in a pageboy, like Joan of Arc was sometimes depicted, or maybe even shorter and a little shaggy, like Amelia Earhart, the vanished aviatrix. So much to think about, so many possibilities to consider. **Pig fat!**

Earlier, Melody Lane drives from the Nash house to the Calvino residence in her Honda, aware that she is possessed, with a full understanding of the nature of her rider. She offers no resistance. She has no fear. Even more than Reese Salsetto, Melody welcomes her rider. She is delighted by the possibilities of cooperation with it, pleased to have the benefits of its protection and its power.

When she was twenty-four, Melody killed her three children—ages four, three, and one—after deciding that motherhood is limiting and boring, and after she learned that humanity is a vile planet-killing plague that Earth can't survive. She saw it on TV. A documentary about the end of the world and about how it is unavoidable. We all have a responsibility. As each brat died, Melody kissed it, inhaling its final exhalation, which symbolized that she was participating in the salvation of the planet by eliminating the CO_2 breathers who were polluting it every time they exhaled. The planet is a living thing. We are lice on the planet.

She murdered **her** louse, Ned, her husband, and made it appear to be suicide. She saw it on the Internet: lots of ways you can make a homicide appear to be a suicide. Her attempt to stage the children's murders as Ned's work deceived the finest crime-scene investigators with all their high-tech devices and scientific wizardry. Not such a bunch of smarties, after all. Her alibi proved ironclad.

This success has enhanced Melody's self-esteem. Self-esteem is the most important thing. You can't make the life you deserve if you don't have enough self-esteem.

Too long, she believed that she was ordinary, unimaginative, not very bright, something of a schlump, as colorless as dishwater. But then she gets away with four murders, and she is doing something socially useful, even important, at the same time. She realizes that, after all, she is interesting, just like Dr. Phil and so many other famous TV hosts have been for so long telling her she is.

Over the past four years, she has murdered three other children, in two different towns. She wishes she could have disposed of dozens, but she is cautious when selecting her targets. The oil companies need new generations to exploit, and if they ever discover she is eliminating their future customer base, they will be ruthless.

All her life, Melody has been ignored by everyone but Ned. And Ned was a bully. He liked her only because she could never stand up for herself and always just hung her head and let him curse her and heap abuse on her—until the night she didn't. They say you are what you eat, and Ned ate a lot of ham and pork and bacon. Now she knows that she is as interesting as most people and more interesting than many, with her secret life.

They say that the meek will inherit the earth, but if that's true, by the time the inheritance is paid, it won't be worth spit, the earth will be used up, burnt out, like Mars. On TV they have all these dance competitions, talent competitions, chef competitions, designer competitions, and no matter what kind of competition it is, the meek never win. The prize always goes to the most aggressive, to the most confident, to the person who has the most self-esteem. Melody has noticed.

She parks in front of the Calvino residence, walks boldly to the door, and lets herself inside, using the key she got from Preston Nash. She has no fear of discovery. Her rider knows where everyone is in the house at all times, and it will guide her through these halls and rooms without an encounter that might compromise her mission.

With a brief conjured windstorm provided by her rider, she makes a dramatic appearance before Naomi Calvino. The rider knows the girl to her core, but Melody knows how to **talk** to the girl. She has always been able to talk to children at their level, to charm them, to tell stories in ways that enthrall them, to make them laugh. This seemed like a worthless talent until she started killing children to save the world, whereupon it facilitated gaining the trust of her prey. Each of her own children giggled in delight when she started to kill it, certain that this was just another of her fun games. Well, it **was** fun, but not for them. They are the plague. She is the antibiotic. We all have a responsibility.

After she finishes the job with the Calvino girl, Melody leaves the second floor by the front stairs, as quiet as a wraith. As she puts her hand on the knob of the front door, the rider departs her to remain with the house.

Melody Lane is aware that the rider will summon her to return, no doubt more than once. She will come when called and will welcome its renewed presence in her blood and bones. When the time to kill arrives, she hopes that Naomi will be hers and that she will be able to suck the dying breath from the girl's mouth.

Meanwhile, the rider has given her several tasks to perform. She must acquire and then make ready certain items, and she understands precisely how to prepare them. Melody doesn't need to be ridden in order to do her master's bidding. For the pleasure of participating in its slaughter of the Calvinos, especially the ruination of the children, she intends to serve it of her own free will.

⸻

Minnie had just gotten a bottle of juice from the refrigerator and was twisting off the cap when she turned toward the French door between the kitchen and the terrace—and saw the golden retriever peering in at her from outside.

Willard had been dead for two years, but she still remembered **exactly** what he looked like. This was Willard, all right, or rather it was Willard's spirit, just like those ghosts at the convenience store except that half of Willard's face wasn't shot off.

He was beautiful, like he had been in life, the best dog ever. Minnie's heart swelled—it actually felt as if it were swelling like a balloon in her chest—at the sight of him. She could feel her heart ballooning all the way up into her throat.

But then she realized that Willard hadn't come back from Heaven to play or to wring tears from her, but to show her something. He was pawing at the glass, not making any noise, but pawing at it anyway. His tail wasn't wagging, as it would be if he wanted to chase a ball or beg for a treat. And the expression in his eyes, in the lift of his upper lip on the left side, meant what it had meant back in the good old days when he was alive: **I'm trying to tell you a thing here. It's so obvious even a cat would get it. Will you please, please, please pay attention?**

Minnie put her juice on the kitchen island and hurried to the door. Willard scampered away as she approached, and when she pushed through the door and stepped onto the patio, the dog was waiting for her on the north lawn.

Willard's forelegs were splayed, his head thrust forward and slightly down, in that partial play bow that meant **Chase me, chase me! You can try, but you can't catch me! I'm a dog, I'm faster than the wind!**

She ran toward him, and he sprinted out of sight along the north side of the house, toward the street. When she turned the corner, she saw him standing on the front yard, looking back at her.

As she raced toward Willard, the retriever faded: first red-gold and beautiful, then gold and beautiful, then white and beautiful, then semitransparent and still beautiful, but then gone. Minnie felt her heart swelling again, and she just wanted to drop to her knees and cry. But she kept going until she stood on the very grass where Willard had last been visible.

On the public sidewalk, as though she had just stepped off the flagstone front walk that led from the porch, a woman in a long gray dress moved toward a car at the curb. She looked like she had come to talk someone's ears off about Jesus, but she didn't have magazines or pamphlets, or even a purse. Apparently she heard Minnie running to the spot on the lawn where Willard vanished, because she stopped and turned to face her.

They were only about twelve or fifteen feet apart. Minnie could clearly see the woman's face. It was pleasant enough but seemed not quite **done,** as if it lacked the final details that would allow you to remember it ten minutes later, a face like one of those in Mom's paintings that was still a stage away from being finished. The woman was smiling sort of absentmindedly, as though she saw Minnie but was thinking about something else and didn't want to be distracted from that.

They stared at each other maybe fifteen seconds, an eerily long time without saying anything. Minnie didn't know why the woman kept staring at her, but she kept staring at the woman because she sensed something not right about her. Minnie kept thinking she was going to figure it out, figure out the not-right something, but it eluded her.

Finally the woman said, "I like your pink shoes."

This statement baffled Minnie for a moment, because she didn't own any pink shoes. If anyone ever gave her pink shoes, she wouldn't even risk saying, **I'll wear them when Hell freezes over,** because you never knew what to expect of the weather. She didn't want to be a marine, like Zach, but unlike Naomi, she didn't swoon about wearing tiaras and diamond-studded capes and pink glass slippers for the rest of her life.

Belatedly registering the stranger's meaning, Minnie looked down at her feet, at her sneakers, which were deep coral, not pink at all. She realized the woman must be color challenged.

"You remind me of a little girl I used to have," the woman said. "She was very sweet."

Minnie was taught never to be rude, and being polite included speaking when spoken to. But in this case, she kept silent. For one thing, she didn't know what to say. More important, she sensed that speaking to this woman would be a mistake for the same reason that speaking to a spirit was a bad idea: Just responding with a single word would be an invitation.

The stranger didn't appear to be a spirit, but she had something in common with spirits that Minnie sensed but couldn't quite name.

After another, shorter silence, the woman in gray took a step toward Minnie, but then halted.

Although they were in a public place, Minnie began to feel alone and dangerously isolated. No traffic passed in the nearby street. No pedestrians were in sight. No kids were at play on any of the front lawns. The sky was pale, the air still, the trees limp, so it seemed as if time had stopped for everyone in the world except the two of them.

Minnie wished Willard hadn't done a fade. She wished he would reappear, not just to her but also to the woman. When alive, the dog had a totally phony but threatening growl, and his spirit still had big teeth even if it couldn't bite anyone.

The woman's dreamy smile, which had been nice enough, now seemed like the fixed smile of a snake, which wasn't a smile at all but only the **shape** of a smile.

Just when Minnie was about to spin away and run for all she was worth, the woman turned from her and went to the car at the curb. She glanced back as she got into the vehicle, but then she pulled the door shut and drove away.

As she watched the car dwindle along the street, Minnie finally realized what the woman in gray had in common with ghosts. Death. They were both about death.

From the journal of Alton Turner Blackwood:

After spending the night disinterring skeletons from unmarked graves in the pine-circled clearing, the boy returned to his tower room before dawn and spent the morning and the afternoon brooding about his discoveries.

An hour before twilight, when he was still expected to remain discreet and to refrain from inflicting his unappealing presence on either the family or the estate staff, he went to the guest house. In half of this very comfortable residence, he once lived with his mother, Anita, where now his mother's sister, Regina, resided alone with her daughter, Melissa.

The boy went with no intention of committing violence. He wanted only to learn the truth. But if necessary, he would use terror and pain to extract the truth from them.

In killing the rabbits and the deer, he had learned there was pleasure to be had in ripping the life from pretty things.

Aunt Regina and Cousin Melissa were sitting at a table on their back patio, in the shade of a mammoth maidenhair tree, playing cards. They were annoyed but not apprehensive when the boy suddenly loomed over them.

Some on the house staff were disturbed by his malformed face and his misproportioned body, were even afraid of him though he had harmed no human being to that point. Regina, however, had never shown the slightest fear of him, nor had Melissa except when she was very young. Fourteen now, the girl regarded him with the distaste and the contempt that she learned from her mother.

Having killed animals, having been acknowledged by a mountain lion as Death personified, he saw things through a new and clearer lens. As a boy more naive than he was now, he had thought that Regina and Melissa were smug, fearless, and uncongenial because they were beautiful. He thought beauty was not only their power but also their armor, that if you were as beautiful as they were, then you respected and feared nothing because you were privileged by natural right and were indestructible. Now he realized that their

superior airs, their contempt, and their
fearlessness were based also on secret
knowledge, on something they knew that he
did not know. He was an outsider at Crown
Hill not just because of his grotesque
appearance but also because of his ignorance.

When he told Regina that he had excavated
his mother's skeleton from an unmarked grave,
he expected her to express shock or grief or
anger that her sister had come to such a fate.
Instead she remained seated at her card game,
unimpressed with his grisly news. She told him
that he had been a stupid boy, that he would
regret digging like a dog for a bone.

Realizing that the truth concealed from him
was even bigger than he might have imagined,
he expected that he would have to choke it or
cut it or beat it from Regina. But though she
kept him standing, she did not deny him the
truth as she denied him a chair. She spelled it
out for him with a cold, acidic glee, and the
longer she spoke, the more the boy realized
that she was insane.

Melissa, smiling and playing cards
throughout the revelations, proved to be no
less insane than her mother. Teejay, Terrence
James Turner Blackwood, patriarch of the clan,
surely must be the maddest of them all.

Having inherited great wealth and built an

even larger fortune, Teejay didn't worship money. He was a singularly handsome man, vain about his looks. He worshipped beauty, which in part was also self-worship.

He worshipped beauty but didn't know how to create it, as his films and his faux castle amply proved. He was still a teenager when his preoccupation with beauty became a burning obsession with—and an unnatural passion for—his younger sister, Alissa, one year his junior. Regina could only guess when he seduced Alissa, but at what cost to Alissa's sanity eventually became clear.

In time, young Alissa achieved fame as a silent-film star under the name Jillian Hathaway. In those days, movies were considered as much of a low-class business as carnivals and burlesque shows. Some early actresses worked under noms de cinema, and swore to embrace invented biographies written for them by the studios that had them under contract.

Jillian supposedly married Teejay in 1926, in a glamorous ceremony in Acapulco, when she was twenty-five and he was twenty-six. They were never wed, however, because they were brother and sister and couldn't document otherwise.

As Regina shuffled her deck of cards and

made this revelation to the looming scarecrow of a boy, he didn't at once see why this long-ago depravity, a wicked union occurring thirty-one years before his birth, should have sealed his fate and guaranteed his life of loneliness, bitterness, and violence.

During the dealing of a new hand of 500 rummy, Regina explained that of course Teejay and Jillian's only child—Marjorie—born in 1929, was a product of incest. Her father was also her uncle. Her mother was also her aunt.

The girl grew to be even more beautiful than her mother—which confirmed Teejay's theory that greater beauty could be distilled from lesser beauty. He believed that a particular human lineage could be improved and refined just as a line of dogs could be tightly bred to emphasize their most eye-pleasing characteristics. Preventing the introduction of lesser genes, restricting mating to specimens with the same desirable qualities, a family might in time produce individuals of such breathtaking beauty that the world would never previously have seen their equal.

Fourteen years after giving birth to Marjorie, when Jillian learned that her daughter was pregnant with Teejay's child, she hung herself in the room at the top of the south tower. To Teejay, this suicide was not entirely unwelcome, as it meant that his efforts to further concentrate his seed would not be complicated by the need to service a wife.

In 1942, when Teejay was forty-two, young Marjorie gave birth to Anita and Regina, fraternal rather than identical twins—whose father was also their grandfather and their great-uncle. The twins grew to be even lovelier than their mother, which Teejay took to be absolute justification of his actions and proof of his theory.

"You would not be born for another fifteen years," Regina told the unwelcome boy on her patio, as she laid the jack, queen, and king of clubs on the table. "And because of you, I and mine will be the only heirs to Crown Hill, to everything."

The boy began to understand the inevitability of his birth in the condition that he must endure. He was on the brink of discovering what he must become and what he must do with his life. The boy was only hours away from becoming me.

42

SLEET TAPPING AT THE WINDOW WAS A RAT-claw sound, sharp bat teeth biting on beetle shells.

Ten days after the massacre of the Woburn family, John Calvino's mood had grown grim. He seemed powerless to improve it. The return of the oppressive presence in their house, which he did not believe he could be imagining, had by its constant pressure infused him with an expectation of defeat and death that he struggled unsuccessfully to overcome.

Even when he was not at home, as now, the bleak mood persisted. Images of a disturbing nature frequently came to him as they never had before—rats, bats, beetle shells—inspired by things as innocent as sleet ticking on a windowpane.

Here in Father Bill James's office in the rectory adjacent to St. Henry's Church, John expected the bleakness to relent if only because of the comparative sanctity of this place. But he remained afflicted by a stubborn foreboding.

He stood at the window, perhaps drawn there particularly because it offered a somber view. Under the stone-slab sky, thin mist drifted like acrid smoke from dying embers. The black trunks and bare limbs of the trees revealed an ugly angular chaos that a drapery of leaves had once concealed.

Father William James arrived with apologies for being five minutes late. About forty, with short brown hair, stocky but fit and quick, Father Bill—as he preferred to be called—looked less like a priest of old than like a physical-education teacher in a high school of any time and place. Now at home, but not always **just** at home, he wore athletic shoes, gray Dockers, and a blue sweatshirt instead of a cleric's suit and a Roman collar, which of course he wore when he felt they were appropriate.

He vigorously shook John's hand and led him to an arrangement of four black-leather Herman Miller chairs—wheeled office furniture but ergonomic, comfortable, and stylish—encircling a round coffee table with a brushed-steel base and a glass top. Another window looked onto more skeletal trees, thin mist, and sleet.

The rectory office was different from what it had been two years earlier, before Father Albright retired. Along with all the Victorian parlor furniture, the quaint paintings and highly figured statuary were gone. Behind the priest's desk hung an abstract bronze crucifix that looked to John like a rag twisted around an old-fashioned four-arm lug wrench.

Here was a place of serious business. This priest understood that in addition to being the shepherd of his flock, he was equally an overseer of parish assets, a promoter of the public welfare, a manager of the congregation's energies in the interest of equitable solutions to societal problems, and much more.

Indicating the sleet that clicked against the window, Father Bill said, "I don't remember an October quite as cold as this."

John nodded. "They say it'll be a short autumn, early winter."

"I suppose weather doesn't make a difference in your business."

"Homicide, you mean? The murder rate rises slightly in extreme heat, diminishes slightly in extreme cold. At the end of the year, we've been as busy as ever."

"And busier in hard times like these."

"Actually, the homicide rate usually falls significantly during hard times, then rises when prosperity returns."

Frowning, Father Bill said, "That seems counterintuitive."

"It stumps everyone from the theorists to guys

like me in the trenches. But that's how it is. Recently, of course, the Lucas and Woburn murders have skewed the statistics."

"Such tragedies. Horrible. They seem inexplicable. Were you assigned to those cases?"

"No," John said. "But they're part of the reason I wanted to see you, Father."

In recent weeks, John had more often retold the story of Alton Turner Blackwood's crimes than in the past twenty years combined, but repetition made it no easier to tell. As with Nelson Burchard and Lionel Timmins, he recounted the destruction of those four families, including his own, without emotion, with only the essential details, as he might describe a crime scene in a court of law. Nonetheless, as always, the words cut him.

With a compassion so respectful that it didn't make John uneasy, Father Bill responded from time to time with expressions of sympathy that never smacked of pity, with condolences as elegantly restrained as they were clearly sincere. When John listed similarities between the murders twenty years earlier and these contemporary crimes, Father Bill was fascinated, appalled. He was alarmed, too, at the prospect of the city besieged by an imitator of the long-dead killer.

The last words of Alton Turner Blackwood, the only part of the story that John had withheld from Nicolette, brought a frown of a different quality to the priest's face. His expression grew more dour as John revealed his fear that Blackwood somehow had been **within** Andy Tane as he had been within Billy Lucas. John methodically laid out his evidence that an apparent supernatural force might be at work—for the first time to someone disposed to believe him—and Father Bill looked like a football coach whose team was on a losing streak and who disapproved of his players' negativity.

"What I'm hoping," John said, "is that I can establish a place of safety for my family to ride out December tenth. If something's in my house—a presence, a spirit, a ghost, I don't know what—but if something is there, and I truly believe, Father, that something **is** there, then I need to know how to get rid of it, how to make the house safe, a fortress. Because I think if we can get through the tenth of December, maybe that will be the end of all this. At least I've got to hope so. I don't know what else to do."

The priest nodded thoughtfully, swiveled his chair toward the window, and watched the sleet biting at the glass as he brooded about what he had been told.

Having fully unburdened himself, having bared his deepest and strangest fears to an audience capable of taking them seriously, John was relieved more than he had expected to be. He wasn't free of worry but the sense of utter helplessness lifted from him, the helplessness that was the pivot point on which he had been turned to his recent bleak mood.

Swiveling his chair toward John, Father Bill said, "Roosevelt was right when he said we have nothing to fear but fear itself. And our fear can only consume us when we face it alone. I can help you with this, John."

Grateful for that commitment, John said, "Thank you, Father. I don't know how it should be done. It's a house, not a person. A ghost, I guess, not something demonic. So maybe it's not an exorcism in the classic sense. . . ."

Father Bill shook his head. "If we believe in the Magisterium of the Church and its interpretations in this area, we don't believe in ghosts. Souls of the deceased can't linger in this world. They pass to God or Purgatory, and they can't return here in any case. Séances and the like are transgressive, unhealthy, dangerous to the mind and soul."

"Yes, I understand, I really do, but if the devil is the prince of this world, as the Church says he is . . . couldn't he perhaps free a soul from Hell to finish something that it started here during its lifetime?"

Father Bill's expression was pained, and his eyes seemed to be full of sorrow. But though he still spoke with compassionate concern, his voice contained the faintest note of impatience. "We've come a long way in the past hundred years, and further with every passing decade. But the full flowering of the faith in our time is delayed by medieval ideas that make the Church seem hopelessly credulous. Faith isn't superstition, John. Superstition is a stain on faith, a perversion of the religious impulse and possibly a fatal corruption of it."

The priest's words didn't fully confuse John but bewildered him. He sought to clarify what must be a misunderstanding. "I assure you, Father, I don't bury statues of Saint Anthony upside down in the yard to attract a buyer for a house that's been hard to sell or anything of that kind. I know some people mix a little voodoo with the faith and don't realize what they're doing. But if ever a man lived who would earn the admiration and assistance of demons, then Alton Blackwood was that man. He was—"

Not with impatience now but in a tone of utmost good-humored reason, Father Bill said, "In an age of nuclear weapons, we don't need Hell and demons, succubi and incubi and hungry vampires on the doorstep. We need food banks, John, thrift shops, homeless shelters, and the courage to express our faith in social action. There was a time when every diocese was directed to have a priest trained in the Ritual for Exorcisms. We haven't had one in this diocese for eight years, and that poor lost soul isn't even a priest anymore."

The light in the rectory office fell in such a way that John didn't cast a reflection in the glass table.

He said, "But Father, can't we have food banks **and** Hell?"

The priest laughed. He sounded relieved when he said, "If you can laugh about this, you can deal with it."

John had asked the question seriously, with no intention of a joke. "You said you could help me. What did that mean?"

"You've lived with this fear of Blackwood's return for twenty years. The trauma of your family's murder and then your face-to-face confrontation with him was so harrowing that it was psychologically formative. When these recent murders occurred, with the coincidental similarities to this monster's crimes, you were virtually programmed to see signs and portents in even the most ordinary things. Like air knocking in a water pipe. A bad smell in the laundry room."

Searching his wallet as he talked, Father Bill found a business card. He dealt it across the table as if a game of poker had begun.

"This is a good man, John. Absolutely first rate. I've had many occasions to recommend him and never one occasion to regret that I did."

On the pale-yellow card were the name, address, and phone number of a psychiatrist named Dr. M. Duchamp.

Prior to this meeting, John had thought the most

embarrassing thing that might happen would be Father Bill pointedly asking why Zach and Naomi and Minnie were not as involved with parish activities as they had once been, and why the Calvinos attended Mass about twice a month when they used to receive the Eucharist every week.

This parenting failure arose after Father Albright's retirement, and John wondered at it and worried over it from time to time. But he had continued to procrastinate about getting the kids in a pew more often, and he had been unable to put his finger on a reason for this less diligent commitment to attendance. Now he understood.

Being pressed about more regular appearances at Mass would not have been half as embarrassing as **this,** as being gently and kindly counseled against hysterical superstition and being referred to a psychiatrist. John was not embarrassed at all for himself, but for Father Bill.

Somehow they were chatting about the weather again, and then about the latest oil crisis and the cost of gasoline.

Soon John was shepherded out of the office, along the hallway, to the front door in a cloud of earnest sophisms, sincere platitudes, and heartfelt encouragements.

Alone on the front porch, he stood at the head of the steps, buttoning the collar of his raincoat and putting up the hood.

A jacket of sleet had begun to encase some of the black limbs of the bare trees, the ice like the ivory shell in a bone scan, the bark like malignant matter in the marrow.

Sleet slanting through the day added no glitter to the scene, as if the ice pellets had formed from dark water.

Just twenty-three days until November seventh. Just fifty-six days until December tenth.

43

AS THE DAYS PASSED FOLLOWING THE EN-counter in the guest bedroom, Naomi's secret grad-ually lost some of its luster, though she polished it with her imagination so regularly and so vigorously that it should have been as bright as a bejeweled di-adem. Over and over, she relived the incident, sometimes with fabulous elaborations and with such hot excitement that the memory melted like a buttery candle, dissolved into a scintillating puddle of incoherent fantasy and pure delight. At other times, in the reliving, the events in and around the window seat struck her as too pat, almost scripted, wooden, even goofball on close examination.

But wasn't it shamelessly ungrateful to wish all her life for a moment of magical revelation and then to doubt its validity when at long last the wish was granted? By worrying that the assassins-of-the-Apocalypse-and-the-imperiled-kingdom rap seemed just a smidgen trite, wasn't she calling Melody a liar? And when you began asking yourself questions like this, as though you were both the detective and the suspect, wasn't that a sure sign that you already knew the answers and didn't much like them? Well, wasn't it? Well?

By the morning of October sixteenth, twelve **exhausting** secret-keeping days after Melody's visit, Naomi realized that all her doubts sprang from a single source: the acts of magic that Melody performed. When you thought hard about them, the opening-and-closing drawers and the flying book weren't so fall-down-in-amazement magical.

Indeed, they were not magical at all. Turning a pumpkin into an elegant horse-drawn coach was magic. Transforming a chameleon into a tiny human being with a seven-word spell was magic. The events in the guest bedroom were mere **phenomena**. Paranormal, yes. Magical, no. Like dowsing successfully for water was a phenomenon but not magic.

Melody was no Merlin or Gandalf. She certainly possessed some kind of power, you couldn't deny that, but it wasn't a talent for magic so fabulous that recruiters from Hogwarts School of Witchcraft and Wizardry would ever be beating down her door. The business with the dresser drawers and the violence with which the book flew across the guest room and slammed into the wall—that seemed to be more like the work of a poltergeist. Paranormal phenomena lacked the charm and the **finesse** of real magic.

By the afternoon of the sixteenth, when Walter Nash drove Naomi to junior-orchestra practice at the civic auditorium, she was a mess. Not physically, of course. Whether or not she might be destined to inherit a kingdom of magic, she would always brush her hair a hundred strokes every day, maintain clean teeth, and that kind of stuff. Her clothes weren't a mess. She wore a blue skirt and matching blazer with a crisp white blouse and a smashing blue beret with a furry red pompon, so she felt stylish but not overdressed. She believed that she looked very much like a first-chair flautist, which was in fact her position in the junior orchestra. She was a mess **mentally** because she couldn't stop tearing apart the story Melody told her, examining it critically piece by piece, even though she **wanted** to believe.

Practice went well enough, but Naomi didn't feel the music all the way down in her bones as she usually did. In one piece, she had a modest solo passage, and the conductor, Mr. Hummelstein, praised her performance. But Mr. Hummelstein was old, and while there wasn't anything wildly wrong with being old, he was one of those old men with absolute **forests** of hair bristling from his ears. So when he complimented your playing, you couldn't bask in the praise because you couldn't be sure that he had heard you clearly.

During a twenty-minute break between two fifty-minute practice sessions, the young musicians always socialized. Naomi was usually a fiend for socializing. She could spin through a chattering crowd with all the energy of—but with far more refined social graces than—a whirling dervish. On this occasion, however, she was subdued, as distracted by her Melody dilemma as she was when participating in the orchestra rehearsal.

At the end of the second session, after she packed up her flute, as Naomi made her way up the inclined center aisle of the auditorium, toward the lobby, Melody was suddenly walking at her side. No wind. No oak. Only Melody.

Surprised, Naomi said, "How did you just happen?"

"Please, m'lady, let's keep moving," Melody said. "I can see Walter right now, with remote viewing. He had no choice but to park at the hateful red curb. You don't want him to be ticketed."

"Remote viewing?"

"I can't turn a pumpkin into a horse-drawn coach."

That statement didn't halt Naomi, although she gaped at Melody, speechless, as they continued along the aisle.

Speaking softly that others nearby might not hear, Melody said, "I can't transform a chameleon into a tiny human being, either, but then, m'lady, please remember that I never claimed to be a sorceress or a white witch."

Her mind racing back through the conversation in the guest room, twelve days previously, Naomi supposed this might be true.

Melody continued, "I only said that you are the one and true heir to a kingdom of bright magic. In your kingdom, **you** will regain magical abilities. But I am not of royal blood. Those of my humble station in the kingdom have only certain **psychic** abilities, such as remote viewing, some clairvoyance, and a little psychokinesis, which is the ability to move small objects—like your book—with the power of the mind."

At the head of the aisle, Melody stepped out of the way of the departing musicians, into the pathway behind the last row of seats.

As Naomi joined her, the woman raised a handsome compact piece of luggage that she had been carrying at her side. "I am herewith consigning this attaché case into your care, m'lady."

Anyone else would have called it a briefcase, and the use of the elegant word **attaché**—not to mention **herewith**—gave Naomi a little shiver of pleasure, renewing her sense that a fabulous adventure must be approaching.

As Naomi accepted the attaché case, Melody said, "It contains items of a most magical nature that you will need on the glorious night we travel. You must guard them until then and **allow no one to see them**."

"May I look in the case?"

"Later at home, yes. Not now. However, you must not unscrew the lid from the reliquary—that is the jar. The precious items in the jar must never come into contact with air until the moment they are needed. Otherwise, all will be lost."

"You can trust me to be responsible with it," Naomi said softly.

"You must swear to keep this secret, m'lady."

"I do. I swear."

"The lives of multitudes depend on your discretion."

"Yes. Multitudes. I swear."

"Finally, m'lady, you must put aside doubt. I'm not offended to be doubted. But when the time comes to make the great journey, you must have full confidence in me. One who doubts will not be able to fly between the worlds. One who doubts will not be able to return to her throne. If you doubt, you will be lost, you and your family, too, and all the people of your kingdom—all will be lost."

Worriedly, Naomi said, "It seems all can be lost so easily."

"So easily, m'lady. So very easily. Your doubt

could kill us all. Find the courage to believe. Now go quickly before your coachman endures the indignity of a citation from some gendarme."

Coachman, indignity, citation, and **gendarme** gave Naomi shivers just as **attaché** had done. Of all the fabulous qualities that set magical beings apart from ordinary humanity, their vocabulary and unusual phrasing were almost as thrilling to Naomi as their special powers.

"One question," Naomi said. "**When** do we fly between the worlds?"

"All I dare say is **soon,** m'lady."

And then Melody did a most disconcerting thing. Their heads were close because they were speaking conspiratorially. A strange look came into the woman's eyes, and she kissed Naomi on the lips.

The kiss was light, not a massive lip-mashing experience, but instead like the brush of a butterfly. It wasn't merely a kiss, but also something else for which Naomi had no name. Having just inhaled before being startled by this intimacy, Naomi exhaled in surprise—and felt Melody suck in her exhalation, seemingly with intent, like a hummingbird sipping the nectar from a flower.

Melody's stare compelled Naomi to meet it, to sink into those molasses-brown eyes as if into dark waters. Just when it seemed that something shocking and even terrible might happen, the woman said, "My sweet lady, go quickly now. The frost is on the briar rose, and the coming twilight is no friend of ours. Quickly, **go!**"

Naomi hurried out of the auditorium and across the lobby, where only a few young musicians lingered.

Opening one of the outer lobby doors, Naomi glanced back, but Melody apparently remained in the auditorium.

At the red curb, Walter Nash waited with Mother's SUV. Naomi often rode in the front passenger seat, to chat with Mr. Nash, but this time she climbed in back because she didn't want to talk. She desperately needed silence and privacy to consider and reconsider what had just transpired.

The frost is on the briar rose, and the coming twilight is no friend of ours.

Naomi had no idea what those words meant, but it seemed as if they must mean **everything**. It was a perfectly fabulous thing to have said to you by someone, especially by someone mysterious who could fly between worlds.

The kiss had been bizarre, even freaky, and the look in Melody's eyes had been so intense you half expected it might set your face on fire. But in retrospect Naomi realized that she couldn't interpret the meaning of the kiss-and-sip or of the stare by the standards of this world. Melody came from another world altogether, from a place of psychic and magical powers. The culture of that world must be as different from this one as this one was different from the culture of a tribe of red-haired dwarf cannibals in a remote South American jungle, supposing there were any red-haired dwarf cannibals. Over in Melody's world, a lady-in-waiting might pay her deepest respect to her princess by just such a kiss-and-sip as Naomi had received.

The ride home seemed as slow as if they had been dragged in a sledge over dry ground by half-dead horses.

Once there, carrying her flute case and her small purse and the magnificent attaché, Naomi flew from the SUV, raced up the back stairs to the second floor, and hurried along the hall toward her room. At her door, she realized she might burst in upon Minnie, and if old Mouse was indeed there, she would be curious about the attaché case and its contents.

Naomi took a detour to the guest room, where she put her purse and flute on the carpet. She quietly closed and locked the door. She placed the attaché on one end of the deep window seat and knelt on the floor in front of it.

The case appeared to be covered in some kind of snake skin or maybe alligator. Of course it might have been crafted not in this world but in the world of her kingdom, where a dragon might have provided the hide.

Even though she was now several days closer

to twelve than to eleven, and even though she was precocious, Naomi found herself for once in a situation where her galloping imagination seemed tethered, pawing at the ground with its hooves, stirring up nothing but dust. She had no slightest idea what "items of a most magical nature" might be in the attaché case, and she couldn't fantasize anything.

She popped the latches. Opened the case. Within rested a four-inch-deep white box that filled most of the attaché, cushioned all around with crumpled tissue paper.

Handling the box as if it contained a treasure both sacred and of immeasurable value, she lifted it out and set it beside the case. Four pieces of Scotch tape fixed the lid in place. She slit them one at a time with a fingernail and opened the box.

Within were ten coins in a small Ziploc bag. Quarters. They had been painted black.

Nestled in soft cushioning paper stood a little glass jar that might once have contained olives. It currently held five dry, round, brown discs only slightly larger than—and approximately twice as thick as—the black quarters. They rested on a bed of cotton balls.

She had been sternly warned not to open the jar. The contents must not come into contact with air until the very moment they were needed.

Otherwise, all will be lost.

In a second Ziploc bag were a tube of epoxy, a ball of string, and a pair of scissors. These things looked suspiciously ordinary. Naomi wondered if they might have been included by mistake, although Melody didn't seem like a person who would accidentally include such things instead of, say, a wizard's monocle that revealed the future.

The final items were the most interesting and quite mysterious. Cushioned in nests of tissue paper were five chicken eggs. Each bore a name printed with a red felt-tip pen: JOHN, NICOLETTE, ZACHARY, NAOMI, MINETTE.

Picking up the egg bearing her name, Naomi discovered that it was light, empty. Each end featured a small hole. The yolk and white had been drained from the shell.

When she turned the egg, a whispery sound arose within. Holding it to her ear, she listened intently, but she couldn't identify the contents, though it sounded rather like a loose scrap of paper—or maybe a dead insect with brittle wings.

To what purpose these objects might be put and what spectacular effects they might create, Naomi couldn't guess. But they were for sure magical. It seemed to her that at any moment they would begin to crackle and glow with eldritch energy. **Eldritch** meant eerie, weird, and spooky all in one. It had been her favorite new word back when she was about to turn eleven and leave the unspeakable awkwardness of ten behind her forever. She hadn't used it in a while, but it seemed the perfect word now.

Reluctantly, she returned the items to the box, exactly as she had found them. She put the box in the attaché case, which she closed and latched.

Melody had explicitly warned that these magical items must be hidden away until the night that she would lead the Calvino family to a new world. Naomi considered a dozen places to conceal the attaché in the guest room, but none of them seemed safe enough.

Even when the room wasn't in use, Mr. and Mrs. Nash cleaned it once a week. They were so thorough that if they had served some Egyptian pharaoh, his mummy would be in perfect condition three thousand years later. They would find the case.

Finally, in the walk-in closet, Naomi climbed a stepstool and placed the precious item of luggage flat on a high shelf. She buried it under spare blankets that were wrapped in plastic to prevent dust from collecting on them when they weren't in use.

No one was scheduled to visit in the near future. Mr. and Mrs. Nash wouldn't disturb the blankets until they needed them for an overnight guest.

Near the door to the second-floor hallway, as she picked up her flute and her purse from the carpet, she thought again of the strange kiss and of the penetrating stare that went so deep into her eyes that she could almost feel it frying her gray matter somewhere around midbrain.

Doubt began to creep into Naomi's mind again, even though all would be lost if she doubted. But then she remembered the cryptic warning—**The frost is on the briar rose, and the coming twilight is no friend of ours**—and she thought of her levitating book and of the green grapes disappearing into the mirror, and she was slammed right back into the breathtaking wonderfulness of it all, so that her tummy fluttered and the nape of her neck tingled.

Naomi stepped into the hall. She went to her room.

At the play table, Minnie looked up from her LEGO project. "I saw this clown once wearing a blue beret with a red pompon."

"Put-down humor is simply **not** your forte, my darling sister. You shouldn't embarrass yourself by attempting it."

"No, I mean there really was this clown in a hat like that."

Putting her purse and flute on her desk, shrugging out of her blazer, Naomi said, "If you say so."

"Was Mr. Hummelstein at orchestra practice?"

"He's the conductor. He's always there."

"Has he trimmed out his ears yet?"

Flopping on her bed, Naomi said, "No, they are

still two great thickets, you expect a flock of ducks to be startled out of them."

"Did you play your solo?"

"Yes. Twice."

"Is that all?"

Mentally reviewing the contents of the attaché case, Naomi said, "All what?"

"There wasn't a standing ovation, applause like thunder, no crowd of admirers with fresh roses at the stage door?"

Naomi thought about eggs. They were very symbolic objects. What might an empty egg represent?

Minnie came to the bed. "What're you up to?"

"What do you mean? I'm lying here exhausted."

"You're up to something," Minnie said, frowning down at her.

"My paranoid sister, if you aren't careful, you'll grow up to be the Lord High Inquisitioner and Torturer to some crazed dictator."

"You're up to something, all right."

Naomi let out a long-suffering sigh.

"Something's going to happen," Minnie said.

"Well, maybe something wonderful will happen."

"No. Something very bad."

"Here comes Miss Gloomy Bloomers again."

"Something's wrong with this house," Minnie said, looking toward the ceiling. "It started with the mirror."

"You painted the mirror black."

"Maybe that wasn't good enough."

Minnie went to the window and stood staring into the twilight.

Sitting up on the edge of the bed, Naomi said, "The frost is on the briar rose."

"What does that mean?"

"I don't know," Naomi said, "but doesn't it make you feel just totally delicious?"

"No. I'm scared."

Naomi went to the window and put a hand on Minnie's shoulder. "There's nothing to be scared of, sweetie."

Gazing at the fading sky, Minnie said, "There's everything to be scared of."

"Sometimes it looks that way when you're eight. But when you're eleven, you have a whole different perspective."

44

FOR A WHILE, EVERYTHING MOTORED ALONG on cruise control, not exactly normal but not in-your-face bizarre, and then Zach began to dream about Ugly Al again—though with a difference. These new mind movies were megatons worse than nightmares. They were so radically real that Zach woke up to throw up more than once, barely making it to the bathroom in time.

The dumb-ass cliché carnival wasn't a locale anymore. These dreams were set in their house or outside on their property, and though they were horror-movie stuff, they didn't have a bone-head horror-movie feel. They felt like documentaries.

In the first of them, Zach climbed into the stupid playhouse high in the stupid cedar, where he **never** went in real life because it was a girl's kind of place. Snow was falling, rungs on the ladder jacketed with ice, and he was bare-chested and barefoot in jeans. He could feel the snow spitting against his face, the slippery ice under his feet, feel it cracking and hear brittle chunks of it clinking and rattling down through the dark branches. Never before had he felt things so intensely in dreams: the texture of everything, the cold, his feet numb yet **stinging** from prolonged contact with the ice.

He could smell everything too, which never happened in other dreams. He smelled the cedar as he ascended through its boughs. He smelled the wet wood of the playhouse—and the blood when he went inside.

In throbbing lantern light, Naomi's severed head stood in a puddle on the playhouse table. Stepping out of shadows, Ugly Al said, "I have lots of uses for her fine little body, but I didn't need her head. You can have the little slut's head." Zach tried to back away, couldn't. Ugly Al shoved the head into his hands. Zach could feel the slickness and fading warmth of the blood, her hair tickling his wrists. All this did worse than terrify him. He was grief-stricken, such anguish, he was sobbing, his throat felt raw from sobbing. His sister was **dead**. Maybe it wouldn't have been as bad if it was only terrifying, but Naomi was **dead,** and a stake through Zach's chest couldn't have hurt as much as this loss. He wanted to put the precious head somewhere safe and cover it so that no one could see brilliant

Naomi like this, beautiful Naomi reduced to this, but Ugly Al gripped Zach's hands and forced him to bring the head closer to his face, closer, saying, "Give her a nice wet kiss."

The dreams got a lot worse after that.

Zach knew that he should tell his parents, because the dreams were so godawful intense and so strange that maybe he had a freaking brain tumor the size of an orange or something. He intended to tell them, but then the dreams got sick in a different way from how they had been, still violent but also way perverse. Disgusting, demented syphilitic-monkey things happened in these supercharged nightmares, things Zach could never in a million years tell anyone about because they would think that he must be a walking pus bag, that he must be rabid-bat deranged if he could even imagine such grotesque stuff. In fact, he didn't think he was imagining any of it, he felt like he was **receiving** this filth, as if it were being downloaded into his brain like a movie from the Internet, but he knew he'd never sell **that** idea to the psychiatrists.

On the night of October eighteenth, any lingering thought he had of sharing his nightmares with his father and mother was vaporized like a teaspoon of water at ground zero in a nuclear blast. Something happened that so shamed him, he had no option but silently to endure this torment until it either stopped or he went into full brain melt.

In the dream, Ugly Al tried to force Zach to do something so evil and repulsive that even Hell wouldn't let him in if he did it. When he refused, Ugly Al produced a meat cleaver and chopped once, twice, three times at Zach's crotch.

Screaming in a dry breathless whisper, he sat up in bed with a lap full of warm blood. After desperately, interminably fumbling for the lamp switch, he discovered that of course he wasn't emasculated for real, only symbolically: He had wet the stupid bed. He had **never** been a sleep piddler as a little kid. Now nearly fourteen, he had turned his bed into a freaking **lake**.

Leaping out of bed as if it were a skillet full of sizzling-hot oil, he peeled out of his saturated underwear and threw them on the bedclothes. He stripped the bed fast, before the mattress sustained damage, and piled everything on his desk after sweeping the blotter and his drawing tablet to the floor. He would have preferred to heap the reeking bundle on his desk chair; but because he had become a godawful paranoid dumb-ass, the chair was bracing shut the closet door.

At 2:20 A.M., in fresh underwear and jeans, operating in superstealth mode, not daring to turn on the hallway or stairwell lights, he carried the soiled sheets and clothes to the laundry room on the ground floor. There he had to turn on the lights to figure out how to load the stupid washer and get it going.

This being the totally wired twenty-first century when every third-world hellhole had nuclear weapons and your cell phone was able to do everything but read minds, you would think a load of laundry could be washed in a minute and tumbled dry in two, but no. He had to sit on the laundry-room floor forever, waiting to be discovered and humiliated—a thirteen-year-old, would-be-marine bed-wetter.

45

ON THE EVENING OF OCTOBER NINETEENTH, complaining about recent bouts of insomnia, John revealed that he had called Dr. Neimeyer, their internist, to request a prescription for Lunesta. He took one and retired early.

Recently Nicolette had been worried about him. He seemed to be preoccupied by his current case to an even greater extent than he had been by previous homicides. He didn't have his usual appetite, either. She was sure he had lost weight, at least five pounds, but he claimed that he felt fit and that his weight was the same as ever.

When he first mentioned having trouble sleeping, she suggested he see Isaac Neimeyer, but for a full checkup, not to obtain pills. Usually he was averse to being medicated. His insomnia must be worse than he had told her.

With John off to bed early and with the kids absorbed in their interests, Nicky returned to her studio. She intended to spend two or three hours with the problematic picture of Naomi, Zach, and Minnie.

As she was laying out her brushes and paints, she realized that the time of year might have something to do with John's condition. His parents and sisters had been murdered on October twenty-fifth, which was just six days away. Every year, he became pensive around that date, somewhat withdrawn. Although John never marked the dark anniversary by talking about it, Nicky knew it lay heavy on his mind. Perhaps he was more deeply troubled this time because of the twenty-year milestone. Time didn't, as advertised, heal all wounds. Although the wrenching immediacy of grief eventually passed, the settled sorrow that replaced it might in its own way be even more intense.

As Nicky completed preparations to paint, her younger sister, Stephanie, called from Boston. Stephie had just gotten home early from her sous-chef job at the restaurant. In this economy, business was off, as it had been for some time. Nicky sat on her high stool with the swiveling seat, turned toward the vase of peach-colored humility roses, and worried with her sister about various economic catastrophes in the news, talked about food, and swapped stories about their children.

Neither of them had ever been awkward with the other, but Nicky sensed her sister circling around a subject that she hesitated to raise. This perception proved correct when Stephie finally said, "Maybe you'll think I'm flaky when I tell you this. . . ."

"Honey," Nicky said, "you've **always** seemed as flaky to me as one of your pie crusts. What's on your mind?"

"The thing is—you do have a really good alarm system there, don't you?"

"A house alarm? Yes. Surely you remember accidentally setting it off during your last visit."

"So you didn't take it out or anything. You're sure it's working like it should?"

"The perimeter doors and windows—they're armed right now. John has a zero-tolerance policy about forgetting the alarm at night. It's a cop thing."

"So then I guess—what?—does your alarm company test the system regularly?"

"Stephie, what is this? All the creepy murders here in the news lately?"

"No. Well, maybe. I don't know. Last night I had this dream about you guys. You and John, and the kids."

"What dream?"

"It was gross. I've never had a dream so gross, and I never want to have another one. I don't want to repeat the gory details, all right?"

"I can probably do without hearing them."

"This terrible thing happened, I think partly because your alarm wasn't working."

"It's working."

"The panic button," Stephie said. "Your system has one of those panic buttons, doesn't it?"

"On every keypad and every phone, too."

"The panic button wasn't working. Isn't that a strange detail for a dream? So specific?"

Nicky swiveled on her stool to look at the painting of Naomi, Zach, and Minnie. Their unfinished faces.

Stephanie didn't know anything about the tragedy John endured twenty years earlier, but after another hesitation, she said, "Is John doing okay?"

"What do you mean?"

"At work, you know. His health. And, like, things between you—everything good?"

"Stephie, things have always been great between us. John is the dearest man."

"Oh, I didn't mean anything like that. I love John, I really do. I meant . . . I don't know. It's the damn dream, Nicky. Been thinking about it all day. Trying to make sense of it. You know how dreams are. They don't make sense, you're not quite sure what you saw."

Nicolette looked past all the kids in the painting, to the half-seen mirror in the dark background. She had not included the shadowy figure that appeared in five of the photographic studies; but she half expected to see it in the portrait.

"I'll call the alarm company first thing in the

morning," she said. "I'll have them come out and test the system. Will that make you feel better?"

"It will, yeah," Stephie said. "It's just a dream. This is so silly. But I'll feel better."

"I will, too, now that you've dropped this centipede down my blouse."

"I'm sorry, Nicky. I didn't mean to spook you. Or I guess maybe I did a little. That dream really walloped me. Don't be angry with me, will you?"

"I couldn't be, Stephie. I love you to death."

"Jeez Louise, don't put it that way."

"Sorry. How's Harry?" He was Stephanie's husband. "Is he still wearing his mother's dresses?"

"His what?"

"His mother's dresses—and then stabbing sexy blondes in their showers?"

"Oh, I get it. Payback for John. I deserve it. No, Harry's still wearing his mother's dresses, but at least he's over the stabbing thing."

A few minutes later, after they hung up, Nicky sat staring at the unfinished painting of her children. John Singer Sargent was an impossible act to follow. Maybe that was the only problem. She put away her paints and brushes.

In the master bedroom, she stood beside the bed, watching her husband sleep, his face in the penumbra of the lamplight. He looked at peace. The Lunesta had done its job.

They hadn't made love enough lately. If the mood was wrong, you had to change it.

Using the front stairs, she went down to the second floor. She knocked at Zach's door, and then at Naomi and Minnie's. The kids were safe, doing their homework, though they all seemed more subdued than usual.

Although John would have walked the house, checking doors and the operable windows, Nicky toured the perimeter. She found nothing amiss.

In the living room, she stood for a while in front of the tall mirror in the baroque frame. Her reflection was considerably smaller than the shadowy form in the photographs.

The house had felt odd to her for so long that she had adjusted to the new atmosphere and didn't feel it as strongly as before. But the difference remained. Nicky couldn't have described the change to anyone; it was something you simply **felt,** for which all words were inadequate.

Suddenly she thought the oddest thing of all was that she hadn't mentioned this sense of wrongness to John, no matter how resistant to description it might be. It was as though the house, employing some strange power that no inanimate object should possess, schemed to isolate them, one from another, within its rooms.

46

THE TWO-STORY YELLOW-BRICK HOUSE STOOD in a neighborhood once a testimony to middle-class success, now evidence of the stalled dreams of generations, proof of the destructive avarice of a political class that promised prosperity while robbing rich and poor alike. Sidewalks were cracked, canted. Iron lampposts, spotted with rust, were overdue for painting. Street trees, untrimmed for so long that they could never be properly shaped by an arborist, stood leafless and raging at the bleak sky with mutant arms and bristling fists.

The house rose behind a spear-point iron fence from which some weapons had been borrowed. In summer the lawn would be nearly as dead as it was on this October twenty-fifth.

Inside, the rooms and hallways provided narrow passages between cliffs of heavy old furniture. In spite of air stale with years of cigarette smoke, John thought that all seemed scrupulously clean.

Peter Abelard, once a priest, still dressed rather like a cleric: black shoes, black slacks, black shirt, with a dark-gray cardigan. For some reason, he wore a watch on each wrist.

Fifty-six, with a lean ascetic face and ash-gray hair combed back from his pale forehead, he was so thin and dry that it seemed he might subsist entirely on the cigarettes that he lit one after the other, the new from the butt of the old.

The house belonged to his ninety-year-old mother. She was currently in the hospital, dying of terminal cancer. Abelard had lived here since the Church finished with him.

After the meeting with Father Bill on the fourteenth, John spent eight days trying to learn who had been the diocese's last exorcist and to locate him. The search became complicated because Abelard's mother lived as Mary Dorn, having re-married after her husband died.

Another three days were required to convince Abelard, by phone and by proxy, to agree to an interview. If he didn't fear policemen, he at least had developed an aversion to them.

In the kitchen where they conferred, the cabinets were pale green. Yellow Formica counters. The old stove and ovens were heavy, as if inspired by foundry works from the long-gone Soviet Union.

Yellow-and-white-checkered oilcloth covered the table at which they sat. A glass ashtray, a pack of cigarettes, a paperback copy of **The Deceiver,** by Livio Fanzaga, and a glass mug of dark coffee stood at Abelard's place. His resting arms had worn the table's oilcloth where he sat, suggesting he spent little time elsewhere in the house.

He offered John neither coffee nor a smoke. On the phone, he made it clear that this would not be an extended chat.

For the fourth time in less than two months, John told the story of Alton Turner Blackwood. He spared himself nothing, wanting to be certain that Peter Abelard had every fact that might matter.

He spoke also about the recent murders and his investigation, beginning with his first visit to Billy Lucas at the state hospital.

"Blackwood will kill another family in thirteen days. If I can't stop him, he'll kill **my** family December tenth. Twenty years ago this very day, I lost my parents and sisters. Not again. I'll do anything to save Nicky and the kids. I'll sell my soul to save them."

Abelard's eyes were the same gray as his hair, as if they had once been another color but, like the rest of him, had been steeped in smoke until they paled to this somber shade. They were clouded pools of sorrow and enduring dread.

"Never offer your soul even as a joke or in frustration. You think no one is listening or will make a deal. Someone is—and will."

"Then you still believe."

"I failed as a priest and as a man. But even in those days, I believed. Now more than ever. That is the horror of my position."

He drank some of the inky coffee, drew deeply on his cigarette, and exhaled a cloud of smoke that wreathed his head.

"Father Bill was right about one thing," Abelard said. "Your true enemy isn't a ghost. Rarely, a suffering soul in Purgatory might, by divine permission, be allowed to haunt this world to seek an intercession that will shorten his time of purification before he may enter Heaven. But no soul in Hell returns of his own volition."

Because Abelard's manner was authoritative but without a trace of pride or pretense, and because his voice seemed to be as haunted by remorse as it was seasoned by tobacco, John offered no argument.

"Blackwood's ritual tells us by whom you're truly confronted."

"There must've been a hundred interpretations of the ritual."

Abelard blew twin plumes from his nose. "Only

one interpretation is correct. The rest are the theories of psychologists. The quarters were symbolic payment to Death for ferrying the souls of Blackwood's victims to Hell, where he intended one day to follow them. The disc of feces was a mockery of the Eucharist, to solicit the favor of his satanic master. Each egg symbolizes the soul of the victim. The eggs contain the Latin word for 'servant,' because Blackwood was sending his victims to Hell to serve him there later. They're supposed to be his retinue, his entourage, his slaves for eternity."

John's voice thickened. "My parents and sisters aren't in Hell."

"I didn't say they were. Blackwood's ritual was his delusion. However, no doubt **he** was in Hell an instant after you killed him."

Homicide investigation was a career in madness. Sometimes John wondered if by association with so many murderous mad ones, he might one day come unhinged.

"What about the three bells he carried?"

Abelard said, "They tell us the identity of your true enemy. It has brought Blackwood with it, but it's the sole entity of power in this game. Do you believe in demons, Mr. Calvino?"

"Three months ago, I probably would have said no."

"You've been one of that 'wretched generation of enlightened men,' as Eliot called it. But now?"

"My life is all about evidence—knowing when it's true and when it's false, how it will play in court. I'm good at knowing all that. The evidence of Blackwood's return—I'd take that into court."

With the dexterity of long habituation, Abelard finessed a new cigarette from the pack one-handed, rolled it across his fingers in the manner of a magician manipulating a coin, brought it to his lips, and lit it from the glowing butt that then he crushed in the ashtray.

"The names of the important demons come from the Bible or have been handed down to us by tradition. Asmodeus, Beelzebub, Belial, Lucifer, Mephisto, Meridian, Zebulun . . . But often in an exorcism, when the exorcist demands and eventually succeeds in getting the malevolent spirit to identify itself, the name is also its purpose or the sin that it most particularly advocates—names like Discord, Envy, Jealousy or like Perdition, Disease, Ruin."

"Ruin," John said. "The word etched on Blackwood's bells."

"He sought the intercession of the demon Ruin to ensure that the souls of his victims were received for him in Hell. Most likely, the only soul he sent there was his own, but perhaps Blackwood's life of murder and nihilism pleased this entity called Ruin, and now perhaps it wishes to see the killer keep his promise to you."

"Why?"

"Why not? Evil doesn't exist to justify itself. It exists for the pleasure of corruption and the destruction of the innocent. Your children are the primary lure. Young and tender."

John half felt as if he were sinking in the smoky air like a drowner weighed down by lungs full of water. He breathed deeper, more often, to keep his mind clear.

"This thing, this Ruin, is in my house. I know it is. Can it be forced out with an exorcism?"

"Sometimes a residence or other buildings are exorcised, but not often. A demonic presence in a house can do little real harm. Noises in the night. Footsteps. Doors opening, closing. Foul smells. At worst, poltergeist phenomena—levitating furniture and that sort of thing. A demon isn't long satisfied with such simple play."

Gesturing, the hand with the cigarette was as pale as a ghost's hand except for two nicotine-stained fingers that were the singular greenish-yellow hue of the tissue of a corpse in a particular early stage of decomposition.

Peter Abelard said, "When it's in the flesh, however, the entity can do unlimited damage, both to the one possessed and to others. If this demon has brought Alton Blackwood's spirit from out of time into time once more, to keep the killer's promise, then it won't kill your family using the house, Mr.

Calvino. It will kill the family using someone in the house whom it has possessed."

John wanted to get up from the table and step out of this soiled atmosphere, onto the porch. A cold front as hard as ice itself had come in from the north the day before. Although the sky hung as dark as iron, the air was polished bright, invigorating. But a desperate hope kept him in his chair.

"Who is at risk of possession?" he asked.

"Anyone," said Abelard. "Perhaps not one who lives in a truly saintly state. Though even if I knew such people, I wouldn't need all my fingers to count them."

"But it must be easier to control a corrupt man like Andy Tane, to force him to commit murder and even suicide."

"You're speaking now of two different things. When the intention of possession is for the corruption and destruction of the one who is possessed, one weakness of character or another is enough to open the door to the entity."

With ashen eyes, Abelard watched as he tapped the burnt end from his Marlboro into the glass ashtray.

He continued: "The demon can exert such total control as you suggest only in those who have turned away from grace and isolated themselves from redemption."

"Billy Lucas was a fourteen-year-old boy. And not a bad boy, judging by the evidence."

"According to the law," Abelard said, "how old must a murderer be to stand trial as an adult?"

"In most jurisdictions, children are generally presumed to have the capacity to form criminal intent by the time they're fourteen."

"Then let's suppose they haven't fully developed the capacity to make sound moral judgments until that age, either. And even then, if they received no previous spiritual guidance, might they not be as vulnerable to total control as this Andy Tane you mentioned?"

"But surely an innocent child—"

"Most children may be innocent. Not all. You must have known or heard of a murderer even younger than Billy Lucas."

"This case several years ago. He was eleven."

"Who did he kill?"

"A ten-year-old playmate. And brutally."

With thumb and forefinger, Abelard plucked from his tongue a shred of tobacco that was stuck to it. He flicked it in the ashtray.

"You mentioned Mrs. Lucas's belief in the healing power of herbs and obelisks and geodes. There might be medicinal value in certain herbs but not in crystal animals and the rest. How passionately did she believe in this?"

John shrugged. "I don't know. She bought a lot of that stuff."

"Some of it voodoo."

"No. I didn't see any evidence of really bizarre stuff like that."

"Didn't you say the shop sold High John the Conqueror and wonder-of-the-world root?"

"They sold hundreds of herbs and powdered weeds. Those names stuck with me because they were unusual."

"They're both voodoo powders. Oh, I'm sure the shop isn't a nest of wild-eyed voodooists and that its proprietor has no malevolent intent. Sounds as if they sell the golden calf in a large variety of forms, and no doubt with the sincere conviction that they're doing good."

Events of the past few weeks had in a sense broken the world as John knew it into colorful fragments that, like the bits of glass at the bottom of a kaleidoscope, kept shifting to form an increasingly complex reality.

Abelard said, "But if Mrs. Lucas had true, deep faith in the efficacy of these things, perhaps her son came to share that faith."

"Maybe he did," John said. "He had several of these things in his room, but neither his sister nor his grandmother did. Why does it matter?"

For a long moment, Abelard watched a ribbon of smoke serpentine from the end of his cigarette, as if it might take form the way that the vapor from a magic lamp morphed into a genie.

Finally he said, "Have you ever heard that using a

Ouija board is dangerous because in trying to communicate with spirits, you can open the door to dark forces?"

"I've heard it often. I thought it might even be a warning on the Ouija-board box."

Abelard smiled thinly. "I don't believe the government's gone so far yet as to require that. There are many ways to open the door to that waiting darkness. And there are things we do that both open the door and also leave us vulnerable not merely to possession but also to loss of control. This Reese somebody you mentioned . . ."

"Reese Salsetto."

"He worshipped money and power," Abelard said. "That opened the door but also made him vulnerable to full enslavement. Likewise, an obsessive blind faith in material things—crystals, herbs, geodes, powdered weeds—can sometimes be like consulting a Ouija board. And if you believe only an obelisk and wonder-of-the-world root can save you, if you insist on attributing supernatural powers to objects that of course do not embody them, then you're not merely vulnerable. You are utterly without defenses."

As if so much talk of doors had opened one in the sky, a sudden wind blew down into the yard, conscripted an army of dead leaves into its service, and assaulted the nearby window with them, so that John startled, though Abelard did not. The wind's second breath was less ferocious than its previous one, and as the leaves fluttered away, the first snowflakes of the season flurried against the glass. They were as large as silver dollars and as intricate as lace mantillas.

John said, "If I unknowingly invited it, could I be possessed?"

Watching the snow at the window, Abelard murmured, "That's not the question you really want most to ask."

After a silence that drew the ex-priest's stare to him, John said, "If I was possessed, could I be controlled so completely that I might be used . . . to kill even the people I love the most?"

Through the haze of cigarette smoke, Abelard searched John's eyes and offered his own for searching. "I don't really know you that well, Mr. Calvino. I don't know you well enough to say."

"On December tenth, when I believe we're all at risk . . ."

"Yes?"

"Will you spend those twenty-four hours with us. In our home?"

"Eight years ago, I was unfrocked. Not excommunicated, but stripped of my priesthood and all authority."

"You still know the rituals of exorcism."

"I know them, but it would be a sacrilege for me to say them in my present condition."

With the nimble fingers of his free hand, Abelard extracted a fresh cigarette from the pack on the table, conveyed it to his lips, and lit it from the butt he was discarding.

John listened to himself talking as if listening to a third man at the table. "I'm terrified that I might be as defenseless as Billy Lucas. As defenseless as Andy Tane leaping from that window with Davinia. What if I feel it clawing into me . . . and I don't have the clarity of mind to do what Brenda Woburn did, the clarity to kill myself before it can take me and . . . use me?"

Peter Abelard savored his new Marlboro, blew a stream of smoke at the ceiling. Then he leaned forward in his chair, forearms on the table where the oilcloth was worn, and at last said, "You aren't alone. Remember, the forces of darkness are balanced by the light."

"I pray," John said.

"Good for you, Mr. Calvino. So do I. But beyond that—don't let fear blind you to every saving grace you're offered."

"Such as?"

"Such as any that may be."

"Please, for God's sake, I need more than riddles."

Abelard considered him for a long time, his eyes seeming more steely now than ashen. At last he said, "The vast majority of people who think they need an exorcism or who appear to need one—

they're suffering only psychological illnesses of one kind or another."

"This isn't just psychological."

"I didn't say it was, Mr. Calvino. I've done many exorcisms over the years where the demonic presence was real. And there were times when the demon was so powerful and so firmly embedded in its victim that no matter how often I performed the Ritual, no matter how very profound the prayers I employed, regardless of repeated blessings with the sacramentals—water, oil, salt—I failed utterly to force the possessing presence to depart. But then . . ."

His voice had grown quieter as he spoke, until his last two words were a whisper. And his stare drifted down from John's eyes to the smoke curling off his cigarette.

"But then?" John pressed.

"In each of those instances, when all seemed lost, I witnessed a divine visitation that expelled the demon from the afflicted. Divine visitations, Mr. Calvino. Is your willingness to believe so elastic that it can stretch that far?"

"I've seen the demonic. If it's real, so is its opposite."

Abelard said, "We don't live in Biblical times. God doesn't appear in burning bushes and the like. Angels no longer materialize in all their winged glory. I think the divine has taken a few steps back from humankind, perhaps in revulsion, perhaps because we don't deserve to look directly upon holy beings anymore. In my experience, when the divine enters the world these days from outside of time, it manifests discreetly through children and animals."

John waited as another smoky silence unraveled with Abelard lost in thought, but at last said, "Tell me, please."

"With the Ritual, I repeatedly failed to evict the presence in a twenty-year-old man whose possessor had caused him both terrible physical maladies and deep depression. Then a neighbor boy knocked on the door and insisted he could help, though the parents of the afflicted twenty-year-old had never breathed a word to anyone about my visits to their home or my purpose. This child was only five—but had a tremendous presence. He brought with him a hush, a sense of peace I can't convey with words— and he brought an ordinary drinking glass. He went to the bed and pressed the open end of the glass to the chest of the afflicted young man and said simply, 'Come out.' I watched a darkness rise out of the young man's chest and fill that glass, not like smoke or like anything but itself. The boy turned the glass over, and the darkness rose from the glass and hung in the air half a minute, less, before dissipating. The victim instantly cast off his long depression, and the horrible impetigo sores that antibiotics couldn't cure healed in minutes as I watched. In another case, a beautiful stray dog that no one had ever seen before wandered into the house and lay beside the afflicted, its head on his chest, and a similar cure was effected."

When after another silence Abelard made eye contact again, John said, "And your point?"

"Don't let your fear blind you to every saving grace you're offered," Abelard repeated. "Look to the children around you, animals if you have any. One of them may be an avatar of the divine."

As if Abelard had been unnerved by recalling these incidents, his hand trembled when he brought his Marlboro to his mouth.

John tried once more: "Even if you couldn't perform an exorcism or anything, if you could stay with us that day just to provide . . . your counsel."

As he smoked, Peter Abelard held John's stare again, this time as if daring him to look away. Eventually he said, "So . . . do you know why I was defrocked, Detective Calvino?"

"Yes," John said, and with dismay he realized that although he meant to manage his expression, a trace of disgust surely could be read in his face by anyone as perceptive as Abelard.

"That I broke my vow of chastity is bad enough. That I was drawn so strongly to teenagers is perhaps the more damning factor. Boys or girls—it didn't matter."

John looked at the window. The first fluffy wheels

of snow had spun away, and smaller flakes drove through the day.

When he could look at Abelard again, he said, "It's just that, I've nowhere else to turn."

"The watch on my right wrist," Abelard said, "keeps perfect time. The day in the date window is correct. The watch on my left wrist has no batteries."

He extended his left arm for John to look at the dead watch on his thin wrist.

"The date in the window has to be reset from time to time. You see now—it's set eight weeks and three days ago. I reset it every time I fall. It's my reminder of how weak I am. It shows the date on which I last had sex with a teenager."

Colder than the day beyond the window, John said, "Eight weeks, not eight years."

"That's right. I no longer get what I want by manipulation and by the betrayal of trust. I pay for it. I struggle to resist. I pray and fast and subject myself to pain, needles acutely placed, trying to force my mind off the path I am about to follow. Sometimes, I succeed. Sometimes not."

The pain in Peter Abelard's voice was exceeded only by the self-loathing. John could hardly bear to meet the man's bleak eyes as he listened to his confession, but he knew too well how anguishing it was to despise oneself, and he could not look away.

"Then I go to those parts of the city where men

go for this," Abelard continued. "You know the places I mean. Any policeman must. I seek out the young ones, the runaways. Boys or girls, it still doesn't matter. They're already selling themselves, so I haven't taken their innocence. I've just corrupted them further, as if that matters much in the ledgers of Hell."

John slid his chair back from the table. He didn't quite have the strength to get up at once.

"No demon rides me, Mr. Calvino. There's only me in me. I seek redemption so imperfectly. You have a boy of thirteen. My eyes roam over what they wish, as if I've no control of them. Does your eleven-year-old look a bit more mature than her years? There's no demon in me, but God help you, Mr. Calvino, you don't want me in your house."

John got to his feet.

Abelard breathed dragon plumes upon the table and said, "Can you find your own way out?"

"Yes."

As John reached the doorway between the kitchen and the hall, Abelard said, "If you really pray—"

"Yes, I'll pray for you."

"Not for me," Abelard said. "For my mother suffering with the cancer. Pray for her. Surely it'll mean more coming from you than from me."

As John followed the canyons of the crowded house, the looming furniture seemed more Gothic than before, hulking and dire, and the scent of cigarette smoke on the air seemed now as bitter as ipecac on the tongue.

Outside, the frozen sky, the freezing air in brisk motion. The cleansing sluice of falling snow. The black arachnid limbs of dormant trees in falling snow. Barren yard and battered fence and broken concrete and falling snow.

At the curb, he stood beside his car, reluctant to get in behind the wheel. The cold pinched his face, and snow lasted on his lashes until he blinked.

Twenty years to the day.

Twenty years and counting.

Breathing in snow, breathing out the stale scent of cigarettes, he could not at once get rid of the smell of smoke.

Overhead, wind whispered through the naked limbs and shook the younger branches, rattling them like the fragile bones of small dead things.

Twenty years to the day.

And he had nowhere to turn for help.

The time had come to sit with Nicolette, to share with her his once irrational-seeming fear that Alton Turner Blackwood was in the world again, to tell her the one thing he had withheld from her about his confrontation with the killer on that long-ago night. The time had come to make some plan for the tenth of December, if any plan could possibly be made.

He got in the car, started the engine, drove into the street.

This evening, he would pray for Peter Abelard's mother, for Abelard as well. He would pray for his lost family, for his family still alive, for himself, for everyone who knew pain, which meant everyone who wore a human face.

From the journal of Alton Turner Blackwood:

The awkward boy stood on the patio, in the shadow of the big maidenhair tree, which in those days he believed had been named for the two maidens who sat playing cards at the table before him: the beautiful Regina, his aunt, and her even more beautiful daughter, Melissa.

Smug Regina took a wicked pleasure in educating the boy about his family history, which was in part buried in the secret cemetery that he had found in a woodland clearing. So Jillian had given birth to Marjorie, and out of Marjorie had come Regina and Anita, the boy's own mother, all fathered by Teejay. When Anita and Regina, fraternal twins, were in their turn impregnated, Regina produced Melissa, whose exquisite beauty seemed further proof of Teejay's insane theory about selective inbreeding. But the boy's arrival hardly a month later was a dramatic refutation.

Teejay wanted to kill the newborn boy and bury him in the woods—or at least commit him to an institution, but Anita rebelled. If Teejay wanted to continue his experiment with her, if he wanted to father other children with her, he must allow her son to live. And thus the boy's mother bought his survival.

In the decade following, Regina gave birth to three sons, but Teejay had no interest in sons, who could not bear his children and thereby help him distill his unique genes into a perfect beauty never before known on earth. He smothered them in infancy and buried them in the woods.

"Why do you let him?" the boy demanded.

"What use do I have for sons, either?" Regina asked.

"I mean, why do you let him touch you?"

"It's what I've always known. I've known nothing else. It's his religion, and it's mine. What do I have if I leave? What do I have if I tell and destroy everything? There's luxury in Crown Hill, and I'm accustomed to luxury."

The boy thought that the estate staff must know, but Regina was amused by his naiveté. People routinely blinded themselves to truth, she said. Besides, each year, there were a few three-day weekend parties at Crown Hill, and among the houseguests were men who might have seduced a young girl. Teejay's daughters also traveled with him from time to time, and perhaps he was not a diligent chaperone during those excursions. Teejay had been born at the turn of the century, when midwives attended virtually every birth, and he himself midwifed the births at Crown Hill; no physicians ever saw that the "stillborn" male children were, in fact, smothered in the crèche. If a member of the staff became suspicious, he might be retired young with a most generous pension, an irresistibly fat monthly check that made his easy life dependent on his silence. Or perhaps he would leave his position without notice—to trade his handsome room and private bath in the comfortable staff quarters for a new bed and a long sleep in the woodland clearing.

"In the woods," the boy said. "My mother, your sister."

"My competition," said Regina.

Under the maidenhair tree, in the privileged afternoon, in the golden light of a sun swelling toward the horizon as if to burst, the awkward boy stood as though rooted, the ugly boy, towering and rough and shatter-faced, watching the elegant hands of the beautiful women as they dealt and received the cards, moisture beading on their tall glasses of iced tea, lemon slices and leaves of mint, their skin as flawless as that of the bisque-porcelain figurines in the drawing-room display case, and the ugly boy was pierced by a sharp yearning as the women ordered their cards, not yearning for the women but for something he could not name, watching as Melissa put upon the table four threes, one in each suit, and with them won the hand, watching as Regina totaled their scores, the fluid shuffling of the deck, the languid dealing of the cards, their grace and catlike confidence, their glittering eyes as Regina recounted how her sister, the mother of the ugly boy, wound up dead and buried in the wildwood.

47

THE CITY HAD KNOWN SNOW IN OTHER OC-
tobers, but usually only flurries, at most two or
three inches. The forecast called for this storm to lay
down six inches, which would make it one of the
deeper snows of October but not a record blizzard.

While the kids were in the library, enduring math
with Leonid Sinyavski, John and Nicolette sat in
armchairs in his ground-floor study, where the
gallery of birthday photographs confronted him
with a poignant reminder of all that he might lose.
Beyond the window, the sky was invisible now, scattering white petals by the million, and toward the
back of the yard, the deodar cedar had begun to
robe itself in winter.

Quietly and without excuses, John told Nicky
that he was in his second thirty-day leave, that he
had been pretending to go to work as usual but instead had undertaken an investigation of a personal

nature. As crisply as he would lay out the facts of any case to Nelson Burchard or to an assistant district attorney, he presented them to her, beginning with his first visit to Billy Lucas at the state hospital.

She realized why he had hoped to spare her the worry of all this until he understood the situation as fully as possible, and his secrecy neither offended nor disappointed her. Like all good artists, Nicky could empathize with the fear and anguish of others. Like every **great** artist who had been able to maintain a human perspective, she didn't believe that she was the center of the world, to be included in everything first above all others; she lived instead with the conviction that her talent and her success required of her both humility and a generosity of spirit.

And at last he told her the one thing he had withheld from her all these years, the last thing Blackwood had said before John shot him: **You'll be a daddy someday. Then I'll come back and use your wife and kids harder than I used your slutty sisters here tonight.**

"I never told you more than that I shot him. Well . . . I shot him point-blank in the face. He was dead as he fell. But I stood over him and emptied the gun into his head. I shot him and shot him, Nicky, I shot him until he didn't have a face at all."

"Good," Nicky said. "And good that you didn't tell me the last thing he said to you. Why should that have been in my head all the lovely months I carried Zach, Naomi, Minnie? I only love you more for sparing me that craziness—until you couldn't anymore."

Although John expected her to be understanding, Nicky surprised him by her readiness to accept the possibility of a supernatural threat, but then she **stunned** him with the revelation that she, too, sensed something uncanny if not malevolent in the house and that she'd had experiences that felt occult in nature. The man glimpsed in the mirror—**Kiss me**—before it seemed to explode in her face. Perhaps the same man again in the photographic studies for the portrait of the children.

Nicky's inability to finish that painting, her distressing sense that somehow it had become a study of loss and despair, rocked John so hard that he felt as if some many-legged horror crawled the nape of his neck. When reflexively he reached back to clap the nonexistent insect, he discovered that his hands had gone cold and clammy.

Too disturbed to remain seated, he got up from the chair. He stepped to the window, peering intently at the snow-flocked backyard, half expecting to see some scaled and horned and lantern-eyed demonic beast slouching through the storm, forty-seven days ahead of schedule and hungry for children.

Nicky said, "It's like the house—or whatever's in it—has been working damn hard to keep us isolated from one another, playing to our fear—and our love—in just the right way to turn each of us inward."

He heard her get up from her chair. When she spoke again, she sounded as if she was at the gallery wall, but he didn't turn toward her. For some reason, the storm increasingly disquieted him, and he didn't want to look away from it.

"You never read Blackwood's journal?" she asked.

"No. He was dead. I didn't want to read his self-justifications, his craziness. I didn't want to let him even deeper into my head. I don't know . . . it would have been like being there in the house again with everyone dead."

"He couldn't have written about that before you shot him."

"No. He couldn't. But that's how I felt. The therapist at the orphanage got a Xerox of it from the police. He read it to better understand Blackwood, to get some idea what my confrontation with him might have been like. He told me a little about it, but he never read to me from it."

"I want to read it," Nicky said. "I mean . . . I don't want to, but I have to. How can we get a copy? Would the therapist still have it, do you think? Or the police back there?"

"Maybe. I don't know. That website where Billy Lucas got the photos of my mom and dad, my sisters. It's devoted to serial killers and mass murderers. Maybe you could look there."

"Do you remember the name of the site?" When he gave it to her, she said, "Let's use your computer," and he heard her going to his desk.

Turning from the window, John said, "That's all ancient history. The only thing it can do for me is just twist my nerves tighter. I'm already so jumpy I can't think straight anymore. And I damn sure need to think straight." He glanced at his wristwatch—3:38. "Better tell Walter and Imogene to leave early. The streets are already a mess. They need to get home before there's an accident clogging every intersection."

At the desk, Nicky switched on the computer. "I'll let you know what I find."

"Crazy is what you'll find. Madness, evil, the dark side of the moon. You won't have much appetite by dinner."

As he opened the door to the hall, she spoke his name, and he turned to her.

"There's never been anything we couldn't get through together," she said. "We'll get through this somehow. Father Bill isn't the whole Church, and neither is Peter Abelard. We've got forty-seven days. We'll make a plan. You and me against the world—that seems like a fair match to me."

Her smile charmed even now.

John said, "I love you," and refrained from saying, **Baby, it's not just you and me against the world. It's you and me against Hell itself.**

The website offered a free side and a pay side. Of course the former proved to be a tease, and the latter contained the deep archives.

When Nicky discovered that Alton Turner Blackwood's handwritten journal was available for viewing by subscribers only, she used a credit card to sign up.

The first thing she noticed about the document was that the killer's handwriting was so neat as to be almost fussy, as though he believed that meticulous penmanship imposed rationality on his insane musings. And he dotted each letter **i** with a little zero.

After sending Walter and Imogene home for the day in spite of their insistence that they were leaving too much work undone, John went to the second floor, to the library, intending to suggest that Professor Sinyavski might also want to leave early to avoid the worst of the snowstorm. Instead of a math lesson in progress, he found the library deserted, the lights off.

In his current state of mind, any variation from the children's routine alarmed him. He hurried along the hallway to the girls' room, knocked, received no answer, knocked again, then opened the door. No one there.

He crossed the hall to Zach's door, rapped sharply, and was relieved to hear his son say, "Come in."

John opened the door, leaned into the room, and saw Zach with a drawing tablet. "So you've learned all the math there is?"

"Just about. But Professor Sinyavski wanted to leave early. He won't drive in snow. Remember last year, his girlfriend brought him on snowy days, the one with the huge hair and—"

"Where are the girls?"

"Naomi was doing her full Naomi thing about the first snow of the season. I think Minnie went outside with her."

Downstairs, John hurried from window to window, searching for the girls in one yard and another—but he found them in the mud room, where they had just taken off their boots and hung up their coats. Their noses were red, their cheeks pink, and their eyes lively.

"It's just too little snow yet, a pathetic fleece, you can't **do** anything really memorable," Naomi explained. "You can't even make a good snow angel yet, and just forget a snowball fight."

"I told her," Minnie said.

"She did. She told me. She always tells me."

"I'm waiting for when you listen," Minnie said.

"You better be a good waiter, Mouse."

"And I'll probably have to live like a hundred years before it happens. Don't call me Mouse."

"Don't either of you go out there later without me. All right?"

"You want a snowball fight?" Minnie asked.

"I always win them, don't I?" John said.

"We were littler last year," Naomi said. "We'll whup your butt this time."

"Maybe you will. Until then, stay in the house."

⁂

Freed early from the unspeakable torment of math class, Naomi felt her spirits soar to rare heights. But then she was brought down again by the crashing disappointment of the too-slow snow and the humiliation of Sister Half-Pint being proved right. Oh, she wasn't depressed, never depressed, she didn't have time for that, but she wasn't exactly in the mood to tie a dozen ribbons in her hair and cartwheel through the halls.

Nine days had passed since mysterious Melody beamed up or down, or sideways, or whatever, smack into the civic auditorium to give her the totally splendid attaché case full of the so-called magical items that, in all fairness, were pretty convincingly magical-looking. The frost might be on the boring briar rose, but Melody didn't seem to know one thing about how to **pace** a truly thrilling adventure. Melody would never be Louisa May Alcott. At this rate, by the time they flew between the tedious worlds, Minnie **would** be a hundred, and

Naomi herself would be too senile to be the princess of anywhere.

After coming in from the useless wisp of a snowstorm, Naomi was at loose ends for forty minutes, not sure what she wanted to do, just bumping around the house like a thoroughly frustrated moth looking for an open window. But then at 4:20, she bumped her way into the library, and she decided the best of all best things to do would be to read the **third** novel in the series about Drumblezorn the dragon and his not-anymore-completely-savage young student, the Joan of Arc wannabe.

As she located the novel and took it from the shelf, someone tapped on her shoulder, and when she turned—speak of the devil—there was **Melody**! Her dress was as drab as ever, but her face seemed more animated than Naomi had previously seen it, her eyes virtually shining with excitement.

"M'lady, I am proud of you—that you have put your kingdom above your family and kept the secret of the attaché case."

That didn't sound quite right to Naomi. "Well, I'm a zippered-lips champion at keeping secrets, but I wouldn't put my kingdom above my family, and why would I have to, anyway?"

"But you have, and that's the glorious thing. Because . . . the time has come. Tonight's the night. Very soon, we fly between the worlds."

48

NICOLETTE SAT AT JOHN'S DESK, READING Alton Turner Blackwood's journal in a hologrammatic format on the computer, at first with academic interest but then with grim fascination. As she turned the electronic pages, a steadily intensifying dread gripped her. Her respect grew for the formidable threat that the malformed man had been during his lifetime and might still be in death.

She had not expected to be so rattled. Yes, she believed every word John told her. And she'd had uncanny experiences of her own. And Stephanie's worried phone call on the night of the nineteenth, six days earlier, must have been something like a heads-up warning from Providence. Yet Nicky hoped that in reading the journal she would be relieved to find that, like most sociopathic killers, Blackwood was essentially a bug intelligence, bright perhaps and dangerous, but as narrowly focused as a praying mantis stalking prey, as a spider whose world was limited to its web. If his inner landscape was like those of uncounted butchering maniacs before him, it would be harder to credit the notion that he, of all such bloody-minded bugs in human form, should be the one empowered to return from Beyond, with or without demonic assistance.

She was a woman of faith but in a modern sense that until now allowed for Heaven but doubted Hades, that welcomed the notion of angels but relegated devils to cartoons and horror movies. After half an hour of reading Blackwood's lurid account of his origins, however, she knew in her bones that she needed to take seriously the idea of his enduring spirit. He wasn't as easy to dismiss as Big Foot or vampires, or the Loch Ness monster. He was like the presence you felt in the dark when you woke past midnight, that was still there but not visible when you switched on the lamp. He was akin to the thing that pricked your intuition at twilight in a lonely place, pricked it so sharply that you felt something like flukes twitching in your blood.

Beyond the computer screen, at the other end of the room, she half saw someone hurry past the window, through the snow, across the back terrace. Maybe Walter and Imogene hadn't left yet, and he was tending to some final task before heading home to beat the worst of the storm.

A minute later a door closed so quietly that Nicky

almost didn't hear it. Then quick soft footsteps along the hallway.

She looked up, expecting someone to push open the study door, which was three-quarters closed. As the footsteps passed and then receded, she called out, "John?"

Whoever it might be, he evidently hadn't heard her. He didn't double back to see if she wanted something.

Although Blackwood's journal fascinated her in a deeply morbid way, she was spending too much time on the early pages. She could go back later and read with more care if she wished. Now she skimmed through the seemingly endless lines of painstaking penmanship, in search of what the killer had written about his reasons for switching from single murders to the destruction of entire families.

⎯⎯✦⎯⎯

Preston Nash is sitting alone in his basement apartment, eating corn chips with salsa, drinking beer, and playing Grand Theft Auto, really **living** the action, when suddenly for no reason at all, he says out loud, "Come to me."

The next thing he knows, he's got the key to the Calvino house in a pants pocket, and he's driving his parents' second car, which he is forbidden to operate even though he's thirty-six and a grown man.

Preston has suffered fugues in the past, when because of drugs or booze he slips into a dissociative state. Then he does things of which he's less than half aware, hours of activity that later he dimly remembers or can't recall at all. But he hasn't chugged enough beer or popped enough pills to be in that condition now.

Besides, this is different from a fugue. Weirder. He's acutely aware of what he's doing, and he doesn't want to be doing it, but he can't stop. He's compelled to get to the Calvino house. He feels as if his life depends on it, but he doesn't know why. In spite of the storm, the world around him isn't blurred and remote. It **is** black-and-white, which has nothing to do with the snow and the bare trees, because all the other vehicles on the road are either black or white, or a shade of gray, as are all the signs for businesses and all the clothes that the pedestrians are wearing. The only color in the world right now seems to be Preston, what he wears, and the car he drives.

He isn't frightened. He thinks he ought to be in a fear sweat, vibrating like one of those coin-operated massaging beds in a cheesy motel, but something tells him that he should remain calm, that he's all right. The times he's ever been afraid, he's always been sober. This thing that's happening to him isn't like being drunk, yet it's just **enough** like being drunk to keep the tangles combed out of his nerves.

So he parks a block from the Calvino house. He walks to their place as briskly as a punctual man with an important appointment to keep. He is not a graceful guy. Most of the time, the world seems to Preston to be the deck of a ship in a storm, and he is pleased with himself if he can just stay on his feet and not be washed overboard. But now he strides along the snow-covered sidewalk without a misstep. Onto the lawn and along the north side of the handsome white-brick house. Across the back terrace to a windowless door. It's locked. He uses his key.

Taken.

The rider mounts this horse for the first time since the fifth of October, and though it rode Preston secretly back then, it makes itself known to him now. He submits to control instantly, even more obedient to his master than an avatar in a video game is obedient to whoever holds the joystick, and color floods back into the world around him.

Leaving his key in the door, Preston enters the mud room. The girls' boots stand on a rubber mat that glistens with snowmelt, and their coats hang from wall hooks. Preston closes the door behind him. Along one wall is a utility cabinet with upper doors, drawers below. Preston, who has never been here before, opens exactly the right drawer and removes from it a claw hammer.

Two inner doors lead out of the mud room, one to the kitchen, one to the ground-floor hallway. Preston enters the hall and hurries as quietly as possible toward the front of the house.

As he passes a nearly closed door, Nicolette Calvino calls out, "John?"

He could stride into the study and smash her skull to mush. But he understands that she is a most desirable bitch and therefore must be used first. Later, when she's begging for death, it might **then** be fun to hammer her face.

Preston has no problem with that if it's what his rider wants. It'll just be like one of his porn films crossed with one of the **Saw** movies except that it'll be fully 3-D and more intimate.

The foyer features a small walk-in closet. Preston steps into it and quietly closes the door behind him.

Using Preston's voice, the rider tells him **"Stay,"** as if he were a well-trained dog. In this condition, he's more like a car than like a dog, a reliable Honda left in park with the engine idling. He is just Preston now, not Preston and Alton and Ruin, but he's Preston in stasis, like a guy in a movie on the TV after the viewer presses the pause button. He knows he's Preston, and he knows that he's in a coat closet, and he is aware of holding a claw hammer. He also knows that, whatever happens, he won't really be responsible for it, more of an observer than a participant, although a keenly interested and easily entertained observer. Preston has been an observer all of his life, rather than a participant, so there is nothing new about his current circumstances, except that he can't go get a beer anytime he wants one.

⸺⸎⸺

Minnie stood in her room, beside her play table, staring at the LEGO thing. White, about three inches thick, six inches in diameter, it resembled a big rice cake, except smooth, and stood on edge like a coin. It shouldn't hold together. It should spill apart into a bunch of pieces, but it didn't.

For two years, she had been doing this LEGO thing; she didn't know why. It started when she got home from the hospital after being so sick everyone thought she was dying.

Well, in a way, it started while she was in the hospital. . . .

She had a high fever that the usual drugs couldn't lower. Fever but also chills, drenching sweats, terrible headaches. The thirst was almost the worst of it. Sometimes she was so thirsty, as though she'd eaten a pound of salt, and she couldn't get enough water. Most of the time, they were giving her fluids through a needle stuck in a vein in her arm, but that didn't relieve the thirst. They had to monitor her water intake because sometimes she would drink until her belly bloated painfully, and in spite of the pain, she desperately wanted to drink still more—even in her dreams.

She had a lot of strange dreams in the intensive-care unit, some of them while she was awake. Before she went into the hospital, she didn't know what the word **delirium** meant, but she sure could define it by the time she got well and came home. The dreams, whether she was awake or asleep, often had to do with thirst: deserts where every promise of water turned out to be a mirage; pitchers and spigots from which poured only sand; being chased by some kind of monster on a hot day along dry riverbeds; a forest of parched dead trees surrounding a dusty clearing where brittle bones were scattered in the withered grass, where the only water was pooled at the bottom of an open grave, but when she scrambled into the grave, **that** water proved to be a mirage, as well, and something started shoveling spadefuls of chalky dirt onto her, the same half-seen monster who had chased her along the waterless river.

Delirium was funny, not ha-ha funny, but weird funny. Delirious, you were sure that not only were monsters trying to kill you but so were some people who were actually trying to help you, like Kaylin Amhurst, the intensive-care nurse. In Minnie's hallucinations and nightmares, while in the ICU, she thought Nurse Amhurst was trying to poison her.

Sometimes, usually near the end of Minnie's worst nightmares and hallucinations, Father Albright appeared. She loved Father Albright very much. He was the super-best person she knew besides Mom, Daddy, Naomi, and Zach. He retired not long before Minnie became ill, and Father Bill took his place, so maybe she gave Father Albright a role in her fever dreams because it was the only way she could see him anymore. He was the one good thing in the dreams. He always gave her water, and it never turned out to be salt or sand.

That was a bad year, not just because of her illness. A month before Father Albright retired and went away, Willard died. Daddy and Lionel Timmins were almost killed by a bad guy, too, and though they got an award for valor, Daddy was nevertheless nearly killed, which scared Minnie for a long time. Maybe the only good thing that year was Zach deciding he just **had** to become a marine.

Minnie didn't know whether the LEGO shapes were a good or a bad thing. She first saw them in her fever dreams, except they weren't made of LEGO blocks. They were just shapes seen from a distance; then she found herself walking around on them, as if they were buildings, and eventually she was walking around inside of them. On these tours, she knew that she had shrunk like Alice in Wonderland, until she was the tiniest thing in all of creation, and that the strange shapes she explored were what lay at the bottom of the universe, holding it up.

Her mother said that three great powers kept the universe going. The first and strongest was God. Each of the two additional powers was as strong as the other: love and imagination. Of the three, God and love were always good. Imagination, however, could be good or bad. Mozart imagined great music into existence. Hitler imagined death camps and built them. Imagination was so powerful that you had to be careful because you could imagine things into existence that you might regret. Everything in the universe was an idea before it was real. Walking inside the shapes in her delirium dreams, Minnie knew they were the ideas from which everything had started, although she didn't know then— or now—what that **meant**. After all, she was only eight.

Turning away from the LEGO construction, she went to the window and watched the snow falling through the bare limbs of the scarlet oak. The weather forecast was wrong. They would get more than a foot of snow, not six inches. She didn't know from where this certainty came, but she was confident about her prediction. It was just one of those things she knew.

Since shortly after coming in from the snow with Naomi, Minnie had been in a spooky mood. This was one of those times she sensed unseen presences so strongly that she knew sooner rather than later, they would become visible to her, like at the convenience store, the guy with half his face shot off. This time would be worse than that.

Something moved on the south lawn, at first partly screened by the branches of the oak. Then it came into the open, and she saw that it was Willard. He looked up at her in the window.

"Good old dog," she whispered. "Good old Willard."

Willard stood looking up through the falling snow for a long moment, and then he approached the house.

Minnie lost sight of him. She wondered if he had come inside.

Roger Hodd, reporter for the **Daily Post,** has a date to meet his wife, Georgia, for dinner after she gets off work. She has suggested his favorite restaurant, though it isn't a place she particularly likes. From this, Hodd infers that she intends to ask for a divorce over dessert. She has long desired her freedom from him. Because of his temper and caustic wit, she hopes that she will be less verbally abused in a public place than in a private one. She won't be abused at all because Hodd is going to let her sit in the restaurant alone until she realizes she's been stood up. He'll give her a divorce, but only after he's made her **desperate** for it.

He's in a hotel room with a hooker, whom he's paid in advance, and he's undressed only so far as unbuttoning one cuff of his shirt, when he says, "Come to me." The girl on the bed is wearing nothing but her panties, and she says with all the seductive allure of Miss Piggy the Muppet, "Why don't **you** come to **me**? I'm **really** ready." He's already buttoned his cuff and snatched his heavy leather coat off the armchair. He says, "I've just discovered I've got a lower tolerance for ugly than I thought," and she curses him as he leaves the room.

He's hurrying along the hotel corridor before he fully realizes what he has just done, and he has no idea why he did it. She wasn't ugly. And even if she was, he's got a reasonably high tolerance for ugly if the rest of the package is okay. He's been drinking since eleven this morning, but not heavily. Sipping. He's not drunk. He's been drinking so long that he hardly ever gets drunk anymore, not that he realizes.

By the time he's in his car, piloting through billowing waves of snow, he feels like Richard Dreyfuss in that old science-fiction movie **Close Encounters of the Third Kind**. He's obsessed with getting somewhere, not to some remote butte in Wyoming where the mother ship is going to land, but somewhere he can't name. He ought to be afraid, but he's not. For one thing, he's never afraid. He's one tough sonofabitch. Anyway, he's been trying to slow-kill himself with booze and neurotic women for years, which is a far more gruesome way to go than setting yourself on fire. For another thing, every time the weirdness of this compulsion makes him breathe fast and his heart races, this soothing voice in his head sort of croons a wordless lullaby, and he grows calm once more.

He parks in an upscale neighborhood, near a white-brick house, which is apparently his destination. He walks around the back of the place, through the snow-covered yard, across a terrace to a door in which a key sticks out of the deadbolt lock. As he opens the door and extracts the key from the lock, a cold black something slams into his head, or at least that's how it feels. Then it's **inside** his head but his skull is intact. He screams, but it's a silent scream because he doesn't control his own voice anymore.

As he steps into a mud room and closes the door behind him, he keeps trying to scream, because he's terrified as he never was during the trip here. Fright overwhelms him as he proceeds out of the mud room into a kitchen, through a dining room, toward the front of the house, and a cold sea of horror rises over him because he's not hard-assed Roger Hodd anymore, he's now somebody's bitch.

Naomi stepped out of the walk-in closet in the guest bedroom and offered the attaché case to Melody. "You'll see everything's exactly the same as when you gave it to me. So the eggs—what're they about, with our names on them? And there's something in them, I couldn't figure what it is. Eggs are very symbolic, they can symbolize about a thousand things. Are these symbolic? What's magic about them, how do they work? Is the frost still on the briar rose, and what does that mean, anyway?"

"M'lady, all your questions will be answered soon. Tonight we travel on the storm."

"On the storm?" Naomi said, liking the sound of that—**travelers on the storm.**

Melody's pretty-enough face was so animated now that she became truly beautiful, much more full of **life** than she'd been before. Her molasses eyes were amazing, bright and quick, as if shining with an inner light. And her voice, always captivating, always musical and positively dripping with mystery, sounded more enchanting than ever:

"This is not a natural storm, m'lady. This is a conjured snow that falls hereabout but also accumulates in the lonely space between worlds, drifting sideways across time until it bridges this place to your kingdom, so we can glide home as smoothly as oil on glass, as quick as quicksilver."

Naomi thrilled to every word but one. "Glide? I thought we were going to fly between the worlds?"

"We do both at once, m'lady, as you'll understand when you see the cross-time sleigh with all its great sails filled and taut with the winds of time."

Naomi was so dizzy with language and fantasy and possibilities that she couldn't speak. Then she remembered a word that a kind of witless girl in **The Tale of Despereaux** often said when bewildered, and it amused Naomi to use it to express her stupefaction: **"Gar!"**

"Now you must accompany me at once to the top of the house to make further preparations, m'lady. Come, let's go, while there is no cat afoot to espy our destination."

Melody flew to the guest-bedroom door, and Naomi hurried after her, wondering if she would ever be able to speak as fabulously as did, apparently, all the people of her kingdom.

They dashed along the second-floor hallway to the back stairs, hastened to the third floor, breezed across Mother's studio, darted through another door onto the landing at the head of the main stairs.

When Naomi realized that Melody intended to enter the master bedroom, she said, "Wait! That's my parents' private space. You need an invitation to enter."

"We must make the preparations at the top of the

house, m'lady. Later, we can only leave from the top of the house."

"The studio is also at the top of the house."

"But the studio is inadequate." Indicating the master-suite door, she said, "Anyway, there's no one within."

"How do you know?"

"I know as I know."

"At least we have to knock," Naomi said. "It's the rule."

Melody smiled mischievously, fisted her right hand, and rapped silently on the air. Before them, the door swung open magically.

Against her better judgment and in violation of the rules, but giggling with delight, Naomi followed Melody into the master suite and closed the door behind them.

Here at the end of the afternoon, with twilight nearing, the world outside was white with whirling snow, but the master bedroom lay mostly in shadows. As Melody approached the bed with the attaché case, both nightstand lamps switched on as though attended by an invisible chambermaid, and there was just enough lovely soft light.

"You're going to have to teach me stuff like that," Naomi said.

"Your powers will return when your memory is restored, m'lady. And this evening you will learn many things. Many amazing things. You'll learn more this evening than you have learned all your life so far."

Melody put the attaché case on the bedspread and then patted the spot beside it, indicating that Naomi should sit there.

Naomi perched on the edge of the bed, legs dangling. "Now what?"

"Now you will wait here, right there exactly where you're sitting, while I go downstairs and manifest quite dramatically to each member of your family, convince them that this is a night of magic, and bring them here one at a time."

"Can't I go? I want to see you manifest quite dramatically."

"I must do this as it is written it must be done," Melody said with a faint note of admonition. "All must be done according to the guidance of the royal mage."

With that, she stepped lively across the room, exited onto the landing, and closed the door, leaving Naomi alone.

Naomi wished that she could shut off her overloaded mind for five minutes and allow her **legions** of spinning thoughts to slow to a speed that wouldn't dizzy her. At least a thousand thoughts were in motion, each rotating on its axis but also revolving around the center of her mind like planets around a sun. All of them were such dazzling thoughts, too, all of them wonderful, except two or three fraidy-cat thoughts that simply weren't worthy of her, compliments of Minnie's infectious pessimism. Naomi was determined not to let those yeah-buts or what-ifs grow into ugly little mind warts that would spoil the mood and the magic. She was a positive person, a believer in believing, a first-chair flautist, and though she didn't know much about math, she knew an enormous amount about magic.

She watched the snow falling diagonally past the window. The wind had gentled to an easy breeze. The ceaselessly unraveling snow was a calming sight.

A deep quiet filled the master suite. Naomi tried to let the quiet seep into her noisy mind.

<hr>

With a growing disquiet, John roamed the ground floor and the basement, not exactly searching for anything, but half expecting to find something important or even ominous, though he had no idea what that might be.

Eventually, in the kitchen again, he used the security-system keypad beside the back door to set the perimeter alarm. Night lay almost an hour away, but none of them had a reason to go out in this weather. He had told the girls to stay inside. Zach had seemed happily occupied with his drawing tablet. John felt better with the alarm on. He didn't allow himself the illusion that they were now perfectly safe. No one anywhere was ever perfectly safe.

Forty-seven days remained before the tenth of December. John should not yet feel that a countdown clock was urgently ticking—but he felt it anyway. He could almost **hear** it.

When darkfall came, the lighted house would be a fishbowl to anyone outside in the night. He decided to close all the draperies and pleated shades, starting in the kitchen. As he went, he checked to be sure that the door locks and window latches were engaged.

This was the anniversary of the worst night of his life, and each window he inspected reminded him that his parents and sisters perished while he lived because of his selfishness and weakness.

On school nights, Marnie and Giselle went upstairs to bed at nine o'clock. John's parents were teachers, early to rise, and they were usually asleep by ten.

Because he was fourteen, John was permitted to stay up later, but that night he pled weariness and retired when his sisters did, at nine. He sat in the dark until he heard his dad and mom close their door at nine-forty.

His room lay on the opposite side of the hall from his parents' room. His window looked onto the front-porch roof.

He slipped out of the house through the window and slid shut the well-waxed bottom sash. Because it wasn't latched, he could open it without difficulty when he returned.

During the past few months, he had sneaked out often. He was so practiced at it that a cat couldn't have split the scene any more quietly than John did.

The thick limb of a tree overhung the north end of the porch. He reached up, grabbed it, lifted his feet off the roof, and went hand over hand just far enough to be away from the house. Then he dropped to the grass. When he came back, he would climb the tree to the porch roof and enter his room, so ready for sleep that he would pass out as his head hit the pillow.

Her name was Cindy Shooner. She lived two blocks away, and he could be at her place three minutes after leaving home.

Mr. and Mrs. Shooner were dysfunctional, Cindy said. They hated their jobs, they hated their relatives, and they weren't that fond of each other, either. When they didn't drink, they fought, so because neither of them was a mean drunk, they started drinking early each evening as a way to have some peace in the house. Most nights by ten o'clock, they were either about to pass out, already passed out, or in bed watching wrestling on cable channels because muscle-bound men in brief costumes appealed to both of them.

Their bedroom was on the second floor, and Cindy's was on the ground floor. She could escape her house even more easily than John could slip out of his.

In early August, when this started, they would take a blanket into a nearby meadow and lie under the stars.

Then Mr. Bellingham, who lived two doors from the Shooner place, was asked by his company to take a nine-month assignment in another state, to help turn around a problem factory there. Mrs. Bellingham decided to go with him. They didn't want to rent their house, so they closed it up and paid Cindy a little money to look after the place, to do some dusting and vacuuming every couple of weeks.

After that, she and John didn't need the meadow anymore. They could have candlelight, music, and a real bed.

She was sixteen, a year and a half older than John. She was the first girl he'd been with. He wasn't her first guy. Although still a girl, Cindy was in some ways a woman by then. She had assurance, attitude, appetite, and birth-control pills that her mother got for her because her mother hated the idea of a grandchild more than she hated her job or her husband.

Cindy was bad for John, though he didn't think so at that time. In fact, if the wrong person had told him that she was bad for him, he would have had his fists up in an instant.

In truth, he was bad for her, too. He liked her well enough, and he definitely liked being with her, but he didn't love her. If a girl wasn't loved a little bit, without the depth of affection that might at least be **mistaken** for love, she was being used, and no one was the better for being used.

He stayed with her that night from shortly before ten o'clock until later than usual, until three forty-five. After making love, they drifted off to sleep in the Bellingham place.

By the time he said good-bye, hurried home, climbed the tree, and returned to his room, it was four o'clock.

He might have stripped, dropped into bed, and fallen instantly asleep. He might have awakened in the morning, self-satisfied with his secret escapade, only to find that he had been sleeping in the house of the dead.

As he quietly slid shut the lower sash of his window, he heard bells ringing somewhere on the second floor. Silvery, eerie, alien to this place. After a pause, they rang again. In the dark, he moved to his door to listen just as the bells rang a third time.

Easing open the door, he saw light in the hallway. Issuing from his parents' and his sisters' rooms.

On the hallway floor stood a black satchel. Beside it lay a pistol.

John knew guns. His father, a good marksman, hunted deer in season and taught his son. This wasn't his father's weapon.

A homemade silencer was fitted to the barrel. He removed it.

Odd noises in his sisters' bedroom told him where the intruder must be.

The noises were not weeping or screaming, and he knew what the silence of the girls had to mean. If he thought about that, he would freeze or he would not have the strength to act, so he focused on the pistol and what he needed to do with it.

Weapon in hand, he eased to the open door to his parents' room. They were lying in the bloody bed. Shot in their sleep. Something on their eyes. Something in their hands.

His rabbit heart, fast and timid. But no going back.

After a silence, the bells rang again.

John sidled along the hallway, holding the pistol in a two-hand grip. He hesitated a step short of the girls' room.

Again the bells.

He stepped into the doorway, the light, the bleak future.

Giselle on the floor. Dead. Worse than dead. Marnie. Little Marnie. The suffering. Beyond comprehension. Blindness would be a blessing, to have been born without eyes.

John wanted death. Cover each girl with a blanket, lie down between them, and die.

Crouched over Giselle, the killer rang the bells one more time. Tall, as strange as a cockroach, quivering in his excitement. All bones and hands. Brute bones and greedy hands.

As bell-cry echoes still sang faintly off the walls, the beast raised his head, looking up from Giselle's body, his freak-show face boiled bright by a hideous rapture, his mouth smeared red from cruel kisses, those black-hole eyes that drew entire worlds to destruction in their crushing depths.

The sinister voice shattered John with words: "This little girl said you were gone to Grandma's for a week."

Had he known that John would be coming back, the killer would have been waiting in his dark bedroom. Even in her terror, Giselle had the presence of mind to save her brother with a clever lie. She died that John might live.

Rising from his crouch, folded bones unfolding into pterodactyl ghastliness, the killer said, "Your lovely sister, your Giselle. She had such pretty little training-bra breasts."

John's arms were straight in front of him, elbows locked, pistol in a good tight grip, but his slamming heart shook him, and the gun shook with him, the sight jumping, jumping on the target.

Taking a step toward John, the killer said, "You'll

be a daddy someday. Then I'll come back and use your wife and kids harder than I used your slutty sisters here tonight."

The sound of the first shot was huge and hammer-hard in that confined space, a cannon blast, concussion waves bouncing wall to wall to wall, and the bullet sucked the splintered cartilage of the nose backward into the fevered brain as the killer staggered, stumbled, fell.

John stepped into the bedroom, stood over the fallen beast, and emptied the pistol's magazine into the hateful face, obliterating the eyes that had seen his sisters in their agony and despair, shredding the mouth that had profaned them. He heard no shot after the first, but watched, seemingly in silence, as the demented face dissolved from miscreation into chaos.

John had no memory of going downstairs to the den. The next thing he knew, he was loading one of his father's handguns with the intention of putting a single round through the roof of his mouth, that his shame and grief might be blown out with his brains.

His sister died with no hope but that John might live by virtue of her lie about his visit to a grandmother. He could not repay her love with a coward's exit. His penance could be nothing less than that he must go on living.

The taste and the weight of cold steel were on his

tongue when he heard the sirens that the gunshots had summoned.

They found him on his knees, and sobbing.

In the dayroom, where Walter and Imogene Nash ate their lunch and did their planning, John was lowering the pleated shades when Nicolette located him.

She had been on the computer, reading Alton Turner Blackwood's journal. Her face was as pale as the white-gesso ground with which she prepared a new canvas before painting.

"Your family shouldn't have been the fourth. He meant to kill the Calvinos third, the Paxtons fourth."

He stared at her, not fully comprehending what she said but instinctively alarmed.

"The therapist who read it. He never told you. Yours was the third family on Blackwood's list. When he came to your house that night, a police patrol car happened to be parked on your street. Two officers in it. Probably just taking a break. Blackwood spooked. He went to the Paxton place instead. Thirty-three days later, he came back for your family."

John felt targeted. In someone's gun sight at this very moment. The bullet in the barrel.

"If we're **third,**" Nicky said, "we don't have until December tenth. We have just thirteen days."

"But why would he revert to the original order?"

"Why not? He wants to do it like it should have been done. But John . . . my God."

"What?"

"If he can change the order, why stick with thirty-three days?"

"Serial-killer periodicity. Who knows why? They don't understand it themselves."

She shook her head. "But today. **Today,** John. It was twenty years ago today. If he can change the order, put us third, he can change the day. **This** day might be sweeter to him than waiting."

From the journal of Alton Turner Blackwood:

As Melissa flicked the cards facedown across the patio table, Regina gathered up hers not one at a time but only after the full hand had been dealt, and it seemed to the boy, as he stood listening to the story of his mother's murder, that the beautiful girl had cast his fate in the seven cards and that the beautiful woman held his fate in a fan of numbers and royals.

After giving birth to Melissa, fertile Regina had produced three sons who were now only baby bones in the scattered earth of excavated graves. But after giving birth to the malformed boy, Anita failed to conceive again during the next nine years, though Teejay relentlessly bent her to the task. The old man lost his patience with her, and one night when Anita pressed him too insistently about granting greater privileges to the boy, whom Teejay preferred to keep sequestered, he struck her with the iron poker with which he had been jabbing at the logs in the master-bedroom fireplace. Seeing the damage that he had done to Anita's face in that moment of unchecked anger, he used the poker to finish her.

So the boy's mother did not abandon him, after all, and what he had been told about her growing revulsion at his appearance proved to be only another lie in the wilderness of lies that was Crown Hill and the Blackwood family.

With Anita dead and unable to lobby for her child, Teejay might have considered killing the boy at last, but instead he banished his only living son—who in the twisted limbs of the family tree was also his grandson and great-grandson—to the lonely tower room, as a vivid and living reminder to himself that in the quest to refine beauty into perfect beauty by incestuous breeding, the rose can be plucked only at the risk of an occasional thorn.

After drawing a card, Regina took three queens from her hand of eight cards and put them on the table.

"I tell you all this because Melissa and I, each of us, is in her first month with a new

child. I've come to feel I've done enough—
more than enough—to earn all that I should
have coming to me."

The awkward boy stood staring at the three
queens, and in his mind he saw the cards
bearing the faces of his beautiful mother, his
beautiful aunt, and his even more beautiful
cousin.

Not finished putting meld on the table,
Regina revealed two threes that she augmented
with a joker.

"While you're deciding what all this means
to you and what if anything you should do
about it," she continued, "you must remember
three things. First, that I'm your mother's
sister. Second, that Melissa is not only your
mother's niece but also her half-sister. Third,
of everyone at Crown Hill, only I—not even
your mother—only I have ever told you the
truth."

Later, the boy understood that she expected
him to kill Teejay. Instead, that night, he
packed a knapsack that included only what he
thought essential—including the photograph
of naked Jillian hanging from the rafter. He
forced his way into Teejay's private suite and
with a knife demanded money. He had no
intention of harming the old man—who was a
hardy seventy-three at that time—because to

do so would make him a fugitive and ensure that he would be hunted down. He wanted freedom more than revenge. Teejay had twenty-two thousand dollars in a wall safe. The boy also took ten antique coins worth perhaps fifty thousand more.

At midnight, the boy set out along the driveway toward the front gate of Crown Hill. The raven had given him the night, and the night had been his tutor.

The boy now knew everything that the night knew, lessons for the life he would henceforth make for himself. Everyone was born to die. Sex was death. Death was sex. Being a predator was better than being prey. Hell must exist because there was an urgent and abiding need for it. He had no need of Heaven because he would secure a place of honor and privilege in Hell.

Mere minutes after midnight, the boy passed through the main gate, into the world beyond Crown Hill. At that moment, he became me. I am Alton Turner Blackwood, and I am Death.

49

AFTER LEAVING NAOMI IN THE THIRD-FLOOR master suite, Melody Lane—talented spinner of tall tales about other worlds and cross-time sleighs with billowing sails, the willing and eager servant of Ruin and therefore a kind of spiritual sister to Alton Turner Blackwood—descends the back stairs to the ground floor. As she opens the door between the stairwell and the kitchen, she hears voices, the anxious mother and the father, coming from the nearby dayroom. She remains in the stairwell, behind the door, which she holds ajar, listening. When John and Nicolette hurry away somewhere, Melody enters the kitchen.

They have many handsome and meticulously sharpened knives to choose from: bread knife, butcher knife, turkey carver, pot-roast slicer. . . . They are good customers of Williams-Sonoma, and they buy the best quality. Though she admires their purchases, she believes they might be consuming more than their fair share. We all have a responsibility. Well, tonight their consuming ends. When she opens a drawer and sees the cleaver with the flat-grind blade, she picks it up and considers her reflection in the polished steel. For a child a year old or younger, Melody prefers drowning in a bathtub. For a child between two and four, smothering or vigorous strangulation. Blunt objects for any age. But for a fit boy of thirteen, who has been made wary by his recent experiences, an edge weapon wielded aggressively seems more advisable.

After closing the knife drawer, while still gripping the drawer pull, she asks for guidance, because she isn't now being ridden and therefore does not share Ruin's omniscient awareness of the family members' whereabouts. The boy is in his room—and in a moment the youngest girl will join him there. The tender girl must be saved for later, and Melody will receive assistance with Minette's bloodless detention. The boy is hers, and this reward excites her. He will be the oldest child that she has killed to date, and when she drinks his last exhalation, she will lick every wisp of it from the deep recesses of his ripe mouth.

Holding the LEGO wheel-like thing against her chest with her left arm, Minnie rapped on Zach's door with her right fist. "It's me and it's important."

He invited her in, and she found him sitting at the slantboard on his desk, just closing the cover on his drawing tablet.

"What's up?" he asked.

"Something bad is going to happen."

"What've you done? Did you break something?"

"Not me. I haven't done anything. It's in the house."

"Huh? What's in the house?"

"Ruin. Its name is Ruin."

"What kind of name is Ruin? What's the joke?"

"Don't you feel it in the house? It's been here for weeks. It hates us, Zach. I'm scared."

He had risen from his chair as she talked. Now he walked past her to close the door that she had left ajar.

Turning to her, he said, "I've had some . . . experiences."

Nodding, she said, "Experiences."

"I thought I was going freaking nuts."

"It's been waiting for the right time."

"What's been waiting? Who is this Ruin guy?"

"He's not people like you and me and Naomi. He . . . it . . . whatever, it's a kind of ghost I think, but also something more, I don't know what."

"Ghosts. I'm not so big on ghost stuff, you know. The whole idea seems stupid."

Minnie could see that he didn't really think ghosts were as stupid an idea as he might have thought they were back in September or August.

"What've you got there?" he asked, pointing to the LEGO wheel-thing she had trapped against her chest with her left arm.

"I built it from a dream, except I don't remember how I could have put it together."

Frowning, he said, "You can't lock LEGOS together like that, not everything round and smooth and layered like that."

"Well, I did. And we've got to keep it with us every minute tonight, 'cause we're gonna need it bad."

"Need it for what?" Zach asked.

Minnie shook her head. "Damn if I know."

He stared at her until she shrugged. Then he said, "Sometimes you're a little spooky yourself."

"Don't I know it," she agreed.

<hr />

In John's study, Nicky had not switched off the computer. A page from the hologrammatic journal of Alton Turner Blackwood waited on the screen. John glanced at it, surprised that an apostle of chaos could have recorded his crimes in such neat handwriting. Of course, evil of the most refined variety had a respect for certain kinds of order—enemy lists, gulags, extermination camps.

From a desk drawer, he retrieved the holster and the pistol that he had put there before he had settled in the armchair for a nap.

As he slipped into the rig, he watched Nicky unlock the tall gun cabinet in the corner. She unclipped a 12-gauge, pistol-grip shotgun from its rack braces and passed it to him.

Most of Nicky's friends in the art world were wary of cops and afraid of guns. They seemed to like John and assumed she married him because he wasn't much like other cops, when in fact **she** was at heart as much a cop as an artist. She did her work not only with emotion but also with intellect, not just intuitively but also analytically, considered it a career but also a duty, and felt above all the need to serve Truth even more than art. He had known many good cops whom he would have trusted to cover his back, but none more so than Nicky.

As she grabbed a box of shells from one of the bottom drawers, she said, "Where are the kids?"

"In their rooms, I think." He accepted a shell from her and loaded it in the breach. "I told the girls not to go outside again."

"We've got to stay together," she said, passing him the first of three more shells. "I swear, it wants to keep us apart, that's what it's been doing. We're stronger together. Where in the house is easiest to defend?"

"I'm thinking." He loaded one, two, three shells in the tube-type magazine. "Give me some spares."

From the computer speakers came music. A recording of one of Naomi's flute solos of which she was particularly proud.

John and Nicky turned to the monitor. The page of Blackwood's journal blinked off the screen. A photo flashed up. The same photo of John's mother that had been in the file labeled CALVINOI on Billy Lucas's computer, which he had gotten from this same serial-killer site. That photo flashed away, and one of John's father appeared.

Nicky said, "What's happening?"

John's dad blinked away. Replaced by his sister Marnie. Then Giselle. Then the faces appeared one at a time in rotation: fast, faster, blindingly fast.

John glanced at the gallery of his children's birthday pictures, at the familiar furniture, the walls, the ceiling. Their house, their home. Not theirs alone anymore.

The screen blanked. Still the flute music. A new photo. Zach. Now Naomi. Minnie. Nicky. John.

"It's starting," he said.

"Screw this. We'll stop it," Nicky said almost savagely, and switched off the computer. She put the entire box of shells on the desk. "But how? John, it's crazy. How can we defend against a thing like this?"

Stuffing four shells in one pants pocket, four in the other, he said, "Abelard told me it can't really hurt us with the house. It has to get into someone and come at us that way."

Nicky looked at the pistol in his rig, at the shotgun in his hands, and he could read her thoughts.

Billy Lucas had killed his family. The enemy within.

"I shouldn't have all the guns." He handed the pistol to her. "You're a good shot. It's double action, just pull through the first resistance. It's stiffer than you're used to, but you'll be fine."

As she stared at the weapon in her hands, abhorrence distorted her lovely features.

John could read that expression, too. "Nicky, listen, you watch me for any sign, any slightest sign that I'm . . . not me anymore."

A tremor softened her mouth. "What if I—"

"You won't," he interrupted. "It can't get in you, not **you**."

"If I were to do anything to one of the kids—"

"Not a woman as good as you," he insisted. "It's me that I'm not too sure of. I'm the one with a history of . . . letting the team down."

"Bullshit. You're the best man I've ever known. And it won't be the kids. Not our kids. It'll come at us from somewhere else, in someone from outside."

"You just watch me for any sign," he repeated. "Any slightest sign. And don't hesitate to pull the trigger. It'll look like me, but it won't be me any-more. And if it's in me, it'll go for you first because you have the other gun."

She grabbed the back of his neck, pulled his face to hers, and kissed him as if it might be the last time she ever would.

———

In the past twenty-one days, Lionel Timmins hadn't been able to find any hinges to open doors on the Woburn investigation. There was the link between Reese Salsetto and Andy Tane, but day by day it seemed to be a link that didn't connect with **this** chain of events, just a coincidence. The more he probed into the weirdness on the night of the fourth—culminating in the furious violence at the hospital—the less sense it made.

And day by unnerving day, with increasing seri-ousness, Lionel reviewed his memory of the curious atmosphere in the Woburn house and the experi-ence with the screen saver that had formed into a blue hand on Davinia's computer. The repulsive cold squirming against his palm and spread fingers. The sharp nip as if a fang had pierced his skin. His persistent sense of being watched. The sound of doors closing on the deserted second floor, foot-steps in empty rooms.

Alternately questioning his sanity and assuring himself that he was merely gathering information with which to set John Calvino's mind at ease, Lionel found his way to the yellow-brick house of the former exorcist late on the afternoon of the twenty-fifth. He didn't call ahead for an appointment, but used his intimidating physique and his badge to batter at Peter Abelard's resistance to grant an interview. Lionel didn't look much like a cop in his wool toboggan cap and navy peacoat, but the ex-priest relented.

When he learned that John had been there earlier, Lionel was not surprised. He was amazed, however, to discover that this smoke-saturated man who bore no resemblance to his idea of a priest was nonetheless eerily convincing. The interview chilled him.

In the street outside Peter Abelard's house, as Lionel stood watching the white sky come apart and drift down in cold crystals, he stuck out his tongue to catch the flakes, as he had done when he was very young, trying to remember what it had been like to be a boy who believed in wonders and in Mystery with a capital **M**.

Now, in his car, a few blocks from the Calvino house, he still didn't know if he was aboard the superstition express all the way to the end of the line or if he would get off at the next station. Whatever happened, he owed John Calvino a longer and more serious discussion of the evidence, and he owed it to him **now.**

Sitting on her parents' bed, beside the attaché case, watching the glorious snow falling outside, hoping that the hush of the room would seep into her noisy brain and bring her clarity of mind, Naomi thought that she heard a chanting voice, as if from a radio with the volume set low. On the nearest nightstand stood a clock radio, but it wasn't the source of the rhythmic murmur.

The chanting repeatedly faded, although it never went entirely away. Each time it returned, the volume was never louder than it had been at its previous loudest, and she could not make out the words. Pretty soon, curiosity got the better of Naomi, which was only what curiosity was **supposed** to do, to her way of thinking, because without curiosity there would be no progress, and humankind would still be living in grotesquely primitive conditions, without iPods, nonfat yogurt, and shopping malls.

She was pretty sure Melody had told her not to move from her perch on the bed. She didn't want to be one of those graceless people who used her status to justify all kinds of obnoxious behavior, but the inescapable fact seemed to be that if there was royalty from a far world in the house, it was not Melody. She Who Must Be Obeyed was instead a certain eleven-year-old going on twelve. She got up from the bed and followed the sound, turning her head this way and that to get a bead on it.

A short hallway opened off the bedroom, with a walk-in closet on each side. Naomi switched on the hall light. The chanting didn't arise from either of the closets.

At the end of the hall, the door to the bathroom stood ajar. The room beyond was almost dark at this hour, little of the storm light penetrating the clerestory windows high in the walls.

The rhythmic sound was definitely chanting. A male voice. But she couldn't quite make out what he was saying.

Naomi wasn't an impetuous girl given to **flinging** herself into harm's way. This chanting might be weird but surely it didn't arise from an ill-intentioned person. Melody wouldn't have brought her up here if anything were amiss. No doubt the chanting had something to do with the preparations for departure. Magicians were always chanting.

She pushed open the bathroom door, felt for the light switch, and the room brightened.

The most desperate-looking man sat on the floor, knees drawn up to his chest, arms wrapped around his legs to pull himself into a ball like a pill bug. His tarnished-penny eyes were so wide with terror, they looked as if they might fall out of his sockets. He bobbed his head up and down, up and down. As if trying to convince himself, he muttered, "I'm

Roger Hodd of the **Daily Post,** I'm Roger Hodd of the **Daily Post,** I'm Roger Hodd of the **Daily Post.** . . ."

⚬⚬⚬

John with the shotgun, Nicky with the pistol, hurried along the ground-floor hall toward the front stairs, on their way to the children, who should be upstairs.

The doorbell rang.

She said, **"Don't answer it!"**

They were just past the foot of the main stairs, with only the foyer between them and the front door, so that John clearly heard the **clack** of the deadbolt sliding out of the striker plate in the door frame.

"No," Nicky said, and raised the pistol.

John brought up the shotgun as the front door swung inward. The perimeter alarm had been engaged. The siren should have sounded. It didn't. A meddling phantom had invaded the system.

The door swung wide, but no one stood on the threshold. A taunt. A lure. Someone might be out there, to the left or the right of the doorway, back pressed to the wall of the house, waiting for John to step into a trap.

There was no music, flute or otherwise, and the breeze barely murmured, but snow whirled as if waltzing on the porch, flung off thin veils that fluttered silently into the foyer, sparkling in the chandelier light.

For eighteen years, John had dreaded this moment without fully recognizing that on an unconscious level he believed implicitly the impossible would happen, that the killer of his family **would** return from the grave. Two years previously, when Minnie seemed close to death, her illness was so mysterious that John then became conscious of his conviction that Blackwood's promise to him would be kept. As Minnie lay in delirium, her fever uncontrollable, Blackwood prowled the edges of John's imagination, and it became easier by the day to believe that a spirit, not a virus, was killing her. Since then, his dread had grown, and now it almost seemed that he'd drawn Blackwood back into the world, that by so often imagining the worst, he had issued an **invitation**.

Now the open door and the vacant threshold argued for boldness on his part, because he would be the **last** victim on this killer's agenda. It wanted him to witness the brutalization of everyone he loved before slitting him open to steam in the winter night. At this moment of the open door, Nicky far more than John was in danger.

"Go upstairs to the kids," he said. "I'll check this out."

"No. I'm with you. Do it fast. Do it now."

Zach was near the door that he had just closed, Minnie stood beside her brother's desk, and Willard materialized through the wall.

Always, when Minnie thought about Willard as he had been, she thought about play and fun, laughter and love. Even the sight of Dead Willard could lift her heart, though the truth was that the dog did not come back into the world to play or to make her laugh. He wasn't scary like the ghost with the blasted face in the convenience store, but you didn't want to cuddle Dead Willard, either. He wouldn't feel soft, furry, and warm anymore. You might feel a coldness when you tried to touch him or nothing at all, which would be worse. The sight of Willard scared Minnie now, because he meant trouble was coming.

The dog raced to her, dashed to Zach, disappeared through the door to the hall, and at once returned by the same route.

"What's wrong with you?" Zach asked Minnie as he watched her watching the ghost dog that he couldn't see.

Willard barked, barked, but even Minnie couldn't hear him. She could see only that he was trying to bark out from his reality into theirs.

She said, "Zach, get away from the door."

"Why?"

"Get away from the door!"

The dog did his best. Nobody could blame good old Willard when the gray-dress woman from twenty days earlier, the woman who might have been a door-to-door Jesus-talker but wasn't, burst into the room and swung a meat cleaver at Zach.

⎯⎯⎯◦⊰⊱◦⎯⎯⎯

Roger Hodd was told, with his own voice, to **Stay**. He finds that he can't disobey. He is a dog, not a man anymore, just a dog with a master who has him by the short hairs of his mind, and minute by minute his sanity is melting away. As a reporter, he gets to ask the questions, and you either have to tell him the truth, lie, or say "No comment," and no matter what you say, he can characterize it as either the truth or a lie, as he sees fit. That is his authority, his power, but no longer. He doesn't get to ask questions here, and this thing that has controlled him like a marionette, that isn't in him at the moment but that can still make him **Stay,** is going to do something monstrous with him, then **to** him.

The girl pushes the door open wider, turns on the lights, and gapes at him from the threshold. She asks if he's all right, if he needs help. How stupid is the little gash? Of course he needs help, he's dying here. He wants to tell her that she's a brain-dead future whore, that she's dumber than the load she probably has in her pants, but then his rider returns, fully controlling Hodd once more, and he says to the girl, "You are a sweet treat, aren't you? I want my sweet candy. Give me some tasty candy, you ignorant little bitch." As abruptly as it mounted him, the rider dismounts, for it has business elsewhere, but Roger Hodd remains on **Stay**.

<hr />

Swaddled in the odors of wool coats and fake-fur collars and sheepskin linings, Preston Nash waits in the lightless closet, like a Level 3 threat in a video game, the claw hammer ready in his hand. He remains unafraid. After almost twenty years strung out on drugs and drink, he has so often walked with Death along one brink or another that his capacity for fear is burnt out, until the only things that can at times frighten him are his worst hallucinations. Long-term users of ecstasy—a drug Preston dislikes—lose the ability to know joy **naturally** because their brains stop producing endorphins. As they must rely on their drug of choice for happiness, he relies on his for terror that the real world—a faded and threadbare place to him—no longer can supply. So he waits for his new and interesting companion, the sharer of his flesh, with pleasant anticipation.

He is idling on a **Stay** command with nothing to do but think, and he likes what he is thinking. Although not in control of his body, he has the benefit of all his senses when his spirit driver gets behind the wheel and takes him for a spin. Preston's vision, smell, touch, taste, and hearing remain as sharp as ever, but the intensity of these experiences will be beyond anything he, as a lifelong observer rather than participant, has ever known. He has killed thousands in the virtual worlds of games, but **this** will be real and intense. He has bedded women, mostly those for whom he's paid, and he's seen thousands of women used and roughly abused in adult films, but he has never raped or beaten one. He suspects his spirit driver will inspire him to do things this night that will be more outrageous and thrilling than anything he's ever seen on film. He hopes he'll be allowed the wife. But certainly the girls. What lies before him now is the opportunity to play with the real world as he has previously only played with virtual ones.

As Preston listens to John and Nicolette Calvino in the foyer, his spirit companion returns.

————

John went from the foyer to the porch as he would have cleared a doorway in any murder house where the killer might still be found: low, quick, shotgun tracking with his eyes to the left, right. The porch was deserted. He surveyed the autumn-brown lawn that lay half-concealed under its first coat of winter white, saw no one either there or in the street.

Stepping inside, he looked at Nicky and shook his head. He closed the door, twisted the deadbolt turn, and watched the lock for a moment, waiting for it to disengage.

"The kids," she said worriedly.

He went to Nicky, peered up the stairs beyond her, and said, "Let me take the lead. Stay a few steps back, so we don't make one target of ourselves."

"You think someone's in the house already?"

"The alarm is set, but it didn't go off when the door opened. Maybe someone came in earlier and it didn't go off then, either."

He had never seen her face this grim. She looked at the pistol in her right hand and said, "There's no way we can call the police, someone you know."

"I knew Andy Tane. The only cop you can trust is me—and maybe not me, either. After we've got the kids safe with us, we'll bar the doors or nail them or something—then sweep the house room by room. You with me?"

"Yeah."

"Remember—stay behind me. Two targets, not one."

He climbed three stairs, glanced back, and saw

her surveying the foyer ceiling as if this were not her home but instead a cave unknown to her, in which hung bats and other rabid threats.

⚬⚬⚬⚬

Ridden again, Preston thrills to the vicious rage of his demon master, a hatred so exhilarating that it's like an infinite roller coaster without rising inclines, only breathtaking plunges, one after the other, allowing but a moment to shudder in anticipation of the next free-fall into fury.

He quietly opens the closet door, steps into the foyer, and sees John Calvino climbing the stairs, his attention on spaces above, and Nicolette turning away to follow her husband. Just a rich-bitch, tight-assed, art-school phony, vomiting her pretentious swill onto canvas after canvas, a baby machine pumping out more little phonies to live in this oh-so-precious fantasy life of hers. She needs to be taught how the world **really** is, needs to be brought down and broken and forced to admit she's just filth like everyone else.

Preston's rider finesses from him a stealth and swiftness that he—always awkward and so long enervated—has never shown before. The woman doesn't hear him coming. He raises the hammer as he closes on her, dismayed that he is going to be allowed only to kill her. But the dismay lasts just an instant, because he is **in the game,** in it as he has never been before, no longer merely a player sitting in an armchair. Although ridden by Death and a demon, Preston feels more alive now than ever before, and he knows that when the claw end of the hammer cracks through the top of her skull and gouges the art out of her brain forever, his pleasure will be an order of magnitude more intense than anything he has felt before, orgasmic.

He swings the hammer down.

If Nicky heard the squeak of a shoe or the rustle of clothing behind her, she didn't consciously register it, but she smelled bad breath—garlic, beer, rotten teeth—and strong body odor, and she instinctively ducked her head, hunched her shoulders. Something cold and curved brushed along the nape of her neck and apparently hooked in the collar of her blouse. She was jerked backward. Off balance, she fell against her attacker.

". . . ignorant little bitch."

Roger Hodd of the **Daily Post** didn't have the voice of the thing who spoke to Naomi from the mirror back in September, but Naomi had no doubt that they were one and the same, that nothing was the way she had thought it was, that she had been less perspicacious than foolish.

She turned to run, in front of her the bathroom door slammed shut, she seized the knob, it wouldn't budge. Trapped.

———— ∞ ————

When Minnie told Zach to get away from the door, he instead turned toward it, to see what was wrong, and there was the woman.

Minnie screamed as the blade flashed.

Zach dropped, tucked, rolled as the cutting edge sliced the air with a **whoosh** where he had been. As he sprang to his feet, he heard the cleaver chop into the carpet inches short of him. The freaking maniac had swung it so hard that she cut through to the wood beneath and needed a moment to free the blade, spitting and keening like a rabid weasel or something.

Clutching her LEGO wheel to her chest with both arms, Minnie backed away from the desk toward the hall door, screaming again. Man, he hated to hear his sister screaming, it tore at him. Zach snatched up the desk chair, throwing it at the maniac to buy a few seconds. Struck, the woman stumbled backward, and by the time she regained her balance, Zach had the Mameluke sword.

Lizard-fast in spite of her long dress, the shrieking lunatic came at him before he could draw the sword from the scabbard, came at him in a fury, and he didn't even **know** her. He used the sword and sheath defensively, as a cudgel, holding it by both ends and thrusting it forward to meet the descending blade. The cleaver rang off the polished-nickel scabbard, and the force of the blow almost vibrated the Mameluke out of Zach's hands. She swung left to right, horizontally, under the sword, almost slashing his belly. He danced back, she slashed right to left, and the blade snagged his T-shirt and flashed away with a quiver of light but with none of his blood.

The smooth curved back of the claw slides harmlessly along the nape of the bitch's neck, and the two sharp talons snare her blouse. Preston jerks, ripping the collar, pulling her against him. With his left arm, he encircles her throat. As her right arm comes up, maybe trying to shoot backward at him, he swings the hammer at her hand. He strikes the gun instead, it flies out of her grip, thuds off the area rug, clatters across the floor.

At the feel of her, the warm delectable body, Preston's rider wants her, after all, and so does Preston, he wants to take her and kill her with a knife **while** he's taking her, which is more extreme than anything he's seen in the roughest bondage films. Time the killing cut to the moment of his orgasm. This is his rider's desire, as well, for it believes that Death is the best sex.

The husband is coming down the stairs, the pistol-grip shotgun raised, but he can't take a shot without killing his rich-bitch baby-making machine. She's kicking at Preston's shins, clawing at the arm that encircles her neck, but he feels no pain, he is supernaturally **strong**. He's a match for any of the superheroes in all those movies that he has watched repeatedly while rooting for the archvillains.

Using the woman as a shield, he drags her along the hallway, toward the back of the house, grinning at Calvino, who follows them with the shotgun ready, the big tough cop with his door-buster gun, but his badge and his gun don't matter now.

"Shoot me through her," Preston taunts. "Go ahead. Blast both of us to Hell. You won't want her anyway, when I'm done with her. You know what happened to your other hump? That hottie, Cindy Shooner? She committed suicide five years ago, she's waiting for this bitch in Hell. They can compare notes about what a one-minute wonder you were in bed."

Preston wants the cop to threaten him, to beg for her, to try some half-assed psychology, because it will be sweet to hear the terror in his voice. But Calvino says nothing, just shows him the muzzle of the 12-gauge and follows, waiting for an opportunity, but he's not going to get one.

At the study, Preston drags his prize of fresh meat

out of the hall, backward across the threshold. The cop quickly closes on them and tries to shoulder through the door, thrusting the shotgun ahead of him. But if the house cannot be used to kill, it can be used to hamper. The door closes hard against Calvino, pinning him to the jamb.

"The house is mine now," Preston declares, grinding himself against the rich bitch's tight butt, "and everything in it."

Although the cop strains to break free, the door is unrelenting, denying him further entrance, squeezing him hard until he will have to retreat. Swinging his right arm past the wifey, Preston strikes at the husband's face with the hammer, Calvino jukes, the claw gouges a chunk from the door frame.

The bitch hasn't stopped tearing at Preston's left arm. But suddenly she seizes the handle of the hammer, ferociously twists it, so surprises him that she takes the weapon. Trying to snatch it away from her, he unintentionally relaxes the arm around her throat. She starts to slip down and away. He grabs a fistful of her hair to yank her back. For a moment his head is fully exposed.

Face flushed and clenched with the effort to squeeze farther into the room, Calvino gains two inches. He thrusts the shotgun forward, over his wife's head, into Preston's face. The flash—

Backed against his desk, Zach desperately blocked every swing of the cleaver with the Marine Corps sword, but was given no opportunity to draw it from its scabbard. The crazed woman chopped high, chopped low, lunging with every slash of the wicked blade, which could probably render an entire chicken in five seconds flat. His heart pounded so hard he could hear it, a hollow **ba-boom ba-boom** that seemed to enter his ears by a back door, could feel it knocking against his sternum, his ribs.

Minnie had backed away to the hall door. But she seemed frozen in fear.

Zach shouted at her, "Get out! Get help!"

Reminded of Minnie, the whack job with the cleaver relented for a moment, glancing at her, maybe thinking she should chop the easier target first and demoralize Zach by killing his sister. He instantly took advantage of her mistake, didn't attempt to draw the sword from the stupid scabbard, but just swung the whole thing at her head. The sound of the blow was hugely satisfying, one of the best things ever. Dropping the cleaver, the freaking lunatic collapsed to the floor on her back, possibly dead but probably unconscious.

Zach snatched up her weapon and stowed it in a desk drawer. He dropped onto one knee beside her, pressed fingertips to her throat, and found a pulse. He was relieved. He didn't want to kill her if he didn't have to. Maybe she was only crazy, not evil. And he was just thirteen, not ready for this. Maybe he could drag the nutcase into the closet, brace the door shut, and then call the cops.

Only as he pulled open the closet door did he realize that Minnie was gone.

———— ❧ ————

As Minnie stepped into the hallway to shout for help, the LEGO wheel-thing was heavy, at least ten or twelve pounds when it ought to have weighed maybe twelve **ounces**. And it seemed to be getting heavier by the second. She was terrified for Zach. She loved him, she didn't want to grow up without him, so her legs were already rubbery. The weight of the weird LEGO thing caused her to totter, but she knew that she should let it out of her hands only if she was in extreme danger, though she didn't know **why**.

Exiting Zach's room, she opened her mouth to shout for help—and saw Professor Sinyavski, his wild hair wilder than ever, lurching out of the storage room at the east end of the hall. But he'd said he was leaving early because of the snow.

With his bushy eyebrows, rubbery nose, and big belly, he usually looked funny in a nice way, but he didn't look any kind of funny now. His lips were skinned back from his teeth in a snarl, his face was twisted and hateful, and his eyes seemed to be burning and icy at the same time. Maybe Professor Sinyavski was peering out at Minnie from somewhere behind those eyes, but she knew at once, for sure, Ruin looked at her from within the mathematician—and it wanted her.

Voice rough with anger and slurred as if he had been drinking, the professor said, "Piggy pig. Come here, you dirty piggy pig, you dirty pig." He started toward her, staggering, and for the first time Minnie realized how big the Russian was, not just overweight but big in the chest and shoulders, his neck thick, more muscle under the fat than she had realized before.

This was extreme danger, all right. Reluctantly but without hesitation, she put the LEGO wheel on the floor and ran toward the front stairs.

<hr />

"I'm Roger Hodd of the **Daily Post,** I'm Roger Hodd of the **Daily Post. . . .**"

The inside of the bathroom door had a thumb-turn deadbolt, but that wasn't holding it shut. No matter how furiously Naomi wrenched at the knob, jerked on it, the door didn't even rattle against the jamb, as if it was steel and was welded in place.

She glanced back at Roger Hodd, still on the floor, doing his pill-bug imitation. No less terrified, the man now appeared deranged, too. This time, a shaky humorless laugh punctuated **"Daily Post,"** and Naomi knew that soon, any second—**Oh God, Oh God**—he would return to the subject of tasty candy, and she shuddered at the thought of his hands on her.

As Minnie reached the stairs, a shotgun boomed on the ground floor. She had intended to go down. Instead she went up to the third-floor landing. Into Mother's studio. Across the studio to the back stairs. Don't glance behind. Looking over your shoulder wasted time, slowed you down. She just prayed and ran, hoping God would help her if she helped herself by running her butt off. She had to be faster than big old Professor Sinyavski. She could do the math, he'd taught her to do it. She was eight years old, he was maybe seventy, so she should be almost nine times faster than he was.

The door released John, and Nicky embraced him. She didn't look back, didn't want to see faceless Preston Nash or the room fouled by a spray of blood and brains.

"The kids," she said, and together they hurried once more along the hall toward the front stairs.

A dark primitive part of her despaired that this would never stop, that Nature was a pagan beast that devoured everyone in the end, that the unrelenting idiot evil of Ruin-and-Blackwood had the power to turn the entire world against her family, one person at a time, until finally it got what it wanted. But a more profound part of her, the believer who was an artist and who **knew** that imagination could create something from nothing, insisted that the world was not a cancerous maze of infinite malignancies, that it arose from an intricate matrix of exquisite design, which made it possible for hope to be fulfilled. If only she and John did the right thing, the smart thing, they could save the kids, all of them, and get out of this damn box.

In the front hall, she retrieved her pistol. John hurried toward the second floor. Nicky followed him, realizing that the nape of her neck still felt cold where the convex curve of the hammer claw had slid along it, and she shivered.

Once, in a true-crime book, while browsing in a bookstore, Naomi saw a picture of a murdered girl. A police photo or something. A girl younger than Naomi. She had been raped. Punched in the face, stabbed. Her eyes in the photo were the worst thing Naomi had ever seen. Wide pretty eyes. They were the worst thing because they were the saddest thing, they brought tears to her own eyes there in the store, and she quickly closed the book and put it back on the shelf and told herself to forget she ever saw that poor face, those eyes. She worked hard to forget it, but it showed up in a dream once in a while, and now as she struggled with the bathroom door, the dead girl's face haunted her once more.

Breathing raggedly, making strange noises, little whimpers, which frightened her because she sounded like someone wholly different from herself, Naomi figured-hoped-prayed she might be all right as long as Roger Hodd continued to drone about who he was and where he worked, showing no interest in her. But then she heard him moving, and when she turned, she saw him rising to his feet from the floor.

She gave up on the door, she couldn't get it open anyway, and if Hodd was on the move, she didn't dare turn her back to him. He swayed as he chanted, not looking at her or at anything in the room, for that matter, but his words had a different rhythm from the way he'd been saying them, and a new tone entered his voice. The self-pitying note and confusion became impatience and petulance, and he emphasized the word **am** as though arguing with someone: "I AM Roger Hodd of the **Daily Post,** I AM Roger Hodd of the **Daily Post**. . . ."

Minnie raced down four flights to the landing at the ground floor, where she halted at the door to the kitchen, held her breath, and listened. The stairs were quiet. Professor Sinyavski—or the thing that had once been the professor—wasn't thundering after her.

She looked down the next flight of stairs. All remained quiet—but then something drip-drip-dripped onto the carpeted treads. Red. Thicker than water. Blood. She glanced at the ceiling above the stairs and saw a long line, a slash in the plaster, like a wound, blood oozing out between the lips of the wound, as if the house were alive.

Her heart fluttered. She told herself that the blood wasn't real. The only reason she saw it was because Ruin wanted her to see it. This was like a delirium hallucination except that she wasn't feverish in a hospital bed. Or if it was real, it didn't come from a body somewhere above the ceiling. It was like the tears of blood that a statue of the Holy Mother might weep during a minor miracle, though this was dark magic. If she allowed herself to be frightened by this, then she would be **inviting** Ruin to torment her with other visions, maybe with a lot worse than merely visions. But her heart fluttered anyway.

The stairwell lights went off. In the absolute darkness, the drip-drip-dripping of blood became a noisier drizzle, and she could smell the metallic odor of it. She was overwhelmed by a fear that the noise of spilling blood masked the sounds of something approaching from above or below. But this was less her imagination than it was a suggestion **pressed** upon her by Ruin, and if she succumbed to panic, that also would be an invitation.

Easing open the landing door, she surveyed the kitchen, saw no one. She stepped out of the stairs, quietly closing the door behind her.

First, find Mom and Daddy, get help for Zach. Minnie wouldn't think about Zach being hurt, let alone dead. Nothing good could come from worrying about that. Zach was smart and quick and strong; he would take care of the crazy cleaver woman.

Whether or not Minnie found her parents, she could help Zachary if she had a weapon, and she could protect herself, too. She slipped across the kitchen to the drawers in which the cutlery was kept. She chose a butcher knife. She couldn't imagine using it as a weapon, but neither could she imagine just letting someone hack her to pieces with a cleaver and not fighting back.

She closed the drawer, turned, and Professor Sinyavski seized the knife, took it away from her, threw it across the room, scooped her off her feet. She tried to fight back, but he was stronger than an old fat mathematician ought to be. He held her tight under his left arm and clamped his right hand over her mouth to silence her. "My little pretty pig. Pretty little dirty piggy." Minnie's scream stifled by his meaty hand, he hurried with her toward the door to the terrace and the backyard.

———

In Zach's room, John and Nicky found pencils, erasers, and a couple of large drawing tablets scattered on the floor, as if they had been swept off the desk during a struggle. One of the tablets had fallen open, and John picked it up, stunned by the portrait of Alton Turner Blackwood.

From the description of the killer that John had given fifteen years previously, Nicky recognized the subject. She took the tablet from him, paged through it, her shaky hands rattling the paper as she found Blackwood again, again, and yet again.

"What's been going on here?" John worried.

"It's not Zach," she said adamantly. "It's not in our Zachary. He'd never let it have him."

John didn't think it would get into Zach, but it was in someone, moved on to **someone** after Preston's head was blown half off, and it was loose in the house. In the house and hunting down the kids.

From the closet came a voice. "Hello? Is somebody there?"

The door was braced shut with a chair.

"Somebody? Could you let me out of here, please? Hello?"

"That's not one of ours," John said.

"No," Nicky agreed.

"Let her out?"

"Hell no."

They hurried to the girls' room. No one. So quiet. Snow at the window. The whole house was quiet. Dead quiet.

Nicky said "Library," and they rushed to the library. The lesson tables. The reading corner. Between the stacks. No one. Snow beating soundlessly against the windowpanes.

Stay cool. No one screaming. That was good. No screaming was good. Of course they couldn't scream if they were dead, not if they were all dead, all dead and gutted, **servus** and two **servae.**

Guest room. The closet. The attached bath. No one. The quiet, the snow whirling at the windows, Nicky's purple eyes so bright in her suddenly pale face.

Quicker, quicker. Storage room. Hall bath. Linen closet. No one, no one, no one.

———

Zach entered the kitchen by the back stairs, far past anxious and halfway to frantic, searching for Minnie, for Naomi, for his parents. He saw the door standing open, old Sinyavski in the sheeting snow with Minnie, carrying her across the terrace toward the yard in the colorless twilight. Zach didn't know what that was about, but it couldn't be good, even if the professor had always before seemed like a right type, never a hint that he was a god-awful freaking maniac.

On the floor lay a butcher knife. Zach picked it up. It wasn't a pistol, but it was better than bare hands. He hurried to the open door.

⁂

With her back to the door that wouldn't open, Naomi watched with increasing fear as Roger Hodd pulled out drawer after drawer in the master-bathroom cabinets. He still chanted, louder and more angrily with each repetition, the emphasis now on two words: "I'm Roger HODD of the **Daily POST,** I'm Roger HODD of the **Daily POST. . . .**" His back was to her, but Naomi could see his face in the mirror as he moved along the granite counter, and he looked insane, as if at any moment he would start shrieking like a chimpanzee and come at her snapping his teeth in a biting frenzy.

In the next-to-last drawer, he found what he apparently wanted. Scissors. He held them by the handles, the blades shut, as if he were gripping a knife to plunge it into something.

Clutching the scissors, he returned along the counter, staring at his reflection in the mirror as if furious with himself—"I'm Roger HODD of the

Daily POST, I'm Roger HODD of the **Daily POST** "—slamming shut the drawers that he previously opened. At the end of the counter, near Naomi again, he picked up a rectangular box that she hadn't noticed before because it was dark green, sitting on the black granite, against the black backsplash. He took off the lid and set it aside. From the box he withdrew a silvery something that she could not immediately identify until they tinkled, and then she saw they were three bells. Three bells shaped like flowers.

⸺∾∾∾⸺

Leonid Sinyavski is in chains, not his body but his mind, imprisoned. For the last forty years, he has tried to live a good life, to redeem himself for certain things he did in the old Soviet Union before he fled to the West. As a young mathematician working on military projects in a time of deep restiveness among Russian intellectuals, he informed on some of his colleagues who wanted to see Communism fall. They went to gulags, and some most likely never returned. Now his own body is a gulag, and as he carries Minnie toward the arbor, he is shocked by the things he says to her, the threats he makes, and is **sickened** by the images that flash from his rider's mind through his, the cruelties and indignities that he is intended to perpetrate, the mutilation and murder. The chambers of his heart slam, slam against one another, slam like doors, and though his rider tries to calm him, Leonid can't be calmed when he knows for what he is being used. He tries to rebel, to rear up, and the chains around his mind stretch taut, as if the links might break, and again he rears, resists, and his rider bears down harder upon him as they reach the entrance to the arbor. Entering, he gathers all his mental strength, his courage, his righteousness hard-won over forty years, and says within, **No, never, no, no, never!** And on the second **never,** his slamming heart slams one last time and stilled blood pools in its chambers even as he collapses.

───ᴥ───

As he examined the calla-lily bells, Roger Hodd abruptly stopped hectoring himself about his name and occupation. For a moment, Naomi was re-lieved, but then the silence seemed worse than the chanting, especially when she shifted her attention from the silver bells to his reflection in the mirror and saw that he was watching her. A few times, she had seen men look at women this way when they didn't know Naomi saw them, but no man ever be-fore turned such eyes on her, and no man ever should watch a young girl her age like this. It was a hungry look, starving, and furious, and violent.

Grinning at her reflection in the mirror, Hodd

rang the bells loudly once, twice, three times. "You ignorant little bitch. Are you ready? Are you ready to meet your aunts, Marnie and Giselle? You don't even know about them, but they're waiting for you. They're waiting for you in Hell."

He put the bells in the box from which he had taken them, and he turned to her, the scissors in his fist.

Naomi yanked at the bathroom door again, but it was as immovable as before. With a cry of terror, she dodged past Hodd, darted to the farther end of the bathroom. There was nowhere to go except into the shower stall, pulling the door shut behind her. A glass door. Even if she could hold it shut, which she wouldn't be able to do because he was stronger than she was, but even if she **could** hold it shut, it was only a glass door.

<hr />

Bells. Elsewhere in the house. Eerie, silvery bells.

John and Nicky were entering the front stairs at the second floor, not sure whether to search upstairs or down first, when they heard the bells. Upstairs.

The horror of the past was now the horror of the moment, and John was in two places at once, in his house now and in his parents' house that night, racing up the stairs to the third floor but also following the shadowy hallway toward his parents' bedroom, pushing through the door to this master suite but also peering through another door at his murdered parents in a bed of blood, hearing the killer ringing the bells in his dead sisters' room but also hearing Naomi cry out in the master bath.

The bathroom door was locked. Nicky shouted, **"Shotgun, shotgun!"** He was bringing the weapon to bear on the lock even as she urged him to blow it out. Two shells dissolved the lock and the wood around it, but the door wouldn't open. It didn't even rattle in the frame, it was as solid as a concrete block in a wall of concrete blocks. More than a lock held it in place: the fury of Blackwood, the power of Ruin. In the bathroom, Naomi screamed, the worst sound John had ever heard, ever, and here in the hallway, Nicky screamed, too, an even more terrible sound, as much grief as terror, and she clawed at the blasted hole in the door, clawed so ferociously that her fingernails tore and bled.

Zach reached the entrance to the lattice arbor as old Sinyavski staggered three or four steps inside and fell, trapping Minnie under him. Zach had the butcher knife, but when he hurried to the fallen professor, he saw that he wouldn't need it. Last year's roses had been cut back to stumps, the trailers removed from the structure, so even in the fading light and shadows, he could see the staring eyes and the slackness in the face. Whatever had killed him, maybe a heart attack, Sinyavski was no longer a danger to anyone.

Minnie struggled, half under the heavy body, and when Zach freed her, she threw her arms around him and held him very tight. "I love you, Zach, I love you." He told her that he loved her, too. With one hand flattened on her back, he could feel her heart pounding hard as a bass drum, and it was the most wonderful thing he'd ever felt, the **thud-thud, thud-thud** of her heart.

A dry-as-bone, rasping-crackling-snapping noise drew their attention to opposite ends of the arbor, where the lattice appeared to come alive, like scores of flat white snakes, undulating to some music only they could hear. In maybe four seconds the lattice wove shut both exits from the structure, imprisoning Zach and Minnie with the corpse of Professor Sinyavski.

―⊶⊷―

In the second-floor hallway, the wheel stands on edge. Once made of a child's building blocks, it is now something entirely different, transformed, as ordinary things are always transubstantiated when the supernatural enters them from outside of time, in the way that bread and wine become body and blood—or, less exaltedly, in the way that Frodo's Ring of Power is not just a ring made in Mordor, the way that the Ark of the Covenant is not just a wooden box. Making the wheel, Minnie was in the thrall of a higher power, just as the Light ensured that Frodo should be the one Ring-bearer. Minnie is the Frodo in this family, the innocent who sees what others don't, loves others always more than self, and can be a bush that burns without being consumed, a conduit. Here and now, the moment of transubstantiation arrives. The wheel is white, but as it rolls along the second-floor hallway, it becomes golden, so heavy that it leaves a lasting impression in the carpet. Descending the stairs, it makes a more solid sound than might a two-hundred-pound man leaping downward. Along the lower hallway, wood flooring creaks and cracks under it.

⠿

Driven to the edge of madness by Naomi's screams, John threw himself against the door once, twice, without effect, and he knew he could break his shoulder without gaining entrance. Beyond rage, beyond fury, in the iron grip of wrath, he flattened his hands on the door and shouted, "This is **my** house, you degenerate sonofabitch, you worm, you filth, this is my house, **not yours, THIS IS MY HOUSE!**" The door rattled in the frame, and suddenly he was able to push it open.

He grabbed his shotgun and crossed the threshold as the clear safety-glass door of the shower stall shattered into frosted veils and shimmered to the floor. A man was stepping into the shower stall with scissors held high to stab. John got him by the belt and yanked him off the raised threshold. The guy turned, slashing wildly with the scissors, and it was Roger Hodd, a reporter to whom John had given interviews, regarding homicide cases, on several occasions. He was Hodd, but his eyes were not Hodd's eyes, they were deep pits of implacable hatred. John dodged the scissors, shoved Hodd against the wall to the left of the shower stall, shouted to Naomi— **"Don't look!"**—jammed the shotgun into the possessed man's abdomen, and scrambled his internal organs with buckshot.

※

Zach hooked his fingers through the new-grown lattice and pulled hard, but it was as firm a part of the structure as the walls and the arched roof. The twisted tines of the meat fork no longer seemed like a big deal, not compared to this, and he wondered if next the arbor would sprout spiky wooden teeth on all sides and chew them up as if it were a shark and they were chum.

As though she could read his thoughts, Minnie said, "It can't hurt us with things like the arbor, it can only confuse us and scare us with things. It needs to have a **person** it can use to hurt us."

Zach heard something move behind them, and when he turned, he saw Professor Sinyavski's dead body roll onto its back and sit up in the gloom. "Pretty piggy," old Sinyavski said in a voice as hard as gravel and as thick as mud. "My pretty Minnie pig."

To Minnie, Zach said, "A dead body is a **thing**. It's not a person anymore. It's a thing just like lattice is a **thing**."

The professor clutched the lattice wall with one hand, trying to pull himself to his feet. "Pretty piggy, I'm gonna chew your sweet tongue out of your mouth."

※

Clutching her mother's arm, shaken and tearful but recovering her emotional equilibrium quicker than John would have predicted, Naomi came with them, down through the house, as he called out to Minnie and Zach, neither of whom answered.

Earlier, he had thought that perhaps he'd **drawn** Blackwood—and his master, Ruin—back into the world by worrying, especially since Minnie's illness, that the killer's promise would be kept. Had he, by his obsession, **invited** the spirit to haunt him? Had he felt that he **deserved** to be haunted, to be hell-hounded unto death for having been the sole survivor of his murdered family? After the incident at the bathroom door, when he gained entrance merely by the assertion of his ownership, he suspected that indeed he was only as vulnerable as he allowed himself to be, which suggested that if a door had been opened between this world and another, he himself might have swung it wide, even if unwittingly. If he opened a door to the twined entities of demon and ghost, he could close it, close it once and for all. The one thing that scared him now was that he would close it too late, only after a devastating loss—Minnie, Zachary, maybe both of them, maybe still **all** of them.

At the foot of the stairs, where the front hall met the foyer, he experienced again the sensation of a phantom presence brushing against his legs, eager and ebullient. This was what he had felt a few weeks before in the backyard, at night, when the fallen leaves of the scarlet oak whirled and tumbled as though a dog were at play in them. Willard.

"He wants us to go this way," John said, leading them along the hall toward the kitchen.

"Who wants?" Nicky asked.

"I'll explain later. Zach and Minnie must be this way."

The three of them hurried across the kitchen and through the open door onto the terrace, where they encountered a strange sight; and considering recent events, John's threshold for determining anything to be strange was far higher than it had been two months earlier.

In the snowy half-light, a golden wheel, mysteriously powered and as large as that from a Peterbilt, rolled slowly across the snow-covered terrace, leaving a wake of clear dry flagstones. Rolling with a deep rumble more ominous than an earthquake, as though it weighed far more than its size suggested, the wheel seemed to charge the air merely by its presence, and the snow crackled around it as if the flakes became electric particles under its influence. The flagstones cracked and splintered under the wheel, and through the soles of his shoes, John could feel the vibrations from its progress shuddering through the concrete slab on which the stones were laid.

The golden enigma held their attention only until they heard Zach and Minnie shouting for help.

The dead horse offers the rider a clumsy weapon more difficult to use with each degree of heat lost from the cooling brain. But it is a human cadaver and thus still has some capacity for the extreme violence that is one of the key signifiers of the species. It might be an instrument of considerable destruction even for as long as an hour or two, until early rigor mortis sets in, stiffening it beyond easy function. The rider spurs the corpse to drag itself erect by clawing at the lattice wall. The boy steps forward, between the professor and his sister, knife ready, but he will find that the knife is useless, for a corpse cannot be killed with either a slash across the carotid artery or a hundred stab wounds.

⸺

In Zachary's room, the securing pivot pins rise out of the barrel hinges on the closet door and tumble to the floor.

By contact with the door, Melody knows what has been done to assist her, and she strains against that barrier until the knuckles of the hinge barrels separate from one another. One side of the door sags an inch away from the jamb, and now there is enough play in it to work it until the bracing chair slides out from under the knob.

The door falls, and Melody enters the boy's room. She goes to his desk, opens the drawer where he put the cleaver, and recovers that fine piece of cutlery.

⸺

The wheel rolled to a stop on the snow-mantled lawn, near the arbor, having grown as immense as the tire on a giant earthmoving machine, maybe seven feet in diameter. Its weight must have been enormous, because it pressed an eight- or ten-inch-deep trench in the frozen yard.

The new-woven straps of wood on the ends of the arbor would not unweave at John's declaration of his ownership, which had caused the bathroom door to relent. Judging by the look of the lattice, he would need a chainsaw to cut through, assuming wood didn't magically heal behind the wound made by a high-speed chain. If he wasn't in downtown Twilight Zone anymore, he was still in the suburbs.

Fingers hooked in the gaps, Minnie pressed her sweet face to the lattice and screamed, **"The professor died, but he's still after us!"**

———— ∞ ————

Spirit-ridden, the dead professor lumbers forward, the boy lunges, the knife goes deep, but hands that once signed declarations of treason against several young men of promise serve just as well to grab the boy's knife hand and force him to drop the blade. He also grabs the boy's throat to lift him and slam him backward into the farther wall of lattice so hard that the entire arbor clatters, and the girl screams. The dead man is strong but with poor coordination, while the boy is clever and agile and fiercely determined. The boy wrenches his right hand out of Sinyavski's grip, kicks and squirms, thrashes furiously, breaks loose. The dead man turns, grabbing at him, stumbles, almost falls, and lurches two steps into the wall. The lattice cracks, the structure shudders, Sinyavski drops to his knees.

———— ∞ ————

Heart in his throat, breath so hot it didn't just plume from him but gushed out like pressurized steam from a leak in a boiler, John ran back and forth along the structure, trying to understand what was happening in there, as the bad light rapidly got worse. When he thought he saw Zach escape Sinyavski, John thrust the barrel of the shotgun through one of the two-inch-square gaps in the arbor, but the bracketing lattice allowed no lateral shift, he could only shoot straight ahead. No way to take down Sinyavski unless the professor stepped directly in front of the muzzle. And where was Zach? Gloom, moving shadows, chaos, too much risk of hitting Zach.

Minnie shouted, "He's **already dead**! He can't be killed **twice**!"

"He's clumsy, Dad," Zach said. "Dead-guy clumsy. But there's not much room in here."

"Use the thing!" Minnie urged.

On their knees in the snow, face-to-face with Minnie, Nicky and Naomi held fast to the small fingers that the girl hooked through the lattice, Naomi crying. Nicky said, "What thing, baby? What thing?"

"The wheel-thing."

John pleaded: "What is it, Minnie, how do I use it?"

"It's an **idea**."

"Idea? What idea?"

"**The** idea, the idea behind everything. Daddy, it's the drinking glass with the black stuff in it, the stray dog that healed a guy."

Stunned that she referred to Peter Abelard, to a conversation she had never heard, John said, "How do you know about that?"

Zach shouted, "Dad, I've got the knife again."

"Stay away from him! Where is he?"

"On his knees but trying to get up," Zach said.

"How do you know about the glass, the dog?" John asked Minnie.

"I don't know how, but I know."

John heard Abelard in memory: **I think the divine has taken a few steps back from humankind, perhaps in revulsion, perhaps because we don't deserve to look directly upon holy beings anymore. . . . When the divine enters the world these days from outside of time, it manifests discreetly through children and animals.**

Whatever it might be, the huge wheel wasn't exactly discreet, but John said, "What is it, Minnie? Tell me as clear as you can, what is the wheel?"

"It says it's the power that makes a highway through a sea."

"What do you mean **it says**?"

"I hear it now," Minnie declared. "It's the power that makes a highway through a sea, and wakes the dead. It's whatever you need it to be when you need it, and what you need is a door. Isn't what you need a door, Daddy?"

John had extended an invitation, letting an evil back into the world. Only he could evict it. They wouldn't send an exorcist. They were embarrassed by the old-fashioned idea of absolute Evil, of Evil personified, but the answer to this wasn't a food bank, he would not save his family and himself by throwing **food** at this thing, not by giving it a cot in a homeless shelter, not by social action, what he needed here was some really effective **anti**social action or else what was once called a miracle, which these days maybe only a child, like Minnie, had the imagination to envision and the faith to pursue. So be as a child. Put aside pride and vanity. Have the humility of a child who is weak and knows his weakness. Admit fear in the face of the void. Admit ignorance in the presence of the unknowable. A child believes in mysteries within mysteries and seeks wonder, which should be easy, considering that here in this yard, this very moment, John was adrift in a **sea** of mystery, in a **storm** of wonder. What the heart knows, the mind has forgotten, and what the heart knows is the truth. "I need a door," John said, becoming as a child, "I need a door, and I know there must be a door, I believe in a door, please give me a door, God, please, I want a door, please God, **please give me a damn door**."

Zach shouted, **"Dad! He's on his feet! He's coming!"**

⚬⚬⚬

As the last of the twilight slid westward through the icy sky, as a light arose within the enormous golden wheel, Zach cried out. John leaned his shotgun against the arbor and grabbed the lattice with both hands.

Nicky had seen him try to rip it loose before. He couldn't do it then, couldn't do it now.

She knew the shotgun was useless. She wanted to use it anyway, do something, anything. But what?

In the dark arbor, Zach was taunting Sinyavski, trying to keep him—it—away from Minnie. "Over here, bonehead. Over here, you freaking freak."

Fingers trembling against Nicky's fingers, with the lattice barrier separating them, Minnie whispered desperately, **"It's gonna kill Zach."**

The luminous wheel changed from gold to red and acquired a greater dimension, revealing within itself numerous spiraling masses reminiscent of the sky-filling whorls in van Gogh's **Starry Night**. It began to throb, and in the ominous arterial pulses of swirling light and shadow, the falling crystals of snow glittered like sparks.

John shouted something into the arbor, and Nicky didn't at first understand what he meant: "Take **me**. Take **me**. Take **ME!**"

Abruptly the wheel flared brighter, projecting galactic spirals of shadow and scarlet light across the rose arbor, across the yard, across the falling snow, which descended so heavily that it curtained the night.

———

"Take **ME**!" Breaking off a six-inch piece of lattice, making a hole large enough to thrust his hand through, John shouted, "Here, damn you, here I am, here, take **ME**!"

He thought he knew what needed to be done, and if he didn't do it, there would never be an end to the threat. There could be only one reason that some benign force had used Minnie to make the wheel, which was the embodied **idea** of a portal between time and eternity. The door was for him to use, him and no one else. He started this, he must end it. If a door was provided, he must use it and by using it offer himself as penance.

In the arbor, from out of the shadows, revealed by the whirligig glow of the wheel, the Sinyavski thing loomed, a hulk in a dark suit. The face was familiar yet as John had never seen the professor's face before: twisted with a soured and festered malignity, almost deformed with rage. His eyes were pools of distilled hatred, glistening with malevolence, sharp with resentment.

"It's me you really want, just me," John said. "I'm the one who got away."

Rising from where she had knelt to confront Minnie, Nicky said, "What're you doing? John, no, not this."

"Do you trust me?" he asked her.

"Don't." Her misery grew with each repetition: "Oh, don't, don't, don't."

He said, "I trust Minnie, and I trust whoever . . . possessed her to make the door. Trust me, Nicky."

"With everything?" Anguish strained her voice. **"Everything?"**

"Haven't you always? For fifteen years?"

"It's too strong for even you."

She had once told him that sometimes he was all cop when half cop would be tough enough.

He said, "This isn't a half-cop night. It's all-cop or nothing."

Through the lattice, to the thing using Sinyavski's body, John said, "Take me. Tear me apart from the inside out. And maybe you can totally control me. Won't it be fun, using me to kill them? To use them and cut them and kill them? Won't it be fun, Alton? Ruin?"

He heard Nicky say, "Naomi, get behind me."

"Why settle for less than using me?" John asked the thing in the dead professor. "You can't be afraid of me. I killed you, Alton, but you can't be killed again. I'm flesh and weak. You're strong and everlasting. Or are you?"

The professor thing smiled at him through the lattice, a sly and venomous sneer. His eyes were iron-dark and not his own.

John's hand was palm-up, and Sinyavski's hand pressed upon it palm-down. Something cold and eager squirmed against John's skin. He almost recoiled. With effort, he relaxed, offered no resistance. He felt a gelid, twitching presence not against his hand any longer but within it, slithering as far as his wrist . . . but then no farther.

He turned out of his mind any thought of his parents and his sisters, and for the first time in twenty years, he allowed himself to think about Cindy Shooner as he had not dared to think of her since that night. He pictured her naked, her lovely body, her full breasts, and he tried to summon the memory of how she felt under him, the silken rhythms, her deep warmth, the way she rose to meet him, her mouth, her abandon, her insatiable need, her thrilling appetite.

Ruin took him.

Within the arbor, the dead man fell in a heap.

With poltergeist-like power, the lattice at the ends of the arbor unlaced, raveling back into the walls of the structure, freeing Zach and Minnie. As if from a distance, John heard Nicky urgently calling them to her.

Colder than the night, John's mind flooded with

hideous images of Marnie and Giselle being brutalized before they died. His sanity was assaulted by
those eternal memories of Alton Turner Blackwood.
Anguish slammed him, grief wrung him with a
cruel fist. He tried to scream, but he could not
make a sound.

In the whirling crimson snow, John saw himself
picking up the 12-gauge. As he turned toward
Nicky, he became aware of his finger tightening on
the trigger.

He felt as if he were under an immense weight of
earth, buried in his living body, buried as surely as
his dead family, and his terror swelled.

Nicky held her pistol in a two-hand grip, sighting
lower to ensure a chest hit on the upkick.

John moved toward her without hesitation, and
she told him to drop the shotgun, but he kept moving until the muzzle of the 12-gauge pressed into
her abdomen.

An arm's length apart, they stared into each
other's eyes, and despairingly he thought that he
had surely done the wrong thing again. Twenty
years to the day, had he done the very thing that
would cost him this family just as his weakness and
selfishness **then** had cost him?

Behind her, the kids were gathered. Judging by
their stricken expressions, whatever they saw in
John's face, they saw nothing of their father.

Tears welled in Nicky's eyes. "I can't."

Killing him might be her only chance. He had brought them to a precipice above a longer drop than he had intended.

"I love you," she said. "I love you. I can't."

She lowered the pistol.

"I am Death," he heard himself say to her. "You've never had sex with Death before."

As his finger tightened on the trigger, John suddenly rose out of his living grave, throwing off the weight of evil that pressed him down. He sensed Ruin begin to realize that its host had hidden his most private thoughts, and enticed it into him with a pretense of weakness. Before the demon understood that John might have sufficient strength to evict it, he threw aside the shotgun, rushed past Nicky and the kids, toward the glowing crimson wheel, which was not a wheel but a portal, as it had always been a portal waiting to be named.

Racing through snow as bright as blood spray, John saw nothing within the portal except wheels of red light in a red haze. As far as he knew, he might fall through eternity forever, but he sprang across the threshold without hesitation—

—and is in the dark bedroom of his boyhood, only an instant after quietly lowering the bottom sash of the window. The smells of Cindy Shooner are still on him—her perfume and the faint musky scent of sex.

He sees his dark form in the mirror above the dresser, but there is something wrong with it. He steps close enough to see his face as he looked at fourteen.

This is neither a dream nor a vision. It has not one quality of hallucination, but affronts him with the grim texture of horrifying reality. This is the real place, the momentous night, the silence heavy with the weight of murder.

He waits, anticipating silvery bells, and the bells ring.

John moves to the door, and the bells ring again.

Eases the door open. Steps into the hall. Light radiates from his parents' and his sisters' rooms.

On the floor, the black satchel. Beside it, the pistol fitted with the homemade silencer.

This is not memory. This is the moment. This is the past that made his future.

He doesn't understand why he is here. The bells suggest that they're all dead, as before. Therefore, he isn't here to save them.

And if he could save them, he would change his future, perhaps to one in which he never met Nicky, in which his own children were never born.

More terrified now than then, he stoops, picks up the handgun, removes the silencer.

The open door to his parents' room. In there—the blood-soaked bed, the empty eggs in pale dead hands.

As the bells ring again, his frantic heart knocks hard against its cage.

He sidles along the hallway, pistol in front of him, his hands sweaty as they had not been on that night. He hesitates a step short of the girls' room, hears the bells once more.

He steps into the doorway, into the hateful light that reveals the beloved dead.

Blackwood crouches like a feeding raptor, like a sharp-beaked raven over the torn bodies of song-birds. Mouth red and wet and cruel.

The black-hole eyes shift from the tender victims to John in the doorway. The graveyard voice speaks the same words as before: "This little girl said you were gone to Grandma's for a week."

John realizes he is here to do something different from what he did the first time that he lived this night. But what? For God's sake, **what**?

Like some prehistoric missing link between ancient reptile and humankind, Blackwood rises from the girl, the girl forever lost, and says, "Your lovely sister, your Giselle. She had such pretty little training-bra breasts."

Heart slamming, pistol sight jumping on the target, hoping to buy time to think, John says in the trembling voice of a boy, "Come out of there, get away from them."

Blackwood towers over the blessed ruins, hump-backed Death with a bloody grin.

"Get away from them now, you sonofabitch!"

Blackwood takes a step forward, John backs out of the doorway, and Blackwood follows him into the hall.

Without knowing how he knows, John **knows** that if he dies here at Blackwood's hands, he dies for real, and all the life he lived hereafter will never have happened. Nicky will marry someone else. Children other than Zach and Naomi and Minnie will be born. All is at risk and there is no room for error.

The dead can't be resurrected by a mere man. What he's being offered is not the past undone, but instead a chance to disinvite the spirit whose return he encouraged by his guilt, obsession, and ceaseless worry.

Grinning, Blackwood seems not to fear the gun, but approaches, forcing John to back along the hallway as he tries desperately to imagine what he must do.

"Listen to me, boy. You'll be a daddy someday," Blackwood says—

—and John knows in the instant that what he must prevent is the Promise that inflamed his imagination, that haunted him, obsessed him, and made him vulnerable to the undying fury of this implacable spirit and to the thing called Ruin.

He shouts, **"Shut up!"**

Blackwood steps forward, John backward, Blackwood forward, John backward onto the killer's satchel. He stumbles, falls. Blackwood rushes, looms.

John fires up, it's a wild shot that shouldn't score, but score it does, a gut shot. Blackwood staggers forward and falls atop John, a weight of greasy flesh and deformed bones.

Eye to eye, Blackwood says in a rough whisper, his breath hot on John's mouth: "You'll be a daddy someday—"

The pistol is between them, still clutched in John's hand, he can't guess which of them will take the bullet, but he squeezes the trigger. The muffled shot widens Alton Blackwood's fierce eyes, and suddenly he seems twice as heavy as before.

Gasping, making wordless sounds of terror and revulsion, John rolls Blackwood off him, scrambles to his feet, looks down, and in the dim light sees life still shining in those dreadful eyes, and the lips moving to form the next words.

John empties the magazine of the pistol, and Blackwood's face dissolves from one kind of horror to another.

As John backs away from the corpse, the shade of Alton Turner Blackwood rises from it, a transparent image in a silent rage—which folds in upon itself and is gone. A second entity arises from the corpse, far more abhorrent than Blackwood. Asymmetrical, twisted, crookbacked, yellow-eyed, this abomination named Ruin hovers for an instant—then follows Blackwood's shade into oblivion.

The Promise was a curse. The curse is lifted now and forever.

The house is hushed. What was lost is still lost, though not forever, and something has been gained. What the heart knows trumps what the night knows.

John drops the gun, turns away, and as on that long-remembered night, he hurries down the stairs. Back then, he was compelled to find another gun, load it, and kill himself. But now . . . as he comes off the bottom step, he plunges not into the lower hall but through the portal, into a night streaming with crimson snow.

Before him waited his safe and living family. He had done the right thing, after all, sacrificing himself for them, an act of atonement that at last gave meaning to the past twenty years of his life.

Behind him, the eldritch light faded until the portal vanished. The wheel from which it had formed was gone. In days of old, when angels visited or when a bush burned without being consumed, no video cameras existed to record the moments. Likewise, nothing remained to prove the wheel had ever existed—except for the trench through the yard and the cracked flagstones. **Machina ex Deo.**

A flood of joy swept fear away, and the sight of his precious family blurred before him. He started toward them, and they toward him. At the same time, from out of the night and the cascading snow, in a toboggan hat and a navy peacoat, came Lionel Timmins, wide-eyed and speechless. He found himself at the center of the converging Calvinos, which was at that moment a magical, emotional, freaking perspicacious place to be.

⸺⸺⸺

Entering the kitchen with the meat cleaver, with a headache caused by the blow to her head, and with bad intentions, Melody Lane halted when she felt the thread snap. The ethereal line between her and the entity that had once ridden her, that she served even when not ridden, was disconnected. She waited for it to be reestablished, for she was looking forward to drinking life from the dying boy. But after a minute, she put down the cleaver and departed the house by the front door, because without the protection and guidance of the spirit rider, this place was too dangerous.

Melody trudged through the storm to her parked car, started the engine, switched on the wipers to sweep the snow from the windshield. As she drove into the street, she decided to move on to a new place. There were tens of thousands of cities and towns out there, in which millions of children were at this very moment breathing when they shouldn't be. Melody had a responsibility not to future generations but to **eliminate** future generations. We all have a responsibility. Some shirked it, but not she.

As she drove, Melody delighted in the magical scenes through which she passed, the city gowned and jeweled in snow. Her sweet and gentle voice matched the moment when she began to sing "Winter Wonderland."

50

FOR FIVE MONTHS AFTER JOHN DISPATCHED
Alton Turner Blackwood to Hell for the second
time, the Calvinos lived in a rented residence while
the interior of their house was repaired, painted,
carpeted, and cleaned from top to bottom.

On the morning that they returned home, Father
Angelo Rocatelli, the priest from their new parish,
formally blessed each room of the house. He even
climbed into the service mezzanine between the
second and third floors to bless that space. Minnie
loved him as much as she loved Father Albright,
and Minnie's opinion carried a lot of weight in the
Calvino family.

On day one of his investigation, Lionel Timmins
discovered a connection between Preston Nash and
Roger Hodd. The reporter's wife, Georgia, had
been Preston's rehab therapist. Why the two men
would conspire to invade the Calvino home and

terrorize the family, no one could quite say, though theories abounded. Georgia Parker Hodd suggested that her late husband's alcoholism and Preston's addictions gave them something in common, but she theorized no further. It was thought that Professor Sinyavski must have been stabbed by Nash or Hodd and dragged into the arbor after spotting them entering the house with malevolent intent. In any event, John acted in self-defense, and no charges against him were ever considered.

Walter and Imogene Nash accepted a position as estate managers for a magnificent eighty-acre property in California. The Calvinos missed them, but Lloyd and Wisteria Butterfield, who replaced the Nashes, were good workers with sunny dispositions. Mr. Butterfield had once been a United States Marine, and Mrs. Butterfield knitted hats and matching scarves.

A month after returning home, the Calvinos rescued a year-old golden retriever from the pound. Minnie named him Rosco and said that Willard approved of him.

Nicky successfully finished the painting of the children. She hung it in the living room, where the baroque mirror once had been. She continued to imagine scenes and make them real, as she would until the end of her days.

A year after they prevented Blackwood from keeping the hateful promise, John and Nicky flew back to John's hometown, where he had not been for twenty-one years. For three days, they walked the streets that he had walked as a boy. The residence in which his lost family lived had been torn down, another built. It looked like a good house. Each day, they went to the cemetery where the four graves were side by side, and they spread a blanket to sit on the grass. Embedded in each gravestone was a porcelain medallion bearing a photo of the deceased. The sun had not faded them, nor had two decades of weather worn away the glaze. John found the faith to ask forgiveness for having failed them, and he felt forgiven. He no longer dreaded that a moment might come, after the world and outside of time, when he might see them again, because he was able at last to imagine that such an encounter would be about one thing and one only—love.

At last at peace, he and Nicky flew home, where they belonged.

ABOUT THE AUTHOR

DEAN KOONTZ is the author of many #1 **New York Times** bestsellers. He lives in Southern California with his wife, Gerda, their golden retriever, Anna, and the enduring spirit of their golden, Trixie.

Correspondence for the author should be addressed to:

Dean Koontz P.O. Box 9529 Newport Beach, California 92658

LIKE WHAT YOU'VE READ?

If you enjoyed this large print edition of
WHAT THE NIGHT KNOWS, here are a few of
Dean Koontz's latest bestsellers also available in large print.

BREATHLESS
(paperback)
978-0-7393-2865-1 • $28.00/$35.00C

DEAN KOONTZ'S FRANKENSTEIN:
DEAD AND ALIVE
(paperback)
978-0-375-43472-3 • $25.00/$28.95C

RELENTLESS
(paperback)
978-0-7393-2851-4 • $27.00/$32.00C

YOUR HEART BELONGS TO ME
(paperback)
978-0-7393-2809-5 • $27.00/$32.00C

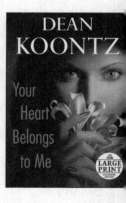

Large print books are available wherever books
are sold and at many local libraries.

All prices are subject to change. Check with your
local retailer for current pricing and availability.
For more information on these and other large print titles,
visit www.randomhouse.com/largeprint.